Caitlin Crews discovered her first romance novel at the age of twelve and has since conducted a life-long love affair with romance novels, many of which she insists on keeping near her at all times. She currently lives in the Pacific Northwest, with her animator/comic book artist husband and their menagerie of ridiculous animals.

Rachael Stewart adores conjuring up stories, from heartwarmingly romantic to wildly erotic. She's been writing since she could put pen to paper—as the stacks of scrawled-on pages in her loft will attest to. A Welsh lass at heart, she now lives in Yorkshire, with her very own hero and three awesome kids—and if she's not tapping out a story she's wrapped up in one or enjoying the great outdoors. Reach her on Facebook, Twitter (@rach_b52) or at rachaelstewartauthor.com.

If you liked *Teach Me* and *Getting Dirty*
why not try

In For Keeps by Taryn Belle
Under His Touch by Cathryn Fox

TEACH ME

CAITLIN CREWS

GETTING DIRTY

RACHAEL STEWART

MILLS & BOON

First Published in Great Britain 2020
by Mills & Boon, an imprint of HarperCollins*Publishers*
1 London Bridge Street, London, SE1 9GF

ISBN-13: 978-0-263-27749-4

MIX
Paper from
responsible sources
FSC™ C007454

This book is produced from independently certified FSC™ paper
to ensure responsible forest management.
For more information visit www.harpercollins.co.uk/green.

Printed and bound in Spain
by CPI, Barcelona

TEACH ME

CAITLIN CREWS

MILLS & BOON

To Rose, in hopes you'll perform this one, too.

CHAPTER ONE

SHE WAS IN.

Finally.

Erika Vanderburg tried to breathe as elation and anticipation coursed through her in equal measure, as if in time to the deep thump of the music that wound its way around and through the crowd and seemed to rest against her clavicle. Like a heavy hand.

The notion made her warm. Maybe too warm.

Concentrate, she ordered herself.

She'd worked too hard to get in the door to waste her one chance…fluttering.

No one could simply walk into the infamous Walfreiheit Club, though many tried. The line of hopefuls stretched for acres on its once-a-month semipublic exhibition nights, like tonight. Some waited outside every night and never got in. And though Berlin was a city filled with sex clubs to suit any mood or experimental phase—or all of the above, all at once—Walfreiheit was its most exclusive.

Erika had been trying to get in the door for going on six months now. She would fly in the night before, then spend the day treating her jet lag at the Hotel Adlon Kempinski Berlin, her favorite hotel in the city. She liked to take her time selecting an outfit from the high-end shops on Friedrichstrasse before relaxing in the hotel's five-star spa. The routine was familiar now, and got her ready for a long night of waiting in line with the rest of the hopefuls outside the converted old building in East Berlin. All of them trying to look *appropriate*, whatever that meant when the place in question was an upscale bondage club. And when the opportunity to enter was entirely at the whim of whoever was at the door.

She had been reminding herself—sternly—that there was a point to all this, despite the annoyance of being denied entry month after month, when one of the terrifyingly calm and formidably solid bouncers had pointed straight at her. Erika had frozen solid.

"You," he'd said in German, then shook his head at the dark-haired woman next to Erika who surged forward. "The blonde."

Erika had been certain that he'd shake his head at her when she moved toward the door, but he didn't. He opened the rope and waved her through. It was on her to somehow…not fall apart with sheer giddiness as she was actually let in.

The Walfreiheit Club specialized in kink. Specifically BDSM, though it was whispered that definitions were kept loose to better serve the imaginations and desires of its exclusive clientele. Members played as they liked within the walls, and membership was never automatic. No amount of money could buy someone a place if the other members didn't vote them in. Unanimously. There were always stories about this or that celebrity or tycoon trying to buy his way in, only to be summarily denied, because the club did as the club liked. Always.

In the same vein, on exhibition nights, the men on the door made their selections from the vast line outside according to their fancy. Selected hopefuls were brought inside to the large, cavernous foyer where Mistress Olga waited, dressed in full fetish gear—though what was actually terrifying about her was the arch amusement she wore on her distractingly beautiful face.

Erika had not been prepared for Mistress Olga. She wasn't sure a person *could* be prepared, especially because the bouncers outside were only collecting a group of potentials for the mistress to sort through. Which she did.

With brutal precision.

The tiny yet ferocious woman reputed to be the most sought-after Domme in Berlin threw out most of the people who'd waited in that foyer with Erika at a glance. She sauntered down the line, flicking a finger to dismiss each person she didn't like. She nodded at a stunningly pretty-looking man. She studied a woman with a bowed head, then murmured an assent. By the time she'd reached Erika, she'd gotten rid of most of the people who'd been let in. And she stood there, magnificent in her spike-heeled boots that stopped midthigh, training her very cool, assessing look all over Erika until Erika rather thought she might scream. Or otherwise embarrass herself beyond repair.

She would never know how she managed to just… stand there.

"You will do," Mistress Olga pronounced, in crisp German.

Erika had been ushered into a smaller foyer, this one in all black. She and the other two selected were met by another woman, this one clearly not a Domme. Or so Erika assumed from the way she bowed her head to Mistress Olga. The three of them were made to fill out extensive paperwork, were given bright yellow wristbands that they were warned sternly not to take off, and were then treated to a long list of the club's rules and regulations.

The truth was Erika would have agreed to absolutely anything to get inside.

She'd played around with various outfits for months. How did a person broadcast the necessary submissiveness required in a place that took its sexual roles very seriously while also making sure to advertise to one specific person exactly what he'd been missing all these years? She'd fiddled with different attempts to hit that sweet spot every month. Tonight she wore a strappy little top that cupped her breasts and lifted them up, but left most of her shoulders and her midriff bare. And a tiny little skirt that flirted with the bottom curve of her ass. The only other thing she wore was a thong that peeked up over the waistband of her skirt.

It wasn't her most subtle outfit. But what was subtle about sexual escapades that started with a frank negotiation of terms, needs, expectations, desires and limits? Erika had decided to fully embrace what she was walking into.

Though that had seemed more like a power move before she was actually doing it.

"All right," she muttered to herself beneath her breath as the huge doors were opened and the three lucky selections were led through into the wall of noise and simmering dark. "You need to settle down."

The main floor of the club was big, soaring up from the open space where most of the crowd was gathered to a second-floor gallery that offered views of the action down below. And, the club submissives had told them, private playrooms. Not that a person sporting a bright yellow guest wristband would be allowed up there.

There was a bar against one wall, though that, too, was subject to strict rules. No more than two drinks for anyone who wanted to play, no exceptions, and no drinks for yellow wristbands at all. *Alcohol is a privilege of membership*, they'd been told. There were a number of small, private seating areas tucked into nooks along the dark walls, and then a wider, more open collection of sofas and tables and comfortable-looking chairs, which Erika assumed were as much for aftercare as for socializing. She'd read all about it.

There was a dance floor, and there were people out there working off their energy and anticipation—

or maybe that was just her—to the seething, brooding electronic music that filled the space. And made everything feel edgier. Cut through with danger.

But beyond that, Erika knew thanks to the hand-drawn map they'd been shown up front, lay the dungeon. *Here there be dungeons,* someone had written in bold letters and they'd all laughed on cue—and had all sounded equally nervous, to her ears.

She pulled in a breath now, then let it out in a rush. Because she knew without a doubt that the dungeon was where she would find him.

And she would finally be able to set her plan in motion.

There were butterflies in her belly as she began to make her way through the crowd, her gaze skimming over couples in leather and latex or jeans, submissives in various chains and collars or merely kneeling at their dominants' feet. She took an extra moment to admire two buff, beautiful men on the end of their top's leash wearing bridles and jaunty tails.

She skirted the edge of the dance floor, her feet bare against the hardwood. It felt strange to be barefoot in a club, but it was deliberate. *Submissives are encouraged to go barefoot,* they'd been told at the desk, where they'd surrendered their phones, wallets, coats and bags, as well as their shoes.

Erika would have worn clown shoes if asked, and had thought it was a silly request meant to make the club more mysterious—but now she got it. The wood beneath her feet felt silky and warm. It was one more sensation to add to the mix. The heat of so many bodies in one space. The cool prickle of air moving over the flesh she'd left uncovered. She could feel her pulse pick up as she wove her way through the crowd, carefully keeping her gaze averted from anyone she passed.

Especially if they had that particular look about them, too calm and too direct, that she knew meant they were dominants.

Erika was wearing the costume of a submissive, and she'd experimented a little with the whole power-exchange thing, but she intended to explore it further with only one very specific person. Starting tonight.

It had taken her six months to get in the door tonight, but she'd spent years working her way here, one way or another. She'd danced nearly naked beneath the desert sky one summer, then experimented in the red-light district out there in Black Rock City. That had been illuminating, if dusty, and it had spearheaded her own little journey. She'd followed her libido wherever it took her, aware that there was a restlessness in her but never sure quite how to address it. She'd tried partying. She'd tried spiritual retreats. She'd done yoga in Santa Monica and she'd surfed in Bali. She'd hiked and she'd communed and still, that restlessness had dogged her.

That had been true since she'd dropped out of university after her second year, but Erika had felt an enormous sense of relief when she'd packed up her things and left Oxford behind. She'd felt less sanguine about her choices when her officious, tight-assed older brother, Conrad—in his role as head of the family that he'd assumed after their father had died, which Erika felt he'd taken to a little too readily and far too sternly—had cut off her financial support.

"I'm not supporting you while you waste your life," he'd said after he'd summoned her to his palatial home in Paris.

She'd rolled her eyes. "I'm actually *getting* a life, Conrad."

"Get it with a job, then," he'd retorted.

And could not be swayed, epic asshole that he was.

Erika had gone right out and found herself a job in a dive bar in New Orleans, because she was sure that would gall her uppity brother, and she'd had every intention of paying her own way to make her own fun. But then her dramatic, theatrically self-involved mother had swept in and restored Erika's access to the family money, because the only thing Chriszette Vanderburg feared was not having strings to pull on to control her offspring.

At first, Erika had resisted, because she didn't want to answer to anyone. Especially not a member of her family. But Chriszette had implored her and Erika had given in because Chriszette was difficult to ignore and harder still to deny, and that was how she'd ended up acting like a paid companion when her mother was between torrid love affairs. And having to find new ways to ask for money without ever being so crass and vulgar as to *ask* for it the rest of the time.

But what she'd really missed in that time was not Conrad, who could shove his tough love up his own ass as far as Erika was concerned. She didn't care if he treated her like a walking disaster, because really, he always had. What she missed was the occasional access to Dorian.

She shuddered a little, involuntarily, as that name—*his* name—rolled through her the way it always did.

Dorian Alexander was her older brother's best friend, stretching back to their boarding school days. They had been thrown together at age eight and had been fast friends from the start. She had heard Conrad refer to Dorian as his brother.

But he was not Erika's brother.

The last time she'd seen Dorian, it had been at the family charity ball his shipping magnate grandfather threw each year in Athens. Erika had gone with her mother, who liked to order her daughter to serve as her date at such things when she didn't have a lover on hand. And yes, if she was honest, Erika had accompanied her mother to an event she could have talked her way out of for the distinct, petty pleasure of flaunting herself in front of her brother.

Conrad had been icily civil. Though Erika had seen that telltale muscle going wild in his jaw and had smugly enjoyed the satisfaction of shooting him an unmistakable middle finger simply by turning up and *not* begging him to reconsider.

Dorian had not followed Conrad's lead. He had been distinctly uncivil when Erika had chirped a greeting his way, and her stomach had knotted up with a strange heat when he'd stared at her. Unsmiling.

"Why don't you dance with me?" Erika had asked him, feeling reckless and daring. Where Conrad was infinitely disapproving and always annoyed by Erika's existence, Dorian had always been…stern. But there was something about the particular intensity of that sternness and the frank way he looked at her—at everything—that had always made Erika feel…silly.

That night she'd decided to lean into the silliness. And besides, she'd been wearing a sparkly dress that bared most of her back and hinted at her ass. Okay, more than *hinted*. She'd wondered how long he'd stay *stern* if he had his hands on her.

"I don't dance with little brats in the middle of temper tantrums," Dorian had said. Calmly.

And she'd never understood how he could do that. How he could look at her in a certain way, usually while saying obnoxious things to her, and it only made her want to giggle. Or maybe melt. Or worse, both, while the knotted heat inside her seemed to thump its way lower the longer he looked at her.

"That sounds like Conrad-sourced propaganda," she'd said, laughing.

Because she was afraid that if she didn't laugh, she'd do something far more embarrassing.

Dorian did not laugh. He was a tall, extraordinarily well built man. That had been true when he was in high school and Erika had seen him on the odd holiday he'd spent with Conrad's family instead of his own. But time clearly loved him. He looked as if he was chiseled from stone, his lean muscle honed to perfection. His dark hair was closely cropped, yet somehow gave the impression he'd only moments before run his fingers through it. His eyes were a cool coffee brown, excruciatingly intense. Powerful. His cheekbones were so high they made Erika think of arias.

And his mouth was always set in that firm line. She'd spent a lot of time staring at it over the years, so she knew its every slight quirk and the raw sensuality that seemed to brood its way out of him no matter how stern he looked at any given moment.

But the look he gave her at that ball in Athens was pitiless.

"Is it propaganda or simple truth that you flounced out of university and refused to return?" he asked coolly.

"I wouldn't call it *flouncing*."

She expected him to launch into a screed on the importance of education. Or to discuss the firsts he and Conrad had received when they'd gone up, because of course they had. She'd wanted him to, really, because surely if he was horrendously boring and too much like Conrad she'd stop feeling so *lit up* when she saw him.

Dorian was not the only person around who disliked Erika, well she knew. But he was the only one whose dislike she *felt* so keenly. And the only one whose dislike did not result in her immediate indifference.

But Dorian did not wax rhapsodic about the dubious charms of an Oxbridge degree as expected. "Your brother has far more patience with willful disobedience than I would," he'd said instead.

"I'm not sure I would consider cutting off his only sister very patient," Erika had replied, not sure why she felt flushed. With a surprising wallop of what couldn't be shame, surely. And something else she hadn't wanted to name. "But I suppose your mileage may vary."

"I don't negotiate disobedience," Dorian had said in that same quiet, intense way. His gaze was fierce and disapproving and, worse, made her shiver. "I punish it."

Erika hadn't known what had come over her then. It was part of that flush that seemed to deepen by the moment. Red and everywhere and what was *happening* to her?

She'd tilted her head to one side. "How would you punish me?"

Dorian hadn't smiled. If anything, he'd looked more forbidding. And harder, somehow, though he didn't move or shift as far as she could see. Erika had felt herself go a little weak, even as she'd felt herself get wet and needy between her legs.

Right there in a fancy dress, in a room where her mother and brother also stood.

And that restless thing in her…settled. Into a kind of expectant stillness she'd never felt before in her life.

"I generally start with a spanking," he'd said very distinctly. "And not the kind you'd think was fun,

Erika. The kind that would encourage you to change your behavior."

"Or what?" she managed to ask, though her voice was barely above a whisper.

His eyes had gleamed. And she could swear there was something like a curve to his hard mouth. "Or I would be even more disappointed with you than I already am."

And it was at that moment that a great many things about her older brother's best friend came together for Erika. With the force of a blow—or, perhaps, that spanking.

Dorian had sauntered away as if nothing had happened. As if Erika was breathing normally and wasn't the least bit overheated and reeling. The genteel crowd had swallowed up that gorgeous body of his, dressed in black tie that somehow managed to suggest that he was from another time.

Her blood had thudded inside her, making her heart feel heavy and her head light. And the sense that he'd spanked her without putting a hand on her only seemed to grow, turning into an ache. An ache that spread, then went deep.

All the whispers that followed in Dorian's wake made a different kind of sense suddenly. The very specific way certain women looked at him, as if they knew a secret about him. Erika had always thought it was simply because he was so powerful, with all that Alexander family money augmented by the tech company he'd gone and started himself after university. Apparently feeling that where there was one fortune, there might as well be two.

And when she began looking specifically for rumors about Dorian Alexander in darker, more shadowy places… Well. That was when she'd really found him. And it hadn't taken a whole lot of digging to learn that Dorian was famous for a great many things in the wider, more civilized world, but when it came to sex he was a king of a whole different sort.

In fact, they called him Master.

Her schoolgirl crush flipped inside out and turned into something far more edgy.

Particularly because, the more she thought about Dorian and spanking—and Dorian spanking her, for that matter—all her vague fantasies and all her sexual explorations seemed to spark into something new. And much, much hotter.

She'd experimented with light bondage and a few tame scenes in clubs in New York. London. Lisbon. She'd spent a particularly hot and steamy winter down under in Melbourne, playing top and bottom games with some new friends. And anytime it got to be too much, playing dominance games with tops who were never quite what she wanted, she thought of Dorian.

Master Dorian, as he was known. Master Dorian, who had used to scene quite a bit in the clubs—especially in Berlin, at the Walfreiheit—but did so less and less these days. Master Dorian, who was a legend and a favorite fantasy of pretty much every submissive she met.

Master Dorian, who had nothing to prove, had never given a submissive his collar and was the only thing Erika could take from her brother that he would miss.

He'd had no use for her as a supposedly spoiled rotten socialite, sure. But would he feel differently about her as a submissive?

It was time to find out.

She felt her pulse pick up when she saw the displays as she made her way into the dungeon. A pretty girl strapped to a table while her Domme applied all manner of wicked-looking clamps to her, murmuring encouragement as she shuddered and squirmed. In the next room, a Dom was working his submissive into a series of intricate and beautiful shibari knots, as if she was an installation piece, there with her ass in the air and her face to the floor. One scene bled into the next. Threesomes. Fireplay. Suspension. One erotic fantasy brought to life after another.

But the biggest throng of onlookers had flocked to the biggest space, toward the back, and Erika headed in that direction. Even though she felt something shiver over her, like foreboding.

Because she knew what she would see. They'd all heard the whispers out there in line, that Master Dorian was picking up his whip tonight for the first time in ages. That he was putting on a show.

But God help her, she wasn't prepared.

Dorian stood on a raised dais, facing a Saint Andrew's Cross. A woman was strapped to it, straining against her bonds, moving her head back and forth in erotic distress. That alone made Erika's belly quiver.

But Dorian took her breath away.

He looked darker and more dangerous than she remembered him, dressed in dark trousers, boots and a black T-shirt that managed to hug that remarkable chest of his like an obsessed lover. Every single one of the muscles she'd marveled at when he was clad in black tie was on display. And more, like his mouthwatering expanse of sheer abdominal fitness.

And it was hard not to appreciate his glorious corded arms as he wielded that lethal, deliciously terrifying whip.

Erika's mouth went dry. She felt her eyes go glassy, but she couldn't look away. She felt rooted to the spot as surely as if it was her up there on the cross, writhing, tears wetting her own cheeks while cuffs kept her exactly where he wanted her.

Meanwhile, Dorian made the whip dance.

He was murmuring in a low voice and the woman responded, and it took Erika some time to understand that he was telling her exactly where each strike would land. Then he waited as she writhed, moaned.

But each time she quivered. Then said distinctly, "Yes, Master Dorian. Please."

Yes, Master Dorian. Please.

The words jolted through Erika like a live wire. Like the kiss of that terrible whip, landing precisely where he said it would.

He was controlled, precise. Beautiful and terrible, like an angel. He moved like a furious dancer, a dark and mighty cloud, and Erika thought the whole crowd was as breathless and undone as she was.

And for the first time since that party in Athens, Erika thought to ask herself what in the hell she was thinking.

All her little sex games were just that. Games. But Dorian was very plainly the real thing. She'd been charging up a gentle slope and calling it a mountain, and it was only now that she understood the enormity of her error. She wanted to poke at her brother, not…this. A whip and a crowd and that hungry, greedy thing she could feel turn over inside her and bare its fangs.

She didn't want *that*. Erika felt exposed, even though she stood with everyone else, and knew no one was looking at her. Still, she felt vibrant with embarrassment and panic. Most of all she felt deeply, remarkably silly. Foolish.

The brat he'd called her, and more.

She needed to leave. Now. Before she made an even bigger fool of herself.

But she couldn't seem to tear herself away. The scene on the dais went on. The whip licked over the submissive on the stage, bringing her closer and closer to that brutally perfect end that Erika could feel all over her. Her own nipples were hard. She was much too wet. She wanted to *squirm* but she didn't dare move. Or she couldn't move.

And then, finally, he asked and was answered with a sob. But a *yes, Master Dorian, please*, all the same. Dorian shot out his arm. The whip cracked.

Then landed with merciless precision on the submissive's exposed clit.

The girl on the cross screamed, her body shaking wildly as she arched into a climax, her body like a bow against the cross. Out there in the dark of the audience, rooted to the floor and still bright red with the realization that she shouldn't have come here at all, Erika felt her own body clench and tremble, as if she was on the same slippery edge.

That was when Dorian stopped. He looked out toward the crowd and the murmurs of appreciation. He looked as if he might smile.

But then he saw her.

She felt the impact of those fierce, intense eyes. She saw the flare of recognition.

And without a single hand upon her—without anything but that outraged gaze of his—Erika felt herself catapult straight over that edge.

Hard.

CHAPTER TWO

HIS BEST FRIEND'S little sister was coming right there on the floor of his club.

That it was impossible—that she shouldn't be in the club, or dressed like that, or witness to his particular enthusiasms without his knowledge or approval—didn't change the fact that it was happening. Right there before Dorian Alexander's astonished eyes.

Her climax rolled over her, and he could see entirely too many things about little Erika Vanderburg, then, that he understood in a flash he would never be able to unsee.

Her plump, high breasts and her hard and proud nipples that poked out from behind the top she wore, begging for his mouth. Or better yet, his clamps. Her exposed abdomen, a sensuous display of softly toned female flesh that quivered with the force of her orgasm. And low on her hips, so low he could see her thong poke up above the waistband, she wore a skirt so tiny it hardly deserved the name, making him think that if she shivered *that much more* he might actually catch a glimpse of her pussy, too.

The mental image he'd carried around forever of little Erika, maybe age ten, with pigtails he wasn't sure she'd ever actually worn, went up in smoke.

His gaze shot back up to find hers. Her eyes were heavy-lidded and flooded with arousal. And something else the dominant in him was delighted to see looked a whole lot like the kind of panic that made a good scene sing.

Dorian had been reasonably aroused throughout his whipping demonstration, because he loved what a whip could do to a trembling, beautifully bound woman who let it kiss her and carry her off into bliss. He didn't understand anyone who claimed they didn't.

But looking at Erika—and that ferocious orgasm that still held her in its grip—he was suddenly as ragingly turned-on as if instead of a demonstration he'd been deep in a scene he expected to end in his own release.

That's Conrad's little sister, something in him protested, but his body didn't seem to care. His body saw only a lovely submissive, flushed and wide-eyed and panting—just the way he liked them—and all she'd been doing was watching him whip someone else.

Dorian couldn't permit himself to focus on that, so he focused instead on what he was supposed to be doing on that dais in the first place. Which was demonstrating one of his hobbies for the assembled club members and tourists here on one of the club's exhibition nights. Only a split second had passed, he was sure of it, despite the fact that to him it felt like a lifetime or two—but it was still a loss of focus.

It didn't matter how long it was. His lapse of attention galled him. He was no novice, for God's sake.

He moved over to the cross, murmuring to Angelica as he released her from her cuffs, soothing her as they both waited for her permanent dom to climb up to the dais and take charge of her aftercare. Dorian had to make himself focus the way he should have been already, because what was important here was caring for Angelica, not a bratty little sub—

Sister, he snapped at himself. Bratty little *sister*. Of his best friend. A man who was more family than friend, as a matter of fact, and who Dorian knew would be distinctly unamused at the idea that his wild-child baby sister knew a club like Walfreiheit existed. He didn't want to think about Conrad's reaction to the news that she was going around climaxing in public and, worse still, because of Dorian.

When Angelica was off the cross and in her dominant's care, Dorian's responsibilities to her were finished. He handled his equipment and packed it away, then straightened. He turned slowly, not entirely convinced that Erika hadn't been a figment of his imagination. Though why he would conjure up such a maddening little brat he spent very little time thinking about unless she was right there in front of him, he had no idea. He searched the crowd, half expecting to find no trace of her. He would find a blonde sub who reminded him of Erika instead, and the good news was, he would know exactly what to do with *her*. He would tie her up, make her scream and cry and come, and exorcise this strange demon he hadn't known lurked about inside him.

But Erika was right where he'd left her. The actual Erika Vanderburg, his best friend's little sister, in the disturbingly succulent flesh. She stood stock-still on the hardwood floor, gaping at the stage.

At him.

When their eyes met again, Dorian could feel the temperature rise, then sizzle.

He told himself it was sheer outrage.

Her eyes widened. Dorian lifted an arrogant brow in reply. It was usually sufficient to make submissive knees bend. Hers appeared to tremble, which sent a kind of shock straight through him. And even up on the dais he could see the gulp of air she took in.

He wasn't surprised when she turned around and dived through the crowd as if she actually believed she could run away from him. Here in this club that in some seasons had operated as his second home. He wasn't *surprised*, but still, the fact she was trying to escape him made something in him, dark and hungry…wake up.

Then focus. On her.

Intently.

He jumped down to the floor, following her through the crowd. He was aware that the people parted before him to let him through, the way they always did. He was vaguely cognizant of the usual congratulations and sultry little come-ons from the hopeful unattached submissives who followed him around in packs on nights like this, but he was focused on his quarry. He stalked her through the crowd, feeling a kick of satisfaction as she looked around wildly—then turned deeper into the dungeons rather than out toward the bar.

He followed, nodding at his friends as he passed. He was in clear pursuit of Erika, and he didn't have to say a word to explain himself. Master Dorian stalked no submissives when they all flocked to him, and here he was, going after this one.

She might as well have worn his name around her neck.

A not-unpleasant thought.

Which really should have horrified him.

It did, he assured himself. Of course it did. No matter why she'd come here.

Though the notion that she might have come tonight to play with others filled him with a hollow sort of heat that took him a moment or two to realize wasn't simply temper.

It was deeper. Richer.

He recognized his own rare possessiveness—and should have turned around right then and there.

But he didn't.

She was walking faster, very nearly running while doing her best not to look as if she was doing any such thing. Dorian followed, taking the opportunity to control his breath. To settle himself down. To make sure that he was in complete control of himself, as he always fought to be, no matter what

Erika Vanderburg was doing here or that bright fire that burned in him and seemed to spell out her name.

Erika made another mistake, cutting toward what he imagined she thought was a hallway. And it was, but Dorian knew the far door was locked on a night like this, when nonmembers roamed the premises and didn't have permission to wander all the different areas of the Walfreiheit Club as they pleased.

He slowed down, checking in with his control again and trying to separate the dominant in him from her older brother's best friend—no matter his cock's take on the matter. By the time he made it to the mouth of the narrow hall that usually functioned as a shortcut to the club's offices, Erika was already turned back around, clearly having realized there was no escape.

Then she saw him.

She jolted as if he'd used his whip on her, which, predictably, made him imagine doing exactly that—though that was a privilege she would have to earn.

No, he reminded himself. *Not her. Not Conrad's little sister.*

Dorian followed her into the hallway, casually blocking any possible exit. The hall was narrow and not exactly brightly lit—but not so dim he couldn't see that her eyes were wide. And he wasn't sure how he'd never noticed before that they were a particular shade of blue that reminded him of his grandfather's island nestled out there in the Aegean Sea.

He couldn't say he cared much for the comparison now.

He stopped when he was a foot or so away from her. He folded his arms over his chest, widened his stance and waited.

And Erika quivered. He could see the pulse in her neck, banging out exactly the sort of rhythm he liked best. She shifted her weight from foot to foot, betraying her anxiety. He had made a study of the female body in various degrees of erotic distress and he could read her easily. And still, she pulled out that careless, reckless smile of hers that she had to know always put Conrad's teeth on edge.

It reminded him, as nothing else could, what an eternal pain in the ass she was and always had been.

"Oh," she said carelessly, as if this was a chance meeting at some desperately boring society event. Some overdressed, overstuffed ball or other. "Hi, Dorian."

He knew distantly how he ought to feel about this. Unamused, certainly. Even annoyed, because this was a complication he hadn't foreseen and Dorian liked surprises only when he could control their outcome. Which was to say, he didn't like surprises. His childhood had cured him of that. He should have been thinking through how best to break the news to Conrad—and, of course, how quickly he could bundle Erika out of the club, into some decent clothes, and then dispatch her back to wherever it was she had come from. He knew that was what Conrad would have wanted.

He knew how he *should* feel, but instead, the things that beat in him were all too familiar…for very different reasons. She looked flushed and ready, her feet bare and her skin exposed, her pretty breasts thrust toward him while she fought to catch her breath. She looked like a brand-new submissive in the grip of the frenzy that often made them adorably reckless. She looked good enough to eat.

And Dorian might have found himself jaded and restless of late—wondering if it was time to stop playing and start thinking about settling down into the life his grandfather wanted for him, and wanted to see before he died—but a pretty blonde submissive with that particular hot awe in her eyes and a slight tremble to her lips…

Well. *He* wasn't dead yet.

"Try again," he suggested softly.

She shifted from foot to foot again, and it took every bit of his considerable willpower to keep his hands to himself. But Dorian was anything but newly minted. He knew very well the power in simply… waiting. Expectantly.

He studied her as he did, wondering how it was he'd never paid such close attention to Conrad's little sister before…

But even as he thought that, he knew that wasn't true. He'd certainly seen her when she'd turned up in a backless gown at his grandfather's charity ball in Athens one year, enlivening an otherwise staid and boring gala. There had been that split second when he hadn't known who she was, but he'd wrestled *that* under control. And done nothing more than chastise her a little.

He certainly hadn't let her get him hard.

The Conrad's-little-sister part, of course, had always governed his reactions to her, as well it should. He had to be ten years older than her. But when had she become this lush? With all that smooth, apparently blemish-free skin that made his mouth water as he considered how best to leave his mark—

No. She's Conrad little sister. She might as well be yours.

But that thought didn't really land. It certainly didn't impress his cock.

Because he could remember that dress much too distinctly. Erika had worn it for the precise purpose of rendering her brother apoplectic, that much was clear. Dorian remembered murmuring something soothing to his friend, likely about the established brattiness of younger sisters—not that he had any personal experience in that area. Then he'd glanced over and found his eyes drawn to the mouthwatering line of a beautiful woman's graceful back, bared entirely by a dress that flirted with the curve of her ass.

He could remember it in stark, unwavering detail. Even now, years later.

Maybe he'd seen Erika all along.

That night it had taken one second, maybe less, before he realized he was looking at precisely the dress that had his friend in fits. One second before he'd understood he was looking at Erika. He'd sternly reminded himself that Erika was ever and only a brat. Ungrateful, immature. Forever embroiled in her juvenile attempts to poke at Conrad. Pigtails. Freckles. Stuck in amber at ten years old.

That was how he knew her. It was the only way he knew her.

But now his cock was heavy, she was in his club, and he couldn't pretend he hadn't eyed her then exactly the same way he did now. Like a dessert he couldn't wait to get his teeth in.

A sweet little bite he wanted to taste. Over and over again.

Some men saw a pretty thing and wanted to lock it away in a tower somewhere. Dorian, on the other hand, wanted to mess it up. But only if she begged.

He almost had to adjust himself.

"This is *so* funny," she was saying, brazening her way through this in a way he almost had to admire. She squared her shoulders and held his gaze boldly, as if she was up to any challenge he might put to her. Which he doubted very much. "What a surprise to run into you, of all people. I'm in town for the weekend. One of my friends was talking about his favorite clubs a month or so ago and I couldn't resist checking them all out. There's one in Singapore that—"

"Do not lie to me, please." His voice sliced across hers and stopped her dead. "You're well aware I live in Berlin."

She dared to roll her eyes at him, and Dorian's brows rose in sheer astonishment. He couldn't recall the last time a submissive in this club—or anywhere else, for that matter—had presumed to treat him with such blatant disrespect. They were usually far too intimidated. He should have been furious. He was. But even so, that spark in him bloomed into a hotter, darker fire.

"It's a big city, Dorian," she declared, lifting the stubborn chin that anchored her heart-shaped face—and he really should not have been noticing things like that about her. "I had no idea that if I wanted to find you, which I didn't, all I had to do was poke my head into the nearest den of iniquity."

"No one pokes their head into Walfreiheit. You had to wait in line. You had to be dressed appropriately, yet evocatively. And then you have to make it past Mistress Olga, who has an unerring eye for posers and too-casual visitors. Would you like to try telling the truth?" Her lips parted, and he enjoyed watching her cast around for an answer. And enjoyed it even more when she didn't. "My mistake, Erika. I assumed this must be some kind of social call. That you'd come here to seek me out specifically."

"Of course not." But the pulse in her neck told him otherwise. Interesting. "Why would I? I already know that you're Team Conrad. I prefer to avoid his minions whenever possible." Again, that reckless smile. "You know how it is."

He understood she was trying to provoke him. And she was—only not in the way she likely imagined.

"How fortunate, then, that you should run into a familiar face," he said quietly. "In the midst of your heretofore unknown exploration of power exchanges in all their glory. I had no idea you were hiding a thirst for submission beneath your fluffy, spoiled exterior."

Her eyes widened further. She started to say something, but it came out as a breath instead. He liked it. Poor little submissive girl. So afraid of what she wanted.

Dorian needed to remind himself that she wasn't just another new submissive. She was Conrad's baby sister. And this couldn't happen.

But he didn't walk away.

"Well," she said nervously. "I mean, I can't say that I *wanted* to see a familiar face here. Nobody *wants* to see a familiar face when they're watching a grown man whip a naked woman until she..."

Her voice petered out. Dorian only watched her, keeping his expression just this side of a scowl until she flushed again.

"Until she came," he supplied. "And so did you." He smiled faintly when her throat worked, but no sound came forth. "If this is not a specific social call, that means you are here to play like anyone else. And I regret to inform you that you have already shown me entirely too much disrespect."

"What are you talking about? You're the one who followed me down a dark hallway to loom over me and frown dramatically. Maybe *you* should be concerned about respecting *me*."

Dorian studied her, unsmiling. "This is primarily a BDSM club and you present as a sexual submissive. Do you know what that means?"

"Of course I know what it means."

"Is that an incorrect label for you? The girls at the door are usually much better at teasing out our visitors' secret wants and needs. Surely they told you that the pink wristband you're wearing announces your preferences to all and sundry."

She scowled down at the wristband in question and tugged at it. It sat next to the yellow wristband that announced she was here only for the night, which was why she had no bright blue wristbands, one for each alcoholic beverage patrons were allowed if they wanted to participate in any play.

"I can't hear you," he prompted her. "Is that the wrong wristband?"

"This club is obsessed with labels. You know that, don't you?"

"Indeed it is. Let's be clear that you as a person can be as complicated and contradictory as you please outside these doors. In here, however, everything is boiled down to its essence. What you want. What you need. And what you are prepared to negotiate to get it."

Her rebellious chin lifted. "Plus neon wristbands."

"If you are certain a label cannot contain you, perhaps you had better ask yourself if that's the truth. Are you so terribly complex? Or are you terrified that if you took the trouble to look inside yourself you would find that at heart, where it matters, you are remarkably simple after all?"

She jerked at that as if he'd slapped her. And he wondered if she knew how dark her eyes got, telling him secrets he doubted she wanted to share.

"The only thing you know about me is who I'm related to," she threw at him, as if he'd mounted a vicious personal attack. He filed that away. "So maybe you should take the opportunity to ask yourself why you're such an egregious asshole to a person you hardly know."

Dorian smiled. "Is it clear to you that I am a dominant, Erika? And was that clear from the moment you saw me here tonight?"

"Yes," she snapped. "But I..."

"Kneel."

Dorian was in absolutely no doubt of his own power. He enjoyed playing with the wielding of it. And he might have been thrown by the sight of Erika Vanderburg dressed like a submissive wet dream, but he didn't think it was a coincidence that she was in Walfreiheit. He didn't believe she was on a club tour and had accidentally happened on him here.

Couple that with her complaints about "labels" and he had no particular reason to think that she was submissive, either.

Or more accurately, he knew she was a submissive. He could see it every time she looked at him. That longing to yield, but only to a worthy dominant force. To pit herself against his will and chase her own surrender into all the places polite society feared to tread. What he didn't know was whether or not she would allow herself to play with that need in her, or if she was the sort of person who preferred to pretend she never entertained any dark fantasies there in the privacy of her mind.

There was only one way to find out.

"What did you…?" she managed to get out while goose bumps marched down her arms and told him more truths.

"Do you need me to repeat myself?"

He watched, more fascinated than he wanted to admit, as she waged an internal battle. He could see it. Ordinarily he would have no trouble admitting he was fascinated and hard, but this was different. Because while watching a woman fight to do the very thing they both wanted—when she was as aroused by the notion as she was afraid of it—was one of life's greatest pleasures, in his experience, this was Erika.

He didn't know if she would do it.

Or what would happen if she did.

Dorian kept his expression impassive as he watched her struggle there before him. Her pretty face broadcast every last one of her emotions, making it easy to watch her cycle through defiance, longing, fear and a bright flash of straightforward need.

He didn't help her. He only waited, wondering how exactly she would handle this if she was not, in fact, as submissive as he thought she was.

"Did you say…kneel?"

She sounded almost hopeful. As if he might change his mind.

"You do not have to do anything you don't want to do, Erika," he told her, his voice low and his gaze hard. "*Safe*, *sane* and *consensual* aren't simply words we throw around for fun. But I should warn you, this is not a club where submissives balk at something as simple as kneeling to show respect. You can negotiate high protocol with whatever Dom you like, but they will all expect you to kneel. You might as well practice, don't you think?" He waited a moment while she breathed a bit too hard. "If submission is what you want."

"I just… I mean, I only…" Her eyes were slicked over with panic, but he could see the way she kept dancing from toe to toe. Dorian knew this dance. He knew that if he reached between her legs he would find her wet and hot. Better to let her dance it out. "I mean, maybe…"

"Is it our personal connection that has you so flustered?" he asked. Pitilessly. "Would you prefer I summon one of the other masters?"

She appeared to like that even less.

Which he could admit he liked a great deal more.

"I guess… I guess I thought there would be more of a buildup. This feels a lot like going from first to fourth gear in about twelve seconds, doesn't it?"

"Erika." Her name made her shiver, then still. "If this isn't what you want, I will escort you to the bar. You can have as many nonalcoholic drinks as you like, perhaps dance to the music, and feel exhilarated that you were this close to so much edgy deviance. We always expect a certain number of tourists on nights like this. There's no shame in it. But you need to tell me what you want."

"I want…"

"If you don't know how to say it, you can start the

conversation very simply." He tilted his head, indicating the ground beneath her feet. "Simply kneel."

She moved her hands to her belly, as if her stomach was knotting up. Or fluttering. Or any other of the lovely, delicious reactions she could have been having.

She shot a glance behind him, almost wistfully. But Dorian didn't move.

And in that moment, when she pulled her gaze back to his and her cheeks got even redder, Dorian had to ask himself what it was *he* wanted. Did he want her to kneel? Or did he want her to break, flip out and prove that she had come here only on one of her bratty excursions calculated to irritate Conrad more?

It was more than a little confronting that he didn't quite know the answer.

Liar, something in him whispered. *You know what you want.*

As if she heard, Erika blew out a breath.

And then, as Dorian watched, his best friend's little sister sank to her knees on the floor before him, tilted up her face and surrendered.

CHAPTER THREE

ERIKA HAD NEVER knelt before a man in her life. Not... just to kneel. And certainly not because she'd been *told* to kneel. If she'd ever been in this position before, there had been action. She'd been *doing* something. Usually something that put all the power back in her hands. Or her mouth, more likely.

This was not a blow job. This was...completely different. It was electrifying.

She couldn't breathe, and she wasn't sure that she would ever be the right temperature again. She felt much too hot, nearly feverish, though she knew she wasn't sick. It was that fire in her that seemed to burn and burn and burn, hotter and wilder the longer he looked at her so sternly. Erika was sure that her face was the color of ripe tomatoes. She was shaking, everywhere—inside and out—as if she'd done something extraordinary.

And all he did was gaze down at her, his expression uncompromising.

"Very pretty," he said after a moment.

Erika wanted to say something sarcastic. Poke

at him, maybe. Or perhaps make a joke. Anything to lighten the mood, or make the fire in her dim a little, or counter the bizarre sense of *relief* she felt that he'd complimented her, but that didn't seem to be possible. She couldn't make her mouth do what she wanted it to do.

Because the more he gazed down at her, apparently perfectly happy to stand there all night, the more she was aware of all the other parts of her body. The way her thighs felt, splayed wide beneath the short, short skirt she'd chosen to wear. The cool kiss of the floor beneath her knees and shins. Her bare toes were cool, and it felt like a notable, erotic contrast to how confined her chest and her breasts felt in the strappy top. When she'd put it on earlier, it had felt almost loose, but not now. Now she thought another deep breath would pop the straps, and expose all of her to him.

That notion should have scared her, but it didn't.

Or it didn't *completely* scare her.

She could feel her heart, beating so fast it thudded in her ears like her own personal drum. And like a thick pulse in her pussy, a staccato beat in her nipples and a riot in her chest. Everywhere else, her exposed skin felt much too warm.

Erika didn't really understand any of this. She didn't understand the reaction she'd had to Dorian with a whip in his hand. A *whip.* She didn't understand the roaring, greedy thing that had walloped her in that crowd, that had made her come and then made her run, like opposite sides of the same too-hot coin.

She'd thought that she was so edgy when she'd played around with handcuffs and a blindfold and a soft little flogger thing, but she'd been kidding herself. This was like a completely different language, and she didn't know how to speak a single word of it.

She couldn't find the words, but he'd told her to kneel and she had.

And really, Erika didn't understand why kneeling before a man didn't make her angry. Why, instead, what coursed through her felt a whole lot more like that same dark, greedy hunger that had taken her over earlier.

When Erika had always preferred her orgasms sweet and quick, spring showers to dance in rather than the crash and immensity of a sea that could eat her alive.

"I normally prefer submissives to keep their eyes lowered at first," Dorian said in that low voice of his that somehow made it sound as if what was happening between them was normal.

Because it was, she reminded herself sharply. And maybe with a touch of panic. For him, this was any old night at the club. The only difference was that she was his best friend's little sister.

Something about that fact—which she'd known full well while she'd spent all these months trying to get herself into this very position, not to mention most of her life—twisted in her differently now. It made her feel even hotter suddenly.

Erika tried to focus on what he'd said.

"Why do you want their eyes lowered?" she demanded, and she did not avert her gaze. Instead, she glared at him. "Because you hate women?"

"Because I love what it does to a woman when she surrenders herself into my hands," Dorian said. "By her choice. And your impertinence is noted. If I were you, I would rethink that glare."

That shouldn't make her thighs clench, but it did. And for a moment, she thought her pussy might take over again, catapulting her toward another climax she didn't want and couldn't make any sense of. She tried to fight it back.

And that gleam in his dark eyes made her think he knew exactly what was happening inside her. When he couldn't. Could he?

"But I can tell you're brand-new, Erika," he said then, and he had to know how riled up she was, or why else would he sound so *satisfied*? "So I will give you more leeway than I would otherwise." He tilted his head slightly to one side, that assessing look as cool as it was stirring. "And I find I quite like the way you look at me."

Whatever snarky remark she'd meant to throw at him died there in her mouth. Because she couldn't help thinking he looked more like a wolf. Poised to take the leap that would take his quarry down.

He looked as if he could pounce at any moment.

And it was hard, once again, to catch her breath.

"Let me tell you the rules," Dorian said.

"They told us at the door," she all but threw at him, filled to the brim with a kind of desperation she didn't recognize. Did she want to poke at him—or please him? "Green light is *yes*, yellow light is *I'm not sure* and red light is *stop*."

"Are you satisfied with that system as your safe word?" He studied her and he was so *thorough*. It made her ache. "Let me backtrack. Do you know what a safe word is?"

"Of course I know what a safe word is," she said. Or really snapped. Making no effort to modulate her cranky tone. "I read *Fifty Shades* like everybody else."

Dorian did not wince. Not exactly. And yet she was in no doubt that he'd come as close to rolling his eyes as she'd ever seen. "This is not the place to mention that book, if you please."

And Erika realized that she hadn't...*forgotten* she was kneeling, necessarily. It was impossible to *forget*. But it had changed into something else.

She felt quivery, the way she had before. It seemed to go straight through her, as if kneeling on the ground at Dorian's feet had plugged her into an electrical current and it kept pouring into her. Making her sizzle and burn.

But the panic was gone. She felt calmer, somehow, when surely it should have been the opposite. Surely she should have been too outraged and weirded out to stay in that position—but the longer she stayed there, exposed and vulnerable, the more she started to feel something utterly contradictory.

Safe.

"What are your hard limits?" Dorian asked in that cool way of his. But not quite clinically, she could see. There was that intensity in his gaze. The way he held hers.

It was as if she was nothing but a bright pebble closed tight in his fist.

She had no idea where that image came from. Or why she reacted to it the way she did, everywhere—from a breath that shivered out too hot to that melting, aching fever in her pussy.

"My hard limits?"

"Repeating a question is not answering it, Erika. Try again."

She thought she might be sweating. "Um. I mean..."

"I'm not familiar with those sexual practices. Enlighten me."

"There are just so many things," she said, because she had to say something. Even if it was desperate.

"Then perhaps we should narrow it down."

One of his dark brows rose, and she had the vague notion that it made him look demonic. What it did not do was detract in any way from his appeal. Maybe, she thought wildly, there really was something the matter with her. But she didn't rise from her knees. She didn't bolt again, the way some part of her wanted to do.

But only so he can catch you, a voice inside her whispered, like another bolt of electricity.

"Do you want me to tie you up?" Dorian asked, his voice somehow managing to be matter-of-fact and silky at the same time. It felt like an assault. It made her think of that whip, arcing through the air and yet landing like a kiss. She couldn't seem to stay still on her own knees. "Cuffs? Chains? And what would I do once I did tie you up? You seem to like the looks of the whip, but that's hardly for beginners. A paddle perhaps? Or maybe you'd enjoy it if I gave you that spanking you so richly deserve?"

For no reason she could think of, Erika suddenly wanted to cry. She felt emotion well inside her as if she was bruised from the inside out. She didn't know what to do with her hands, and found them lying open on her thighs, as if in supplication.

She thought she should do something about that, but she didn't.

And she didn't understand how the swelling emotion inside her could be so intimately connected with the greediness between her legs.

"I don't think…" she started faintly.

But he wasn't done. Dorian shifted position to lean against the wall before her, as if he'd never been so relaxed in all his life. She thought she might hate him.

Maybe she did hate him, but that was its own bright heat, like a lick. Right where she needed it most.

"There are so many things to choose from," he was saying in that mild tone at total odds with the stern intensity in his gaze. "Cattle prods. Ball gags. Nipple torture. Watersports. Total sensory deprivation. Pony play."

She was panting as if she was running. She still wanted to cry. And also slide her useless hands between her legs and make herself come hard enough that all these *feelings* went away. "I have a yellow bracelet on."

As if she was brandishing a rosary at him.

"That means you cannot exchange bodily fluids, Erika. It doesn't mean I can't, for example, secure a ponytail in your ass, clamp your nipples and make you ride a spanking bench until you come. After making sure your ass is a nice bright red. Does that sound like the sort of thing you had in mind when you came here? On this magical mystery tour of your newly kinky sexual appetite?"

Her head shorted out a little, as those images tumbled around inside her. She felt as if she was drowning, the parts of her body he'd mentioned tingling as if he'd already done the things he'd said he would, though he still hadn't touched her. She felt her own fingers digging into her thighs, but she was caught by the expression on his face.

A little too hard. A little too amused.

She got it, then.

He was trying to frighten her away.

And nothing that she'd felt tonight made any sense. Nothing since she'd found him on that dais, wielding that whip like a song. She'd come. Then she'd run. Now she was kneeling on the floor, staring up at him as if he could save her, when she was very much afraid that no one could. Because clearly she didn't want to be saved, or she would have left the minute she'd seen that bullwhip in his hands.

But she already knew what would happen if she

backed down. Dorian would be patronizing. He would call Conrad, who would be livid. And she would have wasted these months and accomplished nothing.

Erika couldn't quite accept that she could have gone through what she'd already gone through and get nothing out of it.

"That all sounds great," she said bravely. Mutinously. "I saw a pair of ponies on the way in. It looks…intriguing. Bridle and all."

And then, for the first time in as long as she'd known him, she watched Dorian laugh. Not smirk. Not raise those brows of his. But actually *laugh.*

It was a rich, profoundly male sound. It slid over her like chocolate, thick and dark. And the strangest sensation washed over her, centering between her legs again, and she almost thought she might come again. Just from hearing him laugh.

"I believe you'd do it," he said. And he shook his head. "That's not a compliment. If you can't articulate what you want and what you don't want, you shouldn't jump into it blindly. There are many places on this planet we can be coy about sex, but this isn't one of them."

"I'm not being coy."

"No, you're being thoughtless. Reckless. As immature as ever, and with far higher stakes than a backless gown at a charity ball we both know you wore to irritate your brother."

That was exactly why she'd worn that dress, but that wasn't the only reason she shuddered. "I'm glad you remember a dress I wore two years ago."

"I remember the controversy." The way his eyes gleamed made her stomach flip, in that peculiar mix of fear and hunger she was learning to associate with this man. "You enjoy controversy, do you not?"

"It's Conrad who enjoys controversy, since he's the one who causes it. I don't know why you can't see that, as his best friend. But that doesn't make it any less true."

"If you were here for reasons that did not involve your brother, I would handle all this insolence, Erika," he said, quietly. "But you are not, are you?"

And there was something about the very quietness that made her think of that whip again. Precise. Intense.

"I don't know what that means."

"I'm allowing you to keep your eyes raised. I'm allowing you to talk back to me, glare and conduct yourself as if this isn't a power exchange. These are gifts I could rescind at any moment."

Could he see her heart slam against her ribs? "I thought I had safe words."

"Do you feel that you need one? All we're doing is discussing terms."

"I haven't agreed to anything."

"You don't need to agree to anything to employ simple courtesy, Erika." And this time, his voice was a lash. A stark command. "When you're on your knees or otherwise involved in a scene with me, you call me sir. Or Master Dorian. And I'll expect you to address me that way every time you open your mouth."

"That's ridiculous."

But she remembered where she was. They weren't, in fact, standing on a ballroom floor in Greece in sight of her mother and disapproving brother. She had chosen to come here. She'd known what kind of club it was. That brow of his inched upward and she shook deep inside.

Even as her pussy flooded all over again.

"That's ridiculous," she said again. *"Sir."*

Because over her dead body would she call him Master anything.

"Thank you," he said, and she was certain that was an unholy amusement in his dark eyes. But his mouth remained stern, the way it always did. "It is not ridiculous. And no, I'm not on a power trip, which I'm sure is the next thing you plan to say. As insolently as possible."

"Oh, come on. Surely your whole thing is a power trip." His eyes flashed and she remembered herself. *"Sir."*

"I'm interested in power, yes," Dorian replied. "But it's not a trip. There is no power without surrender of one sort or another. A fist is only as strong as the delicate fingers that make it up."

"I don't know what that means," she said crossly. But she was thinking of a hard little stone cupped in a palm. Fingers wrapped around it, making that fist. "And I don't think any man ties up a woman if he doesn't want power over her." She saw his expression. "*Sir.* I thought that's what is hot about it."

"I do not want power over a woman," Dorian said,

very distinctly. "I want her to surrender her power to me. It's the difference between demanding that you kneel before me or waiting for you to choose to do it yourself. Do you understand?"

And she wanted to rage something back at him, but even as she opened her mouth to do it, there was that emotion welling up inside her again. Still. That bruise getting bigger, making it so much harder for her to breathe, making her eyes prickle.

She felt protected, yet she was terrified. Overwhelmed, yet so wildly turned-on it was like she didn't know her own body. And it hadn't escaped her notice that he hadn't laid so much as a finger upon her.

And sobbing on this hallway floor, she knew, was no way to do what she came here to do.

"I didn't know you were this…" she started to say without thinking.

An odd look moved over his face then, and she would have called it regret on someone else. But not Dorian.

"I am all this and a good deal more than you can comprehend," he said.

He pushed off the wall and moved closer, and it was better and worse at the same time. Sharp, impossible, until she felt heavy with longing and whatever kind of fear this was that made her head spin and her pussy wet.

He reached down, and fit his palm to her cheek, and to her horror, she felt tears well up in her eyes.

"I know why you came here, Erika. I imagine

you thought you would simply show up before me wearing as few pieces of clothing as possible, and I would fall like a stone. I imagine this is the effect you're used to having on men."

"I didn't—"

"Quiet."

And as if shushing her wasn't enough, he slid his thumb over her lips, and kept it there. Shutting her up whether she liked it or not.

And like everything else, she couldn't tell.

"My desires run a bit deeper than a hot body," he said, low and dark. "My needs require very specific outlets. I can fuck like any selfish fraternity brother you might have encountered out there, and I'll get off, but it won't truly satisfy me. So this offering of yours, while sweet, is doomed to disappoint you. You can't give me what I need, Erika." He studied her. "And even if you could, I will not be used as a tool to slap at your brother."

Erika wanted to bite him, but she couldn't seem to muster up the will to do it. Much less slap his hand away. Or really anything at all but sit there, his hand hot and strong as it curved around her face, wondering what on earth was happening to her.

Or how he'd seen through her so easily.

"I never said I wanted to use you."

"Time's up, kitten," he told her, and it wasn't until she followed his gaze down to her hands on her lap that she saw she was digging her own nails into her fists. *Ha ha*, she thought, angrily. *A kitten with claws.* "You're not here to play, which means you need to go."

"But…"

She could see from the look on his face that there would not be a second chance. She would never get back in through the doors of this club, that was certain. And she doubted it would matter if she tried to find him anywhere else. His office. His home. Whether he had her turned away by others or turned her away himself, he was done. His expression reminded her a little too strongly of the one he'd used on her all her life. Dismissive. Patronizing. Not at all the heat she'd seen before.

This was her only chance. And she might have misjudged things here, but it was only a matter of degrees, surely. The reality was that she'd watched him bring a woman to climax, and had come herself already. That alone was worth experimenting with.

She could handle him. She was sure she could.

"What if I want to play?" she asked.

"Very well."

He stepped back, taking his hand and his warmth with him, and she was afraid those tears really would spill over from behind her eyes. Would he do what he'd threatened to do? Or had that been a promise? Erika didn't know which part of it shot off the most sparks inside her. A ponytail? Or that spanking that had been haunting her since he'd first mentioned it two years ago?

Dorian's dark eyes blazed. "If you want to play, you must prove it."

"I'll do whatever you want."

His mouth curved. "Don't promise things you can't deliver."

He indicated the hallway behind him, and the club waiting for them, filled with people and music and all the kinky things Erika could imagine—plus a great many she couldn't.

"Prove how much you want this," Dorian ordered her. "Crawl, on your hands and knees, down this hallway and then out into the club proper. Keep going until I tell you to stop. You should be aware, of course, that the tiny little excuse for a skirt you're wearing will almost certainly flip up on your back as you go. Does that thong cover you well, do you think? Or will everybody who looks at you be able to see exactly how wet and eager you are? With your ripe, juicy pussy right there for everyone to see and touch and comment upon—"

And it was too much. Pony play was outlandish but what he was talking about was a humiliation she could envision all too easily, all those eyes and *him* and the *display* that was all her and yet not at all in her control…

"Stop," she managed to gasp out, while her heartbeat nearly bent her in half and that fever in her about took her head off. *"Red light."*

"Yes," Dorian said with far too much grim satisfaction. "Red light. Enough of this game, Erika. It's time to take you home."

CHAPTER FOUR

DORIAN MAINTAINED A penthouse in a quietly moneyed neighborhood that seemed far too settled for a man with his predilections. He was so kinky Erika had imagined he would live somewhere desperately cutting edge within walking distance of his club, but instead his penthouse reflected the old money he came from and the fortune or two he'd made himself. His place sprawled across the top of a luxury building that seemed a lot like a five-star hotel, which, once Erika thought about it—once she was capable of thought, that was—made sense for a man like him.

Edgy, yes, but also pedigreed.

He had taken her out of the club with a swiftness that left her off balance. But then, everything he'd done since she'd seen him on that dais left her reeling. He'd reached down and taken her hand in that hallway, pulling her to her feet as if she weighed less than a euro cent coin. And as far as she could tell, he'd been utterly unaware of the way the touch of his hand against hers…stormed through her.

His dark eyes had swept over her, through her,

seeing everything with that same uncompromising gaze. Seeing things Erika couldn't have articulated if her life depended on it. But oh, could she feel it.

He'd pulled her around until she was in front of him, then kept her there with a hand on the nape of her neck as he guided her back to the club proper. It was louder than before, or she was more sensitive to the sounds. The crack of leather against flesh. Moans and screams blending in with the pumping, seductive music.

Erika felt drunk. Wildly intoxicated, spinning and strange, when she was actually far more sober than she usually was in a club. Maybe that was why she did…nothing. She simply let him guide her, shivering a little because he was either really good at it or she was remarkably attuned to every little press of his strong fingers. Both, probably.

She was vaguely aware of him saying something to someone when they left that little hallway, but she didn't think anything of it. She didn't *think*, really. There was a riot inside her and his hand heavy on her neck, and she was still lit up from what had happened—and what hadn't happened—between them. He led her through the crowds, past the bar and into a different foyer from the cavernous one she'd entered before. This one was all dark stone and dim lights, and all the things she'd surrendered earlier were waiting for her.

"Put on your shoes," Dorian ordered her in an undertone, his mouth so close to her ear that she could *feel* the words.

It didn't occur to her to disobey. Or even to discuss it with him.

Everything seemed dreamlike, or feverish. Or again, so deeply intoxicating that strands seemed to wrap around each other outside time. What she remembered was not how she bent and slipped her feet into her shoes, but instead that moment when she'd glanced up in the middle of it to find Dorian staring down at her. His face had been set in the same stern lines, but an odd gleam in his eyes made her wonder what tenderness looked like on a man like him.

And more, what she could do to earn it.

His hand settled on the nape of her neck again, and that was what she remembered most of all. The heat and the heaviness. The separation between his thumb and his fingers, and the way his middle finger rested on her pulse as if he was monitoring every last beat of her heart.

She had the strangest thought, as she simply allowed him to guide her out into the Berlin night, that she'd never felt quite so safe in all her life.

Though that thought didn't make sense. Because whatever she was, it certainly wasn't *safe*. Not with Dorian.

Surely she knew that now.

There was a car ride through the sprawling city outside her window, alive and kicking no matter the hour. The brash, almost punk-rock east gave way to the plump wealth of the west, the history of Berlin—torn apart and sewn back together—rolling out before her. It wasn't until they arrived at his building, and he led her across a too-bright lobby into an elevator that required he release her to use his key, that she gathered her wits about her enough to remember that she had her own hotel room.

She realized that wasn't accidental. He'd let go of her, ergo, she could suddenly think straight.

Erika stood across from him as the lift soared upward, knowing she needed to open her mouth. She needed to say something—anything—to break this spell.

But she didn't.

She told herself it was natural. She was curious, that was all. She wanted to see how a man like Dorian lived. Was it whips and chains in a red room? Or a medieval dungeon in the lounge?

By that measure, the expansive apartment that appeared when the elevator doors lid soundlessly open was a disappointment. If a person wasn't looking for iron spikes and spanking benches, it was exquisite.

Erika followed him into the great room, blinking as Dorian switched on lights. Then he moved farther into the apartment, seeming to pay her absolutely no mind as she looked around the loft-like space, with dark wood walls and concrete floors. She hugged herself as she stood there, taking in his aesthetic of clean, modern pieces mixed in with the odd, sumptuous rug that would not have been out of place in a sultan's palace. There was astonishing, confronting art on an otherwise bare wall. Across the room, another wall was taken up with bookshelves that somehow managed to look clean and spare despite the tremendous number of books they held. So many books it seemed possible he actually *read them*, and wasn't using them as a design element.

She didn't know why it was so hard to imagine Dorian simply sitting down and reading in one of the deep, wide leather chairs or sofas that made up different sitting areas in the great room. He seemed too powerful to ever really be at rest. As if he had to be in constant motion, or standing over her the way he had in that hallway—or back in that ballroom in Athens, for that matter—or he would sputter out into darkness.

Erika didn't realize she was staring intently at his books, looking for clues to mysteries she wasn't sure she could name, until he walked back into the room.

And she didn't hear him come back in. She knew he was there without having to hear his foot against the floor and without having to glance over her shoulder. The hairs on the back of her neck prickled, like his hand had settled there again. She felt that now-familiar heat bloom in her all over again, coiling low in her belly and into her pussy. Only then did she look up.

Dorian stood in the opening where one room bled into the next, with massive windows all around so she could see the sparkle of Berlin out there in the dark.

"It's late," he said shortly. "I suggest you get some rest in one of the guest suites. They're all located on this floor. I'll call your brother in the morning."

He might as well have slapped her back into awareness. Or doused her in ice-cold water.

Either way, Erika's fingers curled into fists again and she suddenly felt much less fuzzy.

"Or, you know, you could also not call him."

Dorian gave the impression of sighing and shaking his head without actually moving at all. Impressive for a man doing such a terrific impression of a stone wall. "That was a statement of fact, Erika. Not an invitation to negotiate."

"All right, then." She held his gaze, even though there was that part of her, quivering and soft inside, that wanted to lean further into all those things they'd only brushed against in the club. The part of her that wished she'd crawled before him the way he'd requested she do, exposed for all to see. She fought off a telling shiver. "You go right ahead and call Conrad. I'll call your grandfather. He's always had a soft spot for me."

Dorian stared back at her. Erika felt the tension in the room surge toward an almost unbearable breaking point. But she refused to break. *She refused.*

Meanwhile, Dorian looked as arrogant as he did… astounded.

"You little shit," he said in a kind of awe that she chose to interpret as affectionate. Or close enough. "Are you threatening to *tattle* on me?"

"I assumed that's what we were doing here." Erika was pleased she managed to sound, if not as calm as he did, far calmer than she felt. "If you're going to tattle on me, why wouldn't I return the favor?"

He tilted his head slightly to one side, his dark eyes focusing on her so intensely she thought she might bruise. But that wasn't half as scary as the way he did nothing but…breathe. One breath, then another. She watched him visibly relax. Gaining his control, then slamming it back into place, she realized as she watched.

It was the hottest thing she thought she'd ever seen. No yelling. No insults. No other reactions—just Dorian handling himself.

She wondered what it would be like to be handled *by* him.

Her knees went rubbery. And far worse—or perhaps *worse* was not the right word here—it made her pussy clench, then ache.

"You are an inventive, insolent girl," he said quietly enough after a moment.

It was not a compliment. And it took her a beat to understand what that note in his voice was, tangled up with the darkness in the disapproval.

She could swear that was disappointment.

Her heart thudded hard against her ribs at that, and there was something almost dizzying that tore her up, then settled in her stomach like regret.

Erika tried to ignore it. "So you keep telling me."

"You are reckless. Immature and impetuous. And in so far over your head it's a wonder you haven't drowned yet." He said those things calmly. As if he was making a grocery list, when she could see that particular intensity in his gaze that indicated otherwise. It was too controlled to be temper, but it lashed at her all the same. "You come into my club, you claim you're there to play, but you can't handle even the lightest conversation. That's breathtakingly foolish."

"I thought that was what exhibition nights are for."

"What if it hadn't been me?" he demanded. "What if it had been some other dominant who hasn't known you all your life?"

"Then I imagine I'd be coming my brains out right now," Erika shot back. "Instead of being lectured to death by my older brother's irritating friend. You don't know me at all, Dorian. You know Conrad. Maybe you haven't noticed, but I'm not the little girl he thinks I am."

"Then I invite you to stop acting like one."

His voice was rougher then. Much darker in a way that made her breasts feel full again, with that sharp pinch in each that meant her nipples were already hard.

Why did everything Dorian do get to her like this? When he clearly thought so little of her?

"I don't know what makes you think you get to tell me what to do." Erika eyed him, then dug into her story, because she had no intention whatsoever of telling him the truth. Not now. "Everyone knows that Walfreiheit is the best BDSM club in Berlin. Maybe in the world. How was I supposed to know that Conrad's school friend would be there the night I got in, flinging a whip around, and then up for a spot of bullying?"

"Oh, little girl," Dorian said with a dark amusement that licked over her, then knotted up inside her. "I haven't begun to bully you."

"You're the one who keeps threatening me with my brother. Do you run back to him and tell him every last thing that you do? Or do you only feel you need to report on me? I'm all grown-up, Dorian, and Conrad lost his right to comment on what I do with my life when he kicked me out of my own family."

This time he really did roll his eyes. "Your mother seems to have cushioned that blow nicely."

"And look at that. One more thing that's entirely my business and not yours. At all."

"You have no idea what you're doing," Dorian told her. In that calm way that made her want to scream, though she didn't. "Do you? Standing in my home and hurling accusations at me at three in the morning is not a particularly smart way to convince me of your maturity, Erika."

"I don't have to convince you of anything, *Dorian*. You're not my friend. You're not my brother. And when I tried to do the BDSM thing like anyone else might have in that club—"

"You safe worded out."

But his voice changed. It took on that ruthlessly uncompromising quality she remembered from the club. And more, it had an instant effect on her. Her breathing changed. Her chest felt tight.

Suddenly she couldn't seem to tear her gaze away from his.

"I was momentarily overwhelmed." She said it distinctly. Almost loftily, trying to convince herself as well as him. "I didn't realize that using a safe word meant being dragged out of the club into the street. You should have made that clear."

"Careful," he advised her. "Or you might get what you're asking for. And then what?"

"Then let me be more explicit," Erika threw at him. She stood straighter, ignoring that pulling sensation in her breasts, her pussy. Her whole body. "I went to that club for a BDSM experience. Not an older-brother's-best-friend-acting-like-a-dick experience, because I've already had that, thanks. So if you'll excuse me, I think I'm going to leave, go back and tell them I was spirited away against my will."

"Really." There was even more of that amusement then, so dark and dangerous she could feel the edge against her skin like a blade. "And what will you do when you're there?"

"Whatever I feel like doing." She smirked at him and knew the moment she did it that it was a mistake. But she committed to it anyway, because she was nothing if not brazen when it was only going to get her in trouble. "You don't get to decide how I behave, Dorian. You don't get to decide a damn thing I do."

"Erika."

His voice was a crack, like that whip of his. Erika felt her breath go out of her in a rush. All he'd said was her name, but it hit her like a command. Like his hand wrapped against the nape of her neck, guiding her where he wanted her to go.

All she could do was stare back at him, mutely, entirely too aware of her pulse going wild and her breath sawing in and out of her lungs.

"You don't need to go back to the club to have a BDSM experience," he told her. "Lucky for you, I'm a BDSM experience all by myself."

"Lucky me," she said. Faintly. Because the floor

appeared to be tilted beneath her feet and she knew that couldn't be real. It only felt real. "But maybe I want…a different experience. Far away from you and your threats to involve Conrad."

His mouth moved into a curve that was in no way a smile.

"Tonight you have two options. Me, or sleep."

She hoped he couldn't see the way she quivered deep inside, and stood straighter to hide it. "This is Berlin. There are clubs everywhere. I can—"

"Erika, hear me on this if nothing else. You will not get into any BDSM club in this city. Tonight or ever again. It will take one call."

Her breath went a little ragged, but she believed him. She'd heard entirely too much about his reputation over the past two years to think he couldn't do exactly what he said he would.

"Me," he said again. He angled his head toward the hallway that stretched off behind her. "Or sleep. Choose now."

She was choosing sleep, obviously. She would meekly shuffle off to a bedroom like the biddable girl she'd never been, count to a hundred or something, then leave. Or maybe she would just leave now, without the charade. Because there was no way she was taking the other option. No way in hell. That little scene in the club had been more than enough—it had been too much, thank you.

But…something deep inside her whispered. *But what if…?*

After all, she'd spent so long getting here. And

she might find this—him—more overwhelming than she'd expected, but there was no denying the fact it turned her on. Just as he did. And he was supposed to be the best. Maybe here in the privacy of his home, he wouldn't scare her the way he had in that hallway. Even if he did, there wouldn't be a crowd of witnesses.

And she still couldn't think of a better way to stick it to her obnoxious older brother.

Blah, blah, blah, that voice inside her commented. *What matters is that you're wet. And very, very hungry.*

Maybe that was the real point of all of this. The things that had happened tonight had left her balanced precariously on the edge of a very high cliff, and despite everything, Erika…wanted to jump.

She met his gaze again and wasn't at all surprised to find him watching her in that intent, edgily patient way of his.

He didn't pressure her. He didn't have to. He was a wall. All she had to do was walk toward that wall or away from it.

"Have you decided?" he asked, as if he'd offered her a glass of water.

She nodded. Jerkily.

"Use your words, please."

Erika swallowed, but her throat stayed dry. Half of her screamed at her not to do this—to get the hell away from him—but the other half was far too curious. And much too focused on that need between her legs.

That and the dangerous gleam in his gaze that she could feel *inside* her.

"You," she said. "I choose you."

And this time, the smile that spread over his stern mouth washed over her like heat. Or maybe she was already regretting her choice—

"Excellent," Dorian said, and she thought he sounded pleased. It amazed her how much she wanted to please him. He didn't move farther into the room, and she could have sworn he loomed over her all the same. "Let's start by addressing your disrespectful attitude, shall we? On your knees. Eyes on the floor."

"But—"

"You will speak only when spoken to," he said, his voice that calm force that made her feel giddy and terrified at once. "You will answer any question I ask, and, Erika, let me be very clear. I expect and require total honesty. On your knees. Now."

He didn't raise his voice. He didn't sound particularly sharp or angry. If anything, he sounded even calmer than before.

And still, that power he wielded hit her like a blow. That was the only way she could describe the massive force that seemed to push her forward, almost against her will. She didn't think it through and worry over it from every angle. She sank down on her knees and found her hands on her thighs again. And it was easier than she'd imagined to cast her eyes down toward the ground.

Then there was nothing but her breath. Her panic

and anticipation, tangling around into something else. Something hot and liquid that streaked through her, lighting her up and settling like a weight in her pussy.

And because she wasn't looking at him any longer, he seemed bigger. As if he filled the vast room, taking up all the space and air. He made her shake, and he hadn't done anything yet. She'd done it to herself.

She got it then, in a way she never had when she'd been playing with party favor floggers before. He made her *want* to do this to herself. He made her *want* the roller coaster of sensation and emotion.

It was like an adult magic trick. And she was still shaking.

"Very nice," he said from across the room, and his approval made her flush, then feel as if she was *blooming*, somehow. "Obedience looks good on you."

She thought he was goading her, but she was determined that he wouldn't succeed. She glared at the floor and ordered herself to keep her hands *out* of telltale fists.

"Let me be clear about what is going to happen now," Dorian said, almost conversationally. If she ignored that kick of command and heat wrapped up in his words and the way he delivered them. "I'm going to spank you. Your behavior tonight has been disgraceful. Keep those eyes down, please. And I would strongly caution you not to say whatever it is you're about to say."

Erika jerked her head back down, her heart

pounding hard in her chest. She felt outraged. Insulted. How dare he call her *disgraceful*?

Her mind veered away from the *spanking* part.

"I want you to listen to me, Erika," he continued, pitiless and relentless, and in exactly the same calm tone. And the steadier he sounded, the more wildly out of control she felt. Her eyes were blurry, and she told herself that was why it seemed as if her hands were shaking. "Ignore the noise in your head. Ignore all those lies you like to tell yourself and everyone else. Focus on me. Only me. Here, now, and until I say otherwise, the only thing you have to worry about is doing exactly what I tell you to do. Do you understand me?"

She sucked in a shaky breath. "Yes, but—"

"*Yes* is a complete sentence, kitten."

She had to bite her own tongue, actually bite it, to keep from snapping back at him. He was maddening. How could he sound so blasé when he was saying something so…

But she was the one who was still kneeling. She was the one who kept doing as he said. She was the one he'd threatened to *spank* and here she was, still kneeling here like she had no choice. When she had every choice. When this *was* her choice.

"We will use the same safe-word structure as before. I want you to tell me what that is, now. With no editorializing."

"*Green light* means everything is good, fine. *Yellow light* means I'm not sure about something. Or I want to pause. And *red light* means stop."

"Very good."

He moved then, and she could track the sound of him, but she didn't dare look up. It was more than that—it felt as if his hand was on the back of her neck again, holding her head down, when he wasn't even near her.

It was only when she heard the sound of his big body against leather cushions that she realized he'd sat himself down on the wide couch that faced her.

"Come here," Dorian commanded. "And I want you to crawl."

Was she really going to do this? Erika slid her hands off her thighs, not surprised to discover they were damp. She leaned forward, putting her palms on the ground, and then she froze.

"Now, Erika," Dorian said in that same implacable way. "And I already told you how I'd like it to look. I want to see that ass bared. There's no one here but me, but go ahead and imagine you're back in the club. The only thing you should be focused on, there or here, is me."

She told herself he was a narcissist. A lunatic. An asshole of the highest degree.

But she was the one who slid her hands forward, then dragged her knees along behind. Once. Again. And then, without even meaning to, really, she was crawling across the floor.

She couldn't say she remembered the last time she'd crawled anywhere. She felt foolish. Exposed again, and it didn't matter that they were alone here. Her skirt slid to her waist, and she couldn't seem to keep herself from imagining the picture she made: a wanton little slut, crawling across the floor to obey him.

The thought nearly made her come again.

She made it over to him, and found herself at his feet.

"Look at me."

His voice was gentle enough, but with that steel beneath that made her feel as if she was on some kind of leash. She lifted her head.

And the look in his eyes took her breath away.

Dorian reached over and brushed his fingers over one cheek, then slid his palm to hold her there. Once again, the touch of his hand got beneath her skin. It made her want to squirm. Or worse, beg.

"Thank you for doing as I asked," he said, and again, the approval in his voice made her heart skip a beat.

His palm was warm, but the gleam in his dark eyes was hot. And she felt stretched between the two, flushed and obvious and so needy it hurt.

"I expect you to take your punishment exactly like this," he told her, as if he could read her mind. Or her greedy pussy. "I'm going to spank you. It's going to hurt. This is not for your pleasure, though I expect pleasure might be one of the things you feel. You don't understand boundaries, and I'm going to teach them to you. Thank me."

She had to fight the wave of dizziness. Of shame and fury and still, that horrible curiosity that she was afraid was the truth of her.

"Thank you," she gritted out, somehow.

His gaze was cool. One brow rose. "Thank you, who?"

At least she knew this one. "*Sir.* Thank you, *sir.*"

"I find that grudging tone disrespectful." But his thumb moved over her cheek almost tenderly. "Such a pretty face, and yet, so deeply insolent. You told me you were a grown woman, did you not? Now is your chance to prove it."

She opened her mouth, but something in the way his eyes gleamed stopped her.

"You have said a great many things tonight." Dorian's voice was even quieter, like thunder that rumbled so deep inside her only she knew what a catastrophe it was. And she couldn't tear her eyes away from him. She couldn't seem to do anything but breathe too hard, too fast, and burn. "But that's what you do, isn't it? You've spent your whole life writing checks with that mouth that your body can't cash. Tonight, we're going to settle your accounts."

He dropped his hand, then sat back. "You may stand."

Suddenly, crazily, Erika didn't want to stand. She wanted to stay where she was, there on her knees at his feet, where it was safe.

When she knew full well there was nothing safe about kneeling in front of this man.

Dorian watched her intently. With that armored, intense patience that made her want nothing more than to do what he wanted. However he wanted it.

Something spooled out inside her, then, that had

nothing to do with the way her mind raced. It felt long held. Secret and certain.

And the more it unwound itself within her, the less jittery she felt, even when she knew he wasn't kidding around. Dorian had every intention of hurting her. Deliberately. Spanking her like a child, because he thought that would teach her something—

No, that thing inside her corrected her. *Not like a child.*

Because this was about sex and this was about submission, and ultimately it was about her choice to combine those things and let him pick the path they took. She could use her safe word at any time. She could be up and walking away from him right now.

The issue wasn't that Dorian wanted to spank her. It was that deep down, Erika *wanted* to let him spank her.

Or she wouldn't be here, at his feet, fighting herself while he waited. And watched.

And Erika couldn't tell if she was shuddering because she couldn't bear the thought, or because she was terrified of what she might actually learn from this. Who she might become when he was done with her.

But either way, she stood.

"Lovely," he said, and it made her flush with that same strange pride. Then he patted his thighs, his dark gaze its own command. "Now lie down."

CHAPTER FIVE

ERIKA MIGHT HAVE thought she was on the verge of being sick, if it weren't for that blazing fire in her pussy that made a lie out of all the other sensations that sloshed around inside her. Her heart jolted, her stomach dropped, her skin felt stretched too tight… But still she burned.

And all Dorian did was sit there, almost lazily, watching her intently as she battled herself.

He did nothing to encourage her. He did nothing to hurry her along.

He only waited as if he was in absolutely no doubt that no matter her struggle, she would do exactly what he'd told her to do.

Because you want *to do it*, something in her whispered.

She was that hard, small stone in his palm, and he would make a fist only if she admitted it. If she allowed it. If she laid herself across his lap and submitted the way she wanted to, with every last part of the melty, swoony thing currently burning up inside her.

"Were my instructions unclear?" Dorian asked, mildly enough.

But nothing about the intensity in his dark gaze was mild.

Erika let out a breath that turned into something like a sob, and then she lowered herself over him.

It was awkward. His thighs were much too hard, and she was too...*aware* of everything. The way her breasts pressed into the leather cushion and how weird it was to crawl over another person like this in the first place. Much less for the reason she was doing it.

"I want you to lace your hands behind your head," Dorian said, and she instantly felt calmer and more on fire at the same time.

It was like the more she melted, the more of her there was to melt.

And it was a lot different to hear him talk now. In this position. She shifted, and his hand came down to the small of her back, holding her there. Firmly, yet light enough that if she'd wanted to, she could have rolled away from him. Thrown herself on the floor, run for the door—

But she only exhaled. Loudly.

And stayed where she was.

"Hands, please," he said calmly. But there was no mistaking the power in his voice.

God, that *power*.

Erika had spent her whole life careening about from one so-called authority figure to the next, always laughing when they tried to control her, because they couldn't. They always backed down, or lost track of her, or proved easy enough for her to control. They had the position of authority, but not the power to back it up.

Dorian had the power. And she'd given him the authority, hadn't she?

And she knew without having to ask that there was no possibility that she was going to control this, or him, or anything at all unless and until she uttered that safe word.

But she really didn't want to do that.

Her skin was so oversensitized she thought she might come from the faintest breeze, and it seemed to get worse with every breath. Or maybe she meant *better.* She threaded her fingers together behind her head, and that changed things all over again. It thrust her breasts into the leather cushion beneath her, abrading her nipples through the strappy top she wore and making them pull tighter.

But she was far more focused on Dorian. His rock-hard thighs beneath her, muscle like stone, that made her feel deliciously weak. And that hand in the small of her back, holding her in place so easily—though it felt like a heavy length of chain to her. She could feel his heat. His strength. That power that she'd already spent two years chasing. She felt surrounded by him, and it made her body shudder in reaction. Or longing. It was hard to tell.

It was all the same, and she melted, and everything was much too hot—

He smoothed his other hand over her ass, flipping up that tiny skirt. She tried to imagine what he saw. Her bright red lacy thong stuck between her ass cheeks, painting him a picture. She could *see* herself and it made her hips rock a little, as if that could help her aching clit.

It didn't. Especially when he widened his legs, effectively preventing her from rocking herself against him for any kind of relief.

More than that it reminded her, wordlessly, that he was in control. Complete and utter control, and saw everything. Every little wriggle she tried to make. Every expression on her face. Every flush that stained her skin.

For someone who had spent a whole life being both too visible and yet forever ignored, it was… gratifying. Terrifying. *Electrifying.*

"I'm going to pull your thong down," he told her matter-of-factly, as if he was narrating the weather to a disinterested party. "I want your ass entirely exposed. It looks as if it's never been touched. Has it?"

"No one's ever really spanked me, sir," she said to the leather beneath her. "If that's what you mean."

"I'm not surprised to hear that," he said with what she thought might be a measure of satisfaction. "You've needed a good spanking as long as I've known you."

She shuddered at that, and his hand moved, rolling her thong down over her hips. She expected him to pull it all the way off her, but he only left it tangled there above her knees.

Confining her, she realized. Making her feel dirty,

tied down and, for some reason, so turned-on she wanted to cry.

Then he didn't say anything. He stroked her ass in silence, warming each cheek with his palms. Roughly. He explored her, running his hands where he pleased, even delving into the furrow between her cheeks to press against the opening there.

Something arced through her, white-hot and greedy, a dark little gas fire of fear and longing.

"Has anyone taken you in the ass before?" he asked with that damned calm.

"N-no."

"What a shame. Why not? Is it a hard limit for you?"

She wanted to kick him, but she couldn't seem to move. "No. I don't know."

"Pick one or the other."

"It's supposed to hurt," she said, scowling at the cushion beneath her. "Why do something that hurts?"

Though it occurred to her that the question was pretty silly, given her current situation. To his credit, though she had the sense he smiled, Dorian didn't laugh.

"Because pain is temporary and, if employed deliberately and well, enhances pleasure." He pressed against her tight bud again, then moved on. He rubbed his palms restlessly over her upturned cheeks, laying in a pinch here, there, then holding her down when she jumped. "I promise you that if I hurt you, when I hurt you, I'll also make you come. Eventually. You may thank me."

"Th-thank you, sir," she managed to say, while she melted and burned, raged and wanted to sob.

"And you didn't answer my question. Is anal play a hard limit for you?"

Erika felt the strangest trickle of something like relief then, when that didn't make any sense. Why would she feel *relieved* when she was still waiting for a spanking of all things? And he was going out of his way to make sure she knew he never forgot a damned thing?

But in the next too-quick breath, she understood. That was why. He didn't forget. He didn't let things go. If he asked her a question, he expected her to answer.

He would not forget her or any detail about her, down to the dress she'd worn two years ago at a party in Greece.

He would not, for example, swan off to Cap Ferrat for the season as her mother had done one winter, forgetting that she'd left Erika alone on the estate south of Melbourne where they'd spent a span of years. She'd been seven. The staff had been lovely, but her mother hadn't deigned to return until Erika lit a fire in one of the old, empty barns and the butler had finally given his notice, as he wasn't a babysitter.

Erika had no idea why that weird, old memory was cropping up now. While she was close enough to naked and tossed over Dorian's lap all these years later and in Berlin.

"Erika. Don't make me ask you again."

"No," she whispered. "It's not a limit. I would try it."

"If I asked."

"If you asked," she agreed, her heart so loud inside her it hurt. "Sir."

She felt humiliated and excited in turn, and the contrast lurched around inside her, making her squirm. And pant. And want to die—but not before he kept that promise that any hurt he dished out would come with a hefty dollop of pleasure, too.

Erika thought she might die if he didn't keep his promise.

And then, to her horror and her delight, he reached beneath her and cupped her pussy in his hand. That was all he did. He simply...held her there.

She was the one who was quivering, sensitive and sweating with the force of a need that felt like madness.

"Look at this," he said, sounding dark and approving all at once. "You can't wait, can you? You're desperate. Soaking wet. As if you've been waiting your whole life for someone to finally take you in hand. Is that what you want, Erika?"

She wanted to fight. She wanted to argue. And more than both of those things, she wanted to thrust herself backward and somehow make him move his palm hard against her, because she knew it would take only the slightest graze of her clit against him to make her explode.

But she didn't dare misbehave like that. And he

didn't move his palm. As if he knew exactly what it was she wanted most.

"Yes, sir," she made herself say, squeezing her eyes shut as storm after storm rampaged through her. She kept her cheek pressed hard against the leather, gripping her own fingers behind her neck—even though all that did was press her breasts harder against the sofa beneath her.

Everything she did made it worse. Or better.

"I want to hear you say it."

"Yes, sir," she said again, desperation making her voice shake. "I've waited my whole life for someone to take me in hand."

"Not someone. Me. You want me, specifically, to teach you boundaries. To demand respect. To be the only person you've ever met who doesn't allow your insolence to go unheeded. Don't you?"

"Yes, sir."

And it came out a moan, though he hadn't really done anything yet.

All she was doing was lying here, in this remarkably exposed position, with his hand resting gently in *almost* the perfect place. And yet she was as turned-on as if he was fucking her. She'd had orgasms that were less intense than this. She was stretched out, gripping her own hands too tightly behind her neck, every part of her tense and waiting and so, so needy—

"You are in luck, little girl," he told her, with a certain erotic menace that made her pulse kick at her even as she melted all the more. "Because I have no intention of going easy on you. I'm going to spank you. You're going to count. You can sob, but you will lie still. You can cry out, but you will not fight me. If you use words, they will be of gratitude or your safe word and nothing else. Do you understand me?"

It was all storms and riot inside her. Why wasn't she calling this off? Why wasn't she rolling away from him, protecting herself, doing something to stop this?

Erika had played games before, with handcuffs and funny little floggers that tickled, and she'd thought she was practicing for this. But she'd never doubted that she was in complete control. Not once. The men she was with had teased her, but never hurt her.

This was different. Dorian wanted to hurt her. And would.

Or maybe it wasn't that simple. He wanted her to *allow him* to hurt her, because the crazy thing was, she wanted him to do just that.

He saw her. He could list her sins, and had. He was the only one who could punish her for them—and then grant her absolution, too.

She might not be in control of him. But she was here because she wanted to be here.

It was as simple and as wildly, impossibly convoluted as that.

"Yes, sir," she said and shuddered with the force of what she was agreeing to—but it felt as if she *needed* this. As if he was right, and she'd been looking for it all her life.

"Are you a reckless, thoughtless, selfish girl who needs this punishment?"

It was as if he could read her mind. She tried to control her breathing, and failed miserably. "Yes, sir."

"Do you trust me to punish you as you deserve?"

She gave up on her breath, because she was sobbing. Big racking sobs rolled up from somewhere deep inside her, and made her body convulse. Her eyes were wet, her fingers so tight they were cramping behind her neck.

And still, all she could focus on was that blazing heat between her legs.

And him. Dorian.

At this moment, he was the whole of her world.

"Yes," she managed to get out. "Yes, sir."

He moved his hand from her pussy, and did it without so much as grazing a single part of her that would have kicked her deeper into that fire. And when his hand moved over her ass again, she could feel her own wetness.

The first smack shocked her.

It *hurt*.

"Count, please," he ordered her.

"One," she managed to get out. "Thank you, sir."

"Excellent," he said, and he was already rubbing the place where he'd smacked her, almost soothing it. But not quite enough to keep that deep red ache at bay. "Just like that."

And then he got to work.

It was shocking. Excruciating. His hand was big

and impossibly hard. And he was thorough. The pain of each precise smack jolted through her, making her kick her legs, but she didn't roll off him. She stayed where she was, no matter the sting and the ache of it.

Erika counted. And thanked him.

And cried.

And he kept going. First he spanked one cheek, then the other. He smacked her in the crease where her ass met her thighs. He continued until her whole butt felt bright red and agonized, and then he started the same painful pattern all over again.

Again and again, until she wasn't even pretending that she was doing anything but sobbing her eyes out.

She sobbed and she sobbed and he spanked her, and it fucking hurt. And she was strung out somewhere between the white noise in her head and the way her nipples were still too hard as they moved with the force of his smacks against the leather beneath her. Her ass was on fire, the pain outrageous and bright, and still, her clit ached and her pussy was so wet she hardly knew what to do with herself.

Dorian, by contrast, did not thrash about. He spanked her, that was all, but he did it in the same calm, considered rhythm as when he'd started. He didn't speed up. He didn't hit her harder or taper off into something lighter. He was laying down a lesson.

And all Erika could do was count. And sob for all the memories she didn't want in her head right now, but seemed lodged in her chest anyway.

Though Dorian seemed determined to spank them right out of her.

When she counted all the way to twenty, he stopped.

It took her a moment to realize that, because she was still sobbing. He picked her up, so easily that it occurred to her he'd wanted her to crawl into that position with as much strained awkwardness as it took.

But that was something she would have to think about later, when she wasn't so beside herself. He pulled her to him, cradling her against his chest. And then he murmured words that didn't quite penetrate as he held her there, her ass sore and hot against his thighs and her face tucked against his collarbone.

For a long time, Erika cried. And it wasn't until she was sniffling and calming herself, that it actually hit her that she was in Dorian's arms.

And not only that, all the pain in her ass seemed to be radiating out and setting that raging fire in her pussy into some kind of inferno.

"If you keep squirming against me like that," Dorian said, his voice so close, so dark, it made her shudder, "I will take it as an invitation to continue the lesson."

She shuddered out a breath and stopped.

And then he lifted her, gripping her by the upper arms and holding her just far enough away from him that he could stare directly into her eyes.

The world outside had disappeared. There was only sensation, Dorian and that intense gleam in his eyes.

"You please me, Erika," he told her, his voice grave. "You took that well."

She couldn't seem to think. Or speak. All she could do was hold his words close, unexpected light that made her heart feel bigger than it had been.

She pleased him.

Maybe that was enough.

And then, all she could focus on was that ache between her legs, made ravenous by the hot red ache he'd given her.

He set her on her feet then, there between his legs. Erika cast her eyes down without being asked, but she could feel the smile in his voice when he spoke.

"Turn around, please. I want to admire my work."

She shuddered, but obeyed.

"Hold up your skirt, please."

And she could hear her own breathing again—not quite a sob any longer, not simply a breath—as she stood there, staring at those books again. Pretending she wasn't holding her skirt up high, her thong still tangled around her knees, baring the ass he'd spanked to his view. And also unable to think of anything else.

She knew he sat forward when he gripped her hips, then moved his hands painfully over her ass cheeks again.

"Stay still," he ordered her.

And she tried. She really did try.

"Your ass is beautifully red and hot," he told her after a moment. "I like all those tears on your face, Erika. I'm feeling magnanimous and very well pleased. Ask me for what you want. I might just grant it to you."

She didn't even think. She didn't have to think. She knew exactly what she wanted.

Erika couldn't have imagined that it would all go down like this, that he would scare her, then spank her and make her purge herself of some ugliness she wasn't sure she even wanted to look at straight. But she knew what she wanted.

She'd only ever wanted one thing from him, above everything else. It was funny how clear it was now. All the world had seemed to narrow down to just one thing.

"Look at me," he said, and she did.

She looked back over her shoulder to find his dark eyes blazing with the same intense heat she could feel coiled so tightly inside her.

"Ask me," he ordered.

"Please, sir," Erika said softly in a voice that sounded like belonged to someone else, but she couldn't think about that now. "Please. Fuck me."

CHAPTER SIX

DORIAN HADN'T MEANT to do anything but scare her.

But then she'd stuck her chin in the air, gave him that challenging look, talked about finding herself a different kinky club and… No.

He couldn't allow it.

And somewhere in there, it had all changed from a lesson he could have imparted to anyone who needed to understand what a firm hand and some discipline could do, to…this.

His cock was so hard he thought he might burst. When he was never, ever out of control. Never with submissives. Never anywhere, for that matter.

She's different, something in him whispered, but she was Conrad's little sister, so that was impossible.

But at the moment, he couldn't bring himself to think about all the ways he had already betrayed his oldest and best friend tonight, because he wasn't done yet. He had made Erika a promise.

And Dorian did not break his promises.

She couldn't possibly know the picture she made,

Dorian thought as he gazed at her now, or how badly he wanted her.

He had spanked her hard and she'd pinkened beautifully, so that high, round ass of hers was bright and getting redder by the second. He could see the pouting lips of her pussy when she bent forward slightly, still holding up that skirt to give him a better view. Her blond hair was a tousled mess from all that thrashing around on the couch, her face was tearstained, and her eyes were wide and glazed.

But best of all, bratty little Erika Vanderburg was looking at him as if she'd seen God. And better still, wanted some hard, wild communion.

He was so hard it hurt.

He'd never intended to do more than spank her. Teach her a lesson.

Liar, something in him laughed.

But she was looking at him with awe and greed and he felt the same thing return—and then some. And he couldn't think about all the reasons why he shouldn't do exactly what she'd asked him to do.

"Hands and knees," he ordered her in a growl. "Right there."

She rushed to obey him, and he almost laughed at the sight. She was so wound up, it hadn't yet occurred to her how much she'd changed between the hallway at the club and here. How eager she was to obey him, with her pupils dilated and her pulse wild.

Erika liked a hard hand, he'd discovered. She bloomed under discipline. He made a note of that as if he planned to expand on that discovery—

But this wasn't the time to second-guess himself.

Dorian reached into the drawer in his side table and pulled out a condom. He knelt behind her, freed his aching cock from his trousers and sheathed himself. Then he gripped her lush hips, making sure his hands pressed into her reddened flesh. She made a whimpering sound, but pushed back to get closer to him.

It made him smile.

"I'm going to fuck you," he told her, wanting to sound cool but coming out gravelly instead. But that worked, too. "You may come whenever you like, but if you do not, you're out of luck. You can't touch your clit. You can't rub yourself against me. I want you to submit, take it and see what happens. Do you understand me?"

Her head fell forward, as if she could no longer hold it up. As if the idea of submission on that scale made her weak.

"Yes, sir," she whispered.

Dorian lined himself up with the entrance to her pussy, pressing his fingers into the curves of her ass because he knew it would sting. And remind her what she'd already taken. She shuddered, and he could smell how wet she was. How ready.

God help him, but she was a wonder.

He took a split second to admire her, there on her hands and knees, her ass red from his hand and her pretty pussy on display and ready to be split wide-open by him.

It was almost perfect.

"Put your face on the floor," he told her. "Hands behind your back, please."

She blew out a breath, then obeyed with a certain graceless alacrity that pleased him more than studied grace would have—because it meant she was too excited to contain herself. And better still, his grip on her meant he kept her pussy right there, pressed against his wide cockhead. As she shifted, he coated himself in her and had to hold himself back, hard.

When her hands were behind her back and her forehead was nestled against the oversoft, cushy rug beneath them, he wrapped one hand around her wrists and held them there. Maybe a little higher than she would have naturally, to make it fun.

"Thank me," he commanded her. "For showing you this consideration and allowing for the possibility of your pleasure in the midst of this punishment."

He felt the shudder work its way through her, and he loved the way goose bumps prickled all over her skin. She was so responsive. He was already thinking of all the wicked things he could do to make her shudder like that, over and over again.

Dorian hadn't been this pleased and impressed by a submissive in a long, long while.

"Thank you, sir," Erika moaned. "Thank you, thank you."

And with absolutely no warning, he slammed himself home.

She came instantly, violently, with a scream that was like music to him.

He didn't wait for her to ride it out. Dorian pounded

into her, hard and deep, claiming her and taking her over and over. He fucked her through the wallop of that first orgasm, then straight on into a second one.

Erika kept screaming, prettier every time.

And still he kept fucking her at the same, ferocious pace, until her sobs and screams changed. And turned into his name.

"Please, Dorian. Please, sir. Please—please—please—"

He couldn't have said what she begged for. Only that he took it.

Again and again, he took and she gave, and that was the beauty they made between them. That was the discipline and the desire, the coming together of two halves to make something much hotter, much brighter than either one of them alone.

Dorian made her come once more, and then, with a roar, he took his own pleasure at last.

And as he fell, he had the distinct notion that this time, he was well and truly damned.

Dorian did not typically spend a lot of his time questioning himself, his motives or his actions, because he'd spent a lifetime committed to honesty and openness in all things and that generally meant there was very little to question.

He was renowned for ferreting out secrets in the club and in the boardroom by dint of…simply asking. Then demanding honesty in return.

It was amazing how rare that was. So rare, in fact, that he'd heard it discussed in his office as his superpower. He'd always rolled his eyes at that, because if he had a superpower, he was pretty sure it had more to do with the kind of sex he preferred than a simple round of honest conversation.

Some people liked to claim he had been born confident, and he couldn't dispute that. Dorian had always had a deep, invariable sense of who he was, what he wanted and what he was prepared to do to get it. That had come to him honestly. His father had been the disappointment in the Alexander family, lazy and addicted and good for nothing at all—but his inability to live up to the standards set by Dorian's grandfather had merely given Dorian a good example of what best to avoid.

He did not lie because that was all his father ever did. He did not cheat because he had seen the pain his father's various forms of cheating had caused, whether in his relationships or in the business. He was bracingly honest with everyone he came into contact with—especially himself.

But that was before his best friend's little sister had turned up in his favorite club, sank to her knees and made something deep inside him hum.

As if he'd been waiting all this time to truly come alive.

He shook that unsettling notion off. And he concentrated on the practicalities instead.

Erika lay on the floor in a heap. Her eyes were closed, her face was still flushed, and her lips were parted. She was in the position he'd left her, as if she'd simply…folded into herself. Fully surrendered, fully his.

The woman of your dreams, a voice inside him pronounced.

Dorian rubbed a hand over his face, amazed to find he was less steady than he ought to have been.

He tucked himself back into his trousers, amazed that he had come so hard. He couldn't remember the last time a woman had gotten to him like that. And he didn't feel empty and restless the way he did more and more these days, especially after sex. He wasn't already thinking about the work he had to do or what his next extreme BDSM feat would be should he find a willing submissive to test it with him. He wasn't already thinking about who that might be.

He wasn't thinking about anything except Erika and that was…new. Like the feeling of deep stillness inside him that he knew he'd never felt before—and yet recognized, somehow.

Dorian didn't know where the hell to put all that yet, so he shoved it aside. He reached down and plucked her up from the floor, shifting her to hold her in his arms. Then he carried her up the stairs to the master suite that took up most of the second floor. Her head was a soft and welcome weight tucked there into the crook of his neck, making the stillness in him feel like something else. Like religion, maybe.

He moved down the hall past his study, personal gym and sauna, and he didn't bother to turn on any lights. Berlin was bright outside the many windows, casting the room in a dim kind of glow. And when he looked, he could see the first signs of dawn in the sky.

It should have been no more than another well-spent night in this anything-goes city. But that wasn't how it felt.

Not when she was still groggy as he set her on her feet, there against the side of his bed with its four steel posters that he would very much like to tie her to. So groggy she hadn't arranged her features in the usual way. She looked sweet. Defenseless. Wide-open and guileless, and Dorian's ribs seemed to shrink. It was hard to breathe for a moment.

He couldn't say he liked that at all.

Erika murmured something incoherent as he stripped her few clothes from her body. He laid her out on the mattress and left her there, murmuring a quiet order for her to stay where she was.

And she was exactly where he'd left her when he came back. He'd gone downstairs to the kitchen to fix her a little snack and a glass of water, with an electrolyte powder mixed in for when she was recovered sufficiently to tend to the inevitable postscene drop. He'd also found his preferred salve in the play bag he brought to the club, though he hadn't used it in a while.

But that was one more thing he didn't want to think about, because it felt…fraught. Fragile, almost, in this strange blue light of almost-morning with a woman he shouldn't have touched soft and undeniably his in his bed.

Dorian shouldn't have touched her, but he had.

And that meant he had responsibilities. The kind of sex—and sex games—he liked meant there was no hit-it-then-quit-it option afterward. Especially not when things had gotten so intense between them.

Some submissives didn't like to be touched afterward, but Erika had snuggled into him as he'd carried her. He wondered if she would feel that way with one of the fantasy dominants she'd imagined she'd find in the sex clubs he had every intention of banning her from—or if it was specific to him. To them, because she knew him.

Dorian really didn't want to think about how he knew her, or how long he'd known her, and he was all too aware that the things he didn't want to think about were starting to feel a lot like lying to himself. He wasn't all the way there yet, but he had the creeping suspicion it was gaining on him. His jaw clenched on its own accord and he made himself loosen up as he sat down next to her on the bed.

She was soft and warm beneath his hands, and she smiled as he turned her over onto her belly. He took his time rubbing the liniment into the marks he'd left on her ass, taking more than a little satisfaction in the heat of her reddened flesh beneath his palm.

"I can't decide if that hurts or feels good or both," she said softly, as much to the mattress as to him, and when he looked up, her eyes were closed. As if she was talking in her sleep.

"Then it's working." He finished with the lotion and set it aside, then ran a hand down the elegant line of her back that had entranced him for a split second long ago—and that he had the sneaking suspicion would haunt him for a lot longer now. "Are you okay?"

Her eyelashes fluttered as she blinked at him. "Define *okay*."

"Do you feel exposed? Vulnerable? Emotional?"

Her gaze was steady and much too blue. "Yes."

And to his surprise, Dorian found himself smiling. "Good."

"You wanted to make me feel things," she said after a moment. "Didn't you?"

"We can talk about it later," he told her gruffly.

And normally he was remote, if caring, during aftercare. He tended to any wounds and made sure there were no physical complications. He held subs on his lap if necessary, made sure they got their energy levels up again. But he was not cuddly. He was Dorian Alexander. He did not *snuggle*.

And still, without thinking too much about why he was doing it, he crawled up onto the bed beside her. He pulled her to him and held her there against his chest. Which meant he was going to have to find another word to describe what it was he was doing, because it felt too good to be *snuggling*.

She shifted, and for another moment that made his chest too tight, he thought she might pull away. But she didn't.

Instead, she settled against him, tucking her head against his chest and letting out a long, slow exhale.

And a knot in Dorian's chest he would have insisted wasn't there, because it never had been before, eased a little.

Unfortunately, that gave his mind leave to spin about at will.

Dorian had accepted his particular kinks and quirks a long time ago. Unlike some of the dominants he knew, he had never agonized about the things he wanted. His only concession to his supposed deviance had been to go out of his way to make certain that whoever he played with wanted the same things he did. The dynamic. The exquisite give to his take.

He took joy in the initial negotiation, the setting of terms and expectations. He reveled in building scenes and taking submissives on a ride. And even if he'd begun to feel more like one of those shabby old American theme parks of late, that didn't change what he liked or who he was. All it did was make him more selective. It was edging up on a month, maybe two, since he'd gone to the club before tonight—when there had been a time he couldn't get enough.

Dorian knew people thought it was a sickness, even in these so-called enlightened times. His father, for example, who had discovered his son's predilections early and had spent years throwing it in Dorian's face—and not only when he was out of his head. Dorian had been grateful for that, all things considered, because it had made it that much easier to cut his father out of his life. The way his mother and grandfather had done before him.

For him, always, it all came down to this moment. After the storm of play and passion, the simple trust of a well-pleasured, well-spanked woman. It was everything to him. It was the point.

And he had always enjoyed this moment, when surrender was absolute, and only trust remained. He didn't *snuggle* through it, normally, but he always liked it. And tonight he couldn't help noticing that he'd never felt so complete before. As if she wasn't the only one who'd put an integral part of herself out on the table here tonight.

As if she wasn't the only one exposed.

He didn't like that thought at all.

And he *really* didn't like, once it took hold, how that thought bloomed. And cascaded, because this wasn't a random submissive woman he could have met in a club. It wasn't only a surprisingly intense scene that had veered off and become something he hadn't quite intended.

There was no getting away from the fact that this was Erika in his arms, naked, with a red ass he'd given her himself. Erika Vanderburg. Conrad's little sister.

Dorian had never hidden his nature from his friend. There was no point when his father liked to trumpet it to the world at every opportunity. And, in fact, Conrad shared a number of his inclinations.

But he doubted very much that Conrad would find it even remotely acceptable for Dorian to be exploring those inclinations with Erika.

Erika seemed to be in some doubt about the situation with her older brother, but Dorian knew what she didn't. Conrad loved her. Fiercely, stubbornly and perhaps too sternly—but he loved her. Dorian had been with him when he'd received news of their father's death. And Dorian knew that one of Conrad's major concerns, then and now, was how he was going to raise his spoiled, fragile little princess of a sister the way his father would have wanted.

Conrad had done his best to fill his father's shoes.

Erika had flounced off and started referring to him as her enemy.

And Dorian, who had witnessed his friend's struggle and had taken a dim view of Erika's behavior himself, had repaid his friend's trust and friendship by defiling the little sister Conrad almost viewed as more of a daughter.

Plainly, Dorian was fucked.

In his arms, there against his chest, Erika stirred again. Dorian needed to distance himself. He needed to repair the walls he should have kept between his cock and what he owed his friend—and fast.

But her face, her beautiful face, was open and vulnerable when she tipped it up to his. Her blue eyes were sleepy. And suddenly he couldn't abide the idea of any walls.

"Lie down with me," she said, and though she phrased it like an order, he knew it was a question. And an uncertain one at that.

Obviously Dorian didn't cuddle up with his subs and sleep with them that way. He'd always imagined that kind of thing was better left to long-term relationships—which he had always been deeply allergic to.

Allergic? asked that same voice inside him. *Or uninspired?*

But all that unfettered emotion on her pretty face was easily the most beautiful thing he'd ever seen.

And the fact he was digging his own hole was clear to him. But he didn't do anything to stop it. He set her aside and rolled from the bed, and she curled into a ball against his pillows and watched him strip out of his clothes.

He waited for that restless itch to wash over him, and told himself he would handle it for however long she slept because it was the least he could do for this woman he shouldn't have laid a finger on—much less spanked and fucked and made cry. But it didn't kick in.

Not when he crawled into the bed and pulled her tight to his front, one arm slung over her soft warmth. Not when they lay there like that, wound together like roots too tangled to ever be pulled apart.

She sighed a little as she burrowed beneath the covers, and he knew that sound. Surrender and safety. *Beautiful*, he thought.

And just this once, just because it was Erika, he let himself go.

Dorian held her close, matched his breath to hers and then, for the very first time, fell asleep with a woman in his arms.

CHAPTER SEVEN

DORIAN WOKE UP with Erika wrapped around him, tangled up in every possible way with her legs between his and her mouth against his neck, and stopped lying to himself.

She slept heavily and deep. He knew her scent now, and the heat of her skin, as if she was tattooed on him. And the memories of what they'd done the night before were now interspersed with what it was like to sleep in a sweet knot with her, turning this way and then the other as if they'd choreographed it.

As if he, a man who never slept easily or at all with another, couldn't sleep unless he was in contact with her.

As if you will never sleep well without her again.

He could feel that weight in his chest, thick and deep.

But this morning, steeped in the reality his body had already accepted—since he had slept with this woman tucked up next to him and wound around him as if they'd done it a hundred thousand times before—Dorian stopped pretending he didn't know what that weight was.

He had always been honest to a fault. It was part of what attracted him to BDSM and why he flourished in a subculture that prized communication, candor and authenticity above all else. He saw no reason to stop now, no matter that this kind of sudden awareness wasn't exactly what he'd planned for this weekend. No matter how inconvenient the truth that lay there, beautifully naked beside him.

He took his time easing away from her because he wanted her to stay right where she was, her cheeks flushed with the force of her dreams and that ass of hers still red from his hand. He was hard, but then, he suspected that might simply be the Erika effect. If he claimed her, if she was his, he could look forward to mornings like this. To waking her up in whatever method he could devise to best take advantage, and his imagination when it came to the care and erotic torture of women who liked to kneel before him was boundless. And endlessly wicked.

Something thudded through him, and he had the distinct impression that it was the last of his defenses disappearing.

In what felt to him like a plume of smoke. Or maybe a bonfire.

There was no *if* about it, he acknowledged.

He had every intention of claiming this woman. If he hadn't, he would never have fucked her.

Because deep down, he knew what he wanted. He always had.

His restlessness of recent months—the past year—had been because he'd stopped believing that he could get it. It seemed impossible that he could ever combine the two parts of his life. The heir to the Alexander shipping fortune needed to marry an appropriate wife. Dorian had always known that. Even his own father had done his duty in that respect, though Dorian doubted his brittle, elegant mother—now married to a sedate London financier who she could depend on to bore her in exactly the same way for the rest of their stodgy lives—would thank him for it. And Dorian had certainly met his share of kinky, delightfully debauched debutantes over the years, God bless them.

But none of them had inspired him for more than a night. Or in his case, a part of the night. The ones who played as hard as he did weren't interested in anything but playing. And the vast majority of them were better at playing *at* debauchery than really giving themselves over to man who could lead them through the darkness of anything real.

He stood there, one hand on the steel post that he really was going to tie her to, one of these days. It was almost as if he could see it. As if it had already happened, when he knew it hadn't.

Yet.

That word echoed in him like a premonition. Like a vow.

He pulled a light blanket up and over Erika's body, little as he liked covering such mouthwatering nakedness. He would much prefer to lie back down, roll her over and lose himself in her again and again…

But he had some thinking to do. Some serious thinking to do.

And he doubted very much that he would get any of that done while he stood here, *this close* to slipping back into that bed, holding her hands over her head so her breasts jutted toward his mouth and waking her up the way he wanted to do.

Dorian showered, and toweled himself off, choosing not to handle his cock—because he had plans. He grabbed a pair of jeans and a T-shirt on his way toward the stairs, and dressed before he jogged down them. When he reached the main floor, he found his mobile and checked his messages and email. There was the usual influx of work-related things he intended to ignore as much as possible. And there were also three messages on his personal voice mail.

All from Conrad.

And if he'd had any lingering doubts about the conviction he'd woken up with, it vanished then. Because Dorian knew he needed to have a frank conversation with his best friend today, but what he didn't feel was any sense of guilt or shame.

Fuck that.

He padded into his modern, streamlined kitchen, and set about fixing himself his morning coffee. He answered the one or two emails that couldn't wait, then tossed his phone onto the counter. Then he stood there, drinking his coffee and staring out his windows at his beloved Berlin. His grubby, beautiful, sprawling and unknowable city. He had lived here over a decade, had no plans to relocate and still found something new every time he walked down the street.

That was what BDSM had always been for him. Adventure and home in one. A refuge for a boy who had grown up on a steady diet of his father's chaos, and a place where the man he'd made himself—uncompromising, brutally honest and as demanding as he was protective—was appreciated. Lauded, even.

And still, lately, he'd been thinking he was going to have to give it up. Because he needed to marry to carry on the family line in the time-honored fashion, he had no intention of treating any wife of his as shabbily as his father had treated his mother, and he didn't believe that there was any possibility he would be lucky enough to find an heiress to please his grandfather who would also please him.

After all, it was notoriously difficult to please Master Dorian. His entire reputation was built on that essential truth.

And then here, last night, with the least likely person he could ever have imagined, he'd felt that particular stillness inside him.

Erika had pleased him. Deeply and completely.

And as she had told him already last night, his grandfather already loved her.

Dorian might have preferred a direct blow to the face rather than the sucker punch that realization felt like this morning, but he was nothing if not capable of rolling with what he found and making the best of it. It was what had made him his second fortune. It was also what made him popular at the club.

He didn't have to glance at his mobile to see his best friend's name again. Conrad's name was emblazoned inside him, and the idea that a man he considered a brother would hate him for this disloyalty ate at him—but Dorian had never been one to hide from hard things. Hiding was akin to lying as far as he was concerned.

And the liar in his family was his father, not him.

He made himself a second cup of coffee and started thinking about solutions.

Conrad was an issue, but bigger by far than his best friend was the issue of Erika herself. Dorian knew she'd needed what had happened between them last night—desperately. Her submission to him had been real and raw and truly one of the most beautiful things he had ever seen. He wanted nothing more than to protect her. Help her.

And get them both off while he was at it. Repeatedly.

It was what he was made for.

He wanted to do his level best to use this particularly kinky spark between them to make them better people together than they could ever be alone. It was the sweetest, most dangerous game. It was the crux of the power exchange. He dominated, she submitted, and somewhere in there, her strength humbled him even as his power melted her.

It was Dorian's favorite kind of fire, and he had never felt it burn as hot and as wild as it had last night.

Because while clubs like his existed all over the world to create safe spaces for like-minded individuals to play at burning, it was still just play.

And what Dorian had discovered last night, when that fire had led him places he'd never thought he'd go, was that he wanted real. He was done with playtime.

But was Erika?

Because he could sit here and think through a thousand different scenarios to energetically explain his point of view until she surrendered the way he liked best, but if the only reason she was here was because she wanted to hurt Conrad… Well. That didn't exactly fit in with all the futures he was building in his head.

He sat with that for a moment. And didn't like it. Not when she'd given herself over into his hands so beautifully, so completely.

Dorian was hard just thinking about it. Hard and something more—in a kind of awe, really, at her ability to kneel. To submit. To bend to his will, and find herself brighter and more beautiful on the other side.

Fundamentally, he didn't believe—maybe he *couldn't* believe—that what had happened between them hadn't gotten to her.

He figured it was possible she'd come after him for revenge, then found herself on her knees, significantly more compelled by their dynamic than she'd planned. Because the bedroom games she'd played before weren't the same thing as the true, real connection that had blazed between them. No game could touch it.

And that connection was worth anything and everything, as far as Dorian was concerned. Especially when, until last night, he had truly believed that he would have to pack these needs of his away, meet a perfectly nice girl by regular means instead of in his club, where he could ask her for a list of her soft and hard limits, and sentence himself to a life devoid of all this glorious color.

He could get off by having vanilla sex, if he had to, as he'd told Erika last night. He had before, and he'd told himself that he would again. There had been times when he'd assured himself it wasn't even a great sacrifice. Not when he had found it so difficult to find that true connection he craved out there in the clubs, and Lord knew that even vanilla sex was better than going without.

That was what he'd told himself. And he'd been more than halfway to convincing himself that he really, truly believed it. He'd even assured his grandfather that this would be the year he would start looking seriously for an appropriate wife.

And he had. He'd gone on a few perfectly nice dates with lovely women who did absolutely nothing for him. And he'd been gearing himself to simply… choose one and commit himself, if not to his own happiness, then to hers.

But today he found himself standing in a life that looked exactly the way it had yesterday, but was wrecked from the inside out. Changed entirely.

By one mouthy, spoiled, impossible brat who made his cock hard and his heart kick, even now.

Dorian set down his second cup of coffee, ran his hands over his face and accepted his fate. It was done, as far as he was concerned. And Master Dorian did not dither when he'd made up his mind.

He set about getting what he wanted.

And one thing Dorian was very, very good at was getting what he wanted.

He needed to get Erika to admit what had happened here between them, by whatever means necessary, and no matter what revenge fantasies she might have been cooking up in that fascinating little mind of hers.

He also needed to call his best friend, tell him what had happened—or at any rate, a highly sanitized version of what had happened, complete with a full accounting of Dorian's intentions—and accept whatever reaction Conrad might have. Even if it was violent.

Dorian fully expected it to be violent.

But he was prepared to accept the consequences. If he hadn't been, he wouldn't have done it.

He blew out a breath, picked up his mobile and dialed Conrad's number.

Because there was no way he would be able to conduct the conversation he needed to have with Erika in the way he wanted until he talked to her brother.

"You're not going to believe this," Conrad said when he answered his phone. In the background,

Dorian could hear the sounds of a major city. Paris, if Conrad was at home. Though in truth, the man traveled as much as Dorian did, and could be anywhere. Dorian hoped, given what he expected Conrad's reaction to be, that it wasn't Berlin. "Really. You're not going to believe it. I'm getting married."

"Funnily enough," Dorian said, because there was no point doing any of this unless he was all in, "that was what I called to talk to you about. And I'm pretty sure you will believe it even less."

Erika woke up when sunlight streamed in the windows, bright and warm on her face.

She knew exactly where she was.

Berlin. Dorian's massive penthouse. *Dorian.*

For a moment, she let herself lie there as she was, curled up naked in his bed with the most extraordinary feeling that she...belonged there.

That she was safe at last. Cared for the way she'd always dreamed. And right where she was supposed to be.

But Erika knew better than to let herself get carried away with dreams that could never come true, no matter how at peace she felt in this bed. In this home.

She sat up gingerly, expecting there to be pain, but the ache in her butt was minimal and really almost... pleasant. Her pussy felt sensitive. Not exactly fragile, more...greedy. If anything, she wanted more of it.

More of everything. More of *this*. And more of him.

She shoved her hair back from her face, looked

around and wasn't surprised to find herself alone in the massive bedroom.

Images from the night before chased each other through her head, one more vivid than the last. Different emotions buffeted her, but it was as if she'd stuck her head out the window in the middle of a storm. She could feel the wind, but it didn't sweep her away. And when she took a deep breath, then let it out again, she found herself smiling.

Because she felt like a new person.

She crawled out of the bed, running a hand down one of the dauntingly thick and sturdy posters, pretty sure she knew exactly what Dorian did with them. To her surprise, even after everything that had happened the night before, the notion sent a thrill spinning through her, pulsing its way down into her greedy pussy.

When she would have sworn up and down, her body rejected the very idea of morning sex, as a matter of policy. Apparently not Dorian's kind of sex.

She padded into the bathroom and took her time in the oversize shower, letting all the many showerheads send hot water pounding into her as she slicked a body gel over her skin that made her smell like him.

She smoothed her wet hair back from her face when she got out, and wondered if it was because she knew Dorian that she felt so comfortable helping herself to his hairbrush. His products. And even one of his shirts. She tried to imagine what it would be like to wake up like this in the house of the random dominant man she'd pretended she wanted to find last night, but she couldn't. She doubted very much that she would have stayed overnight. And if she had, she certainly wouldn't have slept like that, crashed out in the deepest sleep she could remember having since she was a child.

Because when have you ever felt safe? a voice inside her asked.

Erika didn't want to answer that. Because she knew the answer, of course, and it made her sad. She pressed a hand against her belly as she wandered downstairs, cataloging the faint pull here and whisper of something there, reminding her that she'd had a long and eventful night.

Had she ever.

She wished she was a lot more sore, she realized as she crossed the great room where she'd cried and come and had learned things about herself she'd never known were there. She wished her ass was far more sore than it was. She wished she could *feel* him, so long and thick and demanding as he'd pounded into her. The scrape of her breasts and her cheek against that rug as she'd come and come, his cock hammering into her to make sure she kept on going.

Erika wanted to wear him on her skin.

And she didn't really want to ask herself if that was healthy, because it felt right.

She was too warm again when she padded into the kitchen, so bright with all the light of midday pouring in, and found Dorian there.

He was dressed in a T-shirt that made a symphony out of those arms of his that she appreciated a whole lot more this morning. And in new ways. Because of the pain he could inflict, the pleasure he could wring out of her, and the safety she'd found only and ever there.

But she kept that to herself as he fixed her with a dark, simmering look.

She could feel the tumble inside her. Something defiant that lit her up, and made her want to poke at him—though it was at odds with that shimmering thing that wound around and around, settled in her pussy and made her knees feel weak.

"How do you feel this morning?" Dorian asked, his voice polite. Cool.

Irritating, she thought and glared at him.

"I'm *great*," she said. "Never better. You?"

"Erika. That wasn't a random pleasantry. I want you to provide me with a detailed and honest inventory of your feelings. Can you handle that?"

And all that light tumbling around his sleek, pristine kitchen made her silly. Or bold. At the very least, it reminded her that it wasn't last night. Not anymore.

"While I'm cataloging my feelings, maybe you can ask yourself why it is you have to be so incredibly patronizing."

"I'm not patronizing you. You seem euphoric. I want to make sure you're not peaking on your way into a serious drop."

"I thought that's why you brought me a snack last night."

"What happened was intense," he said gently, as if she might not have noticed. "Emotional responses to that kind of intensity and vulnerability often show up later."

It was the way he said that, maybe. As if he knew things she didn't—about herself. Erika found herself crossing her arms, even though she knew it made that shirt of his ride up her thighs.

Or maybe she wanted to linger for a moment in the way his dark gaze moved over the extra bit of skin she'd revealed. Because she felt a little bit like a junkie, desperate to see that flame blaze in his eyes again.

"If you have feelings about last night that you'd like to share with me, this is a safe space to do that," he said in a remote sort of way, as if he was conducting a seminar on BDSM and was modeling appropriate behavior. And suddenly Erika was flooded with emotion, all right. Assuming fury counted. "No need to observe protocol. You can simply tell me how you feel, ask me questions or share any thoughts you might have that you think I should know."

"I *feel* that you're being unnecessarily condescending to a woman you had sex with when most people pretend to exchange numbers, have three seconds of awkward conversation and then leave. Will there also be a questionnaire? An exit interview?"

His dark eyes gleamed, and the power there almost made her gasp. But all he did was smile. Slightly. "Is there a way that you can share those sentiments without resorting to name-calling and insolence, do you think? Right now that's a question. The next time I get you naked and on your knees, however, you may find there are consequences for such responses."

Erika hugged herself a little bit harder. "All your life, you've been just like this. Aloof. Arrogant. Even when you were a teenager."

"I'm delighted you were paying attention."

He moved to an espresso machine that had its own countertop, and pulled two shots. Then he pulled out a carton of cream from his great steel refrigerator, poured a hefty dollop into the cup and slid it to her.

And Erika's stomach twisted a little as she stared down at it.

"How do you know how I like my coffee?" Her voice was faint.

"You're not the only one who pays attention."

She felt shaky, suddenly. She wished she had something better to wear than one of his shirts with the sleeves rolled up. She wished her hair wasn't still damp and clinging to her neck. She wished she could, just once, control herself *before* making a mess.

"I really am fine," she made herself say. She lifted the coffee he'd made her and took a sip, then forced a smile. Because, of course, it was perfect. Exactly how she liked it. "Better than fine, now."

"Why am I not surprised to hear that?" Dorian asked, and the lightness of his voice was at distinct odds with all that intensity in his gaze. It made her worry. It made her wet. "Most people have intense reactions to their first real BDSM experience, but not you, of course. Not Erika Vanderburg, recklessly careening through life, heedless and untouched by anyone or anything."

And she might have described herself that way yesterday, but she didn't like him doing it. Not today. It felt like a slap of his hand, and not because he was teaching her a lesson, but because he wanted to hurt her. A crucial distinction.

"I do not *careen*. I travel. I *explore*."

He smiled again, but it didn't exactly soothe her. He slid a plate in front of her, and it took her a few moments to realize it was…food. He'd put together a typical German breakfast of rolls, cheeses, meats and sausages. There were jams and honey, butter and mustard. Even boiled eggs.

And as she stared at the feast he quietly set out before her—matter-of-factly, really, as if he served her food every day of her life—Erika realized she was ravenous.

He'd known that, somehow. He'd known it in the same way he'd known exactly how to touch her last night to make her break, then burn.

Something deep inside her quivered.

But it didn't keep her from eating.

"Why did you leave university?" Dorian asked, conversationally.

It was a strange question, but she had warm German bread and she couldn't seem to concentrate on anything else.

"It wasn't the right place for me," she told him.

"Was it not for you or was it another way for you to practice self-sabotage?" he asked, his voice so mild she was starting to smile at him before his words penetrated. "That is what you like to do, is it not? You were a decent student, by all accounts. I believe your brother even praised you after your second-year marks came in—and you couldn't have that. You only like attention when it's negative."

She swallowed, carefully, and set her roll down. Suddenly she wasn't hungry any longer. "What is this?"

And though she was standing there at the counter across from him in his bright and happy kitchen, she felt as if she was back in that hallway. What was wrong with her that she wanted to kneel while he took her apart? *Again?*

Yes, please, something in her whispered.

But he wasn't finished.

"When your father died, you went off the rails. Your brother took on all the responsibility, and you chose instead to make certain you were the enduring thorn in his side. I assumed that was because you were as thoughtless and empty-headed as you've acted over the years, but you're not, are you? You only want people to *think* you are."

"People think what they want." She scowled at him. "And I never asked Conrad to take responsibility for me. It seems to have escaped both his notice and yours that I actually have a living, breathing parent."

"Your mother might be the most truly self-centered human being I've ever met, and my father is an addict."

He wasn't wrong about Chriszette, and yet hearing him say that about her felt like a betrayal. Erika might complain about her, or want to complain about her, but she didn't like Dorian doing it. Especially because he was right.

Now he was studying her like she was a book he was reading and finding lacking. Deeply, profoundly lacking.

For once in her life, Erika didn't know what to say.

And the longer she stood there, gazing at him—or scowling at him—the more that feeling of well-being that she'd woken up with eroded.

Stupid, she thought, the sharp little voice in her head far too much like her mother's. *Always so stupid.*

Because it really hadn't occurred to her until this moment that while she had gone on a significant journey last night, he'd been…doing what he did. To Dorian, there was no connection between a moment in a ballroom two years ago and today. He wasn't the one who had taken it upon himself to search her out. He hadn't done "research" all over the globe, trying to figure out how to get next to her. While she felt profoundly altered by what happened last night, he didn't.

Clearly.

Because the Dorian who stood there across a granite countertop from her looked exactly the same as he had when he'd tried to cut her down to size in Greece.

And suddenly, everything that had happened between them seemed dirty. And not in the hot way. *Soiled*, not sexy.

Why had she gotten on her knees? Why had she *crawled*? Why had she, a grown woman, let this man spank her like a child and then fuck her like some kind of whore?

And how had she curled up in his arms like all of that was a gift, then slept more soundly than she had in years?

She could feel her pulse everywhere, her heart in her throat as if she might get sick.

"Oh my God," she said, soft and horrified, her eyes wide. "You *hate* me."

Something changed, there in the intensity of that dark-coffee gaze. "I don't hate you."

"I think you do," she said, shaken. "I should have realized. Here I was, thinking this was some kind of connection, and you were just…"

Dorian leaned forward, keeping his gaze trained on her, and she wanted to run away. Get away. But she couldn't seem to move.

"Were you chasing a connection when you came into the club last night? Or was it something else?"

She laid her palms on the cool countertop, hoping it looked as if she was doing literally anything but what she was actually doing, which was holding herself upright. "What other reason could I possibly have?"

"I've wondered that myself since the moment you showed up," Dorian said in that same relentless way of his that made her want to cry and made her want to touch him and left her messy straight through. "And the only conclusion I reached was that you really, really want to stick it to your brother and thought you'd use me to do it."

Her heart was stuck in her throat. Or pieces of it were. And she didn't understand why it was involved in the first place. "Because nothing could possibly be worse than getting tangled up with me, obviously, whatever the reason."

"You're beautiful," Dorian told her, and what was *wrong* with her that she felt like the sun had come out from behind a cloud. "You're smart and quick and funny. And I watched the strength you have in you, Erika. Over and over again. I watched you fight yourself. I watched you struggle and suffer, and I'm not being patronizing when I tell you that it was truly humbling to see you give yourself wholly and completely. To me."

Her throat was dry, then. And her heart was a lost cause.

"But," she prompted him.

Because if she knew anything, it was that when it came to her, there was always a *but*. Always.

You could be so lovely, Chriszette had sighed at her father's funeral, *but you're so* emotional. *No one likes that much* drama, *Erika.*

I know we've been friends for years, her supposed best friend ever had told her in boarding school, *but I don't really* like *you, actually.*

I like fucking you, a great many of her lovers had

told her, in one way or another. *But that's all it is. You know that, right?*

You're my sister and I love you, Conrad had said, frowning, after she'd announced she wasn't returning to Oxford after all, *but I can't support this wasted life you want to live.*

There was always, always a *but*.

"But I don't understand how you can be the woman I saw last night," Dorian said quietly, "so courageous in your surrender when you want to be, when the rest of your life is such a disaster."

The more he spoke, the further away she got without moving an inch, and that was a blessing. Her own, personal gift. After all, she was used to being dressed down. Shouted at. She was everybody's convenient punching bag, and there were only two ways to take that. You either curled in on yourself, a sad sack in every regard. Or you practiced your enigmatic smile in the mirror, pretended everything was a *madcap adventure*, and that it all rolled right off you.

Erika had always opted for the latter, because nobody got to see her suffer.

But you already suffered, something in her contradicted. *For him. And happily.*

"What about my life is a disaster?" she made herself ask. And she even smiled. "I have more social media followers than most celebrities."

Because she couldn't help but poke at the wound. Because it wasn't bad enough that she'd woken up feeling safe and at peace, and it was ruined. He'd made an offhand comment to her two years ago and it had changed everything. She'd done nothing but think about him, all this time, and it had all led here. Where she was inviting him to make further cutting commentary, and…then what?

Did she really want to let him haunt her all over again? And probably worse this time?

"I've seen both sides of you now," he said quietly, his gaze so intense it made her *hurt*. "And the woman I met last night was extraordinary. I spent hours this morning trying to reconcile her with this show you put on. You're doing it right now. Why is getting attention the only thing that matters to you?"

"Because it's the only way I matter to anyone."

She said it without thinking. And instantly wished that she could claw those words back, shove them inside her mouth. Chew them up, swallow them down.

Her chest was heaving, and for a split second, Erika honestly and truly wished that she would die right there. Just keel over onto his kitchen floor, and be done with this.

Because surely that was better than suffering through that intent look on his face that she was certain would tip over into pity at any moment.

But it didn't.

"Bullshit," he said. Succinctly.

She felt it like one of those blows he'd rained on her ass last night. Sharp, shocking. Then the sharpness changed, into a dull ache that was almost worse.

When she had been naked before him, her hands

behind her back and completely in his control, she hadn't felt this exposed.

"You're afraid," he told her, his gaze steady on hers, though his voice was soft.

"Oh, please," she threw at him, and it didn't seem to matter anymore that she felt so…ruined. Ripped open, with the stuffing removed and no hope of ever shoving it all back into place. *What the hell*, she thought. "You should talk."

"Me?" Dorian laughed, and it stunned her that she felt *so many things* and he seemed…fine. Just having a conversation while her world was on fire. "Little girl, flailing around throwing out accusations isn't going to change the facts. You live a useless life by choice. I do not."

"Of course not. My mistake. I thought this was supposed to be an honest conversation, not a self-congratulatory stump speech about how virtuous you are, when I'm standing right here, have known you for far too long and certainly know better."

"I talked to your brother earlier," Dorian said. Calmly.

Casually, even.

"Wh-what?"

"Conrad is getting married, Erika," Dorian told her in the same unbothered tone, though his gaze stayed on hers. "He got engaged last night and his soon-to-be in-laws are throwing them a party. In England at the end of the month."

Erika made herself laugh, though it felt like cut

glass in her mouth. "Who would actually marry Conrad?"

And she felt a trickle of something like foreboding as Dorian studied her. For much too long.

"Lady Jenny," Dorian said. He waited, and Erika was sure he could *see* that name fall through her like a sickening stone. "But you know her, do you not?"

Jenny Markham had been on Erika's stair at Oxford when they were first years. They'd become fast friends, had spent their summers together, texted regularly and always got together when they found themselves in the same place. Given that the last text Erika had gotten from Jenny had been a week ago, with no mention of Conrad whatsoever, Erika was skeptical—to say the least—about this news.

But Dorian, who had not looked at her pityingly yet, seemed to be doing so now.

"Of course I know Jenny," Erika said stiffly.

"Here's what I need to know," Dorian said quietly. "Is there any possibility that you can attend their engagement party and be supportive of your brother? And your friend? Or will it be business as usual for you, instead?"

People had thought very, very little of her all her life. There was nothing new in it. Nothing shocking.

But Erika found that further evidence of Dorian thinking the same as everyone else just made her want to sit down on the floor and cry.

She would never know how she managed to stay standing instead.

And he had an idea of who she was in his head,

clearly, so she smirked at him. *Useless. Disastrous. Afraid.* She stuck her hand on her hip as if she was trying to be provocative. Just another example of stupid, attention-seeking Erika Vanderburg. Just what he wanted to see.

"I have no idea," she said, not politely. "Are you going to make me?" She waited for his brows to rise, and that thunder to roll in across his stern, hard face, then made a face she knew he wouldn't care for at all. *"Sir?"*

CHAPTER EIGHT

EVERYTHING WAS GOING as planned.

She'd walked into his kitchen with her hair wet, making her blue eyes look even bigger, wearing nothing but one of his shirts. He didn't think she'd been trying to provoke him. Quite the opposite, this morning. She looked sleepy and sweet, and she gazed at him like he'd personally made the sun rise.

He hadn't known how much he wanted to see her look at him like that. How it made everything in him settle. Then hum.

Now he wanted to see it all the time.

Conrad had not been amused. He'd been silent at first. That had been far better than the lethal clip to his voice when he'd spoken again.

My...sister, he'd repeated. *My little sister and you. In your club.*

Dorian had winced, but that was the thing about taking responsibility, wasn't it? Sometimes it sucked. Sometimes it made people hate you.

But it was always the right thing to do.

I don't know if this will make you feel better or

worse, Dorian had said gruffly. *But I have nothing but good intentions where she's concerned.*

I don't feel anything, you prick, Conrad had snapped, *except homicidal.*

Dorian was glad the conversation was happening over the phone, or he imagined Conrad would have swung on him. And he would have taken it as his due, because he'd not only crossed a line, he'd done it in his own inimitable way. What older brother wanted to think about that?

You can try to kill me all you want, Dorian had told him. *But that's not going to change anything.*

Conrad had made a frustrated noise. Then he'd gone silent.

Is she happy? he asked quietly.

I intend to make her happy, Dorian had promised his best friend. The only brother he had or wanted. *I intend to dedicate myself to the task.*

It had been a vow. And he'd meant it.

But that was the easy part, all things considered. Now he had to do the hard part, which was convincing this dragonfly of a woman—always alighting here, then buzzing off there, always moving, always changing—that he'd found everything he'd wanted in her. In one night. That yes, he knew his own mind and heart. That he'd spent his entire adult life committed to extreme self-awareness.

It was that or follow his father's path. The lies, the self-deception.

Dorian had chosen to face himself in the mirror,

no matter how unpleasant the sensation of cataloging his own flaws and working to change them.

He expected no less from the very few people he let into his life. Conrad had always been one of the few men alive who lived up to Dorian's standards. He had no doubt that Erika would, too. He'd seen what she could be for him and with him last night.

And while he was busy celebrating that unexpected connection that had rocked him to his core, he also needed to make her see that she was worthy.

Of his interest and devotion, which he planned to lavish on her—in the way a man with his particular appetites did, that was—but also of all the other things she'd walked away from. The relationships she pretended didn't matter. The empty life she pretended made her happy. All those things she'd made sure to ruin herself before anyone could take them away from her.

He aimed to give her the tools to take them back.

It didn't take a psychiatrist to understand that a woman like Erika, who hid her truly sweet, soft, longing heart beneath so many layers of attitude and armor, had set out to destroy her relationship with her brother after their father died because that way, she lost him on her terms.

Dorian was ashamed he hadn't recognized that years ago.

Then again, maybe he had. After all, he'd mentioned spanking to her in Greece. Had he sensed, even then, where they would end up?

"I can't make you do anything," he told her now,

watching intently as her bravado faded. "You must choose, and accept the consequences of the choices you make. Are you prepared to do that?"

"Are we talking about my brother's engagement party—or sex?"

"On some level, Erika, I think you and I are always talking about sex."

Her eyes dilated and her lips parted, telling him she'd lost her breath. Dorian felt that intensity snap into place between them, stronger today. Because they both knew where it went. And that meant imagining where else and how hard it could go.

"I thought we were talking about a party," she said, blinking like she wanted to clear her head. *Good luck, little one*, he thought. "And for some reason, you seem to think you can dictate my behavior."

"You should know that I have every intention of dictating a hell of lot more than that." He smiled at her faintly, over his granite counter and the food he'd prepared for her. He liked this. He liked her here, looking uncertain and mulish—and safe. "I'm a bossy man, Erika. Some people pay for the privilege of having me tell them what to do with their business affairs and their messy lives. All I require from you is that you let me. And thank me. Is that so much to ask?"

"Yes."

"Are you sure? You seemed to enjoy it last night. Or were all those orgasms a decoy for your true feelings?"

She scowled at him. "Sex isn't life. It's just sex."

But he could see the way she gripped the counter, her knuckles turning white, and he knew she didn't believe that.

"Not the way we do it," he said. "If I were you, I'd look at last night as a lesson."

"Which part was a lesson?" she asked. "The spanking? Or when you fucked me, came hard enough to take the back of your head off and then cuddled with me all night long? Or maybe you mean *you* learned a lesson."

Dorian was around the counter before he meant to move, and then it was too late. For her. He trapped her there, taking far too much pleasure in the little squeaking sound she made as she found herself with her back against the granite, his arms on either side of her like a cage.

He watched her face flush and her eyes go glassy. He studied the pulse that hammered in her throat. And the rich, sweet scent of her arousal spiced the air between them, making his cock even harder than before.

"I don't like your tone." He leaned closer, smiling when she jumped. He put his mouth on a set of goose bumps that rose along her neck. "Rethink it."

"I don't see why I can't talk to you any way I like," she retorted, sounding awfully tough for someone who was trembling slightly between his arms. And making no attempt to get away from him. "Or do you not see the difference between in a scene and out of a scene?"

"You called me sir, Erika. Do you?"

She flushed at that, and he saw some of that bravado leak away from her. "I was kidding."

"Were you? Or were you trying to goad me into reacting negatively, the way you like to do in all areas of your life?"

Her mouth dropped open, and temper chased something like misery across her face.

"I wanted to explore extreme sex acts, not engage in a group therapy session," she threw at him.

"Too bad, little girl. It's one-stop shopping with me."

She lifted her chin, and her struggle was all over her face. "You're a terrible therapist. News flash—you're not supposed to hate the client."

Dorian stared her down, the dominant in him roaring in triumph when she flushed and lowered her eyes.

"I don't hate you," he told her, using his darkest, most dominant voice, because he knew she would hear him. Even if she didn't want to. "Quite the contrary. I've been waiting for you for a long time, Erika. And now that I've found you, I have no intention of letting you go."

"What do you…?"

She was trembling, her eyes were wide, and she seemed to lose her train of thought halfway through. He liked it.

"But nothing comes easy, does it?" He shook his head sadly. "You found me. And guess what that means? Now you have to contend with me and all my demands. And believe me, Erika, they never get any easier."

"I don't want to *contend* with you," she managed to say. "I just want to fuck you."

"You can't have one without the other."

"Then I'll fuck someone else, Dorian. Many someone elses. Repeatedly and enthusiastically."

He smiled. "And how has that been working out for you so far?"

She flushed a deep, betraying red at that, pleasing him so deeply that it took all he had to keep from hauling her up against him. Her eyes got wetter and he knew that if he reached down between her legs, her pussy would be soft and hot and greedy for him.

"Surrender, baby," he told her quietly. "I'm not letting you go."

And he didn't tell her how fully he meant that. He didn't have to—not when she reacted as if he'd electrocuted her. He could see the fear on her face, and how quickly she covered it up with temper. Dorian had never wanted to wrap a woman in his arms so badly before, for the simple pleasure of holding and soothing her.

Without even paddling her first.

Necessarily.

"If you have such a poor opinion of my character," she gritted out at him, though her eyes were too big and much too dark, "and this driving need to psychoanalyze things you know nothing about, why would you want me to submit to you in the first place?"

His smile deepened. "Because I want you to be the best version of you. I want you to make choices out of strength, not fear."

And it shocked him a little as he said it, because he realized this wasn't new. He'd been uniquely disapproving of Erika Vanderburg for as long as he could remember. But until she'd appeared in his club, he'd never been able to fully imagine her as anything but Conrad's little sister.

"Not that you're a wild egomaniac or anything," she threw at him.

He let his smile cool and his gaze darken, and saw her shiver in response. It was that instinctive response she couldn't control, no matter how disrespectfully she chose to speak to him.

"You have two choices now," he told her with quiet menace. "You can leave. I won't stop you or chase you. I had the concierge find you some more appropriate clothing should you require it, and I'll have a car take you wherever you wish to go. No harm, no foul."

Once more, he watched misery move over her face and had to order himself not to help her. It was her struggle. It was his job—and his pleasure—to make it all that much more pointed, sure, but he couldn't do it for her. No matter how much he might want to.

He'd never experienced this so acutely before. He'd led many a submissive through a scene. But this was her life. And his, if he had his way. *Theirs.*

"Or?" Her voice was husky with emotion, just one of the many ways her body told him truths she wouldn't. Or couldn't. "What if I have a taste for harm and foul?"

Dorian straightened, pushing back from the

counter. He stood at his full height, aware of the way her mouth softened. He could see her pulse in her throat, rapid and obvious. Beneath his shirt, her nipples hardened to needy points.

Her body knew whom she belonged to.

"I'm going to leave the room for a moment," he told her. "When I come back in, you can be dressed in the clothes I left for you on the chair. You can eat. Drink more coffee. I'll leave you to it."

Her breath was a scraping thing between them. "Or…?"

"Or you will be sitting on the table, completely naked with your legs spread wide, eyes closed and your hands behind your back."

He watched her shudder.

"Maybe I have things to say to you," she said, though her voice was thicker now. As was the scent of her need. "And I'm not sure I want all of my sentences to end in *sir*."

"Noted."

He didn't say anything else. He didn't give her permission or argue the point, he just walked away. He went back out to the great room, where he'd left his bag, pulled out the item he'd found earlier and then took his time coming back.

And he wasn't *surprised* to find her right where he wanted her. But he was pleased.

Everything in him went still, then hot. His predatory focus kicked in, hard. He wanted to eat her alive.

He intended to do just that.

"Don't hold your breath," he told her as he moved closer. "I won't be happy if you pass out."

"I'm not going to—"

"Baby, we're deep in it now. Your usual safe word applies. If you continue to speak to me disrespectfully, I'll respond. And I don't think you'll like it."

He roamed toward her, feeling the sweet kick as the beauty of her splayed-open position flooded through him. She sat exactly as he'd imagined she would, stark naked on his table like his very own feast, her body flushed and soft against the hard black granite of the tabletop. Her hands were behind her back, just as he'd asked, making her breasts jut forward and up. Her eyes were shut tight, as if she had to frown to make herself obey. And in between her wide-open legs, he could see her pussy glistening with need.

She was perfect.

All he had to do was prove it to her.

"The only time you seem to behave is when I tell you to," he said as he came closer. "Do I have to parade around an engagement party with you on a leash to make you behave appropriately? Because I think you know I will."

When she only breathed, hard and fast, he reached out to run his palm over her shoulder. Then he took one of her pebble-hard nipples between his fingers. And pinched it.

She hissed, then squirmed, telling him she'd felt it in her pussy, too.

"Answer me, please."

"No…no." She panted. "I don't need a *leash*."

But he doubted he was the only one imagining it, then.

"I'm not punishing you, Erika," he said as he continued to pinch her nipple, raising his other hand to treat her other one the same. She was instantly responsive, arching her back to press her breasts more completely into his palms no matter what expression she wore on her face. "I'm encouraging you. It would please me greatly if you did not take the occasion of your brother's engagement party to make a spectacle of yourself." He frowned when her eyes shot open, mutinous and mad. "Eyes closed. Now."

She shut her eyes again, even as she flushed a bright red that he took for temper. And her reaction to her obedience, if he had to guess.

"I want you to wear something conservative that will cause absolutely no comment at all, unless it is a quiet compliment. The only attention you should be interested in is mine."

She shuddered, hard.

Dorian continued, "I want you to congratulate Conrad, and his fiancée, and if while you're doing it you can work in an apology for past behavior, I will be delighted. Do you understand what I'm asking of you?"

"I understand it," Erika said after a moment while he plucked at her nipples. "But I don't know what makes you think that after you spent all this time insulting me I would do a single thing for you."

"I'll tell you why," he said.

Dorian moved between her legs, enjoying the contrast between her total nakedness and the fact he was dressed. He ran his palms over her thighs, then gripped them to yank her closer to the edge of the table. Only when her ass was on the edge did he again cup her lovely breasts in his hands. He moved his thumbs over her nipples, rougher than before, and enjoyed the way it made her squirm. Then he leaned forward, and put his mouth to her ear.

"You will do it because I want you to," he told her. "Because it will please me. Because I want you to be the person I know you can be."

Goose bumps marched down her neck, toward her collarbone. And below.

"Or I could gently suggest that you go fuck yourself," she said, defiant to the last.

"Let me convince you," he said, his voice a dark ribbon of sound.

Dorian bent down and took one of her nipples in his mouth, sucking hard. She arched into him. Her head fell back, and she made a helpless sort of noise when he moved his demanding mouth to her other nipple, and treated it with the same erotic roughness.

He indulged himself with her taste. She was velvet and rose and he was addicted. He pulled away, then used his hands again until both nipples were dry again. She was so responsive, he entertained himself imagining all the ways he could make her come with nipple stimulation alone.

But that was for another day.

Today, he had other goals. He pulled out the tiny

evil clamps he'd retrieved from his bag. He clamped one nipple, and laughed at the noise she made. Then he clamped the other one, not at all surprised that she lost her head completely, jerking as if she couldn't decide whether she wanted to get away from him or move closer to him, or something in between. Her hands were no longer behind her back, but in those adorable fists at her side.

"Hands behind your back," he ordered her. When she obeyed, he rewarded her. "Open your eyes."

And when she did, all that pretty blue was glazed over.

"That hurts," she said, as if he'd betrayed her.

"You can take it." And to prove it, he tugged gently on the chain that connected the two clamps, making her gasp again. "You will take it."

And before she could say another word, he wrapped his other hand around the back of her head, and then took her mouth with his.

Finally.

He kissed her hungrily, thoroughly. He invaded her mouth, wet and dark and encompassing, the next best thing to fucking her.

And she kissed him back the same way.

Making him wonder why the hell he'd wasted all these years and all this time *not* doing exactly this.

Dorian kissed her until she went limp, and he kept going. He tried one filthy angle after the next until she was trembling beneath his hands, making needy and helpless noises in the back of her throat, and seemed to have forgotten about the clamps entirely.

So he tugged on the chain again, to remind her, and lapped up every greedy little noise she made.

He pulled away then, and stared down at her. She fought to catch her breath. Her eyes looked appealingly dazed, while her mouth was damp from his. Her color was high and good. She looked thoroughly debauched, and the clamps on her breasts made him so hard he almost hurt.

"What was it you wanted to say to me?" he asked her.

Politely.

"I don't..."

"If memory serves, you suggested I was a coward."

He watched her fight to access her brain again. He reached down and pushed her thighs farther apart, to the point where she had to strain the slightest bit to keep them open. Then he held her there, and waited.

"Why so quiet?" he asked her, a gentle taunt. "You came downstairs filled to the brim with insults. I'm beginning to think that all the trouble you cause with your mouth could be averted if you used it to do something other than talk."

An image that made his cock pulse with his own dark need. But she hadn't earned the privilege of sucking him off yet.

"Your rules are convenient," she said, focusing enough to frown at him. "You change them to suit yourself."

"Of course I do. Suiting myself is the whole point. If you concerned yourself less with following or not following the rules and more with pleasing me, it wouldn't matter, would it?"

"But you don't want me to please you," she said, holding herself very still, no doubt because every breath made those clamps tug on her nipples. "You want me to break your rules so you can punish me."

"Baby, I'm going to punish you one way or another no matter what you do." He grinned. "That's kind of the point."

"Not for me," said the woman who was dripping wet and trembling on the edge of an orgasm, all because he'd clamped her nipples. "I'm here for the sex."

"You like your sex with some pain to accentuate the pleasure," he said. He reached behind her and moved her arms, setting her hands down flat on the tabletop. "Ask me how I know."

"Maybe as an experiment," she lied, her eyes wide and full of shit. "Once in a while, as an adventure, and not because I *need*—"

"I think that's enough talking, kitten," Dorian said. Then he bent down, hauling her legs up over his shoulders and bringing his mouth down hard on her pussy in a single, swift movement.

He could feel her reaction go through her as she caught herself on the hands he'd moved for precisely that purpose, but that wasn't quite enough. So he reached up, and tugged on that chain, knowing that it would send that exquisite pain narrowing through her body, lighting her up.

That was how he wanted her.

Lit up, bright red, sweet and soft against his tongue. He tugged on the clamps again, and she got wetter, like dessert.

So he ate his fill.

Dorian ate her hard, as demanding as everything else, because she made the most delicious sounds. Her clit was stiff and proud beneath his tongue, and when he took it between his teeth, she screamed.

He took her to the edge again and again, throwing her over every time, until he had to slide his hands around to hold her steady because she couldn't seem to keep herself upright. He sank two fingers deep into the molten heat of her pussy, curling them around to rub against that rough spot tucked away in there. She made a keening kind of sound.

Then he leaned over her, kissing her so she could taste herself.

She came again, short and hard, with a deep groan that was like poetry to him.

"Promise me you'll do what I want you to do," he said. "Promise me now, Erika."

Her head thrashed from side to side. "I don't want to."

"Do it anyway," he growled.

And he reached down to free his cock, rolled on a condom, then slammed himself into her.

She made herself into a bow, arching up off the table like every wet dream he'd ever had. She was gorgeous, glorious, so he took her hard. She wrapped her legs around him, and met him, thrust for thrust.

And watching her fuck him back was so hot he was tempted to come himself.

But he wasn't quite done.

"Promise me, Erika," he said.

"I thought we were supposed to be done with talking," she managed to gasp out.

And he couldn't help himself. That made him laugh.

And as an extra incentive, he pulled the clamps off.

He knew that the pain would go through her like a shock, and he knew it did exactly what he wanted it to do when she screamed.

Dorian was deep inside her, pounding into her at a relentless pace—long and hard and deep—and he watched her shake like she might fall apart, as if the pain was picking her up and carrying her further.

She came beautifully. She was perfect.

And when she came back down, he picked her up, holding her there against him with his hands gripping that ass of hers that still bore his marks.

"Come," she begged him. "Please, Dorian. Come."

"Please, who?" he gritted out.

"Please, sir," she panted at him. "I want to feel you come inside me."

"Then you know what to do." He pulled out, then slammed himself back in, and her eyes went fuzzy. But she dug her fingers into his shoulders, and held on. "You know what I want."

"I promise," she said, as if it hurt her. "I promise. I'll do it."

For you, she didn't say.

But he heard it.

And when he let himself go at last, deep inside the tight fist of her pussy, she came with him, sobbing out his name.

Already his, he thought with profound satisfaction.

Whether she knew it or not.

CHAPTER NINE

THE FIRST WEEK after Berlin, Erika was…angry.

If that was the right word to describe the intensity of the emotions that jostled around inside her, fighting for supremacy, shifting and changing and sandbagging her every time she thought she had a handle on what was happening inside her.

Because she refused to accept that it had been a full-scale sea change.

She had spent two more days with Dorian.

Two more days filled with…more. With him.

Playing the kind of games she learned were called *playing* and *games* when they weren't really playing at all. Not when they could change a person so completely. So profoundly.

Dorian had tied her up. He'd experimented with cuffs and collars and other binding things. He arranged her on that massive bed of his, attaching her wrists and ankles to the handy chains welded to those steel posters, and he taught her things about herself that she hadn't known were there.

Over and over again.

And afterward, when she was lost in that buzzy, intense space that only he could put her in—where her mind and her emotions and her body were all one, all his—she told him stark truths she'd spent her whole life hiding from.

That she'd thought her father had left her, specifically, when he'd died. She had been the last one to see him and she had learned, during his illness, that good girls were quiet. Silent. Diffident and biddable at all times. And somehow, once he was gone, she'd decided that there was no point in being a *good girl* when people went ahead and died.

So she went in the opposite direction.

Hard.

She told him things she'd never really put into words before. That yes, as he'd suggested, a major part of why she'd dropped out of university was because she'd actually been good at studying and it made her feel like her old self again. Like that good girl she'd lost along the way, or not *lost*. That made it sound like something that had just happened. When she'd deliberately set about exterminating any traces of that girl who longed to please, bit by bit and year by year, until no one remembered she'd ever existed except Erika herself.

And though she never would have put it into words the way Dorian had, she'd shoved Conrad away, too. Because the people who loved her—who genuinely cared for her—died. Her mother was a safe space in that regard because as far as Erika could tell, she truly cared only about herself. Everything else was window dressing. Erika didn't expect anything from her and the beauty of it was, Chriszette never disappointed.

She couldn't believe the things Dorian got her to talk about.

He'd introduced her to a real flogger, not the hen-night jokey versions she'd thought were real before. He taught her the exquisite fear, twined as it was with an almost overwhelming sense of delirious need, for that arch of his brow that promised exactly the pain, punishment and pleasure she wanted.

She discovered she liked anything—sooner or later, and sometimes only because of where they ended up—if Dorian delivered it.

Erika found he could read her body with a fluency that should have terrified her. That did terrify her, sometimes. He knew how far to push her, and it was always further than she thought she could go.

He always asked her if she needed her safe word.

And then, when she gave him the green light, he used it push her limits. Over and over again during those two days that seemed like so much longer to her. Several lifetimes, at least.

Erika found herself caught between her own worst impulses, as if he'd tied her there. Deliberately. She wanted to run. She wanted to kneel. She wanted to lose herself in him on the one hand, and on the other, she wanted to prove her independence. Leap to her feet, storm out and make him regret that he had ever pretended to know her.

In his hands she was made of passion and dark

greed, and rewarded for both. He made her cry and he made her come, and then he held her against him as she sobbed and slept and told him the stories she kept deep inside her and had never told another living soul.

She felt like a different person with him, and that was the real betrayal. In that brief span of time, a single weekend, she felt like the woman she'd secretly always wanted to be. Beautiful. Capable.

Lovable, something kept whispering inside her.

Dorian didn't tell her he loved her and she wouldn't have believed it if he did, but still. There was a look in his dark gaze. A certain gleam when he looked at her that made her wonder what it would be like. To always be here, with him, and a part of this powerful thing they shared. Part of this beautiful dance of mirroring, reflection and awareness.

Mixed in with blistering-hot sex and too many orgasms to count.

It would be a very lucky woman indeed who found herself kept forever by this man, she found herself thinking on that final morning. He'd bent her over the couch, where he'd spanked her that first night, burying his hands in her hair to hold her head where he wanted it. And he'd taken her with a brutal elegance that had left her wrecked in his wake.

Dorian had gazed at her before he'd left, tucking himself away into a three-piece suit that made him almost look like a stranger after the days of T-shirts, jeans and his dominance—were it not for that intensity and power of his that no suit could hide. He filled rooms with every breath, confidence and assurance stamped deep into his bones.

He looked at her as she panted and shook through the aftershocks. He looked *through* her, his mouth unsmiling and too much knowledge in his gaze.

He hadn't said goodbye. He hadn't said he would see her soon, indicating that he expected her to be there when he got back from his business meetings in Zürich.

"When I ring you," he said in that tone that made every hair on her body feel as if it was standing on end, "I expect you to answer."

It was almost as if he knew what she was going to do.

First, Erika had sobbed, there on that leather couch, where he'd first introduced her to herself.

Then she'd left, wearing the clothes she'd come in that first night and not capable of giving a single shit that she was on the streets of Berlin at midday on a Monday with her thong visible, her ass cheeks hanging out and a tiny, strappy little top that might as well have shouted her interest in bondage to everybody she passed on the street.

But it was Berlin, so nobody paid her the slightest bit of attention.

And that stung, too. Because it was impossible to discount everything Dorian had told her when there she was, prancing down the street as if she wanted some stranger to pay her some mind.

He had introduced her to herself, then confronted her with all that meant, and she didn't like it.

She'd gone back to her hotel, packed up her things and gotten the hell out of Germany.

But another fun fact about her madcap existence, about which she bragged to all and sundry as if she loved every second of it, was that she didn't have anywhere to go. Not really. She lived out of hotels, or in the guest suites at friends' houses. She'd been doing it so long that she'd long since stopped thinking too closely to be…rootless.

Untethered. Unattached.

If asked, she called it freedom. *Pure happiness*, she'd said a few weeks back. She'd been on her way to Berlin with a small stopover in Copenhagen to see the sort of friends who asked deep questions over wine, not because they were deep themselves, but because they liked to compete with their answers. The better to pretend their shallow lives had depth.

Erika was fantastic at pretending to be the happiest.

Are you happy? Dorian had asked her. Mercilessly. *Or have you wrapped up* hapless *in a curated social media feed and forgotten that the core of all that glossy performance is emptiness?*

In retrospect, what Erika was happy about was that she'd been gagged when he'd asked that question, because she still didn't know how to answer it.

Nor did the answer come to her as she landed in England, and made her way to Devon, where her mother was living it up in a country manor with her latest conquest, who claimed a Windsor connection and spent as much time tramping about his property with his dogs as he did tending to his gout flare-ups.

Not that Chriszette was ever in the mood to entertain a full-grown daughter for more than the odd meal.

Erika was dispatched to a renovated carriage house far enough away from than main hall that Chriszette could pretend she wasn't about, where she assured herself that she was *perfectly fucking happy*. And then fumed, like it was her job to prove it.

She was angry with herself for putting herself into that situation in Berlin in the first place. What had she been thinking? She was angry with her brother in general for being an overbearing asshole, and specifically for having such terrible taste in friends. She was angry with her mother, who could have taken maybe five minutes from her own narcissism to do a little parenting, back in the day, when her daughter was clearly acting out her grief—but hadn't bothered. And certainly felt no compulsion to make up for that now.

And she was deeply, volcanically angry at Dorian.

Because she couldn't help feeling that the only revenge taken had been against her. By her, which was worse, because she'd been correct in her initial assessment, if nothing else. Dorian was an excellent weapon.

"You'll forget him in about forty-eight hours," she told herself, out loud and with great confidence, when she sat down on the side of her carriage house bed, high in the eaves. "Less, probably."

Because forgetting about men was something Erika was very, very good at. But Dorian wasn't like other men. He didn't fade away, out of sight and out of mind.

For the first time in her life, Erika was plagued with insomnia, hollow-eyed and up at all hours, because her body wanted what it couldn't have. It wanted Dorian's body next to hers, holding her tight, when she'd spent her entire previous life asserting with great confidence that she was the kind of person who didn't like to cuddle while she slept.

She never had, before.

But then, there were a lot of things she'd never done before that weekend in Berlin with Dorian.

And toward the end of that first week and into the second week after she'd left him, Erika mostly just cried.

She felt tossed out to sea and abandoned while wave after wave of old, ugly emotion found her and sank her. Over and over again.

She almost thought it would be easier to drown.

But Dorian didn't let her.

He didn't call every day. Perhaps every other day. Sometimes he sounded terse, busy, and she hated that she felt particularly special that he made time for her. Other times he sounded tired, and she wished she could have the opportunity to soothe him. But he always sounded like *him*. Dark and richly textured and *him*.

"I don't want to talk to you," she said when she picked up the phone, the way she often did. Because even if that was true, she still obeyed him. He'd told her he expected her to answer and here she was, answering. Every time. "But you asked me to answer when you rang. Behold my obedience."

"I never doubted you, Erika." His voice did magical, terrible things to her body. Her nipples pinched so hard she could feel that line of sensation spiral down into her clit. She was wet instantly. Soft and ready for whatever he might do to her. "Are you ready to talk about your feelings yet?"

"I talk about my feelings all day every day," she lied, and pretended she didn't feel a little kick of pleasure when he laughed. "It's true. I stop people on the street and download my every last emotion. I've already made a lot of new friends that way."

That was slightly less of a lie, if a person counted storming about in England's greenest hills and shouting at passing sheep.

She doubted very much the Dorian would count that at all.

"It sounds to me like you've taken a little emotional dip and have stayed there," he said. "I told you that you might."

"Not everything is a pageant of intensity," she snapped, and she was aware as she said it that she clearly didn't believe that herself. Because if she did, she wouldn't be sitting in her carriage house bedroom on her mother's lover's estate, with all the curtains closed tight against the drizzle of another English afternoon. God, she was so sick of her own shit. "And here's a fun fact. Not every emotion I have has something to do with you."

"I'm delighted to hear it," Dorian said smoothly, but still, there was that undercurrent that kicked at her and made her sit a little straighter. "I just landed in London. Your brother's party is this weekend. Now that you're so marvelously recovered from all the intimacy we shared, I hope you remember the promise you made me."

"Go to hell."

Dorian made a tsking sound that blazed through like the warning it was, making her body light up. Wet, needy, naughty—and desperate for the discipline only he could administer.

She wanted to hate herself for that but she couldn't quite get there. Not with his voice in her ear.

"That does not bode well for you, kitten," he said, with that soft, amused menace that made her…glow.

She cleared her throat. "What I do or don't do concerning my brother is no business of yours."

"If you say so."

And she could swear, if she closed her eyes, she could see the look he was wearing on his face when he sounded like that. All that dark, dangerous patience in his gaze. That unyielding power stamped into that unsmiling mouth that made her feel weak in all the best ways. What was it about this man that made her silly straight through?

"Are you touching yourself?" he asked, his voice stern.

Erika froze, because sure enough, she'd reached

down between her legs with one hand, and was pressing the heel of her palm against her throbbing clit. How the hell had he known that? “No.”

“Don’t lie to me.”

Her hand fell away from her pussy as if he’d ordered her to stop touching herself. As if he’d reached over and physically removed her hand, more like.

“I’m not lying,” she said. And his silence felt as sharp a rebuke as a slap on the ass. She sighed. “Now.”

“Good,” he said, and she could hear laughter and satisfaction then. And all that glorious heat. “Don’t. As far as I’m concerned, that’s my pussy and you can’t touch it without my permission. I’ll know, kitten. And there will be consequences.”

“You can’t just say things like that to people, Dorian. Are you insane? I can do anything I want with *my* body.”

“What’s that?” he asked, sounding mild and stern at once. The combination made goose bumps rise all over her skin. “Was that your safe word? Or was it another round of predictable complaints because you like to deal with your uncertainty by shooting off your mouth?”

She wanted to hang up on him. She didn’t. And she hated herself for that, too.

“I’ll see you this weekend,” he promised her. Though it sounded a lot more like a threat. “And I’ll expect you to remember every detail of the promise you made me, Erika. Because you can be certain I do.”

And he cut off the call before she could protest. Deliberately, she was sure.

But something about his voice galvanized her. She got out of the bed where she'd been conducting her experiments in insomnia and petulance. She threw open the curtains and glared out at the gray day. She went down into the kitchen of the carriage house and stared around, uninspired, at the dry cereal boxes that had provided her with the bulk of her nutrition since she'd arrived. Because her mother certainly didn't want her grown daughter taking meals at the big house with her lover. Erika's very existence was a testament to Chriszette's age.

Erika had learned that lesson the hard way. And years ago. Now she accepted the fact that her mother liked to control her in between affairs, but never during them. A situation that had suited them both since Erika had left university.

Does it suit you? a dark voice that sounded suspiciously like Dorian's asked inside her. *Or do you put up with it because she treats you the way you think you deserve to be treated?*

"Shut up, Dorian," she muttered into the empty kitchen.

Her body was still flushed, and wound up, and she thought that maybe she should go ahead and handle her own needs. Because fuck him. Who cared what he ordered her to do? He wasn't the boss of her.

But even when she sat down, then slipped her hand back between her legs, she couldn't do it.

Because you want to be his, something that was

all her whispered, telling her more truths she didn't want to face.

Erika went on a long, punishing walk. When she'd exhausted herself, she trudged back to the carriage house and took a long bath. She soaked in the hot water until she was so heartily sick of herself and her own endlessly cycling thoughts that she thought she might scream.

She wrapped herself in a bath towel, then padded back to the bedroom. She picked up her phone, scowled at it for a while, and admitted that what she really wanted was for Dorian to call her again. Especially now that they were in the same country again.

I'll see you this weekend, he'd said, and she shivered now, because she would see him again.

But that meant she would be seeing other people, too. Maybe it was time to stop recovering from Berlin and start handling her actual life. The one that went on no matter how many hard truths Dorian had marked into her skin that weekend.

Erika pulled up Jenny's number.

So, she texted, what do you think I should wear to your ENGAGEMENT PARTY to MY BROTHER?

Her phone rang almost immediately.

"Oh my God, Erika," Jenny cried when Erika picked up. "I thought you were blanking me."

"I wasn't *not* blanking you."

"Where are you? Are you still in Germany?"

"No," Erika said, her body flushed from her bath. She looked down at herself, caught by that same awareness that had haunted her since she'd left Berlin. That this wasn't *her* body any longer. That he'd made it his. And why was that the only thing that seemed to soothe her? "I'm in Devon with Chriszette and her latest fling. Lord Something or Other. I only stayed in Berlin for that one weekend."

The way she often had, over these last six months. Jenny would think nothing of it. Another weekend clubbing, that was all. And Erika would let her think it, because she couldn't articulate what had happened between her and Dorian to herself. There was no way she could explain it to anyone else.

And maybe that was why, when the silence stretched out between them, she let it. Because she understood it.

"It would be better to see you in person—and before the party," Jenny said after a moment. "Can you come up to London?"

Erika looked around at the carriage house that had become a prison of all the emotions she'd told Dorian she wasn't experiencing. She thought about the fact she'd be seeing Dorian himself this weekend, and all the anticipation and anxiety, need and longing that kicked up. She thought about the promise she'd made him and what that would mean—could she really apologize to her brother?

Her brother, whom Jenny was marrying, for reasons unclear.

"As a matter of fact," Erika said, "I would love to come to London. I could use a break."

She did not add *from me.*

Because that would require explanations she didn't want to give, not even to her oldest friend.

But if she could, she thought the next morning as she caught the train from Cranbrook to London Waterloo Station, she would have left herself behind.

CHAPTER TEN

THEY MET IN the breathtakingly posh bar of an extraordinarily luxurious and exclusive hotel where they'd liked to sneak away to during their Oxford years and imagine what their lives would be like when they graduated.

Erika could almost squint and see all those dreams dancing there in the dimly lit, aristocratically plush surroundings. It made it impossible not to engage in a game or two of what-if.

What if she'd lived these last years differently? Where would she be now? What would have happened if she'd stayed at Oxford and done as Jenny had—because Lady Genevieve Charlotte Elizabeth Markham, Jenny to her friends, was nothing if not dutiful.

In the flattering light of the cozy, quiet bar, Jenny looked as if she could still be the teenager she'd been when they'd met as first years. She sat across from Erika looking as disarmingly approachable as ever, which had always been her secret weapon. She radiated warmth even when she wasn't feeling the slightest hint of it herself. Erika had been drawn to it. Who wouldn't be?

Maybe Conrad could use a little warmth, too, came that dark voice inside.

She told her inner Dorian to go fuck himself.

And then she marinated in memories and more what-ifs while Jenny set about ordering them wine.

Dutiful, well-behaved Jenny had taken the requisite job in an appropriate charity after she'd graduated with her first in classics. Like many girls of her station, saddled with a father consumed with notions of bloodlines and the consolidation of hereditary lands, her charity work had only ever been meant to be a stopgap. A pretty little notation on her résumé. One that she could toss aside the moment she assumed her true duties as a wife of a worthy, wealthy gentleman. Preferably one of her father's choosing.

"You haven't posted a single thing on any social media site in weeks," Jenny said when they were both properly fortified with glasses of wine and a tray of spiced nuts. "I was starting to think the announcement might have killed you."

She smiled as she said it, though her gaze was wary.

"The announcement was a surprise," Erika agreed. And she'd received it not only from Dorian, but from Jenny, Chriszette—and even Conrad's assistant. Lest she complain that she hadn't been invited or informed, she supposed. Things she couldn't imagine doing now but she certainly might have done a few weeks back. She could admit that. “But I survived it intact.”

Jenny sighed as she played idly with her wine-glass. And Erika couldn’t keep herself from studying the enormous, sparkling ring that didn’t quite fit on her slender left hand. It slid as she moved, tipping the great stone this way, then that.

Silence had never been their thing. And Erika was suddenly struck by the unpleasant realization that it was because she’d always filled it. She’d always been perfectly happy to twitter on about herself, hadn’t she? Especially in recent years, when she’d viewed every in-person meeting with anybody as an opportunity to deliver highly curated press releases on how wonderful her life was.

Confront yourself and you conquer your fears, Dorian had told her, the dick.

“Jenny,” Erika said softly now, with more self-possession than she’d ever thought she had. “Tell me how this happened.”

She’d wanted to say *this tragedy*, which she certainly would have before. But something stopped her tonight—possibly the fact that Jenny certainly didn’t look *tragic*. And more to the point, hadn’t asked Erika’s opinion.

It was another little prick of shame that the pre-Berlin version of Erika would have steamrolled right in and bludgeoned half of London with her opinion without caring if anyone had solicited it. How charming.

“As I’ve mentioned before, I’m sure, my father

has never appreciated my passion for charity work," Jenny said, smiling wryly over her glass of wine.

"I would be astonished if your father appreciated passion in any form."

Jenny's smile deepened. "He's quite fond of his dogs."

Erika drank from her own glass. "I'm not sure I can figure out how we get from passionate charity work that benefits children in war zones to… Conrad."

Jenny's smile faded. She frowned down at her wine, but didn't take a sip.

"We were at an event in Stockholm. My father likes me to play his hostess even when it's not his party, so I was with him when he met Conrad. They started talking business, my father liked him, and a few days later he announced that he'd taken it upon himself to set us up on a date." She lifted her gaze. "Which isn't unusual. I've complained about this before. Any day now I expect him to simply announce that he's sold me off."

Erika smiled. Then returned to the subject at hand. "And you went on the date, clearly."

"I didn't dare say no," Jenny said. "I assumed Conrad had either been pushed into it, or thought he could go on a single pity date and then carry on with whatever business dealings he had with my father. But instead, he asked me out on a second date."

"And again, you went?"

"I couldn't say no."

"It's simple, Jen. *No.* See? I did it."

"Erika." And her friend leveled a frank, sad sort of look at her. "Please stop pretending you don't know what my father's like. I've been playing this game for years. He sets me up on a date, and yes, I go on the dates, because that's the price I have to pay for my independence."

"You shouldn't have to pay a price for your independence."

Jenny's smile was sad. "*Should* doesn't have much to do with it, I'm afraid. It never has done."

Erika remembered this from their university days. Jenny's sense of unwavering duty to her stuffy, unsupportive father—or maybe, more realistically, to the nostalgia she'd been raised on. The grand stories about what had made the Markham family great. And wealthy.

Not so long ago, she would have railed at her friend about this. Tonight, she kept her mouth shut instead.

"I know that I could rebel," Jenny said quietly when Erika didn't speak. "Sometimes I dream of it. But that's not who I am. So yes, I went on that second date, because my father expected me to. And I went on the third, and when Conrad brought me back home to my father's house, he stayed for a drink. And proposed marriage, there and then, with this honking great ring and all that… Well. You know what your brother is like. So *sure* of everything."

"I do indeed."

Jenny sent her a reproving look. "And it's all snowballed since. My father was the happiest I've seen him in years. Certainly since my mother died. Later that night, after Conrad left, he fairly waxed rhapsodic about putting me in safe hands at last."

"But, Jen." Erika's voice was soft. Not quite imploring, but close. "You don't love him."

Jenny took a breath, but her gaze was steady when it met Erika's.

"He's kind to me," she said simply. "We want the same things, more or less. He's perfectly happy if I continue working, which isn't something I could say for all the cavemen my father's sent me on dates with. I'm going to have to marry one of them. Conrad is by far the best option."

"Jenny…"

"And besides," she said hurriedly, "sex is not a motivating factor for me the way it is for you."

"That's because you've never been fucked properly." Erika laughed at Jenny's expression. "You know it's true. Or maybe you don't, which is sad, but *I* know it's true. Wait a minute." She narrowed her eyes at her friend. "Are you saying that Conrad's bad in bed? Or are you saying you haven't sampled the wares yet?"

"I can't imagine that you would want me to answer that question either way. About *your brother*."

Erika made a face. "I really don't. But as your friend, it's my duty to ask."

"I haven't slept with him, no," Jenny said, her cheeks red in the dark of the bar. It made Erika wonder how her friend would react if she found herself standing in the Walfreiheit Club one fine night. Or what she'd do if faced with a man like Dorian.

But she couldn't let herself think about Dorian. Not now.

"There's hardly been time," Jenny was saying. "It's all been a whirlwind and my father insisted on throwing this party—"

"You can't marry a man if you don't know what he's like in bed," Erika said. "Really, you can't."

"People have been doing exactly that for centuries."

"And they've been wildly unhappy."

"Not always." Jenny shook her head, and her grip on her wineglass tightened. Visibly. "I don't expect you to understand this decision, Erika. It's a bit like being on a runaway train, if I'm honest. But what's the harm in it? He's not pretending to love me. I'm not pretending to love him. And, you know, there's lots of research to prove that arranged marriages are happier, on balance, than marriages based on romantic love."

"I'll be sure to make that toast at the wedding. Here's to a sexless union of people who don't love each other, but whose financial portfolios match well enough to plod along. Three cheers."

"Just as long as you come to the wedding." Jenny reached over and grabbed Erika's wrist in a fully out-of-character move that made Erika both love her more and worry for her at the same time. "We might not be love's young dream, but we're going to be all right. And I would very much like your blessing."

And a few weeks ago, Erika would have lost her shit. She knew it. She would have said terrible things to Jenny that she'd never be able to take back. She would have called up her brother and shouted a whole lot more things, likely uglier by far. And she certainly wouldn't have been able to sit here and listen to this breakdown of what had to be one of the stupidest reasons to marry another person she'd ever heard in her life. Especially coming from Jenny, who had always been a romantic.

But then, romantic or not, Jenny thought she didn't like sex. Erika had always thought that wasn't quite the truth, and that, really, Jenny had a thing about the man she called her best friend and had therefore never touched that way. Dylan Kilburn had been a first year with them at Oxford, had been brooding in Jenny's direction since day one, and yet Jenny had resolutely refused to see him as anything but a friend. For years now. Erika was chock-full of theories as to why.

A couple of weeks ago, she would have hammered her friend with each and every one of those theories, but she was different now. And Erika wasn't sure she liked that strange awareness deep inside her. She wasn't sure she approved of it. But that didn't matter, because either way, she wasn't the same.

She had always wished that she could choose not to make a mess rather than always and forever trying to figure out how to clean it up. And tonight she found she could put it into practice. She put her hand on top of Jenny's and kept her gaze steady. And she set aside her own feelings on the topic, because it didn't matter what she felt or thought. Jenny hadn't asked her for her theories, she'd asked for Erika's blessing.

"You couldn't keep me away from your wedding," Erika said very distinctly. And found as she spoke that she meant it. "It doesn't matter who you're marrying or why. I will be there, with bells on. You can count on it."

Later, as she was lying in the hotel room she'd taken for the night—curled up on her side with that ravenous hunger between her legs that still she didn't take care of because Dorian had told her not to—she remembered Jenny's face. And how stunned she'd looked that Erika had given her blessing.

And hadn't made the whole damn thing about herself, more likely.

Erika wrapped herself up in her coverlet and pretended it was Dorian's arms around her.

What if this was the strength you brought to every part of your life? he had asked her after another one of his wicked, ingenious scenes. He'd turned her inside out, left her gasping and half-mad, and yet convinced on a deep level that she could take anything he dished out. *What if you controlled yourself out there, and only let outside forces control you when those forces were me?*

And she felt too full there, in another anonymous hotel bed. Alone. Close to bursting and too thick with it for it to be anger. Or anything as straightforward as a sob.

Dorian had held up a mirror to her life and she couldn't pretend she hadn't looked into it. And seen.

Somehow, in surrendering herself to him, he had given her the control now. Out here, in the world. Because she knew what true surrender was like, so there was no reason to submit herself to every passing whim.

Erika had chosen to give herself completely to Dorian because he was powerful enough to keep her safe while she did it, and having done that, why would she bother with these lesser surrenders that never made her feel anything but alone?

She could have a host of emotions about her friend and her brother, but she didn't have to succumb to them.

She could *choose*.

She felt as if she'd been struck by lightning, so bright and hot was the jolt of awareness that hit her then.

Dorian had taught her how to choose.

Erika ran with that over the course of the next few days. She stayed in London, searching for the appropriate outfit. And this time, she didn't want attention in a general sense. She wanted his attention. Only his.

Not just his attention, if she was honest. His approval.

And when she tried on the perfect dress, cut to enhance rather than expose, it felt like his hands on her body. As if he lounged there in the corner of her dressing room, his eyes ablaze and his mouth that unsmiling line that made her heart flip over.

The night of the engagement party, she was

dressed, her hair pulled back into a neat chignon at her nape, and ready to go long before it was time to leave Devon and make the drive to the Markham family's stately home in Wiltshire.

Possibly, she thought wryly, *you are a little over-excited.*

She waited in the ancient gallery in her mother's lover's sprawling house. She stared at the dark portraits that lined the walls, each featuring some ancestor or another of his with the same red jowls he sported himself, and found herself very thankful indeed that her mother's taste in men had been much better when she was younger.

"My goodness, Erika," came her mother's stilted, affected voice from the stairs—as if she'd sensed Erika was entertaining uncharitable thoughts about her and had rushed to remind her why each and every one was true. "Are you ill?"

Erika turned to watch her mother come toward her. As ever, Chriszette was resplendent. An ice sculpture best enjoyed from a safe distance. Her blond hair was swept back from her smooth face and secured with combs. She wore a sweeping, elegant gown that made the most of her trim figure. She was a striking woman with a regal bearing and flashing blue eyes that made everyone around her feel as if really, they ought to curtsy.

And she certainly liked it when they did.

"Do I look ill?" Erika asked lightly. Because there was no telling how her mother would strike. Chriszette was like a snake. She was quite happy coiled up in the sun, until she wasn't. And sometimes she moved so fast you never even saw the strike coming until you bled.

"I have never seen you look so...appropriate," Chriszette said, her accent making her sound sharper than she perhaps meant. Then again, perhaps not.

"I'm going to take that as a compliment," Erika said with perhaps more determination than enthusiasm. "Thank you, Mother."

Chriszette did not like to be called *Mother*. Her blue eyes cooled considerably, which was always hard to imagine as she started out so devoutly frigid. She glanced toward the stairs, and Erika knew that she was looking to see if her lover had heard Erika admit to their relationship. A fate worse than death.

"Darling," Chriszette said with a smile that heralded the coming venom, "only very beautiful and very clever girls can afford to hide their assets. I assumed you knew that." She swept her eyes up and down, taking in every inch of Erika's body. "If you don't put on a little show and make sure they're looking at all that bare skin, they might remember that you're a university dropout who shuffles aimlessly from one place to another, effectively homeless. What is cute in one's twenties is a character flaw in later years. You'd do well to remember that."

The old Erika would have screamed back at her, which was what Chriszette wanted. The more of a mess her daughter was, the more she could make herself the maternal victim. The old Erika had known this as well as the current Erika did, but this was the first time that Erika did nothing but smile back at Chriszette. And fail to otherwise react.

A faint frown creased her mother's brow. "No one likes a born loser, Erika," she said. "But as you know, they are often dazzled by a whore."

"Thank you, Mother," Erika said, and she was shaking a little, but she didn't let it own her. The choice was hers, and she chose to let far more powerful things make her cry. Because *he* always sweetened that pot with a few orgasms. She nodded her mother. "I bow to your example, as always."

And her mother's lover appeared then, cutting off whatever vicious reply Chriszette might have planned to make.

The car swept them off for the long drive to Jenny's father's estate, where the party was being held in as much ancient, feudal splendor as possible. Right down to the selling of the bride, if Erika wanted to get technical.

And it wasn't until she'd followed her mother up the grand stairs that led into the soaring hall, then waited her turn while Chriszette left her coat and fluttered all over her lover, that Erika found herself attacked by her own nerves.

She told herself not to be silly.

Which…didn't really work.

After handing off her own coat, she drifted toward the grand ballroom. Chriszette liked to make an entrance, so the party was already in full swing as she swept inside.

Erika, for perhaps the first time in her life, didn't

particularly want to make a scene. So instead, she headed farther into the house, toward one of the less trafficked entrances to the ballroom. Then she stood there for a moment. Jenny was moving through the crowd, looking beautiful and bright and elegant, as always. Jenny's father trailed along with her, looking puffed up and proud—an upgrade from his usual puffed up and pompous.

And then Erika saw her brother, looking as grim and determined as always.

It had been one thing to find a lovely dress. To take on faith that her mother was wrong and Dorian was right. That she had more to offer than too much skin on display at an otherwise excruciatingly proper party like this one, teeming as it was with the sorts of people who appeared regularly in *Tatler*, yet found their presence in its pages appalling.

She found it was one thing to do the things she'd done with Dorian, and admit the truths he'd wrung out of her.

But it would be something else again to look her brother in the eye. Then apologize for not only disappointing him, but for going out of her way to disappoint *herself*, too. And then taking it out on him. For years.

Her stomach twisted, then plummeted to the marble floor at her feet.

She must have been kidding herself. Or so hopped-up on endorphins that she'd forgotten that Conrad was hardly anybody's idea of the sweet, genial older brother. He wasn't the sort to kick a football about or help his younger sister with her maths. On the contrary, Conrad was a dark cloud of a man. He was so severe. So exacting. And he had a way of looking at a person that reminded Erika of their mother when she was poised to strike. Only worse, because Chriszette prized meanness.

Conrad valued accuracy.

And either way, Erika would end up with a hole punched straight through her.

There was absolutely no way that she could march up to him, make herself vulnerable and expose herself before that piercing blue stare of his.

The very idea made her want to curl up and die. Here and now.

She whirled around, thinking she would just grab her coat, call a car and leave all of this behind her—

But she slammed into a wall.

Except it wasn't a wall, she realized as two hands caught her shoulders, and she tipped her head back to look up acres of broad chest packed into black tie.

It was Dorian.

CHAPTER ELEVEN

"ARE YOU GOING SOMEWHERE, Erika?" he asked, his voice a dark, amused rumble, and with that dangerous gleam in his eyes. "Surely not."

And Erika…burst into flames.

She hadn't seen him since Berlin, and she'd thought his voice on the phone was too much. But this…

She couldn't hold his commanding gaze. Her whole body was a mass of flame and desire, that swamping, impossible need, and something that felt like shame. But it was much darker and less destructive than that, and somehow connected directly to that pulsing greed in her pussy.

Erika hated that they were both dressed in all these *clothes*. She yearned for the simplicity of his penthouse in Berlin, all those modern edges. And the quiet reality of her nakedness before his demands.

She could see those days laid out before her like a tableau. Like a fantasy. Like a wish made real, though she'd already experienced it.

God, how she wished she could go back.

Wasn't that what the past two weeks had been

about? Hating and wishing and wanting, desperate to be in his presence again—

And now she was.

And it was here, at Conrad and Jenny's engagement party. Where he wanted her to do this thing that would break her in half. She knew it would. It would destroy her, and if she was destroyed, she could never, ever go back. She could never have Berlin again.

She could never have *him* again.

Erika felt his fingers on her chin, and then he tipped it up, forcing her to meet that dark, simmering gaze of his. She quivered. And thought she saw the hint of a smile.

"You look beautiful, kitten," he said quietly. "More than beautiful. You look like who you are."

That made her feel more than simply hot all over. It made her want to sigh, maybe. And lean into him. And it felt as if she already had.

"My mother disagrees," she said, concentrating on his strong fingers pressing into her chin. "Demure clothing like this is for very beautiful women or very clever ones. Dumb whores like me need to put on a show. Tits and ass, presumably."

She wasn't sure why she'd said such things to a man who had, until recently, been the most likely to agree with Chriszette's take on her. Until she saw his temper flash across his face, and not at her.

"Your mother is a very small, very jealous woman." Dorian's brow rose, and Erika was conditioned now. She felt the blaze of it go through her, settling heavily in her oversensitive clit. Her nipples ached for his mouth. She *hurt* for him. There was no other way to put it. She already hurt for him, and she would hurt more if he wanted, because the pain was a blessing. It made everything bloom. Especially her.

"And I thought we covered this already. The only opinion you need to consider is mine."

"I can't do it," she said breathlessly. "I can't apologize to him. You don't understand."

"I do understand." He was unyielding and it made her melt even as it made her stomach twist again. "I never told you it would be easy, little one. I only told you that I expected you to do it."

Misery slammed into her, another tidal wave she could do nothing to prevent. "I can't."

She expected him to look angry, but he didn't. He looked only disappointed, which was worse. "That is a choice."

And he had taught her all about choices, hadn't he? He had taught her how to choose. But this didn't feel like a choice. This felt like a death sentence.

"You want to humble me," she said. "Humiliate me. I get that. It's important to you."

And to her surprise, Dorian laughed. "When I want to humiliate you, kitten, you will know. You will not be clothed in full view of the richest men in Europe, one of whom is your brother. You will very likely be on all fours, at my feet, and very, very naked. Understand that first."

She was breathless as he dropped his hand from her chin and then maneuvered her in front of him, away from the crowded ballroom and deeper into the house. He rested a hand on the nape of her neck as if it belonged there, and Erika relaxed into it. The weight of his palm felt right. Good. And after all the turmoil of the past weeks, wave after wave of too much emotion, it took her a moment to recognize what it was that suffused her now.

Peace. Safety.

There was something about this man that felt like home.

He opened a door, and ushered her inside, and it took her a moment to allow her eyes to adjust to the different lighting. It was a very small study, or sitting room, that Erika had never seen on her previous visits here. It was the kind of place the ladies of the house might have retired in latter days to keep up with their embroidery or correspondence. There were delicate, ebullient furnishings, heavy on scrollwork and filigree.

In the middle of so much unrestrained femininity, Dorian was like a brooding, lethal fist. All threat and masculinity, and that uncompromising power that blazed out of him like his very own sun.

That power that she took into her, gloried in and made her own.

Dorian closed the door behind him and then stood there, a narrow, assessing look on his beautiful face.

Inside, Erika felt fizzy. Bright.

He lifted one finger and twirled it in the air, indicating that she should turn for him. And she did, different sensations scudding through her, but all of them ending up in the same place. That delirious, delectable heat between her legs that pulsed out into everything else.

"The trouble with you, Erika, is that you are too beautiful already. And far too clever."

His voice was almost more beautiful than he was, if such a thing was possible. It was his voice that had stayed with her in the time they'd been apart. She'd heard him on the phone and in her head, as if he had a direct connection to her body no matter where he was. As if he owned her, body and soul, mind and pussy, and everything in her exalted in that notion.

Not least because, if he owned her, surely she could own him in return. It was a power exchange after all. Not a power grab.

"When you walk around with your gorgeous body on display, people get silly," Dorian said, his gaze steady on her. "Stupid. They say jealous, small-minded things, as your mother has already amply demonstrated tonight. And people are not always as good as they should be about holding two ideas in their head at once."

"My mother holds a great number of ideas in her head, all of them nasty."

"It is easier to believe that stunning blonde woman with a smile that can light up a room and blue eyes the color of summer must be dumb," he said quietly. "Foolish, at the very least. An easily dismissible whore. I'm not surprised that the people in your life who feel threatened by all that you are would encourage you to dress and act as if you are far less than that."

He pushed off the door at his back and came toward her at last. And then, finally, he was touching her again. He ran his hands over her the way he'd done so many times before, as if he was memorizing her shape. This time, he skimmed his palms down her arms and then held them out at her sides.

"Dressed like the powerful heiress you are, you give all of these vipers no choice but to see the real you. I'm sure they won't like it." He shrugged, that dark intensity in his gaze never wavering. "But as we keep discussing, it only matters if *I* like it. And I do. Very much."

And she couldn't have said why that mattered so much to her. Only that it did. And that further, his praise felt like a crackling fire on a cold night.

"Dorian," she whispered. "I don't want you to be disappointed in me, but you will be. Because I can't—"

"Quiet, please."

It was an order. And on some level, Erika wanted to demand that he make these boundaries between a scene and life clearer to her. But then, she didn't want them clear. She wanted this, the poignancy and sharpness, the intensity and color, and the possibility that every moment with him was a scene.

And only sometimes would actual cuffs, whips and chains be involved.

But she had to shake that off, because she was thinking in terms of tomorrows and she doubted very much that he would want much to do with her by the end of the night.

Because she couldn't give him what he wanted.

"I want you to do something for me," Dorian said, sounding casual when his expression was anything but. "It's not an order. I'm going to tell you what I desire, what I wish, and you may choose or not choose to do it. What are you wearing under that dress?"

It felt as if he'd rocked a boat she hadn't known she was standing on, and she almost felt like she had whiplash as she fought to keep her balance. She expected him to bring up Conrad again and almost asked him why he hadn't…

But his gaze was intent on hers, and over the course of her time in Berlin, she had learned that it was better not to test his patience. She bit back a shiver, remembering the creative things he could do when a naked woman didn't respond quickly enough to an order he'd given her while they were preparing dinner together. One piece of peeled ginger inserted into the right place left indelible memories—and a healthy respect for the limits of his patience.

"Um," she said. She blinked. "A thong?"

"Is that a question? And who are you addressing, kitten?"

She cleared her throat. "A thong, sir."

"Remove it."

She blinked at that, too. Dorian only stared back at her while his brow slowly began to rise.

Erika started to pull at the long skirt of her dress while he stood there and made no attempt to look away. She pulled the skirt up to her waist, then wriggled out of her thong. And when she pulled it down and off, she straightened again to find him holding out his hand.

"I'll take that, thank you."

And it was ridiculous, given the things she had already done with him, but handing him her thong while it was still warm from her body made her cheeks burn. She could tell from the gleam in his dark eyes that he was enjoying it.

She handed them over and was acutely aware, then, that she was suddenly going commando under her dress. Not that it should have mattered to her in the least, when she was normally dressed in much less. But then, that was why the things he did were so diabolical. They could be over-the-top, like a dark pageant in his club. Or they could be as simple as this. Wearing a pretty dress, but knowing she was naked underneath—at his command.

He pocketed the thong, and then pulled something else out of a different pocket, holding it there in his palm like a gift. Erika knew what it was. It was a particularly high-end anal plug, complete with a bejeweled button on the end.

"I bought it just for you," he said, a wicked amusement in his voice. "Thank me."

"Thank you," she whispered, but she couldn't take her eyes off the *thing* in his hand.

"Let me tell you what I want," he said while her heart pounded and her skin seemed to shrink. She would have called it fear or revulsion were it not for her traitorous pussy that ached, soft and hot. "I want you to bend over that breakable-looking chair behind you and lift your skirt for me. Then I want you to thank me when I slide this deep inside your ass. When I'm done, we both know you'll be so slippery that something will have to be done before we go back out there, so I'll have absolutely no choice but to fuck you, hard. You'll want to come, because you always want to come, but you won't, Erika. This time you'll hold it back, for me."

He hadn't moved. He still stood there, doing absolutely nothing but holding his hand out with the plug gleaming there in his palm. And yet Erika was gasping for breath as if he'd thrown her over his lap and paddled her again.

"I told you, this isn't an order," he said. "This is my desire, nothing more, nothing less. You can choose whether or not you want to do it. It's up to you."

And something in that scraped at her, though she couldn't have said why. She felt the way she often had in Berlin, as if she was too big inside, too bright and hot and expansive, and all because he looked at her like that. With that firm, infinite patience that made her believe she could do anything at all. Anything he asked. Anything he dreamed up.

Anything he thought she could do.

They weren't in that apartment of his, with all those clean lines and vast spaces, as if to make room for his dirty imagination. And still, everything else fell away. She forgot that they were in a tucked-away room in Jenny's house. She forgot that her entire family was out there, just down the hall, at a party filled with people who wouldn't take a lot of convincing to think the worst of her.

She didn't care, she realized. Even if they'd all been standing right here in front of her, watching and judging from the fragile-looking settee, she still wouldn't have cared.

Erika saw nothing in Dorian's gaze except confidence that she could and would do anything he asked of her, and that was all she needed. His confidence in her gave her confidence in herself—or maybe that wasn't quite right.

It was more that he saw in her what she had always believed was there, and because he believed in it, she could, too.

She jerked slightly, as if she was coming out of a spell. And still, Dorian watched her as if he could wait forever. And would. She turned to the chair he had indicated, and she flipped her skirt up as she bent over. The arms of the chair were low, and she had to tilt herself at a sharp angle to hold on to them. She was wearing heels, and the simple act of bending over tilted her naked ass high into the air.

"Very nice," he said.

And she dropped her head down, let out a small sigh of satisfaction and waited.

Dorian moved behind her, and she felt his hands on her body again. There had been times over the past couple of weeks that she'd thought she would never feel him again, and she'd never been so happy to be wrong. Her eyes drifted shut as his palms traced down her back, then over the curves of her butt.

Warming her. Greeting her. Both, maybe.

He removed his hands, but his legs were still there, brushing against hers and obliquely reminding her of his strength. His control.

And the particular sweetness of her surrender.

Because giving herself over to Dorian felt like real freedom—not like loneliness.

She felt his hands move into the crease of her ass, rubbing her opening in a way that told he was going to take what she was offering and more, that he expected her to like it. It felt rude and hot at once, especially when she felt something slick and cold on his fingers. He rubbed at her, dipping his finger in and laughing slightly when she made noises she couldn't seem to bite back.

Then she felt the tip of the plug, narrowed for entry before it widened to that thickness her mind shied away from, and she pulled in a deep, scared sort of breath. Scared, electrified—she couldn't really tell the difference.

"Push out," he told her, but he didn't wait for her to obey him. He simply began pushing the slicked-up item deep inside her.

It didn't exactly hurt, though it wasn't at all comfortable. Still, it was thrilling at the same time, because he was relentless. It wasn't about the butt plug. It was his will and her surrender, and the struggle wasn't between her and him, but inside herself.

And the more she accepted that, the wetter her pussy got and the more she pushed herself back against the plug to help him seat it inside her.

"Someday, baby, that's going to be me," he told her, low and fierce.

It made her shudder, her clit pulsing as if she was dangerously close to coming already.

She fought it back, but she was breathless by the time he got the plug all the way in. And she couldn't have said if it was from that cartwheeling, delighted thing inside her because he was here and this was happening, or the laughter she couldn't quite hold back, or all the other things she felt for him—because God, what didn't she feel for him?

And then it didn't matter, because she heard the tear of a condom wrapper.

One hand rested on her low back, keeping her in place. And his cock was there at the entrance to her pussy, as broad and thick as she remembered it.

He thrust himself inside her, hard and deep, and Erika had to bite the tufted pillow in front of her face to keep her scream inside.

"I didn't hear you thank me," he said, and she heard her own crazy breath as she pulled it in, high-pitched and wild.

"Th-thank you…" she managed to get out.

"Who are you thanking, kitten?" came his voice, a dark and silken thread that wrapped around her and pulled tight.

"Thank you, sir," she said.

And she meant it.

His cock was a revelation inside her. The plug in her ass made her tighter, and him bigger, and he was not a small man. She wanted to explode on the spot, so crammed full of him—of Dorian and his demands and his desires—that she shuddered right there on the edge of a climax—

But only in the last moment, remembered that she was not to come.

"Oh my God," she whispered under her breath.

Dorian laughed, and then he began to fuck her.

He took her hard and deep, the way he always did. As if she wasn't tighter than usual. And he didn't slow down. Or speed up.

It was that same, unyielding, relentless rhythm that haunted her in her sleep. It was a greedy, glorious pounding, and normally she would have come twice already.

But she fought it. Erika could feel every inch of him in Technicolor, but she held on.

Her clit ached, and her thighs quivered, and she thought there were tears tracking down her face, but somehow, she held on.

"You're such a good girl," he said, leaning over her, his voice a dark taunt, giving her back those words that no one had said to her since she was a child. Making them new. And his. "You're trying so hard to please me."

Erika couldn't speak. She couldn't do anything but hold herself as tightly and as carefully as possible, because the slightest wrong move—

"But I told you before. Sometimes, no matter how good you are, I'm just going to want to punish you. Because I can. And because it's fun."

And his wicked, terrible hand snaked around, took

her plump, desperate clit between his fingers and pinched. Hard.

Erika went nuclear.

She didn't pass out. Not quite. She was aware that he'd sneaked a hand up and covered her mouth, which is the only reason she didn't scream the house down around their ears. She felt him come hard with a low groan.

But she was ruined. Already destroyed and beyond saving, and she couldn't seem to care.

He pulled out, and she moaned again, because the plug was still there. And she could feel him, still too big inside her even as he removed himself. He laughed again, and she didn't have the energy to do anything but stay where she was, draped over the chair with her ass in the air, completely exposed.

She heard him moving around, and assumed he was disposing of the condom, putting himself to rights. She focused on trying to breathe. Then he was beside her, pulling her to her feet and holding her there before him.

And the look on Dorian's face made the whole world seem to slip to one side.

Tenderness. That was what she saw in those dark, dark eyes of his.

It made her feel inside out. Stripped raw, made new.

He rubbed his thumbs beneath her eyes, and she had the distant thought that she must look a mess, but she didn't care. Not when he was looking at her like that. As if she was his world.

And here, in this sacred space they'd made between them, Erika believed it.

"I don't want you to apologize to your brother for me," he told her, his voice steady. Utterly certain. "I saw him earlier this week. He took a swing at me, and I let him."

She frowned. "That's not right."

"It hurt like hell, and I deserved it." Dorian shook his head. "I'm a grown man."

"Still—"

"I don't need you to get along with my best friend, however nice I might find the idea," Dorian said intently. "I want you to apologize to him for you, Erika. He's your brother. Considering the kind of person your mother is, he's the only family you have. And I know you think he doesn't care about you, but I'm telling you—you're wrong."

"You don't understand."

"I understand completely," he said quietly, and his fingers brushed over her cheek. "You don't think anyone can love you."

Erika felt as if he'd punched her. Revealed her. Destroyed her all over again.

"But I know they can," he said, still gazing at her with all that intensity and power that made her hum inside, then melt. She had no choice but to listen to him, no matter how ruined she felt. "I know it because I do."

It was everything she'd ever wanted and more, because it was him. It was beyond anything she could have imagined. It was every gift she hadn't gotten.

It swept away every time she had been forgotten, thrown away, cast aside. Belittled or ignored.

But it was also impossible.

"Don't tell me it's too soon," he warned her. "You're already in trouble for coming when I told you not to."

And he smiled when she glowered at him.

"Dorian—" she began.

"No, it's not fair," he said, cutting her off. "And yes, Erika, I'm in love with you. I don't need more time to make up my mind. I already know. I've been waiting for you for years. I knew when we woke up that first morning in Berlin that I was never letting you go, and, kitten, I keep my promises. You know this."

It caused Erika actual physical pain to hear him say these things when she *knew* how it would go. How it always went.

"When you get to know me better, you'll regret this." She had to force herself to say it. But the fact was she knew. She knew better than him because she'd seen it play out so many times before. "When you see the truth, you won't be able to get away quickly enough."

And she said it simply. Matter-of-factly. Because she knew it was the truth.

"I've already seen the truth." His hands rested on either side of her neck, his fingers on the nape of her neck and his thumbs on her jaw, holding her where he wanted her. And what he wanted, she delighted in giving him. "What do you think we've been doing?

BDSM is never just the sex, kitten. Not the way I do it. Not if it's right. And this? Us? It's beautiful."

"I chased you all over the planet," she confessed, her eyes filling with tears. "You told me you would spank me in Greece, and I wanted it. I wanted you. Maybe I knew that if I could just find my way to you, you could fix me."

"You don't need fixing, baby." Dorian shook his head, his gaze fierce. "You're not broken. A little lost, maybe, so I gave you a compass. But the journey you take is up to you."

She wanted to fall into his arms and hide there. Instead, she made herself look at him straight on. "How can you love someone you hardly know?"

But Dorian laughed. "You were quick to tell me you've known me all my life," he pointed out. "And even if you didn't, you know all kinds of things about me now. Deep, intimate things. That you can trust me. That if I'm hard on you, I reward it. That I care enough about you to give you the boundaries you've wanted all your life. I demanded total honesty. And you gave it to me. What else do you need?"

Erika swallowed, hard, aware of her heartbeat in every part of her. Even her fingertips. "And if I go out there and apologize to my brother, then we can…continue?"

He muttered something, then leaned forward to press his forehead to hers.

"Baby. I'm not letting you go. If you don't apologize to your brother, I'll be disappointed. And I might take that disappointment out on that fine ass of yours. That's your choice." He laughed when she shuddered. "But you and me? There's only one thing you could do to end this. You'll have to tell me to go, and you'll have to use your safe word, so that I believe it. Is that what you want?"

"No," she breathed. "I don't want that at all."

"Make a choice," he ordered her.

"You," she said, and she didn't even think about it. It didn't require thought. "Of course, you."

Dorian tilted her head up then, and dropped his mouth to hers and gave her the sweetest, most delicious kiss, like something out of a fairy tale. And then he raised his head, his eyes went wicked and he dropped a hand down to her butt and squeezed.

Making her jump, because the plug was still in there.

"Try not to walk as if you have a stick up your ass, kitten," he told her, amusement making his voice that much richer. "You wouldn't want to raise suspicions."

Erika scowled at him, but when he took her hand, she laced her fingers tight with his and felt nothing short of giddy.

She took a quick peek in one of the mirrors they passed out in the hallway, and hardly recognized the person she saw looking back at her. Because finally, after all these years, she looked alive. She wasn't hiding. She wasn't afraid.

She was just…Erika. Herself.

At last.

Dorian drew her back to that same doorway where he'd found her earlier and they stood there a moment, looking in on the assembled crowd. Erika found Conrad quickly in the middle of the throng, looking as buttoned-up and unapproachable as ever. Her stomach twisted, predictably.

"Are you ready?" Dorian asked from beside her.

Erika looked at her brother. And she looked down at her hand entwined with Dorian's.

And she knew it didn't matter what she chose. That he would express any disappointment in her honestly, and present her with consequences, but he wouldn't cut her loose. She could make any choice at all, and he would support her. And possibly paddle her if he didn't agree with it.

But after all this time, after so many years out there, alone, she'd finally found her home. He was her home.

Dorian would keep her safe. He had the power to lead, to demand. But she had the power to surrender. And between them, they had the power to do absolutely anything.

Even fall in love too fast, and then stay there forever.

But she didn't tell him that. Not now. She was certain he would much rather tie her up and make her say it later, when he ran out of patience.

She could hardly wait.

Erika looked up and found herself there in the bright gleam in his dark eyes that was all for her. Only and ever for her.

"I would follow you anywhere," she told him.

And then she smiled, as bright as the sunshine

he made her feel even here, inside and at night. Everywhere. That was the magic they made between them, and always would.

She believed in him. In them. In this, no matter how new.

In the home they made between them, and carried wherever they'd go.

And before he could prompt her, she leaned closer and whispered his favorite word in his ear, so no one else could hear.

"Sir."

CHAPTER TWELVE

ERIKA APOLOGIZED TO her brother, with an openness and vulnerability that made Dorian fall in love with her all over again. And more deeply.

But then, she was good at that.

They'd made a commitment to each other in that frilly, prissy room in the Markham family manor house, but Dorian knew better than to take his skittish little kitten for granted.

It took him two months—and his favorite swing, which he could suspend from his bedroom ceiling—to get her to admit she was in love with him.

He already knew she was in love with him. But he liked hearing her tell him so.

It took him sixteen more months to get her fully moved into his penthouse. Or to be more precise, he moved her in almost immediately because he didn't see the point of being without her, but it took her all that time to finally admit that was what was happening.

He expressed his feelings on her reticence in the language they both understood best.

And Erika set about making his life better in a thousand little ways that had nothing to do with sex. She taught him to feel sorrow for his father's wasted life, instead of outraged about it. She charmed his grandfather and had the old man sparkling like a teenager whenever she was around. Her life had been unconventional in the extreme, but that made her the perfect sounding board for all of the business issues Dorian had never been able to talk through with anyone else. Not completely.

In turn, he taught her how to stand up to her mother—or at the very least, choose not to engage with her cruelty.

She had spent so long acting a part, but the more comfortable she became with him and the safety of the life they made together, the more she began to shine. And she took care of him. She worried about him. For once, Dorian didn't have to be responsible for holding up the whole damned sky and everything in it.

With Erika, Dorian was safe, too. He could allow himself the vulnerabilities he'd always before seen as weaknesses. He could share all of himself instead of chopping himself up into necessary compartments.

He could let her soothe him, too. He could grow, more and more each day, without worrying that the slightest crack in his confidence would send her running.

Because she loved all of him. The dominant, the man and the partner he became, just for her.

Dorian had known he wanted her, permanently,

after that first night. But even he couldn't have foreseen how beautifully in sync the two of them would become over time, until he found that he could no longer remember what life had been before she'd wandered into his club and claimed him.

And now that he had Erika, Dorian lost his taste for club games. He practiced his favorite hobbies on her. He had no need to bring anyone else into it. And more to the point, he had absolutely no interest in sharing her with anyone. He liked all her exhibitions to be for him alone.

Six months into living together officially—meaning six months into getting her to believe that he wasn't going to throw her out, she wasn't going anywhere the next time the whim took her and he really did love her to distraction—she looked at him over the top of the book she was reading one evening. She was curled up beside him, naked as she usually was when they were at home. He sat next to her with her legs on his lap, wearing his typical jeans and T-shirt.

And Berlin was there outside their windows, always beckoning, always bright and unexpected. Much like his woman, Dorian thought.

"I want to do something," Erika said. "But I don't know how you'll like it."

"If I don't like it, I'll tell you so and I will proceed from there." And he grinned at her when she scowled at him. "Is that is advisable way to look at me?" he asked idly. "I haven't played with my whip in a while."

Erika shivered beside him, but her eyes gleamed. She liked to pretend she hated the whip… But they both knew better.

"I want to finish university," she said, surprising him. Because he never knew what she would say or do next, and that was one more reason why he loved her. "Oxford has offered me a place, if I want to do my third year. But it would mean…"

Dorian set aside the papers he was reading, already forgetting whatever tedious report he been making his way through. He reached over and settled his hand on the nape of her neck, calming them both. Connecting them. "And what will you do with this fine Oxbridge education should you finally receive it in full?"

And her smile was hopeful and almost scared, as if she couldn't believe she was daring to do this. To even discuss doing it.

It made his heart hurt.

But then, she was good at that, too.

"I'm not sure," she said. "Anything and everything. Isn't that the point?" Then she bit back her smile, and looked down at her lap. "But Oxford is… in Oxford, not Berlin."

"Let me guess. You want to have a discussion about what it is you think I want. And if I tell you that I forbid it, that gives you something to rebel against, which is far more comfortable than simply telling me what you want. Is that about right?"

She let out a sigh that was half a groan, tilting her head back to lean into his hand. "You know, sometimes, Dorian, I just want to have a conversation. I don't want to scrape back every layer and expose my raw and beating heart to the air."

He pulled her face to his and kissed her. "Tough luck, baby."

"I want to do this," she said, lifting her gaze and keeping it steady on his. "But the idea of missing you, even if it's only during the week and I fly back here on weekends, or whatever, makes me feel… sick. What if I ruin this? I don't think I could bear it."

"You can't ruin this," he told her, keeping her face close to his. "It's not up to you. If you want to go and do this thing, I want you to do it. Not everybody gets the opportunity to reset their past. I'll support you completely."

"My God," she said, there against his mouth. "Do you have any idea how much I love you?"

He did. But he used his whip that night anyway, to measure it.

They found a flat in Oxford, and they made it work. Sometimes she flew out to meet him at his various business affairs. Other times, he came to her. And it wasn't the same as living together 24/7, but it was fine. It was temporary, and they made it good.

And one night, when he waited for her in a pub not far from her last lecture of the day, he patiently turned down the advances of several women. And when he looked up, he found her watching him.

"Jealous?" he asked when she came to him, an odd look on her face.

"As a matter fact…not at all," Erika said, and then

she laughed. "I've worried so much about our separations, but I see now that I shouldn't have."

He traced her lips with his thumb, and felt himself harden, right there on the bar stool.

"Because you strust me implicitly?" he asked.

"That, and the reality of what we are to each other."

She smiled at him, and he felt it then. That she finally saw what he'd seen in her, and helped her bring to the surface. Real power. Their power. And damn, if it wasn't beautiful.

Just like her smile. "A random girl in a bar could never give you what I do."

"Amen," he said, drawing her closer. He made sure to pull her hard against his thigh, so he could press into her pussy, right there where anyone could see them if they looked hard enough. "And remember, please, that your flat is not soundproofed. I wouldn't want your neighbors to call the police this time."

And she still blushed, which was yet another reason he loved her to distraction. But these days, she also smiled. Wickedly.

"Promises, promises," she said.

And then paid for that impertinence, later.

Dorian was there, along with Conrad and his wife—but mercifully not her mother—when Erika walked across the stage and got her degree at last.

Because she could do anything, and would, and he would be right there with her every step of the way. He would put his rings on her finger. She would make him some babies. He knew what he wanted his happy-ever-after to look like, because he was already living it.

She was his. And she was perfect.

Especially when he knew that underneath her graduation robes, Erika wore nothing but his favorite plug that he'd greatly enjoyed inserting earlier—and his handprints, all over her extraordinary ass.

* * * * *

GETTING DIRTY

RACHAEL STEWART

MILLS & BOON

For my sister Louise and her fabulous husband Mark, for inspiring the inclusion of the Highlands with their awesome road trips!

And to my talented editor Sareeta, for loving this storyline when it was just an idea! I hope I've done it justice. ;-) Thank you for being so great at what you do!

Happy reading DAREdevils!

Rxx

CHAPTER ONE

I LOVE MY line of work. People bitch and moan about their careers but not me.

Clients task me with a job and I get it done. I don't run an empire. I don't employ anyone full-time. I only have myself to watch out for and that's the way I like it.

This job earned my family back a shred of their respect a decade ago and I've been dishing the dirt on corrupt arseholes, playboys and spoilt little rich girls ever since.

I didn't set out to be a private investigator. It's a job that chose me when my family needed it most and it turns out I'm a natural. If there's dirt, I'll find it.

And right now, that dirt is sitting across the softly lit room from me.

Only *this* kind of dirt I cannot dish.

It crosses a line that even my skewed moral compass cannot abide.

'Come on, Ash, what gives?'

I raise my eyes from my untouched pint to see

Jackson grinning at me from the other side of the bar. 'Where'd you come from?'

'We're short-staffed tonight. I'm helping out.'

'A bit beneath you, wouldn't you say?'

'Nah, I kind of enjoy it.'

He scans the darkened corners of the room, the various people making out, and barely raises a brow. And why would he? This is his life day in, day out. This is his club—Blacks—complete with sex on tap, catering to the British elite. The upper crust. A circle to which I once wholeheartedly belonged and now wouldn't piss on if it were on fire.

These people have money. Enough to pay for the exclusive membership and the non-disclosure agreement that comes with it. Anything goes within these walls—within reason—and no one on the outside is any the wiser. Including my client. But the presence of my target—*her*—tells me there's more to Coco Lauren than what the world sees. What the press witnesses. And that's what I need to tap into, to expose, if I'm to get what I need and deliver what my client demands.

'Jesus, you need something stronger than a pint, judging by the look of you.'

I barely acknowledge his observation. Truth is, what I need is something that gets her to step out of line, outside of this safe haven where I can't say anything without compromising my friend's business.

He backs up and snatches a bottle from the side with two shot glasses, smacking them down between us. 'You never come here, so I repeat: What gives?'

The truth will only piss him off, and I'm not about to lie, so I stay quiet and his eyes narrow, his powerhouse of a frame turning rigid. If he wasn't my oldest friend I'd think he was about to punch me.

'You'd better not be here on the clock...'

'Hey, easy.' I raise my palms. I knew he'd be suspicious, and he has every right to be—because he's right. I *never* come in here. 'The twisted secrets of this place are safe with me.'

He continues to study me and I know he's warring with what he knows of my work and what he knows of me. I know he doesn't like how I earn a living; we agree to disagree. As far as I'm concerned, these people deserve what they get.

Just like the princess teasing me with her long bare legs, cute little arse and a face that's bordered by a blonde low-swinging bob. She projects such innocence to the outside world, but not now, not in here.

As if on cue she stands and bends over the table to whisper in the ear of her female companion. I clock the feline curve of her body, the gentle swell of her hips, the delicate arch to her back, and then her friend turns and they kiss. Not just a peck. A deep, tongue-sinking kiss that has a spasm of heat ripping through me.

I straighten against it. *Fuck.*

I've seen her dressed for swanky lunch dates, the gym, charity galas and shopping sprees, and now I get to see her half-naked, with an intent that screams one thing: *sex*.

And in surroundings such as these, with soft

lighting, plush grey sofas and the perfect balance of glass and warm wood, she's lending a sophisticated charm that you could lose yourself in. It's only the debauched goings-on here that make it more than just a hip wine bar, and she's smack-bang in the middle of it. Adding to it.

I don't want to see the appeal. The allure. The legs that go on for ever. And that kiss that sears the air, my skin, my blood.

'Ah, now I see…'

Jackson's enlightened murmur snaps me out of it. I pull my gaze back to my pint, chug back a gulp.

'It's a woman that brings you my way—now it makes sense. It's about time.'

I almost choke on the bitter drink. 'Hardly.' He's close, and yet so far off the mark. 'I can't say I care for your choice of clientele.'

He laughs. 'You don't need to care—not for sex. You ought to try it some time…a bit of no-strings fun. Celibacy doesn't suit you.'

'Really?' My brow lifts. Never mind him punching *me*, I'm going to swing for him across the bar, to hell with the doormen flanking the place.

He laughs harder as he pours clear liquid into both shot glasses and slides one across to me. 'Your mistake was letting one get under your skin.'

'One?'

'You know who I mean—Jess.'

I throw back the shot and wince. The harsh hit douses the burn of her—my ex, the woman who left the second my family lost it all. 'Yeah, well, I'd take a woman out of my local over one from here any day.'

'That's not what your face was telling me a few seconds ago.'

I glower at him—but, hell, he's right.

I drag my mind back to the job, to what I should be focusing on.

Coco is clearly at home here, her open affection with the other girl and the show they're putting on for the guy across from them makes that obvious. Nothing in my research suggested she swung that way, but Philip Lauren—my client, her half-brother—had suspected it.

'I'm not sure I'm her type.'

Jackson grinned. '*Everyone's* her type if they can deliver in the bedroom.'

Heat unfurls deep within my gut. I can't pinpoint the cause. Desire, envy, anger… She's just like my ex, I try to tell myself. Only, Jess's vice was money. Coco's is sex. Just as her brother had said.

'How often does she come in here?'

'Depends. You asking for you, or for work?'

'Does it matter?'

It really didn't. It wasn't like I'd put his livelihood at stake. It was the reason her brother was giving me shit. He expected me to have uncovered something by now, and the one thing I'd uncovered was the one thing I couldn't divulge.

'I've promised I'm taking your secrets to the grave regardless.'

'Glad to hear it.'

He's talking to me but his eyes are on her, just as mine were. His expression is thoughtful, almost concerned. And I'm listening, my ears attuned to whatever has him looking so intent.

'It used to be once a fortnight, occasionally once a week, but lately it's been more.'

'More?'

'Yeah.' He looks back to me. 'She's probably been here twice this past week alone.'

'And that bothers you?'

'Not so much bothers me, but you know… This place serves a purpose, and whatever that is for her seems to me she's needing it more and more.'

'It's sex, Jackson. Perhaps she's just on heat.'

I'm purposefully harsh, flippant, but I don't want his concern. It doesn't pay for me to care, to soften towards her, but I can feel it happening. As each day goes by, each new discovery only adds to the appealing enigma that is Coco Lauren.

'It's more than that for people like her.'

Jackson's like a dog with a bone. He's not letting this go. Maybe she's ensnared him too. Not that I'm *ensnared*—unable to douse the attraction more like.

'They come here to get away from it all, and if she's upping her visits, something's bothering her.'

'You sound like you care.'

'She's nice, that's all.' He gives a shrug and his eyes drift back in her direction. I let mine do the same, watching as she walks in the direction of the ladies' room, her hips swaying provocatively. I feel the telltale ripple of heat through my groin and clench my jaw.

'You could be good for her, you know.'

Jackson's tone has a sincere ring to it that makes my blood run cold, as effective as a cold shower ever would be. Never would I go back to a woman like that. They have a knack for taking you to your knees and I've no interest in risking that again.

'If you haven't forgotten how to do it, that is?'

'Shut it, Jackson, or regardless of your bouncers I'll take you down right now.'

I shake my head and neck the minuscule drink. He's hit a nerve and he knows it. Hell, maybe that's why Lady Legs is having such an undesirable effect on my libido.

Who are you kidding? The reason you haven't had sex in an age is because you can't find anyone who does it for you. That is, you couldn't until you started this job, until her...

I look to the closed lavatory door and beat back the thought.

You're here on business, not for sex. And if you were looking for sex it wouldn't be with one of these hoity-toity bitches who remind you so much of Jess.

I'm wired and it's driving me crazy.

Usually I can lose myself in this place. Forget the trappings of my life on the outside and have fun. It takes the edge off—just enough to go back to it and do it all again. Smile, perform, play the part to perfection.

But not now. Not with Granny so sick.

She's the closest thing to a mother I've ever known, and since losing my father two years ago she's been my world.

Nothing can bury the pain. I aim for distraction, pure and simple. But not even distraction is enough tonight.

Caitlin murmurs something in my ear, her dainty tongue tracing its delicate ridge, and I watch as the eyes of the up-and-coming footballer opposite—what was his name? Ryan? Reece? Ricky? I don't know, he's new—turn to saucers. He's out of luck, though. I'm not in the mood, and no amount of Cait's expert attentions are going to do it for me. Not tonight.

I push out of my seat to rise. I take pity on him and give him a view as I lean in to make my excuses to her and kiss her full on the mouth. She tastes of strawberry, the remnants of the daiquiri she's been sipping, and I linger a second longer, urging my body to obey, to want, to overtake this pain with the numbing heat of desire. But…nothing.

With a smothered sigh, I head to the bathroom, triggering a text to my driver to collect me in ten. I'll hit the hard stuff when I get home, knock myself out in my own private domain. I'm not even fearing the hangover that's bound to ensue. Anything to beat off the impending pain of loss that's hanging over me.

A quick pit stop, a sweep of red across the lips and I re-enter the room. Caitlin's chatting to Jackson at the bar and the footballer's long gone. The fact that

I'm not struck with the slightest hint of disappointment tells me I've done the right thing.

The sigh comes full force now and I move off—just as a wall appears in front of me and I smack right into it. A wall of hard, lean muscle that smells oceanic and male, all fresh and inviting, not like the expensive cloying cologne most guys here favour. No this is more natural, more... Just *more*...

My eyes trail upwards from where our bodies are still pressed up against one another. A black shirt, open at the collar, an honest hint of hair... How unusual. A square-set jaw, ample stubble... Nice. A full mouth, firm yet sensual, *very* nice. A strong nose, not too big, not too small. And eyes—

Oh, my God.

I start to lower my lashes, but I've never stood down in my life and force my eyes open. Wide.

Fierce blues pierce me, the coloured rims almost drowned out by glittering pupils. I swallow. At least I think I do. But my throat's still closed tight as my cheeks start to heat. Part of me is aware I should step back. The other part is more than aware that he hasn't made any attempt to either.

I wet my lips and manage, 'Hi,' feeling glad when it's not the squeak I feared.

His eyes rake over my face and then he seems to come alive on a breath. 'Apologies.'

Stepping away, he rubs a hand over the back of his head and my palm tickles like it's mine that's grazing over the dark buzz cut. And then he moves off and the connection is gone, the spell with it.

What was *that*?

Distraction, that's what.

'Wait.' I reach out to touch his arm and feel heat permeate my fingertips, solid muscle flexing beneath the shirt. 'I'm Coco.'

He hesitates as he looks back to me, his eyes still piercing, still ablaze. It's like there's a war raging in his head—he looks angry, even. But instead of being scared I'm drawn in. My body is well aware that this is what I need right now and I can't let it go.

'I know who you are.'

It's a simple statement, but there's an edge to it. I almost want to say it's contempt, and curiosity toughens my spine as I retract my hand and smile. 'You say that like it's a bad thing.'

'Look, princess, you're just not my type.'

I laugh. The sound tinkles, high and easy. I'm already having fun. More fun than I've had in a long time. 'Really…?'

'Really.'

He makes no attempt to leave, though. *Interesting.*

I cock my head to the side, let my gaze travel over him slowly, more brazen this time.

'I hardly think I'm yours either,' he adds, his tone rough and teasing at the electricity already thrumming in my veins.

I lift my eyes to his as I say, 'Let me be the judge of that.'

A pulse dances in his jaw and I wet my lips as I step closer, reaching out to toy with the first fastened button of his shirt. His chest stills beneath my fingers but his face is set hard. If not for the slight flare to his nose and that tripping pulse point I'd think the chest thing was a figment of my imagination.

'You going to tell me your name, or am I to guess?'

His throat bobs and I can sense his need to clear it. I'm not naive when it comes to sex. Sex and attraction. His body is giving me all the signs, even if he doesn't want me to see it.

'It's like that, is it? Hmm… Let me see…' I smile as I ponder and watch his eyes flicker back at me. Am I amusing him? I *want* to amuse him… 'What about… Reginald? Penfold? Archibald…?' I mock pout at his flat expression and catch the slightest twitch to his lips. Definitely amused. 'No? What about Terrence? Bert? Ernie—no, Arnie…? Ooh, yes… Arnie… I can definitely see a bit of Schwarzenegger in you…the whole *I'll be back* thing?'

I tuck my chin in as I deliver my best Terminator impression and my ridiculous comedic act—which, to be fair, makes me look like I sport a double chin—is totally worth it as he rewards me with a grin he clearly doesn't want to give.

'It's Ash.'

He takes firm hold of my fingers, which have just made tantalising contact with the exposed hairs of his chest, and my moment of triumph dampens as I sense the rejection coming.

'And I have to go.'

'Don't be a party pooper, Ash. We were just getting to know one another.' I take another step forward and my breasts brush against his chest as I breathe, my fingers still trapped in his warm, firm grasp.

'And as I said, you're hardly my type.'

He looks away and I follow his line of sight. He's looking towards Caitlin at the bar and I realise what he means.

'She's a friend of mine…a *close* friend.'

He turns back to me. 'So I saw.'

I frown just a little. Is he jealous? Or is Caitlin his type and he means it when he says I'm not? She's the opposite of me—a fiery petite redhead, free and easy. Normally I'd offer to share—to enjoy a debauched night of fun as a threesome. It's something we've done many a time before. But I don't want to. Not this time. Not with him.

I realise he's staring at me, his striking blue eyes penetrating my mind, and suddenly I feel naked… exposed. Like he's reached inside me and can read the very heart of what makes me tick. Which is nonsense. Utter nonsense.

I plaster on my superficial smile—the one I save for the cameras—and his eyes adjust to the change he's seen in me. 'If you're not interested,' I say, stepping away, 'far be it from me to force you.'

I start to pull my hand from his grasp and walk. It's time to go home and do what I intended all along. Now I can add his rejection to my list of things to forget.

'Wait.'

He firms his grip over my fingers and I pause mid-stride. Part of me—the part that felt every millimetre of exposure beneath his gaze—knows I should keep on going. But the devil in me, the pain, needs the distraction more. I look back at him and raise my brow in question.

'I've changed my mind. Let's grab a drink—somewhere else, though. For all Jackson is a mate of mine, his beer sucks.'

'Somewhere else?'

I genuinely hesitate. What I have in mind requires the sanctity of Blacks—this club. These four walls keep everything private. It's why I come here. To let my hair down, to beat off the stress, do whatever I so desire without judgement. Without exposure to the press. Without threat to the great house of Lauren.

'There's a pub not far from here…serves proper craft beer.' He gestures to the bar, where the footballer has returned and is trying his luck with Cait again. 'Bring your friends.'

I chew my lower lip. Would it hurt? Just this once?

But it would only take one photo, one loose tongue, even, and the press would pounce. My reputation would be in pieces and Granny's trust—*love*—would be irrevocably lost.

No, while Granny still lives, I'll be the Coco Lauren she believes in, no matter if it's not the whole story.

Guilt churns away in my stomach—but, hell, I *am* that Coco Lauren in all the ways that matter. Not that she'd see it. She would never approve of my pleasure-seeking side, never understand that I have no interest in relationships and the disappointment that they bring.

No, she would simply tar me with the same brush as my mother and be done with it.

And no one is worth taking that risk for, Coco, no one...

CHAPTER TWO

I LOOK AT her chewing anxiously over her lip and feel something twist inside me. This case is bugging me. There's a doubt I can't shift. A sense that this job is messed-up—that *I'm* messed-up for playing a part in it.

Something just isn't right.

And seeing her hesitate, spying the vulnerability in her glittering green gaze, not to mention the way my body refuses to chill around her, I know I should be ending this now. Walking away from both her and Philip Lauren.

But I've never called it a day on a job before. I've always been careful about which projects to take on, who I go after, who I work for…

But this time you were blinded by the memory of Jess, far too quick to judge.

The idea of another spoilt little rich girl getting her just deserts overrode my good sense. Because that's what Coco is—Christ, *Coco.* Even her name got to me. Dripping with arrogance, money, affluence. Everything I hated.

Or so I thought…

It's not hate that has me standing here hanging on her every word, laughing inside at her sudden playfulness, on fire at her flirtation and delicate touch. No. It's this dogged attraction I just can't shake.

That's not why you're suggesting going elsewhere, though...

I pull her back to me with the hand that's still clutched over hers.

No, you're doing this to get her out of her safe haven. To expose her.

So why does it feel so wrong and so right all at once?

'I'd rather stay here.'

She says it nervously, her lashes fluttering as she stares up at me, her breath making her chest brush against mine once more, her lips teasingly parted.

I've only to duck my head and I could taste her, just as she tasted her friend not ten minutes ago. The urge burns through me. Fire at the memory, fire at her proximity, at the daring shade of her lipstick, all drawing me in.

And then she runs her tongue over her lower lip and my restraint snaps. I forget everything—work, my purpose, my age-old hate. All sense homes in on the gentle swell of her lips as I dip to sample.

Just sample, nothing more.

Nothing that will get out of hand or cut too deep.

But as I sweep my lips over hers, my taste buds come alive. She's all sweet and strawberry-like, tantalising, inviting… And then I hear it, her tiny moan, so slight but definitely there, and it ripples down my ear canal, through my blood, right down to my disobeying cock.

I want to groan at the force, groan at the control I can feel slipping away. *This isn't you. This isn't what you do.* But it emerges as a growl, low in my throat, beating back the judgement.

To hell with it.

She shifts, her free hand travelling down my chest and around to my back as she encourages me closer, her message clear. And then her tongue brushes brazenly across mine and I give up on my sampling. I want it all—every last bit.

I spin her into a darkened recess carved out of the wall. The round table occupying it is the perfect height for her arse to rest as I lift her onto it. She hooks her legs around me, encasing me, hauling me closer. I can feel her heat through my jeans, feel her skirt bunched up to her hips as I rake my fingers down her thighs.

What are you doing? You're in public, anyone can see.

But isn't that the point? You need to get her somewhere you can use it? And with other people—her redhead friend, for starters...

My gut twists tighter, contending with the pulsing heat, and it's a sickening contrast so marked that I gain a second's clarity to tear my mouth away. 'Come with me?'

She shakes her head, her green eyes blazing into mine as her hands take advantage of our parting to unfasten my shirt just enough to slip her fingers within.

'No, I want you here.'

'Why?'

She strokes my skin, her fingers burning a fiery trail down my torso that has my cock pressing harder, eager for satisfaction. Eager for it *now*—not in twenty, thirty, forty minutes. However long it takes to get her somewhere I can use it.

She smiles, all sultry and appealing as fuck. 'Don't *you* have a side you like to keep hidden?'

A side? Christ, I feel like my whole twisted self should be locked away right now.

'Don't tell me the great Coco Lauren fears a little bit of gossip?' I try to sound light, but the words are tight, my teeth gritting against the heat racing through my veins. Desire and my endgame at war.

'This kind of gossip has the power to hurt those that I care about, Ash.'

She says it softly, sincerely, and for a second she's exposed, giving me a glimpse of pain so obvious I feel it against my will.

'Like who?' Because surely she's talking about herself? Protecting herself. Surely, she's aware that this makes her vulnerable to people like her brother. Not that I truly understand his goal.

'People I love.'

My body tenses, the twisting sensation deep inside me increasing tenfold. And then she shakes her head, as though clearing it, and hooks her hands around my neck, her touch searing my skin even as I try to stay focused.

'But I don't want to talk about it—just take my word for it...'

She moves in to kiss me and I pull back, knowing it'll be my undoing. I sense I'm on the cusp of something, of understanding, of getting to the bottom of Philip's intent. Why I want to is beyond me. I should be running from her, from *this*, from the entire job that has me questioning everything, and instead I'm pushing.

'How can gossip of this kind hurt? You're single, available, an adult—'

'And I'm a Lauren—born of a scandalous mother. Believe me, *this* kind of gossip has the power to sow the seeds of my downfall.'

I can feel her withdrawing but I don't stop. Not yet. 'You fear the public backlash? The loss of your golden halo?'

Her eyes flash and her skin pales just enough to tell me I've hit a nerve. 'No, the only eyes I care about are my grandmother's.'

'Scared she'll disinherit you?'

She frowns up at me and I know I've pushed too far. Maybe even said too much. But then everyone would assume she has an inheritance; they just wouldn't all know its value, like I do.

What I don't expect is the sudden movement of her hand as her palm makes for my cheek. I grab her wrist a split second before it collides with my skin and face off the fire in her gaze.

'Apologies.' And I mean it—I do. *Damn it*, why do I care?

Her eyes tremble as they stay fixed on mine and I feel the need to explain. I can't stop myself. 'I meet spoilt little rich girls who put money above love and family all the time.'

'Just because we're born into money...'

She tries to pull her wrist free but my fingers are locked. The contact heats me as her eyes project the same fire.

'It doesn't make us all cold-hearted bitches.'

'No, it doesn't.' It's like she's throwing my own deductions back at me and I almost laugh at the irony of it. 'But if you're so worried about this side of you getting out, why risk it?'

'Because I need to live my life too—because right now she's dying, and I don't know which way is up...'

Her voice cracks a little, her fire dwindling. And, God help me, my gut turns over as I stay locked in her gaze. I knew this too. That her grandmother was sick. I just hadn't anticipated her caring this much.

Now who's the heartless bastard?

I can't speak. Nothing can get past the chaos she has evoked within me.

She wets her lips, takes a shuddery breath. 'Because I thought you were the man who could take that pain away, be my distraction just for a second, just for now.'

Her eyes glisten as they waver over my face and then she backs away from me, shaking her head as my body reels from her admission.

'I can see I was wrong. You're not my type after all…'

She starts to walk, trying to pull free, but I yank her back to me. I'm not even thinking. It's impulsive—a need to take it all away, just as she hoped I would. Because I can't face her pain a second longer. I can't deal with the sickening guilt that comes with it either.

I claim her mouth and force all the guilt out, hanging on to her startled whimper, the swift surrender of her pliable mouth and the heat of her hands as they thrust inside my shirt. She rakes her nails over my chest and I feel a heady sting as she pierces the skin, wild, hungry, desperate. Heat surges through my body. My cock is more than willing to be the distraction she demands.

And what about you? Do you really want to go there with her? She's your fucking target, for Christ's sake!

But she's a target who doesn't deserve to be. This little exchange off the back of all that I've already witnessed is enough to prove that.

But if she's not like Jess—a woman I despise—doesn't it actually make her all the more dangerous? All the more to be avoided?

She bites down on my lower lip and tugs. Pleasure-pain drowns out the inner voice of reason as her fingers move to my belt. *Fuck*, she's undoing it.

'We shouldn't…' I manage against her lips.

'We should.' She nods, her breath coming in short pants. *'Now.'*

I can sense eyes upon us. Does she know we're being watched?

Of course she does—you're in Blacks.

But in that moment I feel like I'm the only person in her world. The way she's looking at me, drowning in me, makes power surge through my veins, and I can't stop my hands from sliding higher, my thumbs caressing the soft flesh of her inner thighs. She feels so perfect; her eyes, her breath, the arch of her body are all so responsive to me.

You don't deserve what she's giving you...

She parts my belt, unfastens my button, my zipper. My cock strains ready and then she slips her hand inside my briefs, her warm fingers taking hold. I freeze. I can't breathe, can't move. I grit my teeth and squeeze my eyes shut just for a second, just enough to regain some control, and when I open them again, she's grinning up at me, her eyes alive with mischief. So much better than the pain seconds before…

She pumps me once and my balls contract—*shit.*

'And there I was, believing I'm not your type…'

She moves over me now, her eyes dropping to take in the sight of her hand gripping me. Masterfully working me. My thighs tremble… My groan is strangled in my throat.

I'm fucked.

She sweeps her thumb over the tip of my cock, sweeping up the pre-cum as more appears. I breathe, ragged, losing it. She runs one scarlet-red nail over my slit.

'Fuck.'

She looks at me from beneath her lashes. I'm so ready to be inside her, so scared I'll shoot my load before I even get there…

'Mmm… I wonder if you taste as good as you look, Ash.'

Oh, Christ, no.

I shake my head, the move negligible with my body pulled so taut, my fingers tight upon her thighs.

'How about I find out?'

She slips forward, forcing me back a step to give her the space to drop to her knees, and I stare at the wall ahead of me, my brain screaming at me to stop her as my cock eggs her on, bucking in her grasp.

She gives a pleased little laugh—and then I feel it, the delicate point of her tongue, sweeping over the sensitised head and my eyes drop. I'm lost to her and all she can do.

Her lashes lift, her eyes lock onto mine and she grips the base of my cock, steadying my length to trace a teasing path around her mouth with my very tip. Like I'm her fucking lipstick.

Holy mother of God.

I fling my hand to her hair and pull her away. Just for a second…just until the wave passes. The wave that's pushing me too close to the edge.

'You know what I think?' she says, looking up at me. 'I think I'm *exactly* your type.'

The words hit home. Harsh, true. She *is* my type. She's everything I've wanted and evaded for so long. Her haughty air, her elegant poise, her perfect fuck-me-now lips.

I bring her back to my cock. 'Less talking.'

I don't need a reminder that I'm destined to walk the world alone because I let my dick pick 'em, thus exposing me to the worst of the female species—the ones who will always feel themselves superior. *Hell*, she *is* superior to me. Because I'm the villain of this piece. I'm the one out to expose her, to break her, all for the money her brother is willing to pay me. And she—

She sucks over me and my mind quits, only a moan breaking through my consciousness. It's not me. It's not her. It comes from someone close behind me. Someone watching. It shouldn't turn me on—none of this should. And still I fork my fingers through her perfect bob and hold her there. Watch as she takes me deeper with every thrust, her cheeks hollowing as she sucks, her eyes bright as they reach inside mine, her soft, feminine scent sailing up to me.

I am fucked. I can't stop this—no matter what I want, or what is right.

I'm going to take all she's willing to give—take it and walk away. Just as Jess would deserve, just as Coco—

Damn it, she isn't Jess.

And that's what's eating at me, even as heat starts to streak through my limbs.

You're the one to be despised. Not her. You're the one blinded by your own pain, your own past, taking it out on her. You're the nasty piece of work.

I groan over the realisation, squeeze my eyes shut,

throw my head back. My balls contract, my release is imminent, and—

Fuck, I should warn her. But pleasure steals my voice, my ability to move. I can only grip her head tighter and try to breathe, try to stave it off. And then I'm gone, my hips jerking forward with the force of my release.

Heaven flows through my entire body, my head falling forward as my eyes open to take her in, wide with shock, with desire, with all manner of mixed-up emotion. And then there's her hum of satisfaction, reverberating around my length as she takes my all. She's not quitting and I don't want her to. She's taking my every last drop, forcing out reality and making me want more. *So much more.*

I soften my hands in her hair, caressing instead of holding. I drag in a breath and then my brain rips through the haze—*you fucking idiot*—and sends guilt and hatred hot on its tail.

And it's not her I loathe. I know that with ice-like clarity now.

It's me—all me.

Something flickers in his gaze, and for a second I worry that it's regret I can see. I don't want Ash's regret. I want the fire back. The same fire that has me all wet, aching, needier than I can ever remember. It's the perfect antidote for life. Powerful, all-encompassing, a perfect distraction.

I release his cock and put right his underwear—but I don't zip him up. I'm not done yet. Not if I have my way. I lick my lips as I stand and take pleasure in his touch as he tilts my head towards him, his thumb and finger gentle on my chin.

'You're pretty talented.'

'Call it practice.'

His eyes flash and his fingers flex. *He didn't like that...*

'I'll bet you've had plenty of practice too.' I throw it back at him and run my teeth over my bottom lip. I want to push him. I want to toy with his obvious conflict. I want this twisted game to go on for however long he will play it. 'I bet your tongue is skilled in so many ways—or do you use your fingers more?'

I take hold of his hand upon my chin and slowly lower it down my body. My breasts prickle inside the confines of my bra as he travels through the valley between them and over my exposed midriff, which has me sucking in a breath.

He isn't stopping me, but that war is back. I can see it in his gaze. At any moment he's going to back away and leave, and the very idea is making my heart beat that little bit faster and urging me on.

I lift myself up on tiptoes and lean into his ear, my free hand working my skirt up, my other hand drawing his hand down. 'Feel how wet I am…just for you.'

I slip his hand inside my lacy knickers, press his fingers into my wetness. His breath hitches in my ear, a curse hot on its tail.

Better. So much better.

My lips lift in victory as I dare to lean back, to

meet his eye, and slowly I circle my hips over his touch, my hand still tight on his.

You're not going anywhere, Ash, not yet.

His lips are deliciously parted and I love it, taking advantage to sink my tongue inside his mouth and coax his own into action. He comes alive at last, his fingers moving of their own volition, his mouth crushingly sweet as he takes control.

He slips his fingers deeper, enters me as his thumb grazes my clit and I buck on the spike of pleasure that runs through me, the continued onslaught of his mouth catching my sigh of ecstasy.

I raise my hands to his shoulders and cling to his body for support, my lower half on a shameless ride of its own.

I struggle to catch my breath as his thumb works me to fever pitch, his mouth endless in its brutal exploration of my mouth. I tear my lips away, press my forehead into his shoulder and remember the audience taking in our brazen display, enjoying what they can see, what they can hear.

I look to where his hand is buried in black lace. His movements are quick and dizzying, his fingers in deep. He's skilled, all right, and I'm seconds away from combusting. My nails bite into his shoulders, my body tenses up and I fling my head back to look at him, to register the blazing heat of his gaze.

'That's it—come for me, princess.'

His words, his hand, his skill… Every muscle floods with heat, my insides are wound so tight, and then I burst from the inside out.

'Fuck...' My eyes clamp shut, my body spasms and he locks his arm around my waist, holding me tight. He won't drop me. I won't fall. It's perfect—perfect and safe.

His thumb rolls over me, slowing against my heightened sensitivity, and then he palms me, his hot heat pressed against my wetness until my body eventually stills and my breathing calms.

My head falls forward, he withdraws his hand and reality seeps in.

Nothing's changed. Life is as it was before. But for those blissful few minutes it was gone, and for that I am grateful.

Slowly I raise my lashes and calm my expression. He doesn't need to join me on the comedown. He doesn't have to shoulder what I do.

'Thank you,' I whisper.

He curves his hand around my behind beneath my skirt. 'You're welcome.'

And then he releases me to fasten his trousers. He steps back, his attention off me. So off me that I'm floundering.

I look away and smooth out my skirt, suddenly awkward, sheepish. Do we just say goodbye? It's what I would normally do. But I don't want to. Already the chill is taking over and the distance is building between us. I want the warmth back.

What's the likelihood of us seeing each other again? I've been coming here for years and never seen him, regardless of his claim that Jackson is a mate. Maybe he's not from London. Maybe he's just visiting.

So many questions burn through me and I can't give voice to a single one.

Regardless of his actions, he said I wasn't his type. Would that still be the case now we'd had our fill?

He's very still and I risk a look. He's staring at me, but I can't read him. He's impenetrable, cold. While his blue eyes seem to pierce me, strip me bare. My confidence is in tatters. Obliterated with the surprising force of my orgasm and his sudden detachment.

Perhaps it's because I could see myself wanting more.

More like what?

A date. A normal, everyday date, like any normal, everyday woman would want.

But you're not one of them. Never have been... Never will be.

The growing chill reaches my heart and I shiver.

'I should go,' he says, smoothing a hand over his hair.

I nod, still speechless, my messed-up thoughts keeping me tongue-tied as I wrap my arms around myself.

He starts to walk and then stops. My heart flutters, my head lifts, I'm hopeful. But then he continues on and I watch him leave…cold, sober, sad.

I turn back to the ladies' room, my head swimming with what's gone down.

You sure you want to let that go...?

I'm already spinning on my heel and heading after

him, but as I break out onto the pavement and scan the street all I see are the doormen. There's no sign of him. Not even a lit-up car about to leave. Where in the hell *is* he?

I look to the doormen, who are doing their best not to notice me. 'Did you see where he went?' I say, and they give me a brief look.

'Who?' one says.

'The guy that left just ahead of me.'

'Afraid not.'

I think he's lying. In fact, I know he's lying. Maybe it's the fact that I'm on the wrong side of the non-disclosure agreement now I'm outside the building that means he won't tell me anything.

I'm about to ask again when I hear a car door open behind me, down the street, and my heart soars. I turn towards the sound.

Maybe he's seen me... Maybe he's coming back for—

'My lady?'

It's my driver. Hope vacates my body, the chill returns, and I wrap my arms around my middle and head towards him. The sinking feeling inside me is ever more pronounced.

It was foolish, anyway. I've read of infatuations that start with such a spark. I've read it in my mother's diary, have been able to feel my mother's lust and then love for my father through the pages. But I always thought such a thing out of my reach. Every boy, teen, man has taught me that aside from sex I'm good for one thing only: *money.*

No, make that two things. Money and a title. I have them both. And because of that I'm destined to become a spinster.

My tombstone:

Lady Coco Lauren
Lived and died
Single and alone

Why did one chance meeting with a stranger make me hope for something more?

CHAPTER THREE

THREE DAYS HAVE gone by since my momentary lapse in judgement.

Momentary lapse?

Monumental fuck-up, more like.

I swear I can still hear her moans ringing in my ear, taste her on my lips, my fingers… I've only to close my eyes and I see her dilated gaze looking up at me, her skin flushed pink, her body moving with sheer abandon in her quick-fire orgasm, my fingers buried deep—

Fuck. There my dick goes, tightening inside my jeans, painful and persistent, nagging for release.

What the hell's got into you?

Stupid question.

She has.

Her taste, her scent, her flirtatious little mouth. She's got under my skin, exposed my inner desires. Making her come while others watched on, her sucking me off, me losing control…

And not only that she's fucked with my job, making me cross a line that I'm struggling to come back from. Making me question everything.

But here I finally am. After three long days of battling my conscience, her insane appeal and every crazy doubt she has instilled, I'm back with it and tailing her. Because I have to. I'm a fucking PI—it's what I do. I don't fall for princesses, and I don't give a fuck. I really don't. I learned that lesson well, and no amount of honesty from her lips is going to change that.

But I can almost hear my inner laughter, mocking me. As if it knows that I'm here because I can't stay away.

It's two thirty in the afternoon and I'm standing in the shadows at an outdoor charity gala for the local children's hospice, my eyes hidden behind shades and once more on her.

I wear a baseball cap, a nondescript hoodie and jeans, my casual clothing blending right in with that around me. But she shines above everyone. Her hair is tied back, highlighting her radiant smile, her effortless grace. She wears a soft pink sweater, white skinny jeans and a pair of trainers. Nothing special, but on her…

To her right is a child in a wheelchair, with no hair and pale, tubes travelling from her nose and arm to a bag of liquid high above. Coco ducks down to talk to her, her smile natural and vibrant, and the girl nods and murmurs in return, her own lips lifting.

They talk a little more and I see Coco's PA start

to get edgy as she watches from the sidelines, her eyes flitting between the watch on her wrist, the tablet she has tight in her hand and the pair talking.

It seems Coco isn't adhering to the schedule, and as I look back to her I can see why. She has the girl laughing now, and the joyous noise is lighting up all those around them. Hell, even *my* insides lift. She doesn't care for her schedule—she only cares for the girl.

And then she stands and turns. For a second I think she spies me, and then I realise she's wiping her eyes. She does it so discreetly, so smoothly, that any ordinary onlooker would probably miss it—but not me. I've come to know her gestures, her smiles, her laughs, those that are forced and those that ring true.

She's crying.

My gut twists and sinks, and I double back.

Guilt. That's what this is. Guilt and another emotion I haven't felt in so long it's almost alien to me now. I don't want to acknowledge it. I just want to get as far away as possible and that means telling her brother I'm out.

You're going soft, comes the mental gibe. The same one that has plagued me since we crossed the line at Blacks. And it's backed up by the sensible argument that I've been blinded by what we did, what we shared. That ultimately she's still the spoilt little rich girl I once had her pegged as—that her brother has her pegged as.

But it's bollocks.

I've followed her enough to know she cares about

these charity projects. Not the front—not the face of it. She cares about these people. And she works hard. She barely stops—moving from one event to another. Even those lunches seem to be more a function of her public role rather than for her pleasure.

No, the only time I've truly seen her do something for herself is at Blacks. That was for her. *All* for her. And I loved being able to give her that. Loved it too much.

And there was her total honesty, her love for her grandmother, her need to bury the pain.

My chest tightens as I fist my hands. I have no choice but to bring this to a close. Even if it could ruin my reputation. Philip Lauren isn't the kind to take my withdrawal lying down, and the more anxious he becomes, the more his nasty side shines through.

How the fuck I didn't see this side to him in the first place, I don't know.

Liar. You didn't see it because you didn't want to; you were too interested in taking down another Jess. Another hoity-toity, good-for-nothing rich girl who only has love for herself.

And more fool me… I couldn't have been more wrong.

I deserve the pain that plagues me now, the sickening guilt, but the least I can do is tell Philip where to stick it. He'll likely do his damnedest to see Livingston Investigations closed down as a result, but I'm not afraid of him or the threat. My PI work exists for a reason: to bury my past and save others from similar fates. It isn't my bread and butter. I have property up and down the country that gets that for me.

Not that I'll roll over in the face of Philip's anger—far from it. I might even have some fun with it. And if I can convince him there's nothing to tell, maybe he'll just walk away from whatever this vendetta is and leave both her and my business alone.

I take my mobile out of my back pocket and send him a text.

We need to meet. Friday. Usual place. Seven o'clock. Don't be late.

I smile as I pocket my phone. It'll certainly give me some satisfaction, watching the guy stew on it as I tell him what I really think of his sister and all that I've learned.

Well, almost all—I'll leave out the finer detail that starts with Blacks and ends with our brief spell of fun.

If only I could forget about it...

Okay, I've officially hit stalker level.

It's been a week since I went all gaga over Tall, Dark and Handsome, and despite several visits to Blacks, he's been a no-show. Which is as I expected, if I'm honest. So last night I swallowed my pride and confronted Jackson. He was his friend. He'd know where Ash lived, and with some gentle persuasion he'd tell me.

What I didn't expect was a grin as wide as the Thames is long and the information that Ash's home address is just around the goddamn corner. It was obvious Jackson was matchmaking, and that gave me hope that whatever this connection between Ash and me is, it's powerful enough for his friend to believe in it too.

So here I am, at six thirty on a Friday evening, nervously toying with my bag as I stare at the exclusive warehouse development before me. It doesn't look like much from the outside, but I'm not fooled. This postcode doesn't come cheap, and whatever's hidden on the other side is going to be just as exclusive...*rather like the man himself.*

And here's another dose of truth: I didn't expect him to be this well-off either. His rough, honest edge hinted at something more normal, something more ordinary—something I wanted to reach out and hold on to so bad.

All I have to do is ring the damn bell and, fingers crossed, he'll be at home and willing.

So why I'm still standing here, ten minutes after my driver opened the car door to let me out, I don't know.

Derek's probably watching me from the car and wondering exactly the same thing. I must look like I'm losing my mind.

I pull my handbag tighter over my shoulder and scan my clothing. Today I'm dressed in black skinny jeans and a free-swinging white shirt—perfectly innocent and a complete contrast to the debauched ideas taking centre stage in my brain. My underwear is bang on, though. It may be white, but the crotchless panties and the revealing lace bra communicate exactly what I'm after.

I take a breath and look to the frosted glass of the double front doors ahead that give nothing away, at the brick archway above that appears far more daunting than it should, and butterflies kick up inside my belly.

What are you doing?

Fuck it, I'm doing what I want—screw the judgement and the doubts. I head for the door. Reality can be pushed away for a night at least. I deserve this. A bit of fun…a bit of—

The door swings open as I reach for the buzzer beside the entrance—the single, solitary buzzer. *Christ, does he own the whole lot?* And then he's there, filling the opening, and I'm gaping like a fucking fool.

'Coco?'

His surprised expression all but does me in. He's even more handsome than I remember, his jaw still unshaven, his eyes just as piercing beneath his dark angled brow, all rugged, rough and—

His brow quirks.

Fucking get with it, Coco.

I straighten, my hands tight over the strap of my bag as I cling to it for solidarity when my legs want to give way.

'Hi,' I say—like this is totally expected, like I *haven't* just stalked the bejesus out of him. 'I thought we could do dinner…if you're free?'

I struggle to hold his eyes. He's doing it again: reading me and all my fucked-up mental chaos. I lower my gaze but stand firm. He's wearing a deep blue shirt and dark denim jeans. Very smart. And as I breathe in, I get the welcoming scent of freshly applied cologne. He looks and smells date-worthy.

Oh, Christ, was I asking him on a date?

My eyes flick back to his and I see my double take reflected back at me.

'How did you find me?'

Not quite the response I was hoping for...

'Jackson gave me your address.'

Fire sizzles beneath my cheeks. *Please, God, let my make-up do its job and stop me from looking crimson.* I'm blonde, I'm freckly, I go red at the drop of a hat.

'It's not like I tailed you or anything. I'm not some stalker.'

I swear his skin pales. *Shit.* He thinks I *am* some stalker.

'Jackson thought you could do with me swinging by.'

'Jackson should mind his own bloody business.'

He scans the street, clearly on edge, and I feel the situation rapidly running away from me.

'Look, it's okay if you're busy.'

'I am.'

'Going somewhere nice?' I try for a smile and gesture to his outfit. He has the same number of buttons undone at the collar, the same hint of hair...

'You shouldn't be here, Coco.'

I realise I'm staring. Right at his chest. My palms are tickling with reignited memories. I pull my gaze back to his face and swallow past the desire-shaped wedge taking up camp in my throat. I hear his words, register their negativity, but there's also his tone, and the pulse working like crazy in his jaw…

Is he really freaked out by me turning up? Or is he fighting the same forceful attraction?

Please let it be the latter.

'No, you're probably right…' I take a breath and give him another smile, wanting to test the water. 'But I can't get our last meeting out of my head.'

His mouth tightens, his throat bobs. He says nothing, but his eyes tell me he's reliving it too and I push on, my confidence returning. 'I thought maybe we could…you know…see each other again?'

'*See* each other?'

It rasps out, but his tough-guy exterior is at odds with the widening of his eyes. The rabbit-caught-in-the-headlights look makes him seem boyish and I give a soft laugh.

'Don't worry, Ash. I'm not asking you for a relationship…or even a real date…' Although the truth was I'd take the date. 'Only sex.'

I straighten on the last word, my chin jutting just a little, like I'm trying to convince him as well as myself.

'You mean more distraction?'

'Yes, if that's what you want to call it.'

'It's what *you* called it.'

'I did.' I step closer and he tenses, backing away.

'I'm not about to go all clingy on you, if that's what you're worried about. I'm not like that.'

'That's not what I'm worried about.' He shakes his head. 'You shouldn't be here,' he says again.

'No? Where *should* I be, then?'

His eyes move over me, hesitant, probing. 'Seeing a counsellor, a professional—someone who can help you deal with what you're going through.'

I laugh. I can't help it. *Is he for real?* 'I don't need a therapist.'

'I didn't say you did. I'm just telling you I understand.'

He says it like he knows it. Like he's lived it with me. And confusion, a sudden surge of sadness, has my temper sparking. 'How can you possibly understand? I came to hook up with you again, not to be lectured. But of course you won't get that, will you? Since I'm just a spoilt little rich girl?'

'No, Coco, that's not… You're not…' He rakes his fingers over the back of his head, turning away in frustration, tension thrumming off him in waves. 'You just shouldn't be here.'

'Why?'

He stares back at me, the nerve in his jaw pulsing. He looks like he wants to say so much and yet nothing is coming.

'Ash, what—'

'You need to go.' He raises his palm to me and avoids my eye.

'Are you going to tell me the other night wasn't

fun?' I'm going to make him acknowledge this, if nothing else. 'Because *I* thought it was.'

His eyes flicker in my direction, that nerve in his jaw ever more pronounced.

'I particularly loved the feel of you in my mouth.'

He sucks in a breath and damn if his cheeks don't heat. The sight has my belly tripping out and the telltale warmth is quick to spread, killing off the sadness, the confusion, the anger. He's like my on-and-off switch and I'm not ready to give up on him.

'Coco, don't do this.'

'What?' I say in mock innocence. I let my eyes drift over him, wetting my lips. 'Or did you prefer sinking your fingers into me?'

'Coco.'

He's so tense, and I'm getting off on it now. Goading him, pushing him where I want him.

'I'm not the man you think I am; you can't play those games with me.'

'Games?' My smile is seductive, calm, the perfect front. 'Who's playing games? I'm being a straight shooter and telling you exactly what I want.'

His breath shudders out. 'Go home, Coco. Before we do something we both regret.'

'Regret?' I frown. 'How can we possibly have regrets? We're just two strangers hooking up. What's wrong with that?'

'*Everything's* wrong with it.'

'Am I missing something? Do you have a girlfriend—or a *wife*?'

He's shaking his head at me but I feel like I'm

missing something huge and I can't begin to imagine what.

'Is that your car?'

His sudden change in tack has my frown deepening and I follow his gaze to where Derek waits for me.

'Yes.'

'Come on. I'll walk you.'

Hell, no.

My laugh is harsh, almost manic. I glare back at him, confusion morphing into anger at his condescension.

'Forget it. I'm not a child. I don't need you to hold my hand. You don't want me—that's fair enough. But don't patronise me while you reject me.'

I spin on my heel and force my stride to be steady as I head for the car. I won't give him the satisfaction of racing off and letting him see how his words, his contradictory behaviour have hurt me. And I certainly won't let him see the tears that come from nowhere.

Because they aren't about him. They're about everything else. His rejection has only served to trigger the whole damn lot.

'Coco...' he calls after me. 'I'm sorry—I didn't mean to upset you.'

And now he's offering out pity? I shake my head. *No fucking way.*

I've heard enough. I don't turn. I don't break stride. I head to my car and get in. I don't dare look back at him until I'm safely locked away behind the privacy glass and the car is moving. Then I look and I see him standing there, confusion in his eyes.

'Where to, my lady?' Derek asks.

The last thing I want is to go home like this. I spent the morning with Granny, chatting with her doctors, the nurses, trying to mask the pain, to be strong. This foolish seduction was to have been my solace, my hope. Now that has failed, and I'm even more messed-up than before. The tears were living proof.

'Blacks…please.'

CHAPTER FOUR

WATCHING HER DRIVE away was hard. *Really. Hard.* But I'd done the right thing, so why did it feel so wrong?

Because you want her. Like you've only ever wanted one other: Jess. And that's why you need to get as far away from her as possible.

But, fuck, there's something about her—that tantalising contrast of vulnerable, innocent do-gooder and hidden temptress.

Philip Lauren's words come back to me full force: *she's no innocent and I want you to prove it.*

Yes, I can prove it all right—but not to that bastard.

No, tonight I walk away from him, the job, her.

Definitely her.

She spells trouble. Messy, heart-screwing trouble.

I squeeze my temples with my thumbs and forefingers. With Jess I was young, foolish and naive. I wasn't foolhardy enough to let it happen again. Nowhere close.

But Coco Lauren…

Damn it, I should have turned away the second

my gut told me to. I swore I would never let anyone get close after Jess. My job has become my lifeline—it's pulled me out of the darkness, given me the drive to move on. I'll never forget, I'll never forgive, but I won't dwell on it either. And I sure as hell won't let myself care about another woman again.

I take a breath and head for my car, reconsidering my choice of vehicle almost immediately. I need the motorbike. A hair-raising blast on two wheels to clear my head before I face off the other Lauren and put this madness behind me once and for all.

But the ride doesn't work.

I'm still mentally delivering my walk-away mantra half an hour later, as I meet the man I'm unfortunate enough to call my client.

'Seriously, Livingston…?' Philip Lauren eyes my casual get-up with distaste and it only makes me grin.

We're in a high-end bar—the kind that insists on a blazer—and the fact that my outfit has already pissed him off is a bonus. 'Don't get your knickers in a twist, Lauren, I don't expect to be stopping long.'

He visibly balks. His princely expression is pained. I swear even his blow-dried golden locks stand perfectly on end at my disrespect. But I don't have time for it. Nor do I care.

'Ah…' His eyes spark now, as though he's had some grand revelation. 'So you have what I need, then?'

I lean back in the rock-hard Chesterfield armchair and raise my leg so my ankle rests over my knee, all casual and to him increasingly disrespectful, I'm sure.

'Nope.' I flick a hand at him. 'There's nothing to give.'

His eyes narrow, his cheeks streak. He's angry. And my gut loves it.

'Look, Mr Livingston, I'm paying you good money to dig this dirt.'

He lowers his voice on the last word, leaning in as he scans the nearby tables, not wanting to be overheard. But I don't even flinch.

'There's no dirt to dig.'

He shakes his head fervently. 'Like hell there isn't.'

He's so certain. Desperate, even. And not for the first time I wonder at his goal, the endgame, why he's so eager to ruin his sister. What does it matter to him that Coco likes her sex on the wild side?

'What makes you say that?'

'A leopard doesn't change its spots, and a whore like her *definitely* doesn't.'

His words hit me like a slug to the stomach and I fight to keep my expression neutral. The slice of pain coming from my tightened right fist tells me I'm losing the battle, my nails piercing the skin of my palm. I unclench it slowly and rub my jaw, as though I'm considering his words and not staving off the need to kill him.

'If you're so sure, why do you need the proof?'

'Because without proof I can't get my hands on what I need.'

'Which is…?'

'None of your goddamn business.'

He quiets when he sees our drinks approaching and the waiter slipping me a questionable stare.

So I don't fit into your la-di-da club? So sue me.

I happily stare the waiter down, and to my amusement he almost spills the drinks as he sets them down before scurrying off.

'I don't pay you to ask questions,' Philip Lauren pipes up again. 'I pay you to get evidence of her sexual proclivities.'

'And I'm telling you there's nothing to report. She's above reproach.'

He laughs and leans back in his chair, whisky in hand. 'You're lying. What I can't work out is why…'

I shift in my seat and take up my own drink for a swig. 'What makes you so certain?'

He eyes the glass in his hand, all thoughtful. 'She and my wife boarded together in their teens.'

'They were friends?'

I want to know more; I can't help it. I'm not one for digging into my clients' reasoning. They give me a job and I deliver. But this case is different. I *need* to know.

'To an extent.'

He lifts his eyes back to mine and they flash with an angry fire that tells me he isn't letting this go—that, whatever his reasoning is, he will keep pushing until he has exactly what he needs. It wouldn't be hard for another PI to retrace my steps. I followed her movements and discovered her visits to Blacks pretty quickly. A few enquiries in the right places and he'd soon have what he needed.

'But that was years ago. Maybe she's changed, maybe she's saving herself for marriage or destined to become a nun—who knows?'

He laughs again. 'You're funny, Livingston. I'll give you that.'

I'm not trying to be funny. I'm trying to put him off—to bring an end to this mission he's so determined to see through. I don't want to care. I don't want to protect her. But I can't stand by while her brother desecrates her reputation for his own gain.

'There's no way she could have changed,' he says, sobering, and his voice is so serious I wonder if he's trying to convince himself of that fact—if his need for her to be as he suspects far outweighs whether he considers it true or not. 'She's just being very careful about it.'

'Doesn't matter how careful she's being. If she was at it—' I hate the words as they form, feel acid riding high in my throat. There's guilt at my lie, at my part in her potential downfall, as well as anger at his conviction. 'I would know. I'd have the evidence.'

'Or maybe you're not as good as everyone says—yourself included.'

He gives me a shit-eating grin and I want to swing for him. He's fucking lucky we're in public. I take a breath instead, flexing the fist that is so determined to ball up, and ask the other question that's itching to be answered.

'Tell me, why is it you want to ruin your sister's

reputation so much? I mean, I have a brother—I get how annoying siblings can be—but this…'

'Again, it's none of your business.'

'There's clearly no love lost between you…not on your part at least.' I see the flash of something—possibly guilt—and jump on it. 'So, tell me, does she *really* deserve this?'

He downs his whisky in one. His eyes water at the hit of booze and lines mar his face, ageing his perfect veneer.

'I don't have to sit here and listen to you question my reasoning, Livingston. I'm paying you to get me evidence, and if you can't do that, then I'll find someone else who can.'

My neck prickles. So much for hoping he would let it go.

But why is it your problem what he does after you're gone? Just walk away and forget you ever met him. Met her.

'Suit yourself.' I start to rise, to leave, to get the hell away, but he shoots up, halting me halfway to standing.

'Wait—just hear me out.'

I look at his pleading gaze. Is he going to open up? Do I really want him to if it means I have to stick around? But what if it means understanding his intentions towards Coco?

I'm already dropping back into my seat, my inner messed-up stance driving my decision.

He lowers himself once more and forks his fingers together on the table, leaning in again. 'Truth is there's no one better than you at this. I know that. You know that. And I *need* this. Believe me, it'll be worth your while.'

'I charge a flat fee. We've—'

'Double. I'll pay you double.'

I don't react visibly, but inside the adrenalin rush has my every sense on high alert. My fee is already substantial—to double it would be laughable. No amount of information is worth that.

Questions hammer ever more acutely through me. What does he hope to achieve? How low will he sink? How much danger is Coco in?

'I mean it, Livingston—man to man now,' he insists.

I swallow back the rising bile. In my mind he lost his man status the second he showed his true nature.

'You get me that evidence and I'll pay you double—maybe more if it's juicy enough and you can deliver it in the next two weeks.'

I have to swallow again and force my hands to relax their death-grip hold over the arms of my chair. 'Why the rush?'

'Time's running out.'

'Why?'

'You need to stop asking so many questions.'

'And *you* need to try answering some.'

'I'll tell you what you need to know and no more.' He reaches into the inside pocket of his blazer and pulls out a folded piece of paper, which he slides across to me. 'Try this place. I hear she's a regular…'

I take the sheet and bite back a curse. I know what

I'm going to see before I even unfold it. But seeing *Blacks* in scrawled handwriting has my gut in knots.

I throw back my drink and pocket the piece of paper.

'Well?' he presses.

I get to my feet and look down at him just long enough to say, 'Consider it done.'

Then I walk away, recounting what I know now.

Time isn't on Philip Lauren's side and he won't stop until he has what he needs. And if he knows about her presence at Blacks then he already has contacts who, with the right persuasion, will give up what he's asking for. Hell, he might even try to gain access himself—not that Jackson will let him anywhere near the place once I've spoken to him.

I'm Coco's last hope. So long as I'm on the job and he's not going elsewhere I can ride this out.

And if he does decide to employ another PI, they will fail, because I'll see to it she stays out of trouble.

And what about you?

Seems I'm destined to walk straight back into trouble...

But in my case, who said trouble couldn't be fun? If keeping her safe means sharing more of what she asked me for earlier this evening, out of the public eye—or, more specifically, out of her brother's eye—then where was the harm?

Yeah, you just tell yourself that...

I slam open the door before the doorman can do it for me.

I just need to keep a lid on it for a little bit longer. I've done it for ten years; I can do it for umpteen more. And once the danger has passed I'll walk away with a clear conscience. I will have kept her safe, and that's all that matters.

I pull out my phone and fire off messages to my researchers. I want to know all there is to know about Philip Lauren. I want to get to the root of his desperation and understand the exact timescale I'm working to. I should have done it sooner, but I had no cause to investigate Philip Lauren when he first came to me.

I see Coco in my mind's eye, see those bright green eyes, too generous by far—too generous and too vulnerable and getting to me more than they should.

Shit.

But I can't walk away—not yet.

In fact, I'll start with her. There must be so much she can tell me herself, if I can coax her into talking a little. And as for Jackson's potential membership leak…that needs flagging now.

First Blacks—then Coco.

'Come on—spill.'

Cait elbows me as she says it.

'You're not jealous that I went off with Ricky, are you?'

She laughs, knowing she's way off the mark. We don't have that kind of relationship. We're more friends than lovers—have been since we went to boarding school together. Our messing around came more from being shafted by the opposite sex than anything else. Sex with each other is safe, fun companionship. She's hot. And she doesn't kiss and tell. Neither do I. It works.

She also knows me better than anyone. And she knows my mind is on six feet, two inches of dark, broody hotness.

'Have you seen Jackson tonight?' I ask. I want to quiz him about Ash. I want to understand him better…try to make sense of his rejection.

'*Not* the question I expected…' She sips at her espresso martini—tonight's drink of choice—as she looks to the bar and nods. 'Jackson was here earlier, doing his thing. I think he teases us on purpose—all that macho muscle and daring cheek.'

She winks at me.

'I'm telling you, I would *so* be on him if he'd shake off that no-dating-the-clients rule. It's criminal, really.'

She frowns into her drink and then her eyes light up as she looks back to me.

'Don't tell me you're after him as well as Tall, Dark and Sexy… What was his name again?'

'Ash,' I supply swiftly, and her grin is back, her brow hitting the roof.

'Ah, yes, *Ash*,' she drawls. 'Now, *that's* the man I expected you to be talking about.'

I shake my head. 'Nothing to tell. He bailed when I offered a repeat.'

'Really?' She pins me with her astute blue gaze. 'Then the man's a fool and—' Her eyes leave me and widen. 'Well, speak of the devil—or rather devils…'

Every nerve ending pricks up. 'What?' I ask. Even though I know.

'They've just stepped in and… Oh, yes, he's spied us…or rather *you*.'

She gives a flirtatious little flutter of her fingers in their direction.

'Cait.'

'Oh, hush—you need to get laid and I need to see the spark back in your eye. That guy can do both.'

Heat creeps into my cheeks. 'Cait, I—'

'Ladies…pardon my intrusion, but I believe I owe this one a date.'

Ash is so close I can feel his body heat penetrate my left-hand side. Cait is now staring in wide-eyed amusement. I don't know whether to turn and smile or blank him entirely. The latter is what I *should* do, for refusing me earlier, but my body has a mind of its own and it turns to him. My eyes are quick to follow as they rise to his… Warm, friendly, apologetic, even.

'You do?'

He smiles and my blasted insides soar, uncaring that he patronised and humiliated me earlier this evening. 'I do. Can we start over?'

I look back to Cait. Her eyes are still wide.

'Hey, don't be looking at me—this is up to you… Not that I mind sticking around, though, if you like…'

She looks him up and down, blatantly happy with what she sees, and I kick her beneath the table. The move earns me a grin as she scoots over, glass in hand, and rises out of the booth.

'Didn't think so. She's all yours, Ash.'

But as she straightens, she fixes him with a glare, her free hand reaching out to poke him in the chest.

'Mark my words, though, buster: mess with her and it's me you'll answer to. I may be small, but believe me, *I can bite*.' She punctuates the last three words with a jab of her finger and then turns and walks away.

Ash watches her go, clearly bemused, and it frees me to look at him—*really* look at him.

You'd think after all we've shared I'd be immune to him by now. Instead my eyes rake hungrily over him, taking in the same clothes he wore earlier, only now his sleeves are rolled back, his forearms deliciously bare, flexing muscle exposed and worthy of salivating over. My mouth does just that.

What the hell is wrong with you? my wounded pride mentally admonishes. *Do you really want to go another round with him?*

'Got your fill?'

Shit. Caught staring. A great start at keeping your cool.

I pride myself for my front—it's never let me down before. I depend on it to get me through each day, to be the perfect Coco Lauren. But it's nowhere now. It's taking a fucking holiday. Maybe that's what I should be doing—hitting a deserted island until I can get this craziness under control.

Or you could go for the far less extreme coping strategy of not giving a fuck?

I smile to hide my mental roller coaster and decide to adopt my trademark Coco Lauren tone—the one I've perfected—and I'm sure as hell going to wheel it out now if it kills me.

'Yes, you can leave now.'

I take my barely touched martini and sip it, the bittersweetness sliding smoothly down my throat as I fix my sights on Cait, now sidling up to the bar.

'Okay, I deserved that.'

I don't react. I keep my eyes on Cait and count to ten.

One, two, three...

'Can I get you another drink?'

Four, five, six...

'An espresso martini?'

Seven, eight, nine...

'Coco, please…'

I don't know whether it's the gentle way he says my name or the fact that he has the gumption to slide into the booth that makes me look at him.

'I don't need another, thank you.'

He scans the bar, smoothing his hand over his hair. He looks nervous now. I like him nervous. It creates a shift in power that I can work with.

'Why are you here, Ash?'

His blue gaze returns to me, all soft and alluring. And, God help me, my clit pulses—instant, acute. I exhale over it, crossing my legs beneath the table and clamping my thighs tightly together. *Behave*. He doesn't need to know the effect he has on me.

'Cat got your tongue?' I raise my brow, arrogant and assured.

No, I'm not going to turn into a hot, gooey mass inside. I'm not.

He runs his teeth over his bottom lip—*definitely* nervous—and I *definitely* like it.

'I came to see you…to apologise for earlier and to…' he opens his palms out to me '…talk.'

I take a small, steadying breath as I smile over my glass. 'Talk?'

His gaze falls to my mouth as I take a sip and I purposely sweep away the remnants with my tongue. If I'm going down, I'm taking him with me.

'*Just*…talk?'

'To begin with, yeah…'

I'm rewarded with a flash of perfect white teeth and a grin that makes my belly flip, upping the low, incessant ache inside me.

'What can I say? I'm an old-fashioned guy.'

The door to the club opens and his grin stills, his eyes flicking in its direction.

'Waiting for someone?' I ask, turning to see a couple walk in.

'No.' He's looking at me when I turn back, but then his eyes flit to the bar, where I can see Jackson talking to his staff.

'You been here all evening?' he asks me, but his eyes don't leave the bar.

'Since leaving your place?' He nods and I frown. This feels like some strange interrogation all of sudden. 'Yeah, is that okay, *Mother*?'

His eyes come back to me, sharp at first, but they soften as he smiles. ‘Sorry, I was momentarily distracted.’

He leans forward on his elbows, giving me his full attention now—a fact my hyped-up body positively purrs over and is more than willing to forgive the little interruption for.

‘How about we take this conversation back to my place?’

I laugh, surprised, delighted, confused. ‘Is that your best chat-up line?’

He laughs too, the sound deep and husky and so fucking erotic he might as well have strummed his fingers over my clit.

‘You answer my question and then I’ll tell you whether it is or not.’

My laugh is real and easy now, and my fingers run through my bob as my body loosens up. I don’t understand his power over me, this dizzying attraction coupled with his ability to put me at ease so readily, but I’m happy to go with it if he gives me a little truth first.

‘What’s changed?’ I ask.

‘Since earlier?’

Like he needs to ask... ‘Yes.’

‘Let’s just say I’ve had a few hours to consider my options.’

‘Options?’

He shifts in his seat and leans even closer, all serious now, and I’m completely hooked, barely aware of the glass in my hand.

'I can walk away from you—abstain from all the delights the gorgeous Coco Lauren has to offer…' He draws his words out, slow, thoughtful, and his eyes are doing their thing again, penetrating my very soul and projecting the heat of such delights.

Then he leans back, and his severity morphs into playfulness as he gives me a cocky grin.

'Which, let's face it, would keep your heart in one piece and avoid the devastating heartache that's sure to ensue when I up and leave you.'

I laugh derisively. 'Oh, believe me, there's no risk of that. My heart is not up for grabs.'

His eyes drop to my lips, the playfulness gone as quickly as it came. 'So you say. In which case, how about we get out of here and stop wasting time?'

'And I thought you wanted to *talk*?'

'Oh, I still want that, princess. I like to know who I'm letting share my bed.'

My laugh turns awkward. 'I'm sure you know enough already, thanks to the Great British press.'

He's quiet for a long moment, like he's waiting for me to say something more—but what? It's true. Not a month goes by without me featuring in some article or other.

'Is that really all there is to know about you?' he asks quietly.

The worry mounts, the hairs pricking at the back of my neck.

'What about the person beneath the public image? Your family? Your dreams? What does the great Coco Lauren want aside from "peace, love and harmony"?'

He's quoting me, from an article published in a gossip magazine last month, and I cringe inwardly. It was a family photo shoot, taken before Granny got too sick to perform for the camera. In it, my pristine white dress is respectable, to the knee and chosen by Granny especially. The string of pearls around my neck was a gift from her. A sedate French manicure, simple white heels and a silky-smooth bob. All just so. The picture of Lauren perfection.

And a total contrast to the girl sitting here now.

My cheeks blaze at the falsity of it, of me, and a sudden spark of anger hits—how *dare* he make me feel like this?

'What's your point, Ash?' My tone is like ice and his eyes narrow.

'I didn't mean to upset you.'

'No? Just like you "didn't mean to" earlier this evening?'

'Hell, no.'

He reaches out, combing his fingers through my hair and holding me there as he leans in. I want to break out of his hold, but already desire is drowning out the anger, more potent the closer he gets.

'I just want to know the real you.'

The real me...

My breath flutters over my parted lips, and then he's there, working them further apart, his tongue gently probing.

'I find you fascinating…'

He sweeps inside, his nose nudging mine as he

encourages me to angle my head so he can delve in further.

'I want to get to know you better…'

My heart sings at his words, and my mouth is quick to follow his bidding. People don't usually want to know me. They want what I can give them. Money, status, connections.

And what if he's just trying to get you into bed?

A giggle erupts and he breaks away to frown at me. I can't help it. I'm heady on his words and the ridiculous mental argument they've sparked. What does it matter whether or not he means it? I only want him for sex, for distraction. There's no getting hurt here. No feelings—just fun.

'Are you trying to wound my ego?' he grumbles.

I laugh a little more. 'I think your ego is impenetrable.'

'Believe me, no ego survives a girl erupting into giggles when you kiss her.'

'Then let me make it all better…' I say softly, leaning in to do just that.

The door opens again behind me and his body instantly tenses, his eyes dart.

It's my turn to frown at him. 'What—'

'Hold that thought,' he says, 'and let's get out of here.'

I'm about to ask what the rush is but he's already out of the booth, his attention on Jackson at the bar. The guy gives him a nod and then Ash offers his hand to me.

'But I haven't finished my drink.'

I'm used to doing things on *my* terms, whether I'm doing it for the public or for me. I'm the one in control. And the fact that I'm losing it more and more in Ash's company is freaking me out.

Admit it—don't you like it...just a little?

'I'll make you another,' he says.

My eyes narrow as I take a leisurely sip of my drink, making him wait. He really is itching to leave. I'd like to think it's because he wants me that badly, but I'm not convinced.

'Are you going to promise me one as good as this?'

'Better.'

I give a soft laugh, loving his confidence. 'Very well.' I slip my hand into his and feel my entire palm come alive at the contact. 'You have a deal.'

I rise up, hooking my bag over my shoulder as I make for the main entrance, but instead he tugs me the opposite way and I frown at him in surprise.

'My car's in the basement.'

'I didn't realise there was parking here.'

'It's Jackson's private garage.'

'Oh.'

I follow him, giving Cait a little wave as I go. Her grin is all-knowing, and then her attention goes back to the bar and more specifically to Jackson. I watch them for a second longer, their easy conversation evident from across the room and I shake my head. The poor guy is going to get eaten alive one of these days.

'You laughing at me again?'

'Your ego suffering again?'

Now he laughs and I follow him out, his husky rumble working its magic over me.

CHAPTER FIVE

'MY GOD, ARE all these Jackson's...save for yours?'

I look at her as she surveys the underground garage, where the line-up of sports cars is impressive even to me. 'It's a weakness of his—he can't resist a new toy.'

Her excited green gaze sweeps to me. 'So, come on, then—which of these babies is yours?'

'Just over—'

'No, actually don't tell me. I want to guess.'

I stop and look at her. 'Okay...' I string the word out, curious at her reasoning.

'I think a car can tell you a lot about a man.'

I fold my arms across my chest and work hard not to look in the direction of any particular car. This is going to be interesting.

Her heels clip against the concrete floor as she starts to walk, looking at each car with open appreciation. Occasionally she dips, caresses a bonnet and then looks to me. It shouldn't be provocative, but with every stroke of her delicate fingers, every dip and rise that she performs, my cock gets harder—to the point that my jeans are suffocating. I adjust discreetly, not taking my eyes off her.

She's teasing me. I think she's about to declare a vehicle as mine and then she moves on and gives me a little shake of her head, her bob swinging and making my palms itch with the need to fork my fingers through it.

She pauses before a blacked-out Range Rover now, private plate, nondescript. It means something to the owner—I know it does, because Jackson takes great delight in explaining this to anyone who asks.

'This one,' she murmurs, turning to face me and resting her hip against it. 'It's big and strong and…' She looks me up and down. 'Safe.'

I bark out a laugh. '*Safe?* Christ, you really know how to kick a man when he's down. You might as well declare me boring.'

She's not wrong, though. I have the exact same model in my garage back at home.

She walks towards me, her heels doing their musical clip again, her body statuesque and so fucking appealing in her white shirt and tight jeans.

'For the record,' she says, pausing before me, reaching out her hand to make tantalising contact with my chest, 'there's nothing boring about being safe.' She strokes her palms upwards, hooking them over my shoulders. 'In truth, I happen to find the sense of security when I'm in your arms quite a turn-on.'

And then she curves into me, her lips brushing over mine, and I'm lost. In her touch, her kiss, her words… I like it that she feels safe with me. I *want* her to feel safe.

She wouldn't feel that way if she knew the truth, though...

I squeeze my eyes shut and cut off my conscience. It doesn't matter what brought us together—what matters is that I'm doing right by her *now.* I wrap my arms around her and pull her tighter against me, my hardness pressing between us almost painfully.

Then tell her the truth—all of it. Let her deal with the threat her brother poses.

I kiss her back, pushing out the foolish idea. I can't do that until I understand what's at stake, what's really going on. And I can't do that until I *know* she's safe. She's all lightness and goodness, and Philip's none of that. God knows what he'll do if he's confronted by her when his desperation is at its peak. And that's exactly what would happen if I tell her—she has the guts to go straight to him and have it out.

Yeah, and what about the shitstorm that will hit when she learns the truth about you? You sure you're not running from that too?

I kiss her harder, desperate not to feel the aching truth of it. All I want is this. This moment. Her body curving into mine…her desire.

She sighs into my mouth. The heady sound provokes a growl of my own and I break away before I lose the last of my control and take her here in the garage, where anyone could see us.

'Come on.' I grab her hand and pull her along, past the Range Rover she picked out.

'But…' She stops, pulling back a little. 'It's not yours?'

'No.' I grin at her. 'This is mine.'

I come to a stop before my motorbike and her mouth gapes.

'You're kidding?'

'Why so surprised?'

'I'm not—well, I am, a little…'

'Is my ego about to take another hit, Coco?'

She laughs nervously, the sound so cute and edgy I want to kiss her all over again.

'No, this bike is all you.'

My chest puffs like a proud fucking peacock; it doesn't matter that I know it's ridiculous to be so pleased at her simple statement.

She strokes her hand over the sleek black frame, her teeth worrying over her bottom lip. 'I've just never been on one before.'

'I'll look after you,' I say, knowing just how true those words are, although guilt pricks all the same.

'I know.'

She flicks me a quick look that tells me she means it too and I struggle to add, 'It's not far to my place anyway…as you already know.'

Her cheeks flush, and the contrast with her over-bright green eyes and her blonde hair makes her appear more fairy than princess. My mind races with all that I want to do to her, to do with her. And all that I wish I could tell her and can't.

Christ.

I throw my focus into action, reaching for my leather jacket and holding it open for her. 'Wear this.'

She hesitates a second before obediently slipping her arms in. Her scent reaches up to me, all soft and floral. I've only had one whisky—courtesy of Philip Lauren—but standing here with her so close I feel punch-drunk.

She turns to face me as she zips up the jacket, and I'm more than just punch-drunk. I feel winded. She looks small, dwarfed by the black leather, but it's not that—it's the hit of possessiveness that comes over me.

'I must look a sight,' she says, suddenly coy, and I realise I'm practically scowling at her—*idiot.*

'Believe me, that's the least of your problems right now.'

She frowns. 'How so?'

I can't answer her. Putting a voice to my thoughts will make them far too easy to act upon.

I take up my helmet and she forgets her question, delivering another instead. 'You're not putting that on me?'

'Too right I am.'

'And what about you? Where's yours?'

'I only have one, and there's no way I'm risking anything happening to your cute little face.'

I expect a laugh, or a rebuke at my overprotectiveness. Instead she drags her teeth over her lower lip, her cheeks flushing deeper. She *must* be used to compliments. People must throw them at her like confetti. So why does it feel like she's hearing them for the first time with me?

The idea pulls at my chest. I focus on putting the helmet on her instead and tightening it. Really. Well. 'You okay in there?'

She nods and tries to smile, the cushioned front to the helmet giving her a hamster expression.

I grin. 'Suits you.'

'Something tells me I don't want to ask why.' Her voice is muffled by her squished cheeks, and I laugh. I can't help it. I laugh even harder when she tries to scowl at me, her green eyes shooting daggers before I slip the visor down.

'Come on.'

I swing my leg over the bike and gesture for her to get on behind me. She places her hand on my forearm as she clambers on and scoots in close, her arms tight around my middle. I try to take a breath, but my chest feels closed in.

She leans her head over my shoulder. 'Ready when you are, bad boy.'

I turn to look at her and curse the visor that hides her eyes from me. 'Bad boy?'

'The car was big, strong, safe…but this bike is badass.'

'If I'm so badass, why are you trusting me to take you back to my place?'

It's a genuine question.

She shrugs and rests her head against my back. Doesn't matter that she's wearing a great big helmet. I feel the gesture like we're skin-to-skin.

'Jackson considers you a friend,' she murmurs, 'and that's good enough for me.'

I shake my head in amusement, bewilderment and a sea of other emotions that I know starts with deception and ends in a twisted, tangled mess around my heart.

I kick the bike into life, pulling back on the throttle and letting its roar fill the garage as well as my head. But I can't shift the weird warmth, the heat that has nothing to do with sex and everything do with her readily bestowed trust.

Coco would be the end of my life as I know it if I let her—of that I'm certain.

Just as well Philip Lauren's timescale is short, because keeping a lid on this is proving harder by the second.

I've never understood the fascination with motorcycles. The idea of being so vulnerable on two wheels and at speed puts the fear of God in me. But with Jackson between my thighs, and the engine reverberating through me, it wasn't fear I felt—nothing close.

I clench him tighter and he calls back, 'You okay?'

More than okay...

But it's impossible to speak. Instead I nod against his shoulder and hold on as he takes us the short distance to his home. It's the quickest few minutes of my life and I find myself wishing he lived a hundred miles away just so we could stay like this for longer.

We sit quietly, the engine idling, as we wait for the garage door to roll up. I'm so lost in the feel of him, of pressing him close, I don't register the inside of the garage as he takes us in.

It's the engine cutting off that wakes me up and I straighten, creating some distance between us and realising just how tightly I was holding him.

'Sorry,' I blurt.

'What for?' He kicks the stand down and I set one foot tentatively on the floor to steady myself.

'For almost squeezing you to death.' I slip off the bike and fumble over the helmet fastening. My fingers are shaking, my thighs buzzing with the lasting effect of the engine.

He climbs off and turns to me, his fingers nudging my own away as he stares through the visor. 'I'd die a thousand times over if I got to go out like that each time.'

His voice is husky, his eyes wicked, and I swallow back the instant hit of lust.

He pulls the helmet up and over my head and I shake my hair out, feeling the air rush over my scalp, teasing at nerve endings already alert at his proximity, his words. I barely finish the move and he's tossing the helmet to the ground, his fingers forking through my hair, bringing me up to the fierce onslaught of his mouth.

Fireworks erupt in my belly; heat uncoils through my every limb.

I'm vaguely aware of the garage door rolling down amidst the rush of blood in my ears, punctuated by our fierce grunts as we rip at each other's clothing. He has his jacket off me, my bag has hit the deck, his fingers are undoing the buttons of my shirt as I tug his own from his jeans.

He rides my mouth, desperately deepening the kiss as he strides forward, taking me back against the hard wall of the garage, imprisoning me between brick and lean, hard muscle. He drops his hands to mine and lifts them above my head, lacing his fingers through mine, pinning them there before breaking the kiss.

I whimper, wriggling against him. I don't want his mouth to leave; I don't want my hands trapped. I want to feel him. *All* of him. But then his mouth is travelling down my neck, searing my skin with its dampened trail. My shirt hangs open and my body arches against the wall, offering my lace-covered breasts to the arrival of his mouth.

He breaks away long enough to stare down at me, to heat me with his look alone. His eyes are dark and hungry.

'You are so beautiful…'

Sheer pleasure radiates out from my core—seeing him, hearing him so sincere, so choked, feeling his arousal pressing between us, hard, eager… Knowing it's real, that he feels it as badly as I do, is exhilarating.

I clamp down on my bottom lip to stop a strangled whimper from erupting and then he's parting my mouth again, his tongue forceful, his mouth ravenous. I squeeze my thighs tight, nursing the budding ache, but it's driving me crazy. I need more.

I lift my leg around him, locking him against me,

seeking out the friction I need. My jeans pull taut, a thick, unyielding layer that frustrates as much as it teases.

'Ash...'

'What, princess?'

He drags his mouth against me as he speaks, his hands raking down my arms to slip beneath my shirt. He cups my breasts, his thumbs rolling over their hardened peaks, already erect and pressing. He works them both, caressing, tweaking, groping. I struggle for air, struggle to keep on kissing him back as the pressure builds through my middle.

My hands drop to his hair, half pushing him down, half holding his mouth to mine. I want it all—his hands, his mouth everywhere.

He tears himself away, resuming his hand's tantalising path down my front, over the swell of one breast, continuing to stroke, to toy, and then his teeth surround one peak and he nips at it. I cry out, pleasure streaking through my veins, my clit pulsing wildly as I clench around the ache. He does the same to the other, alternating between his fingers and his teeth, again and again.

I lower my gaze to take it all in. He's a badass all right, and I'm fucking loving it. My mind fills with carnal imaginings...the things he'll be up for in bed and out of it.

I take in our surroundings. The whitewashed garage walls, the bright overhead lights, the motorcycles, the cars...*the fucking great big Range Rover.*

'I *knew* it.'

He gropes my breast hard and nips at the exposed skin just above the strip of lace with his teeth. 'Knew what?'

'You own a big black muscle car.'

He laughs, the sound ragged with desire. 'So what does that make me? A big, *safe* badass?'

'Hell, yeah.'

He tugs at my shirt, stripping it from me and flicking it aside. His force triggers a fresh swell of heat and then one hand slips to my bra clasp, undoing it with an ease that tells me he's done it many, many times before. A strange prick of jealousy erupts, and I quickly shake it off. I don't do jealousy. He's not mine to be jealous about.

And then all thought dissipates as the cool garage air sweeps over my bare breasts and my bra hits the floor at the same time the hot cavern of his mouth surrounds one peak, sucking me in.

My head drops back and my *'Yes...'* is a breathless pant.

'So fucking perfect.' He brushes the words against my nipple as he releases me, his palm lifting my breast to offer its peak to the flick of his tongue. He rolls his thumb over the protruding flesh, then his tongue. He shifts to the other, sucking it in, his tongue playing before releasing me.

I'm losing my mind on sensation. I tilt my pelvis and ride my body higher against him, my jeans biting almost painfully into my flesh. I just want… I just need…

'Ash...'

He pops open the button of my jeans, then the zip, smoothing his hands around to my sides to shove the restrictive fabric down. I lower my leg to ease his way and he stops the second he can slip his fingers inside.

'*Fuck*, Coco…' He straightens and looks down at me, at where his fingers gently probe. 'Crotchless?'

His voice is a croak, his face strained with tension, his eyes disbelieving and so fucking keen. I'm not sure if it's a question or a statement but I nod anyway.

'Easy access.'

'*Fuck.*'

He slips his fingers through the opening designed for just that. He parts my lips, running his fingers upwards; the second he strikes my clit, I whimper. He rolls over me, his touch so soft he's hardly there. I bite into my lip as I move with him, asking for more. Deeper, harder, faster…

'There are so many things I want to do to you right now.'

I can hear it in his voice: the carnal promise, the ideas merging with my own. He slips back down to my opening, spreading me with his fingers as he dips inside.

'Like what?'

He lets go of a ragged breath and plunges his fingers in deep, his mouth sweeping over mine to steal one rough kiss. 'Like this…'

He pulls me with him to the front of his bike

and places my hands on the handlebars, angling me forward.

'You are beautiful,' he rasps with appreciation, his hands soft as he strokes the curve of my back. 'You know that, don't you?'

Do I? I don't know anything other than the quiver of anticipation running through me and the promise of release, the heat of his palms as he strokes my skin, the crazy stream of sensation along my breasts as they fall heavy in the cool air, my nipples sensitised from his thorough exploration.

'*Don't* you?' he insists, lowering his hands to the waistband of my jeans and working them down my thighs.

'Yes.' I'd say yes to anything in that second.

'Better.'

He smooths his palms over the curve of my arse, his appreciation drawn out, teasing. My skin prickles in his wake. And then he dips low, between my legs from behind, and I moan, *'Yes, more, yes.'*

He dips inside me like he's savouring me. 'So wet.'

I hum as my body sways, the sweet heat of his invasion urging me to spread my legs wider, wanting more. His other hand joins in the attentions, curving around to my front, strumming my clit as he moves within me. I feel a spasm of sheer pleasure deep inside; he has my G spot.

Fuck, yeah.

The pressure is acute, compounded by the perfect rhythm on my clit. I'm panting and crying out at once. It's so good. So intense. I'm going to come—but, no, not yet… I want him with me. I want to tell him to stop, but I can't.

'Come for me, princess. Let go.'

My body rides him of its own accord, its movements rigid and fraught with the tension spiralling through my limbs. I widen my stance again, my jeans cutting further into my thighs an added sensation. Punishing. Powerful. *Yes.*

I lift my eyes to the bike and catch my reflection in the sleek black metal, my mouth slack, my breasts bare, and then I'm coming so hard I fear I'm going to fall.

I drop forward, the cold shield of the bike is sharp against my skin, and then his hands are on my hips, pulling me back against him. I rise and hook my hands around his neck, pressing my arse into his hardness, teasing him as the waves taper off, my limbs fill with sated bliss.

He shudders, his breath ragged as he clamps my lower body tight against him. 'You're so fucking beautiful when you come.'

I turn my head into him, press my lips to his jaw. 'I want you inside me—here, now.'

His cock pulses, his body rocking with it. 'I won't last long.'

'I don't need you to.'

I love that he's honest about it…that the effort it's taking for him to hold himself back has his entire body vibrating against mine. I kiss him again and snuggle my head under his chin as he slips a hand inside the back pocket of his jeans and retrieves his wallet. A condom comes next, and then the wallet joins my bag on the floor, the empty condom packet too.

I lean forward as he unfastens his belt, the jangle of the buckle and the pop of buttons filling my ears, my body reheating with anticipation. I look over my shoulder, desperate to take him in, not wanting to miss a second of his slipping restraint. His cock is bare, pulsing in his grip; his teeth are gritted, his neck corded.

I've done that to him, and I smile as I take hold of the handlebars once more, my arse rubbing against his length and making him hiss through his teeth. I love it that he's so desperate, so keen, and the wetness slips between my legs, coating my underwear. I couldn't be more ready for him.

Slowly he rolls the condom down and grips the base of his cock hard. I nudge back, purposely positioning him in the valley of my arse, telling him without words that I need him now. He grips my hips, steadying me, but he doesn't do what I ask. Instead he slips one hand around my front, beneath the lace, straight to my clit, which is so sensitised in the aftermath that I buck and cry out.

'Patience, Coco.'

'If you want patience you've got the wrong woman.'

'Is that so?' he murmurs, his eyes falling to my arse. 'Guess I'll just have to teach you.'

He flicks over my clit again, but this time he

doesn't stop. It's fierce, brutal, and yet my toes curl, my thighs tighten, and I know I'm going to come again.

'Ash… Ash…'

He keeps up the pressure over my clit as he takes himself in his hand, probing inside the slit of my underwear.

'I love these,' he says. 'White, so fucking innocent, and yet they're so not.'

He rocks against me, the tip of his cock nudging at my opening. He does it again, teasing inside, his hiss of breath as erotic as the movement itself. And then he thrusts so hard, so deep, that he has to use both hands on my hips to stop me from collapsing over his bike.

My nipples brush the cold metal, the headlamp presses against my clit and his cock nudges my G spot. Such a multitude of sensation all at once that my head spins on it, my body hanging on the precipice of release.

His fingers bite into my hips, his tension vibrating through their lengths. His thrusts turn short and jagged and he growls low in his throat. He's so close, but so am I. Every thrust of his body, treats my nipples, my clit, my G spot to a delicious jolt of friction.

My legs tense up and I stop breathing. I give myself over to the mind-obliterating power of it and then I hear him cry out, his release bringing my own.

Together we rock, the movement long, deep. His arms wrap around my middle, pulling me against him, holding me tight. The warmth of his body seeps through his shirt, heating my back as he trails a hand over my front, over the goosebumps now appearing.

'Are you cold?' he says against my ear.

I shake my head. I can't even speak. I would have let him do anything, have anything, in the heat of what just went down. It should scare me. But I'm too content for fear.

I hook my hands behind his head once more, feel his buzz cut tickling my palms. 'I'll take that cocktail now.'

He presses a kiss into my neck. 'I'll take that talk too.'

A man who truly wants to talk—to me, about me…the real me…

The unfamiliar prospect should unsettle me, but with his arm around me, his hand worshipping my front, his back heating me through, I'm anything but unsettled.

CHAPTER SIX

I'M SURPRISED I can hold my hands steady as I craft her the perfect espresso martini. It's a damn good job I could do it in my sleep. My hours as a mixologist in London's high-end bars have taught me well. It was fun, even if the reason I was there wasn't.

'You really can mix a drink,' she says as she leans on the industrial chunk of wood and aluminium that forms the centre island of my kitchen.

She looks too cute, her white shirt buttoned just enough to be decent but not so much that I can't drink in her cleavage every time I look up. Her hair is delightfully ruffled from our antics, her eyes intense as she watches me work; her lips are worked clean of lipstick and they sport a dusky pink tone that reminds me of the inside of a strawberry. And just as tasty.

My cock twitches inside my jeans, gearing up anew, a reminder of just how 'cute' I find her.

I want to say that it's my need to protect her making these feelings more intense—the same kind of protective instinct that had me seeking justice for my family all those years ago. But I'm not convinced.

After all these years I've spent avoiding her type, I'm now powerless to deny I want her in every which way I can have her. I want Coco.

Which is absolutely fine, I tell myself. *You can have her and then walk away.*

She's in this for the sex, and I'm in it to help her, enjoying what she's so willing to offer at the same time.

So why does it feel wrong?

Because you're lying to her. You are becoming the kind of person you despise. The kind you seek to bring down.

I shake the drink. Hard. Fast. I don't want to think about it any more. I just want to be—

'And there I was thinking you were making it up—some corny chat-up line to get me to come home with you.'

Eyes alive with teasing, she takes up a handful of nuts from the bowl I put out earlier and pops one into her mouth.

I grip the shaker tighter. 'I don't make things up.'

Unless I'm on the job, which I am now...kind of...

I feel the brutal force of my confession wash over me, my skin prickling even though it's warm in here.

You've not lied to her, my conscience tries to reason. *You've merely omitted to tell her everything. That's different.*

I pour a little of the mix and then shake again… Pour, shake.

Concentrate on the drink.

'So come on—tell me,' she says. 'How did you learn to do this?'

I almost breathe a sigh of relief, grateful for the question, even if it does mean talking about the past. It beats the internal moral debate and self-loathing that came before it. And, hell, I know everything about her—she deserves to know something of me.

The idea soothes my torment.

'Jackson and I worked the bars together when we were younger. He was plotting his empire and I—well, I just needed to bring in some cash.'

'Sounds like fun.'

'It was.'

If I didn't think about all the shit going down at home: my family's assets being seized, our bank accounts frozen, my university degree forgotten since we had no money to pay for it.

She spins on the bar stool and takes a good look around the room, the high ceiling, the industrial-inspired lighting with black cabling and copper dome lights, the raw wood cupboards against exposed brick walls. It's all designer, high-end, and I anticipate her question before she even asks.

'Something tells me it's not what you do now, though. So what is it, Ash? Software engineer? Financial genius? Entrepreneur?'

My neck prickles with the impending lie that I don't want to tell. 'This and that.'

'This and that…?' Her brow lifts as she mimics me. 'How very specific… Hmm, let me think…'

I can't help but smile. Does she know her nose wrinkles like a rabbit's when she's thinking?

I turn and open the cupboard in which I keep the coffee beans. Taking a couple out, I place one on top of each drink and offer her a glass.

She takes it from me with a cheeky grin. 'It certainly looks the part.'

And then she sips it and I'm lost in the movement. I almost forget the tricky terrain she has hit with her questioning, but then her eyes are open again, pinning me with their inquisitive stare.

I look away and take up my own drink, needing the hit of alcohol, the confidence to navigate what's coming.

'If not for all this I'd say you were in the military—or the police, even…' She tilts her head to one side and her shirt slips a little, stopping at the curve of her shoulder and teasing me with a hint of collarbone that I want to follow with my fingertips, my tongue.

'What makes you say that?' I ask, dragging my eyes back to hers.

'There's your physique for starters.' She gives me a coy smile. 'You're too fit for a desk job.'

I give a short laugh. 'I think there are plenty of businessmen who'd beg to differ.'

She waves a dismissive hand. 'I've met plenty of businessmen and none of them are your Christian Grey variety.'

'Christian Grey?' I frown.

'*Fifty Shades?* You know—Christian Grey, the sexy billionaire who'd have your knickers around your ankles and you tied to a bed quicker than you could beg for it.'

'Well, I'm safe. Knickers aren't part of my wardrobe.'

She rewards me with a laugh that has something inside my chest expanding so fast I can't breathe and my ears straining to capture every last note.

'I don't think you'd be his type either,' she murmurs, her eyes sparkling in the golden light of the kitchen. 'But it's not just that—you have this aura about you…a protective vibe. Like I told you earlier, it's a security thing… Oh, my God, that's it!' Her eyes widen excitedly. 'You're a bodyguard!'

I laugh awkwardly. Christ, how I wish I was that right now. No secrets, no lies…

'Not a bodyguard, then…'

She pouts at me, nose wrinkling anew.

'I give up.'

'You want me to tell you?'

She smiles and nods.

I'm not going to lie. I can't. Truth is there's actually no harm in me being honest. To an extent at least. She doesn't need to know it all. Not yet.

Yes, and it's all about protecting her, not yourself, from what it will do to her, to you, to your relationship.

Relationship? There is no fucking relationship.

'I'm a private investigator.' I say it over the internal rant, louder than it needs to be, and she chokes mid-sip of her drink, her eyes popping out of their sockets as goosebumps streak across my body.

'You're *not*.'

I swallow back the rising panic and the need to confess all, my guilt working its way to the surface. 'What's wrong with being a private investigator?'

I hate myself even as I say it.

'Nothing.' She straightens and wipes her lips with the back of her free hand. 'I'm just surprised.'

'I deal in property too,' I add quickly, suddenly feeling inferior to Her Ladyship in front of me and foolish as fuck for telling her the truth. What does it matter that my job is beneath her? Why do I care?

'So being a PI pays well, then?' she asks, her eyes once again travelling over our surroundings.

'Well enough—but it's the property that really pays…the investment. I do the PI work to help people.'

'*See*—I knew it.'

'Knew what?'

'That you *helped* people. Whatever it is you do, I knew there had to be an element of that in there.'

I smile then, my chest lifting and burying the fleeting sense of inferiority. I do help people. That's why I became a PI and that's why I still am one. There's nothing wrong with my motives. I just misjudged this one case.

'What got you into it?'

'The PI work?'

'Yes.'

She nods eagerly and my smile tightens, my chest falls with the memories I'd like to leave in the past.

'You don't have to talk about it—not if you don't want to.'

'No, it's fine.' I force myself to relax. If I want her to open up to me, the least I can do is the same in return. 'It's a long story.'

'I have all night.' She slips from the bar stool to stand before me, her fingers gentle as they stroke across my brow. 'I want to know what makes your brow do that and take it away.'

I can't breathe past her touch… A weird sensation is lifting inside me.

You're supposed to be helping her, not the other way around.

I chained my demons down a long time ago. The last thing I expect is for them to rush to the surface on her command. But here they are—and more. She's making me *feel* again…something I thought I was long past.

And if I feel, how can I be sure I'll be ready to walk away when the time comes…when she no longer needs me… What if I find I need her instead? What then?

Fuck.

For the first time I see a crack in the solid exterior that is Ash and I'm not letting it go.

He's exposed me in so many ways already, and to see that he's not immune, to see that my playfulness has brought us to this point—I can't let it lie even if I want to.

It's disconcerting to feel this bond with someone I've only just met. I'd blame it on the fierce attraction still burning strong if not for the fact that I've been there, done that. This is something more. It's deeper than sex. And if I understand him I stand more chance of understanding this. Because I've never dared love, never dared risk my heart before. I want nothing less than what my parents had.

Maybe I *can* find that here.

'Let's go and sit down,' he says.

He doesn't balk from my touch, but he doesn't smile at it either. He's all serious and unreadable, but I feel his acceptance, know that I'm about to get what I pressed for.

I lean into him as he curves an arm around my back and leads me into the living area. It has two floor-to-ceiling glass windows made up of square panes and to the left hangs a painting of a dreamscape, its style very familiar.

'Is that… Is that a *Cleveland*?'

His lips quirk at my obvious appreciation. Or is he just happy that we're off-topic temporarily?

'He's a friend of mine.'

'No way—he can't be.'

He grins now. 'Don't ever say that in front of him. He already has an epic ego and he'll never let me live it down.'

'Wow…' I look back to the painting, to the mixture of reds and blues swirling to create stunning shadows and light, shapes that could be trees, clouds, cliffs, water—whatever you want them to be.

'It's called *Illusion*.'

His voice has turned gruff and I feel his eyes on

me. My cheeks warm under his attention. 'It's glorious.'

He doesn't shift focus, and his appreciation is very much on me as I continue to study the piece of art and try to keep at bay the heat simmering just beneath the surface. It would be so easy to roll with it, to get down and naked right here before the masterpiece, but I'd be no closer to understanding what makes this man tick, why my body feels instinctively drawn to him, appreciated and protected by him.

'I'll be sure to pass that on when we next meet.' He reaches out to stroke my hair behind my ear and my lips part just enough for me to breathe.

I turn to look at him, at the heat in his gaze, and swallow. 'Shall we sit?'

He cocks his brow. '*Not* what I was thinking.'

I roll my eyes to break the mood. 'You have a one-track mind.'

'Judging by your colour, I'm not the only one.'

He's not wrong, and I laugh, but I make my legs obey and head for the sofa, knowing he'll follow.

I sink down into the dark cushioned softness, its deep back inviting me in further, and I feel my muscles practically sigh at the comfort. Christ, when did I last just sit, relax, do nothing, think of nothing? I close my eyes, only for a second, and I enjoy it.

The sofa shifts with the arrival of his weight and when I open my eyes he's watching me.

'Don't get to sit down much, hey?'

I give him a small smile, but my head stays resting on the sofa back as I tilt it to face him. 'Such is the life of a busy socialite.'

He doesn't smile. Instead his mouth thins, his eyes narrow. 'Is that all you think you are?'

I shrug softly. 'It's what I am, and I do what good I can with it. My grandmother was—is—the same. She saw it as a great privilege to have inherited the Dukedom. It was no small feat for my great grandfather to get the patent amended to allow his solitary heir, Granny, to inherit, heaven forbid a woman, a non-Royal at that, should be a duchess in her own right.'

'It's about time that whole nonsense changed anyway.'

I nod, relieved that he sees the rules of succession within the peerage as outdated and sexist as I do. 'True, but it's rarity meant extra press exposure and greater interest from the public, which Granny was able to work in her favour to help the causes close to her heart. She has done so much with her role and paid her dues thrice over.'

'And now you want to do the same? Even though your brother will be the one to inherit the title?'

'Yes. Just because he will be the Duke of Rushford it doesn't mean I can't continue the work that I do. Our private fortune is to be split equally and I'll carry on using it to help others.'

'But don't you want more? For you?'

My blood fires with irritation, sending my back ramrod straight, the peaceful moment gone. 'What are you trying to say?'

He riled me when he touched on my public persona back at the bar, so I'm surprised he's dared to go there again.

'Nothing—I don't mean to upset you.'

There's the apology again, and I can see he means it, his eyes turning soft with concern, but my hackles are up and the need to defend myself is riding high.

'I'm just trying to understand what it is you do… what you want to do in the future. What drives you?'

'I want to help people, and with my family's money and connections I can do that. I don't have a degree, a career, a fancy job title. I'm me. Just me.'

He nods. 'I get that—totally. And, yes, you do a lot of good. I know you have your charities and your fundraising efforts. I just meant what do you want for *you*, personally?'

'Oh…' My temper flares, his question poking at an age-old nerve. 'I get it. You think someone my age must want to get married, have children, settle down. Is that it?'

His brow lifts. 'Perhaps…'

I shake my head. I've had this conversation a thousand times over. With Granny, with Cait and, more frequently, with the press. I usually give my well-rehearsed answer, that I haven't yet met the right man to sweep me off my feet. I don't add the truth, that I've met enough to know he doesn't exist.

Although now, staring into Ash's eyes, I find that resolve wavers. Maybe it's that realisation that has me blurting, 'I want the impossible.'

He frowns. 'The impossible?'

'I want what my parents shared—a whirlwind passion and the love that stems from it.' I look into my glass at the frothy topping and smile even as my cheeks burn with my confession. 'You can laugh… It's fine.'

'I'm not laughing.'

No, he's not. He sounds so goddamn sincere I can almost believe that he thinks the same and is feeling the same—it encourages me to explain.

'My mother died when I was two,' I say. 'I only have her diary to go on, but let's just say she was good with words. She loved my father and he never stopped loving her. The day he died he gave the diary to me—said I should learn what I could from her, that she was the role model I should aspire to.'

'I'm sorry.'

I look at him, surprised. 'Why?'

'For the loss of your parents…for not having them with you now.'

I smile wistfully. 'Life would be quite different.'

'You wouldn't have your brother, for a start.'

There's an edge to his voice that startles me, and he looks away, leaning forward to place his drink on the low-slung table before us as he clears his throat.

'At least you have him,' he adds, deadpan now.

My laugh is sudden, harsh, wiping out my concern over his outburst seconds before. 'We're not that close. I think my stepmother fears I might lead him astray.'

I shake my head and brush her away from my mind.

'Why would you say that?' he asks.

Why? There are so many reasons why—starting with my mother and ending with me. 'Because of my mother…who she was, what she did for a living.'

'What does it matter what she did or who she was? You are *you*.'

I don't miss the fact that he doesn't question what my mother did, that he already knows. He's more aware of my family than I would ordinarily expect for a typical guy. Which explains why he knows of that magazine article too. But I won't hold it against him. Why *shouldn't* he know what the press are so quick to dish out?

'If only it were that simple,' I say.

'I can't imagine what life must have been like for you, growing up with a stepmother who sees you in that way. It must have been lonely.'

He reaches over, his hand soft upon my shoulder, his thumb gently caressing, and I lean into the comfort he offers, grateful for it.

'It would've been if not for Granny.'

And it will be again when she's gone.

The pain hits me full force and I take a shuddery breath, trying to let it go.

'You're very close?'

I nod, struggling to talk. 'She's been good to me. Life…life isn't going to be the same when…when…'

I can't finish the sentence, let alone the thought.

My fingers shake as I raise my glass to my lips and blink back the tears that threaten. 'She has only weeks—maybe two months at most. The doctors don't seem to know.'

His hand reaches around me, drawing me in, and his other hand takes my glass from my unresisting fingers to place it on the side.

I don't realise I'm properly crying until I'm against his chest, the dampness of my tears seeping into the fabric of his shirt.

My body shudders with the sobs I've kept trapped inside for so long, and the heaviness eases as I let go. I breathe in his scent, his warmth, his comfort, tuck my hands beneath my chin as I curl into his lap.

Granny's words—*stiff upper lip, girl; never show people you're weak or they'll flock like vultures*—run through me, mock me. But being with Ash isn't part of a show, an act. It's real, *I'm* real and it feels good.

I snuggle down deeper against him and just let go…

If he's a vulture, I'll happily build an aviary to keep him.

CHAPTER SEVEN

I HOLD COCO to me, one hand smoothing over her hair, the other on her back. My heart pounds in my chest, so hard I fear she'll hear every beat for what it is: my guilt, my deception…and something more.

I care about her. There's no use denying it. It's as real as she is in my arms.

I'm starting to get answers too. I'm willing to bet that the Duchess's imminent death is the reason Philip Lauren is so desperate to discredit his sister. It's clear the standard to which Coco believes she has to live her life, her grandmother demonstrated it by example and the slander Philip is after will pull her apart in the eyes of the Duchess. Heaven knows what would happen then. Whether the Duchess would, or indeed could, put family ties—love—over reputation and title.

I want to dig deeper, ask Coco more questions, but I can't just yet. The way she's sobbing suggests she hasn't cried in a long while, and *this* I can do: hold her while she lets go.

'We're not supposed to be talking about me.' She

sniffs eventually, and then gives an unladylike snort that makes my lips quirk.

I bow my head and press a kiss to her hair, the scent of her shampoo teasing my senses and calming my pulse. 'No? What are we supposed to be talking about?'

She wipes her eyes with her sleeve and looks up at me, her big green eyes glistening and wide with so much emotion that it reaches inside me.

'You,' she says simply. 'Why you became a private investigator.'

I give her a small smile. She's right, and I owe her this. I owe her a piece of me in return.

I settle back into the sofa, pulling her with me, my eyes staring unseeing at the window ahead and the dark outdoors beyond.

'When I was at university, a business deal my father was involved in came under scrutiny. It was serious. He was facing a long prison sentence. Our bank accounts were frozen, our assets seized. It was a living nightmare, the kind you so desperately want to wake up from—only you can't.'

She presses up off my chest. 'Was he guilty?'

'Everyone thought so, but it didn't make any sense. My father was a good man…honest, kind; he brought my brother and me up in the same vein. Especially after Mum died. He'd always gone above and beyond. Then his best friend, Clive—he was my godfather too—started sowing seeds of doubt in our minds, telling us Dad hadn't been right since

Mum had passed, that he'd been gambling, drinking, the works…'

I shake my head, remembering those conversations; the nausea that would come, the disbelief and the split loyalty.

'I trusted Clive. He'd always been there for us and I figured he was trying to protect us, prepare us for what the future might hold.'

'But he was lying?'

I look at her. 'Yes—every last word. I overheard him on the phone, talking about the deal to a man I later discovered was his lawyer. I heard enough to start digging. I couldn't go back to university with it hanging over us; I couldn't even afford to go back. I worked in bars to keep some money coming in and I looked into Clive and his dealings. He had no reason to suspect me; made it easy for me, really.'

'What happened?'

'I gave every last scrap of evidence I could find to my father's lawyer and it was enough to get the case thrown out and Clive convicted.'

'Your poor father—it must have destroyed him, being betrayed like that.'

'You could say that; he was certainly never the same. He'd lost his wife and his best friend in the space of a few years. Jake and I were all he had left.'

'Jake?'

'My brother.' I clear my throat, clear the strain from my voice. 'My father retired not long after—got a fishing retreat up in Scotland. He just couldn't face the rat race any longer.'

'I'm sorry.'

I hold her tight against me, press her head into my chest and breathe…just breathe. I haven't talked about it in so long, haven't let the pain back in. Seeing the man you've admired for so long broken by the people he loved most…it's another reason not to let anyone get close.

I should be remembering that, not getting all cosy and exposed with her. But it's too late for warnings.

'Your father's lucky to have such a clever son.'

I laugh softly. 'And your granny is lucky to have someone who loves her as you do.'

She scoffs gently. 'I'm not sure *lucky* is the word she would use.'

I tilt her chin up to me, her green eyes lock with mine and I almost forget what I want to say as the need to kiss her beats into my consciousness.

'What makes you say that?'

'You know that Austen quote—"a single man in possession of a good fortune, must be in want of a wife"?'

'Vaguely.'

'Try it in reverse.'

'Ah…she expects you to be married off.'

She rolls her eyes with a sigh and slumps back against me. 'Has done for years. She can't understand why I haven't brought someone home to meet her yet.'

'No one?'

'No. Anything like that demands public attention,

and it's hard enough working out whether a relationship is going places without having press scrutiny on top. Besides, every guy I've ever met has shown his true colours eventually.'

'What's that supposed to mean?'

'They want what I can give them—money, title, the works. They're not interested in *me*.'

'I don't think that's fair.'

She laughs against me. 'Don't judge people by your standards—you're an exception.'

'I am?' It's so quiet, my own surprise at her knee-jerk remark takes my breath away.

And then she looks up at me again, her eyes narrowed as she considers me.

'I think so. The second you met me, you told me I wasn't your type.'

My lips lift. 'And you're taking that to be a *good* thing?'

She reaches up to cup my jaw, her thumb brushing over my lower lip, her eyes tracing the move. 'Yes. You meant it when you said it. I get the feeling you don't go in for people like me; you like life a little less complicated.'

'And what about you? What do you—'

She cuts me off with her lips, my question answered before I even ask it. She wants *me*. And, Christ, I want her.

I know I have to come clean and tell her the truth—it's too big a lie…*a secret*. But not yet—not until I'm sure of the facts. Not until I'm sure she can't get hurt, sure that her reputation is safe and her brother is dealt with for good. *Then* I can confess. *Then* she can face off Philip and deal with him.

And then she can face off you too...

My blood runs cold—fear, guilt, *what ifs* plaguing my mind—and I kiss her all the more, pushing them away. Her fingers slip beneath my shirt, her exploration rough, hungry, desperate. I return it all twice as hard, twice as needy.

She moans against my lips and I stand, taking her with me.

'Where are we going?' she asks as I pull her along.

'Bed.'

I want her to know how special she is. Not because of her money, her family name—none of it. Only because of *her*.

I turn the lights on low when we reach the bedroom and stop before the bed. I turn her to face me, my eyes locking with hers, and silently I undress her. My fingers are soft and unhurried as I take my time over her and I love it that she lets me.

Her shirt floats to the floor, her bra too. I unfasten her jeans and slip my hands beneath her knickers, smoothing them down her legs, her soft calves, her dainty feet with those delicate red-tipped toes. She steps out, her fingers soft on my shoulder for support, and then I toss them aside and rise back up. She stares up at me…so trusting, so beautiful.

'Let me show you how special you are,' I say into her eyes, and I pull my own shirt over my head, letting it fall to join hers. 'Let me show you it's about you.'

I dip to taste her lips, a sweep of my tongue against hers parting her lips further and taking the whimper that she utters.

'It's not about your name...'

I stroke my hands up her sides, my palms gentle as they cup her breasts, my thumbs rolling over the peaks already tightening against my touch.

'It's not about your status...'

I whisper a path along her jawline to her ear.

'Your money...' I scrape my teeth over her earlobe and she shudders into me. 'Your title...'

I lift her up and she wraps her legs around me.

'This is about you.'

I take her to the bed and lay her down softly.

'*You*, Coco.'

Her eyes glisten and blaze all at once and my chest is fit to burst with the crazy swell of emotion spilling over. I kiss her until it eases, until I can breathe fully, but instead it grows, and she's kissing me back now, pleading for release.

I force myself to slow down. 'Patience...'

'I don't do—'

I silence her rebuke with another tongue-sinking kiss and she moans.

'We've covered that one,' I say, breaking away to sweep along the collarbone that had teased the hell out of me earlier to the curve of her shoulder.

She wriggles and rakes her nails down my back, demanding more. I nip at her skin in return. She tries to unfasten my jeans and I grab her hands, forking my fingers through hers as I press them back on either side of her head.

'Stay.'

She looks like she's going to argue, so I instruct her before she can.

'Every time you move your hands, I'll stop.'

She bites into her bottom lip.

'Understand?'

She nods.

'Let me…'

Let me love you was the shocking phrase that rode my tongue, ready to leap out, and I flick my gaze away in order to regain control.

This isn't love. I hardly know her.

Not true. You've lived in her shadow for weeks...

But I am done with that emotion. I only care because of the part I've played to date, working for her brother's money. It's just my guilt, intensifying everything else.

I can't breathe. The world halted with his words… *Let me...*

Let me...what?

I'm still trapped in the heat of his look. It doesn't matter that his eyes have fallen away. He's still got me. Immersed in the passion I can read. The passion and something more—something visceral that calls to a part of me I've never dared expose before. A part that makes me vulnerable.

He lifts his head and my lashes flutter as I search

his depths, reaching for that same look, that same connection, waiting for his words to come.

'Let me…have this.'

Have this?

It's not the mammoth confession I've surprised myself into wanting. It's simple. It's all I should expect. And it's enough. For all he's done for me in the short space of time I've known him, helping me to feel real, to be me, I'd let him have anything.

I nod and raise my head to his, dutifully keeping my hands pinned, forked in his. He meets me halfway, his kiss soft, tender, and he doesn't stop until I slacken beneath him, my fingers relaxing. He releases one hand to cup my thigh, his palm hot and searing against my skin as he bends my leg. He releases the other hand and does the same with my other leg, spreading me open beneath him, and then he rises.

'Stay,' he commands again, his eyes on fire as they trail down my body.

Anticipation has fire licking through my loins and I nod, my mouth slack as I wait…and wait.

His finger trails a path down my front, around each mound. 'You are so perfect…'

My subconscious wants to scream, *I'm not! I'm so far from it.* But I can't speak. I am so caught in his spell as I lie there, open to his gaze, his touch. He traces my navel and my belly tightens. Beneath, my clit is waiting for that first touch.

But it doesn't come. Instead he backs away and lowers his head. 'I bet you taste perfect too.'

I let out a moan and then he's there, his fingers parting me for the arrival of his mouth, and my belly launches into my throat, the surge of sensation making my body arch as my head presses back, my hands twist to claw at the quilt.

'Fuck…' I curse, my eyes squeezed tight.

He is a master, a true, bona fide expert, with the kind of skill that's born of experience. And, Christ, I'd know. I've given and received enough times. Jealousy claws its way back in but he sucks over me, banishing the unwelcome thought.

He's all flicks and sips, his tongue rough, his stubble rougher. *Oh, hell.* I pull at the bedding, my thighs straining to close, but his hands are there, pressing them wider, and his growl of contentment is working over me.

'Ash…*Ash*…'

I'm practically pulling myself up the bed, the intense streaks of pleasure impossible to control, his mouth unrelenting—and then I am shattering, the explosion inside so intense, so fierce, I can't breathe for it. And even then he doesn't stop. But I'm too sensitive—it's too many waves, too much.

I start to pant, one hand flying to his head, clawing at him, as my lower half bucks with every sweep of his tongue. And then I feel that heated tension rebuild and I can't believe it—it's not possible… Just… not…*possible*! And then I'm not only at the peak, I'm riding above it, and the resurgence of pleasure is so startling, so acute, I can do nothing but grip the back of his head and stare as the sensation builds to an almighty crescendo and then I am convulsing, wild, lost, euphoric.

I rock forward, both hands hugging him to my pussy as I ride it out. Wave after wave. And then he rises up and I pull him to me. I feel raw, exposed, *wanted*, and I throw it all into a kiss. I taste myself on him and tongue him deeper, unable to get enough. His arms surround me and I'm trembling, struck dumb by what just happened. By all of it. By him.

He lies down and takes me with him, our mouths still joined. And I realise I'm not sure I can ever get enough of this—not ever. I want a future. I want it all.

I slow the kiss and break away, waiting for his eyes to meet mine.

Ask him. Just ask him.

The words hang in my throat. I'm scared of rejection. Scared of acceptance.

'I know we said this was just about sex…'

I feel his chest still, spy the sudden tension around his eyes and curse my big mouth.

'Yes.'

I swallow and force my eyes to hold his. 'Well, what about we give this a shot? Try the odd date? I have a charity ball tomorrow night. You could come. It might be fun.'

I'm losing him. I can see it in the crease between his brows, the shutter falling over his expression. And those bloody tears are returning. Now that he's opened the floodgates, it appears there's no stopping them.

I drop my head to his chest, my ear coming to rest over his heart, and I listen to it race beneath me. 'It's okay. I'm more trouble than I'm worth.'

His hand upon my shoulder tightens. 'Don't say that. Don't *ever* say that.'

That passion is back in his voice—so why the shutter, why the rejection that he has yet to put into words?

'It's just… It's just in my line of work, I need to keep out of the public eye—you know, under the radar. No one's going to hire a PI whose face is recognisable to the masses. It'll ruin my business.'

I close my eyes and breathe through the pain. He makes a fair point. I know he does. And he's not rejecting me—not really.

He's not promising you anything more either. In fact, he's telling you it can never be.

But I only have myself to blame for wanting more, for lowering my guard and letting him in. I only have myself to blame for tearing my heart in two.

'We can have this, though, can't we?' I say softly. 'At least for a little while?'

He lifts my chin and looks down into my eyes. The passion I could hear in his voice now flares in his depths.

'For as long as we want it.'

He seals his words with a kiss and I close my eyes. A solitary tear escapes to trail down my cheek but I kiss him harder. I kiss him to block out the sadness. I kiss him to forget the pain. I kiss him to make the present matter more.

I kiss him until he's making love to me and we are as close as two people can be.

CHAPTER EIGHT

I WAKE TO the realisation that I'm not alone—to the realisation that I am more at home in my bed than I have ever been. And I know it's because she's here, her naked body wrapped around mine.

She's snoring softly, fast asleep, and I lie still, not wanting to wake her. Not wanting this moment to end. Even though I know it has to.

A woman like her has a schedule that doesn't stop for the weekend, no matter how much I wish it could. How much I wish reality could be different. How much I wish we lived in a world where she and I stand a chance. But I'm no fool.

The second she learns of my contract with her brother, it will all come to a swift and crushing end.

Won't it?

It has to end—that's a given. But maybe it would be better all round if my involvement with her brother never came to light. If I can see him off with nothing and keep her reputation intact we can just go our separate ways. No harm, no foul.

My chest tightens, my hold around her with it,

and I force myself to relax. It's the only way it can end. Any other possibility leads to her being hurt, and that far outweighs my own concerns.

I ease out from beneath her and set her down on my pillow. She mumbles in her sleep and for a second I fear she'll wake. I stay stock-still. I can't face her yet. Not with the war of emotions so clearly written on my face. Instead she pulls my pillow further down beneath her head and breathes deeply, her body relaxing, her face blissfully at peace once again. And I'm so lost in that look, her beauty, everything she has come to mean.

You need to move. Now.

I slip from the bed and quietly move around the room, pulling on some workout gear and heading downstairs to my gym. I need to work this out of me, focus on pounding the treadmill, the punchbag—anything but the chaos inside.

Not that it works. I'm just as messed-up over an hour later, having showered, donned some tracksuit bottoms and sorted breakfast: freshly brewed coffee and an array of whatever I could muster on a tray before me.

But as I walk through my bedroom door, I find my feet rooted. She's awake and stretching, her beautiful body naked from the waist up. She freezes when she spies me, her eyes widening, her arms still in mid-air, and then slowly she brings them down.

'What?' she says, clearly spying something in my expression—not to mention the fact that I haven't moved or said a word.

Way to go in freaking her out and failing to hide it. And you're supposed to be an experienced PI, for fuck's sake.

I walk towards her and plaster on a smile. 'I'm just struggling with the realisation that there's a beautiful woman in my bed.'

She rolls her eyes and wrinkles her nose in that cute little rabbit move which has my gut flip-flopping—

Your gut? Who are you kidding? Your heart, more like.

'Please don't tell me you're one of those.'

My eyes narrow. 'One of those…?'

'Yeah—one of those men with a woman-free bed.' She goes all dramatic and flutters her hands. '*"Yeah, I'm gonna shag you until you walk like John Wayne, but I won't let you into my bed unless you are the one."* That kind of man.'

She waggles her brow and laughs as she says it, and the move cracks me up too.

'No, I'm not one of those.'

Her laughter dies from her eyes and I see what my admission has cost her. *Shit.* I recall what she asked of me last night about wanting more. Did she want to be the one? Did I want her to be?

Stupid, dangerous question.

But I can give her my honesty. About this at least.

'Truth is I'm not averse to bringing women home…' I see her swallow, her cheeks pale a little, and I push on. 'I just haven't had the inclination in a long time. In fact, if you must know, I can't even remember the last time I got laid.'

I laugh on the last. It's awkward, but it's honest, and her smile, the warmth reigniting in her cheeks, makes it worth it.

'Well, in that case, I'm honoured.'

She's suddenly gone all shy and, God help me, I'm falling so quickly and deeply that my heart pulses in my chest and tells me exactly what I'm feeling for her. It doesn't matter how impossible it all is—it's there. My absolute love and affection for a woman who's been in my life for weeks but doesn't know me from Adam.

I return her smile—although mine is more of a grin—to hide the chaos within, and slide the tray onto the bedside table.

It can't be love—not yet, it can't.

'So, my lady, we have options: coffee, juice, granola, toast and eggs—oh, and fruit. So what's your poison?'

'You.'

My heart leaps and I don't look at her straight away. I know if I do she'll see too much. *Christ*, she probably already has.

'But you'd best make it quick as I have a brunch date with Granny and she doesn't take kindly to tardiness.'

Ah, fuck it—breakfast can wait.

My heart, though… That's another matter. But I'll deal with that when she's safe from her brother.

And from me.

* * *

I let myself into the house and my well-practised mask falls into place.

Our housekeeper gives me *the look* as she bustles into the hallway—the one that says, *Out all night again?*—but I simply beam at her. 'Morning.'

She shakes her head, but her face softens a little as she smiles back. 'I'll bring brunch up shortly.'

'Thanks, Sue.'

I take to the stairs, my mood a weird mix of light and dark. On the one hand I've had the best sex of my life—no, the best *night* of my life. On the other hand I can't keep having it for ever and at some point it has to end.

But that point isn't now, and maybe that's why the lightness is winning out.

I walk along the galleried landing and down the east wing of the house to Granny's room. I can hear voices. It's Philip. *Great.* He won't waste any time before remarking on my night out.

'She hasn't come home again,' he's saying.

'She's a grown woman. I don't expect her to always be here.'

'It's not the fact that she's out all night—it's what she's doing that has me—'

I push open the door and he stops abruptly, turning in my direction.

'You were saying, Philip...?' I say smoothly.

'Ah, so good of you to return, Coco.'

He turns back to Granny, who's sitting ramrod straight in bed, the mountain of cushions at her back helping to keep her there. Her eyes narrow on me, sharp as ever, and then return to Philip as he bends to kiss her forehead.

'I'll call in later to check on you.'

'I have cards with Grace at three,' she returns shortly, sounding like she's delivering an admonishment rather than stating a simple fact.

It's just how she is. *Cards* is code for *treatment*. She does both in tandem. Another Lauren seeking distraction.

'Make sure you don't interrupt then.'

He nods and then walks towards me. 'Where have you been this time?'

He leans in to peck my cheek as I offer it to him on autopilot.

'None of your business.' My response is tight, delivered under my breath, and even though Granny is now staring out of the large balcony window, I know her ears are attuned to us.

I don't give him time to rebuke me. I stride past him and drop a kiss to her paper-thin cheek, my hand gentle on her shoulder, feeling only bone.

'Morning—how are you feeling?'

The door closes behind me, signalling Philip's departure, and I feel my chest ease just a little.

'Old,' she quips, and then she turns to look at me and frowns. 'So, come on—where were you?'

'Out with a friend.'

She thumbs the newspapers strewn across her bed. She already has one open at a page portraying me in an article about one of the charities I front, making preparations for tonight's ball.

She traces the picture with her forefinger. '*Just* a friend?'

I lower myself to perch on the edge of her bed. 'Just a friend.'

She looks back at me and I see her jaw is working. Something is bothering her, and her weight loss is making any sign of tension more pronounced.

'That "friend" put this colour in your cheeks?'

She waves a frail finger at my face, her eyes sparkling as she says it, and I can't help but smile, my guilt shining through.

She makes a low humming sound in her throat and folds her hands on her lap. 'You need to be careful, though, child. You have the weight of the world looking on. And the name of Lauren to protect.'

I have heard this speech a thousand times, and I practically say the words along with her.

'You'll never be far from scandal. Not with a mother like yours. And I need you to be. I need you to be above reproach. And, heaven help him, your brother needs it too.'

Adrenaline spikes in my blood and I have to work hard to keep my face neutral. It doesn't matter how many times they throw my mother at me; it still hurts. My mother loved my father; he loved her back. Whatever she did before then I don't care about. But Granny does. And he chose badly, according to her.

'Philip can look after himself.' I focus on the bit I feel comfortable arguing with.

Her frown deepens, her eyes sad. 'Not when he's led around by that mother of his—and don't get me started on his spendthrift wife. That Clara won't be happy until she has them penniless, and the estate doesn't come cheap. It will need to be maintained, looked after, invested in when I'm gone and—' She breaks off and winces, the breath shuddering through her.

'Please stop worrying. The doctor says you—'

She waves a hand at me, her head shaking as she coughs. 'Dr Know-It-All can zip it. I'll stop when I'm six feet under.'

'*Jesus*, Granny.'

'Language!' she admonishes. 'I need to know I can trust you—that you will take care of things. Philip, or rather those women, won't be able to do anything with regards to the private estate without your say-so. Look out for him, guide him as much as you can, keep him on the straight and narrow and above all uphold our good name, I'm counting on you, Coco.'

She looks to the newspaper page again, rearranges it, then rearranges it some more.

I want to say, *It's just a name—what does it matter? Surely happiness should come first.* But the last time I tried that argument I was sixteen and she refused to speak to me for weeks, persuaded my father to cut off my allowance and vetted anyone who came within a six-foot radius just in case they were corrupting me.

No, I've been brought up to project perfection. To be everything Granny believes my mother wasn't.

How different would my life have been if my mother hadn't been killed in a car accident when I was just a baby? Would she have brought Granny around eventually?

Not for the first time I wonder about giving Granny my mother's diary. Would it make her see my mother as I do, as Daddy must have? I only have to read it to see all the good in her. She had a naughty streak, for sure—her diary makes that clear too—but she was a good person. A person worthy of my father's love…a love that never waned.

But it's private—something my father entrusted to me and me alone.

'Can I ask you something, Granny?'

She looks back at me. 'Of course, child.'

'Why did you dislike my mother so much?'

She's so still and for a second I don't think she's heard me, or she's blanked out, her meds doing something weird, but then she blinks and looks towards the window.

'It wasn't that I disliked her. She just wasn't right for your father—for the Laurens. She was too wild, too young. She was eighteen when Robert brought her home after they eloped.' She shakes her head. 'He *knew* we'd never accept her—not with her… her *occupation*—so he ran away. He figured we'd have no choice but to accept then, that we'd rather not have a divorce on our hands. The press had already had a field day over us—imagine adding a divorce to it.'

'But they were in love,' I say. 'What did it matter that she was a stripper?'

Granny's eyes dart to mine.

'What?' I say, seeing the horror in her gaze. 'It's what she was.'

'Do you have to *say* it?' Her tone is hushed, as though we're in a public room with a judgemental audience listening in. 'How can you ask me that? You're twenty-four—you've been brought up to be a Lauren through and through. You of all people should know that it's not acceptable.'

I shake my head, sadness overwhelming me. 'It doesn't mean that she wasn't a good person, or that she loved Daddy any less.'

I'm a good person and I attend the very kind of clubs you abhor, dear Granny, but it doesn't mean I love you any less.

'Love is for fools,' she quips. 'Look at your brother and the way Clara takes advantage of his love.'

'But at least my parents were happy; you can't say the same for Daddy's second marriage.'

She balks at my mention of it, such is our shared dislike of my stepmother, but I'm not giving in.

'If we go by your standards, that marriage should have been perfect. She had her own money, her own status, and look how unhappy they were.'

Granny's eyes cloud over, and I know some of my words are sinking in.

'And you know why, don't you?' I push on.

She looks back to the window, like it will save her from where I'm heading.

'Granny…?'

She waves a hand at me to stop and it trembles. She looks so weak, so frail, the strength she's mustered to sit up straight seeping from her body as she starts to hunch. I know my father's death weighs heavily on her, that she has always struggled to come to terms with outliving her only child. And I know that talk of his misery in later years will make that pain more acute, but I can't stop. I need to say it.

'Because he never got over my mother—just like you never got over Grandpapa.'

She blinks rapidly and I know she's fighting back the weakness of tears—that even in front of me she doesn't feel able to show that level of humanity. It frustrates the hell out of me, and my own emotions are bubbling so close to the surface that I want to scream them free.

'Yes. And the pain of loving someone,' she says quietly, 'only to lose them, is a burden I wouldn't wish on anyone.'

'*Really*, Granny?' I can't hide my impassioned disbelief. 'You'd really rather never have known that happiness with someone than go through the pain?'

She doesn't answer. She's still focusing trance-like on the window.

'You were so lucky to find what you did with Grandpapa,' I say. 'And Daddy was so lucky to find it with my mother. I'd give anything for that.'

She looks back at me, shaking her head, her eyes bittersweet. 'For ever the romantic, aren't you? I've always worried it will get you in trouble.'

She reaches out to cup my cheek, her bony hand cold against the heat of my skin.

'You have such a big heart…but you have your mother's wild streak in you too.'

'Is that such a bad thing?' I ask softly.

There's a rap at the door that saves her from answering and I push off the bed to open it, knowing it will be Sue with brunch. There's no use fighting this out with Granny. I don't even know what I'm fighting for. To clear my mother's name? To lift the shackles of the Lauren name? I mean, Christ, it's the twenty-first century—who gives a toss about family reputations any more?

I look back at Granny as I pull open the door for Sue. Above Granny's bed is a painting of my great-great-great-grandmother, all prim and perfect. I can see myself in her, I can see Granny in her and I realise that this is what it's about. A legacy that exists long after we're gone, a part of us that travels through the generations.

That's why I can't fight her.

Because I get it.

But I want to live my life too. I want to be happy.

Why can't I have it all?

I smile at Sue as she brings in the laden tray and my mind is catapulted back to another tray, another person offering it up, and my body warms. My heart swells.

I'm an old romantic, Granny's right, and now that I've found a man worthy of loving, have had a glimpse of happiness with him, a glimpse of what the future might look like, I'm going after it.

I just need to make him realise he wants it too and then we can work out the rest together—his job, the public, all of it.

CHAPTER NINE

COCO'S BEEN GONE an hour, tops, and I've been staring at my computer screen, revisiting everything I know of her…of the Laurens. The Duchess's illness, guesstimates of the estate value, including their private wealth, and the business Philip continues to run. Facts, figures—tangible things that I can work with.

But none of it eases the weird angst inside me. I'm edgy beyond reason, and if I stop focusing for a second Coco fills my vision, taking over and making it personal—*too* personal.

I open up an article I have bookmarked and there she is, looking exquisite in a slinky silver number, attending a red-carpet event. Just beneath is a picture of her parents, Robert and Elizabeth Lauren, taken when they were a similar age to what Coco is now.

I keep on reading, even though I've read it multiple times before. It feels more important now—more crucial to my understanding of her and what Philip can hope to gain.

It makes for tragic reading. The sullied reputation of her mother, the open disapproval of her parents' marriage as a result and the sudden death of Elizabeth in a car crash. And her father's second marriage was reputed to have been fiery at best.

I imagine what Coco's life has been like—trying to avoid censure, the kind of slander her mother suffered, coping with the derogatory press coverage of her father's second marriage. Hell, it even makes me feel sorry for Philip, who grew up through it all.

It doesn't excuse his behaviour now, though. Or his mission to ruin her.

And I can say that because I've been there. I lived through it when my father was arrested. It was the biggest case of fraud the country had seen in years and my father was splashed through the media—us too, for a time.

I still don't understand why her brother wants to taint their family name with more scandal. Maybe it's for blackmail purposes or maybe it's something far simpler. I know I said it outright to Coco, but does her brother hope that by ruining her reputation he can somehow get her pushed out, disinherited, cut off? That would explain the timescale pressures, with the Duchess so sick.

My eyes fall from the screen as I shake my head. I can't get my head around it.

She's gone through enough already. Losing her parents. Soon to lose her grandmother. How can her brother be seeking to ruin her too?

I press my fist to my mouth and breathe through the rage clouding my brain; rage doesn't get me any closer to finding answers.

I look at my phone. How long has it been since I instructed my researchers to dig up everything they could on Philip? Thirteen hours at most. Hardly long enough. But a quick chase-up won't hurt.

I snatch it up, but it illuminates before I can do anything, ringing through the quiet.

Philip.

I fight the urge to throw the damn thing down and take another controlled breath before putting it to my ear.

'Philip.'

'Where did she go last night?'

'Hello to you too.' I sit back in my seat, my eyes on the screen, on her. 'She was already under the radar by the time I left you.' That was no lie.

'Have you checked out that club?'

'I swung by.'

'And?'

'And you can't just walk into a club like that and get details—it's going to take time.'

'For fuck's sake, Livingston, I've paid you a fortune already and you've got me sod all.'

'Like I said last night, I can walk away from this and you can find yourself some other—'

'No, no, it's fine. Just watch her. She has a charity gig tonight at the Savoy. Why don't you follow her after? She'll have had a few drinks… She'll be looking for a good time.'

I clench the phone tighter, my hand pulsing around it. I hate the way he says it. But is he right? Would she go to Blacks? Or would she come to me?

The latter was the safest option…for her.

Yeah, you're only thinking of her.

I ignore the mental gibe and focus on my next move. I have her number. I could text, arrange to meet…

'Livingston? You there?'

'I'll be there.'

I go to cut the line, not wanting to listen to his plummy, irritating-as-fuck tone any more, but then I stop.

'And, Philip?'

'Yes?'

'Get off my back or you'll definitely be finding yourself someone else.'

I hear his blustering down the line and my smile is cold as I hang up. People like Philip Lauren respond to a firm hand. The firmer I am, the more he will listen. The second I look weak, he will pounce.

Then I launch Coco's contact details and send a text.

Why don't I pick you up from the event tonight… bring you back to mine? Ash

Her response is swift.

Midnight. Savoy. Don't be late. My dress will turn to rags.

I smile at her *Cinderella* reference.

You could be in a bin liner and I'd still want you. No need to worry about the pumpkin. I'll bring my big, strong, safe car around the back. Tradesman's entrance. ;-)

I can't believe I've just added a wink to a text. I'm still questioning it when her response pops up.

Great. See you then. PS did you get my number from my fairy godmother?

Shit. I think fast.

I won't tell Jackson you called him that. He might bar you.

I'm rewarded with a laughing emoji and an *X*.

I fire an *X* in response and lean back in my chair, realising I'm grinning like a bloody idiot.

But I don't care.

She's safe from Philip for another night and that's what matters.

I've never been more glad to leave an event in my life. I'm like a kid on Christmas morning, giddy and hyper as I sweep through the remaining guests and make for the doors. I've already had a text from Ash saying he's here and I can't wait to see him.

I know how I look. I'm wearing my favourite silver dress—low at the back, high at the front, but with a daring split to the thigh to make up for it. I feel sexy, and I know that's because of him, the way he makes me feel, the things he says, the way he looks at me.

And he listens. *Really* listens. He's not just eyeing me, pondering what he can get. Christ, part of me wishes he was—then I could coax him into something public, something more certain. But I'm not going to debate that now. I'm going to enjoy what I can have: him, naked and beneath me.

I have to ask a passing waiter for directions to the tradesman's entrance and I expect his brow to hit the roof. I mean, I'm giggling like a schoolgirl as I ask. I could blame the champagne but it's not that. I'm drunk on Ash and what the night has in store.

He points me in the right direction and I'm off, as fast as a person can travel on heels as high as mine. Even the weight of 'will we or won't we have a future together' has left me. All I care about is the here and now—and he is definitely *here.*

I thrust at the bar that's holding the double doors shut and burst out onto the street. His car is there, neon headlamps shining, and my heart soars into my throat.

Yes.

I shove the doors back into place and the car door opens. He steps out and I lift the skirt of my dress as I walk faster than the front slit will allow.

He's a silhouette against the lights, his tall, imposing frame so *him*. It's starting to rain, but I barely notice as I come to a stop in front of him and tilt my head back to meet his eyes.

‘Hi,’ I say—and his lips are on mine, feverish, urgent.

The rain starts to pick up, its patter as rapid as my pulse, ruining my hair, my make-up, but I couldn’t care less. All I think about is him, his hands hot on the bare skin of my back, his heat mixing with the wet specks of rain as I kiss him harder. He’s all minty fresh and delicious and I want more. I want it all. He’s missed me. I can feel it. Just as I’ve missed him.

The rain starts to pound, pelting the car, the ground, us. He wraps me tighter against him and breaks his mouth away.

‘Come on—before we get caught doing something we shouldn’t.’

I laugh, delirious on the rush he’s kicked up within me, and hurry in step with him to the passenger door. He pulls it open and helps me in, before closing it and racing around to his side. I get a brief glimpse of him in the headlamps: rakish stubble, shorn hair, strong jaw, glinting gaze, rain running down his face and dressed all in black… I smile.

The second he jumps in, I lean across and kiss his cheek. ‘Thank you for coming.’

He catches my face in his palm, holding me there, his eyes ablaze and all the more intense with the rain beading on his lashes.

‘Any time.’

He strokes away the dampness on my cheeks as I inhale his words. *If only it could be.*

He sweeps over my lips with his thumb, his lips, then settles back into his seat, running a hand over his face and hair to dry it off before buckling himself in.

I do the same. 'You think you could do this every night?' I'm only half joking.

He grins as he puts the car in Reverse. 'For as long as you want me to.'

I give a soft smile. I can't imagine never wanting this—him at my beck and call.

Ten minutes into the journey and neither of us has spoken further. The rain is lashing down, the wipers are beating it back, making him frown with concentration. I haven't wanted to distract him and, to be honest, I'm enjoying the view.

'What?' he suddenly says, flicking me a look.

'Hmm…?'

'You've been smiling like the cat that got the cream ever since you got in.'

I reach out and place my hand on his thigh, squeezing softly. 'It kind of feels that way.'

His leg tenses beneath me and I see his jaw pulse. 'You need to move your hand before I have to pull over.'

I laugh, the sound husky and loaded with the imaginings that have been keeping me company so far, and he looks at me briefly, shaking his head.

'How was the ball?'

'Are you trying to distract me?'

'Yes.'

I pout and pull my hand away. 'It was good. I think we stand a chance of raising more than we anticipated.'

'That's good.' His eyes are fixed ahead now, as he drives. 'Did your brother go?'

My laugh is harsh this time. 'My brother would see it as a waste of his time. If there's nothing in it for him, he doesn't see the point.'

He nods, his fists flexing around the wheel. 'You're very different?'

'We share our father's DNA—that's as close as it gets.'

He has successfully managed to kill my mood. Especially since I have no intention of returning home tonight, and that will lead to further questions from Philip tomorrow. In front of Granny, of course.

'If he had his way he'd see me out of his life for good.'

I expect him to scoff. Instead he frowns at me, serious, concerned. 'That's a bit extreme.'

'Not for him. He'd probably have me dead if it wouldn't dirty his hands too much.'

'That's ridiculous—you can't mean that.'

Did she? No, she guessed not. But… 'He'd see me thrown out of the family without a penny—I know that much.'

'What makes you think that?'

I shift in the seat and smooth out my dress. I feel his eyes flick to my exposed thigh, to the slit that won't be tamed now I'm seated, and he swallows as he looks back to the windscreen. His obvious desire warms me, helps to beat back the chill of our conversation. Cait is the only one with whom I've ever really discussed Philip and his obvious dislike of me.

'He puts a lot of effort into picking apart my flaws for Granny's benefit. Take this morning, for example. The fact I hadn't returned home last night was his topic of conversation when I arrived to visit her.'

'You're a grown woman.' His fists flex around the steering wheel again as he presses himself back in the seat. 'What business is it of his?'

'It's not my lack of homecoming that bothers him. It's what he thinks I've been up to with my time. He'll do anything to have my reputation pulled apart in Granny's eyes.'

'But *why*?'

I shrug. 'To get me written out of her will, pushed out of the family, named and shamed… Take your pick.'

'But your grandmother loves you,' he says softly, clearly finding my reasoning hard to believe. 'Surely she wouldn't take his snide remarks as a reason to cut you off?'

I look out of the passenger window as I consider his question. 'She loves me in so much as she can, but she'll always put the Lauren name first. The family heritage.' I blow out a breath as I turn back to him. 'It sounds crazy, but it's true. "A Lauren must be above reproach."'

I mimic her voice as I quote her and smile. He doesn't return it.

'Sounds cold to me.'

My smile fades. 'It's not her fault. She's a product of her time. It's not Philip's either—not really. He grew up in my shadow; our father always sided with me…doted on me. I was his last connection to my mother and… Well, Philip's mother also struggled with the same inferiority. She was never good enough either. But that was made worse by her nature.'

'Her nature?'

'She's always out for what she can get—Clara too.'

'Clara?'

'Philip's wife.' I grimace as I say it. I can't help it. Her callous, money-grabbing ways are so obvious to everyone but Philip. 'I think he'd grant her anything to keep her happy, to keep her love, if you can call it that.'

'And you really excuse Philip's behaviour because of them?'

I shrug. I know it's hard for him to accept—for anyone to accept, really—but we grew up together. I saw my brother's suffering first-hand and I see his continued suffering now.

He meets my eye briefly. 'So what will you tell them when they ask where you've been tonight?'

'Same as this morning. I stayed at a friend's… And I'll tell them that every night this week if you'll have me.'

CHAPTER TEN

WHEN COCO SAID *every night*, I didn't believe her. I took it as some sort of ploy to get the conversation off Philip and onto us.

But it's now Thursday, five days since the charity ball, and it's the seventh night we've spent together in a row.

I trail my hands along her bare side as she curls into me and presses a kiss to my chest.

'I think you know my every sweet spot,' she murmurs sleepily, and my lips find her hair, breathing in her familiar scent as I kiss the ruffled mass.

'I should hope so.'

It's one thirty in the morning. She'll be up again in five hours. Just like she has been every weekday morning, so that she can get back home, hit the gym and visit her grandmother before she starts another rammed day.

She doesn't rest unless she's sleeping—a fact I've ribbed her about—but she simply shrugs it off.

'Now, sleep,' I say, stretching out my free arm to tap off the bedside lamp.

She's gone in seconds. There's a telltale twitch to her body, a steady rhythm to her breathing. I'm not, though. The longer this goes on for, the bigger my lie—*no*, my omission—gets.

I tell myself I'm looking after her, putting her best interests first. But the more I care, the more I know my reasoning is twisted. Because, yes, I'm doing this for *her*, but I can't deny how much it works for me too. How much I'm enjoying our time together. No matter how borrowed that time is.

And I know it is. Philip is getting twitchier by the day. There's only so long I can keep stringing him along. But I'm getting closer to understanding him. I have enough information to understand the poor state of his finances now, and to know that his wife's spending habits are exacerbating the situation.

I know the family business is struggling too, and that he's under pressure to resign. It appears that Philip has a loose tongue, and the information his golf buddies have been privy to over the years has benefitted them greatly—his company not so much.

How he didn't see the pattern, I don't know, but it's enough to see that pressure to resign becoming an insistence. And Philip won't want that. To be forced out of the company his father left to him would be the ultimate humiliation. And it's the kind of ammunition I need to ensure he stays the hell away from Coco.

And the guy doesn't need her money, surely. Yes, it doesn't come cheap managing the estate he stands to inherit with his title, but there's the Lauren money too. The private wealth, investments, property, including the London residence in which they spend the majority of their time alongside their ailing grandmother. That house alone is worth a fortune even by today's standards. But it truly begs the question: Why sink so low as to go after his sister's money anyway? If that truly is his aim as Coco seems to surmise.

Maybe there's more to it than just money? Resentment, perhaps? By her own admission she was always her father's favoured child, and her parents' marriage was happy, full of love. The same can't be said for the household Philip was raised in.

Or maybe a guy like Philip can never have enough money.

I'd certainly seen enough of that in my time. Clive was a prime example.

But what did it matter at the end of the day? I'm almost ready to turn the tables on Philip. To fight dirt with dirt and get him off Coco's case.

Then I can tackle the truth of what this is between us and whether we have a chance—because it's getting harder by the day to imagine life without her in it.

'What's wrong?'

Her voice startles me, and I realise I'm gripping her tightly. I force my hand to relax, my body too.

'I thought you were asleep.'

'I was.'

Her head moves against me and I can just make out her eyes in the darkness, looking up at me.

'And then you seemed to stop breathing. What's wrong?'

'Nothing.'

'I don't believe you.'

'Nothing for you to worry about at any rate.'

'If it's bothering you, then it bothers me.'

I can hear how much she cares in her voice and guilt claws through my chest.

Just bide your time. You can tell her when she's safe.

I nudge her lips with my own. 'It can wait. Now, go back to sleep. You've another full-on day tomorrow.'

She groans. 'Don't remind me. I'm not sure what's worse—the fact that I have back-to-back meetings or a family dinner to contend with.'

The family dinner gets my vote.

'Just tell your brother you can't make it.'

'I can't. He wants to discuss Granny's care and we're all going—his wife, his mother… I want to be there and make sure they're doing right by her.'

She falls quiet but her fingers are toying with the hair on my chest, betraying her active brain. Is she worrying about the meal? Her grandmother's health? The future?

'Ash?'

'Hmm…?'

'Pick me up after? I should be done by ten at the latest.'

I smile at her soft request. 'Of course.'

Whatever she's thinking about, worrying over,

the fact that she still wants me there at the end of it makes everything feel okay, even though it shouldn't.

Dinner is all one would expect from a Michelin-starred restaurant, but I'm not really tasting anything. The starter was swallowed in silence, the main amidst a smattering of small talk. Clara looks bored beyond measure and I'm doing my utmost to ignore my darling stepmother. I'm eager to get the night over with, so I can make my excuses and hurry back to Ash.

I'm more tired than usual too, and I know I have our nightly antics to thank for that, but dealing with the force that is my brother and the women flanking him is always hard work. His mother even now is raking a critical eye over me and sending the hairs on the backs of my exposed arms prickling. I rub them and do my best to ignore her.

'Are you cold?' Clara asks me, frowning at the move.

'A little.'

His mother sips her wine and offers me a disparaging smile. 'Perhaps if you dressed more appropriately you wouldn't be.'

'You ought to know,' I snap, regretting it as soon as it's out.

My dress is an elegant sleeveless black number, down to the knee, nothing indecent about it. She's just getting at me. But fighting with my stepmother never did me any favours. Normally I can ignore her, but not tonight. This meeting has me on edge and I want it over.

'But we're not here to discuss my attire, are we? We're here for Granny. So why don't we get that out of the way and then we can all get back to our lives?'

'Goodness, you make it sound like it's such an inconvenience, having to talk about your grandmother.' My stepmother looks to Philip. 'Doesn't she, darling?'

'Yes.' His eyes narrow on me. 'Have you someplace else you need to be, Coco?'

I feel my cheeks colour. I know they're baiting me, and I shouldn't rise to it, but it's so hard. Especially having endured them for over an hour already, with their mundane sniping at people about whom they have the pleasure of gossiping.

'It seems you're rarely at home these days,' he continues. 'And I've heard some interesting tales on the grapevine as to what has you so occupied.'

Is he serious? Could he know about Ash? Or is this just another gibe? A continuation of his questioning over my whereabouts in front of Granny?

Both his mother and Clara look from him to me, smiles that send my blood cold playing on their lips. I try to ignore them.

'I've been home enough to spend time with Granny—that's all that matters.'

'You've been just as doting as ever.' He nods, overly sincere. 'As have I, for that matter. But it isn't enough—hence this meeting.'

My sudden panic about Ash morphs into a greater fear now. 'What do you mean?'

'I don't think her living at the London residence any longer is a good idea.'

'But it's her favoured home. It's close to her oncologist, her friends, the h—'

He waves his hand to cut me off. 'You misunderstand me. I think we need to convince her that a hospital—a specialist hospice unit—would be a better place...more comfortable—'

'Is this your doing?' I blurt at my stepmother, my stomach churning over. There's no way my brother would have come to this conclusion alone. He's not *that* heartless.

'Calm down, Coco,' my brother orders. 'It benefits us all to know that Granny is taken care of properly 24/7. She can't even tackle the stairs on her own any more.'

'So? We'll convert a room downstairs for her—one that gives her access to the garden and the—'

'Don't be ridiculous, dear. Which room are you suggesting? The drawing room? The garden room? The library?' My stepmother shakes her head, her perfectly coiffed hair unmoving. 'All that medical equipment will ruin the house; you'd need handrails put in, and there's no bathroom downstairs for her to use. And all for the sake of—what? A month? Maybe two?'

I don't want to listen to her. I don't want to listen to any of them.

'But she wants to be at home—she's *asked* to stay at home.'

'Yes, but our summer soirée is next month and how can we possibly consider holding that with your grandmother under the same roof…or not, as the case maybe.' She sips at her wine, calm as you like, and looks pointedly at Philip.

I stare at her in disbelief. She can't be serious. She wants to put the location of the Lauren annual bash above… No, it cannot be. 'You're not serious?'

'Of course, we can't exactly hold it somewhere else, we always have it in London,' Clara chips in. 'It's convenient to all. Not to mention it's a family tradition.'

'And we know how your grandmother is about tradition,' my stepmother adds.

'*Christ*, have some bloody compassion,' I snap.

She doesn't even smart. 'Compassion only makes one weak, and we know how she feels about *that* too.'

Philip doesn't say a word, only eyes his glass as he rolls the stem of it in his fingers.

'Philip, seriously, you know this isn't right?'

'*Philip* will do what is best for him and his soon-to-be title, he will be the Duke of Rushford and, as such, he needs to start taking the lead at these functions. The soirée is the perfect beginning.'

'But…but she's not even dead yet.'

Philip's eyes lift to mine, a crease between his brows. There's a twisted kind of torment in his face and it betrays his inner fight with what is right and what he is being told.

Clara reaches across the table, her hand resting on his wrist and drawing his attention. 'Come on, darling, it's time you did what you were born to do: take control.'

She runs her teeth over her bottom lip and looks at him adoringly. I can see the power-hungry glint in her eye. She doesn't love him. She only loves what he can give her, and he has fallen for it. Fallen for what I myself have always sought to avoid.

'Please, Philip,' I say, calling his attention back to me. 'Don't do this.'

'It will suit Granny better to be cared for in a specialist unit.' There is no emotion to his voice as he drags his eyes to mine. 'It would be better—easier—if you talk to her, convince her it's the right thing to do.'

I shake my head. I can't listen to any more, can't witness the manipulation that's so obviously in play.

'No, I won't do it. It's her home. She has a right to die there.'

My eyes start to sting and blur, turning them into blobs rather than people. I plant my napkin on my plate and stand. I won't give them the satisfaction of seeing me cry.

'Sit down, child,' my stepmother hisses. 'Dessert is just coming—you're making a scene.'

I blink back the tears and give her a scathing smile. 'I hope for your sake that Philip doesn't learn by your example, because if natural order has its way, there'll come a time when *you'll* be the dying one and he'll be shovelling *you* off to an alien environment against your wishes.'

'Well, really…' she huffs but I'm already looking to Clara now.

'And as for you, I'm not blind to what you are. One day the veil will lift and Philip will see it too, then you'll get what you deserve.'

Her gasp of outrage fills my ears as I turn away and I take some comfort from it. I've hit my mark. But I can't bring myself to say anything more to Philip. I need to be gone.

I need Ash.

My distraction.

It used to be Blacks. Now it's him.

I get that I've only swapped one kind of escapism for another, and that this one has the power to hurt me down the road, but right now I can't worry about that.

I just need him.

I know Coco's upset. Her message tells me so by its urgency.

She's asked me to pick her up two streets down from the restaurant and here I am, parked up and waiting.

I'm surprised she's not here already. And then I spy her, scanning the road for cars, for me. She's pale, sad, her eyes glistening and killing me even from this distance. She sweeps a shaky hand through her hair as she weaves through the pedestrians, the evening rush thick as ever in London.

I reach for the door handle, ready to go and get her, too impatient to wait for her to find me—and then freeze. My eyes zone in on someone else a few beats behind her.

Shit.

My blood runs cold.

Eric Bower.

My number-one rival. I lean back in my seat, as though at any moment he's going to look straight at me and piece it all together.

I try to tell myself it's just a coincidence—that the fact he's walking in the same direction means nothing. But it's bull. Everything about his overly casual stride and wandering eye tell me he's on a job. And what are the chances he's after someone else in the vicinity?

Coco pauses and pulls out her phone.

Bower turns to scan a florist's window.

No, it's no coincidence.

Fuck you, Philip.

I punch the edge of the steering wheel and start the ignition, pulling out into traffic before she can see me. The system in my car announces an incoming text message, and I know it's from her even before I instruct it to read it out loud.

Where are you? I'm here... X

My head drops and I grimace, frustration, anger, guilt making me clench the steering wheel tighter. I try to ease the tension in my shoulders, tell myself

I'll be there for her soon. But I hate it that I've just abandoned her when I know she needs me.

I pull over as soon as I'm out of sight, much to the displeasure of the people in the car behind me, and they honk, but I'm already taking my phone out, my brain racing. Where's safe? Where can I meet her and not have Bower on her tail?

I grip the back of my neck as I think. Blacks—it has to be. Philip already knows she goes there. So long as I stay out of sight and get her to come to me we'll be fine.

I fire off a reply.

Change of plan. Something came up. Meet me at Blacks?

I can't breathe as I wait for her response. What if she tells me to go to hell? But why would she? To her, I've just been held up. I haven't run away because her brother has a second PI on her tail.

Her response is swift.

Okay. XX

The *XX* pulses, stabbing up at me from the screen. Projecting guilt and affection in one.

Time is running out. It won't take long for Bower to know what I know, even with me being careful. We tap into the same resources; it only takes one misplaced word, a flippant comment, and he'll figure things out.

Worse still, it only takes her appearing at my home when I don't expect it—just like she did that Friday night—with Bower on her tail and our relationship will be outed.

I toss the phone onto the passenger seat and pull back into the traffic. I just need to keep things under my control a little while longer and then I can worry about what comes next.

But how, with Bower so close?

Get out of London. Take her away.

It's possible. I have the resources to sneak her out and I have the perfect place too. I'm long-overdue a visit there myself.

But would she come?

I don't like how disappointed I feel at Ash's change of plan.

I know it's not his fault that I've become dependent on him to keep reality at bay. But the second I get his text asking to meet at Blacks instead, the tears escape and I'm drawing attention. The kind I don't need—the kind I'm usually good at keeping at bay.

I pull my coat up around my ears and pick up my pace, heading for the Underground, where I can blend into the background easily enough.

I'll be with him soon; I can lose myself in him and he'll make everything feel okay again.

But for how long?

You can't keep seeking distraction; you have to face reality sooner or later. Granny's dying and you can't change it.

I close my eyes over the pang of pain and realise that's not all I'm running from.

It's my feelings for him too. The risk that he won't feel the same way, that I won't be able to convince him to give us a shot. My feet stall and my heart pulses as my stomach turns over. What if I have to let him go?

I shake my head and focus through a teary haze.

Shit.

I'm being watched. Several passers-by frown in my direction, and a guy's trying to look like he's not, but I see him watching me anyway. Probably a reporter, looking for his latest scoop.

Fuck.

I must look insane, with my mental argument written on my face, and tears too.

I take a breath and move.

Get to Blacks. To Ash.

The rest can come later—much later. Alone, if I have to.

CHAPTER ELEVEN

'THREE VISITS IN one month?' Jackson's brows almost hit the overhanging glassware as I approach the bar. 'This has to be a record, Ash.'

I'm in no mood for his teasing and he clocks that quickly enough. He says no more as he turns away and pulls down two shot glasses and goes for a bottle.

'Save it.' I hold my palm out to him as I slide onto one of his swanky high-backed bar stools. 'Not to-night.'

He turns back to me and rests his elbows on the bar, leaning in to look at me properly. 'Jesus, what is it this time?'

'I need your help.'

'You're telling me? I thought you were finally get-ting some…putting a smile back on that grim face of yours—you certainly looked—'

I shake my head and he stops short. 'What do you need?'

'You found your leak yet?'

'No. People talk—it might simply be a case of

Chinese whispers getting out of hand—but I have my people looking into some of our newer members.'

'Sounds wise.' I pull out my phone and pull up a photo of Bower. 'You had any enquiry from this guy? The name's Bower—Eric Bower?'

He frowns at the screen. 'No. Should I have?'

'He's a PI. I think that bastard Philip Lauren's hired him.'

He cocks a brow. 'In addition to you?'

I nod. 'I wouldn't give him what he needs so he's obviously decided to get someone else on the case.'

'Why do I get the feeling it's not occupational pride that bothers you?'

I swallow. I wish I'd taken up his offer of a drink. I need the hit. I also need something to do with my hands, which are constantly fisting and flexing. But not only do I need to drive, I need my wits about me to ensure we're not tailed.

'She doesn't deserve any of this.'

'No,' Jackson says. 'I tried to tell you that.'

'Yeah, well…consider me told.'

'You're more than told,' he says, squinting into my eyes like he can see right through me. 'You're falling for her, aren't you?'

I shove up from the stool and turn away from him. 'Don't be ridiculous.'

'I haven't seen you this on edge since… Well, since that shit went down ten years ago.'

I flick him a look. I want to flip him the bird too, but, hell, I know he's right. Not that talking about it, thinking about it, is going to help right now.

'Look, she's coming here soon. Do me a favour and send her down to the garage on the quiet? I don't know whether you have a leak or not, and I hope for your sake you don't, but…'

'You don't want to risk it getting out?'

'Yeah.'

'No problem.' He straightens and gives me an assured grin. 'Get yourself down there; you won't be disturbed unless it's her.'

'Thanks, mate, I owe you.'

'And for what it's worth, Ash…' he says.

I've started to head off but I look back at him, knowing I should probably keep on going.

'I'm happy for you. She's a great girl.'

'And she could do a lot better than me.'

He shakes his head, but I'm gone, heading towards the private access that leads to the basement car park. The same way I took her out of the club the other night. Can that really be only a week ago? So much has changed since then…and yet nothing.

I'm still the man hired to dish the dirt on her—on the face of it, at least. But now my focus has changed, my goal is reversed, and navigating that while trying to protect her is messing with my head. Not my heart. Because I can't be in love with her—not yet. Falling, yes. Getting in deep, yes. But in love…?

I slam open the door and sprint down the stairs, wishing I could keep on running, sprint until my lungs burn, until that's all I can think of. Not this crazy confusion and the fear that it's sparked.

No one falls in love this quickly—*no one.*

* * *

Blacks is bustling when I get there and sweep inside, my feet eager to take me to him. Eager to get me out of the public domain, away from the fear of exposure, of saying or doing the wrong thing when my emotions are riding so high.

I enter the main bar area—the place where I first saw him—my eyes desperately scanning, but he's not there. Disappointment fires anew and I take out my phone to send him a text.

'Coco?'

I look up to see Jackson heading towards me, smiling.

'Hey.' I try to smile back but I know it's shaky, and my voice is trembling in its simple greeting.

'Ash is waiting for you downstairs.'

My heart skips. *He's here. Thank God, he's here.*

'This way.'

He gestures for me to follow him. 'Thank you.'

He walks me to the door that leads down to his private parking garage and opens it for me. 'Give him my regards.'

'Will do.' My smile is real now, my voice solid.

Not even my heels can stop me racing down the stairs, and as I burst out into the car park he's there, leaning against the bonnet of his car. He straightens as soon as he sees me, his reassuring form like a welcome beacon, and I run to him.

I don't care about putting up a front, about manners or dignity, only that he's here, and I can let go.

His brow furrows, his eyes question, but he holds

his arms out to me and then I am in them, and I'm kissing him with all the passion and the emotion that's overflowing inside me. And I pray he doesn't stop me—not until I'm ready.

But he isn't stopping. His hands fork in my hair and his mouth is as hungry as my own. He spins me so I'm pushed up against the car, his hands raking feverishly beneath my coat as I grapple with his clothing.

This is what I need. This all-consuming passion that blots all else out. I have no idea how private this garage is. But I'm guessing only Jackson has access, and he's upstairs, and I don't want to stop to ask.

'I've missed you,' I say against his lips.

'I've missed you too.'

The confirmation, the resonance of his tone with mine—it's everything and more.

'Nothing hurts when I'm with you.'

He stills, his hands midway to cupping my breasts. 'What's happened?'

'I don't want to talk about it—not now. Make me forget, Ash.'

He presses his forehead into mine, his blazing blue eyes burning through me. I drop my hand to the bulge in his jeans and squeeze. Air hisses between his teeth.

'That's a dirty move—'

'Too many words.' I cut off his retort with my tongue, dipping inside his mouth, grazing his teeth.

His growl is feral as he pulls my thigh up, exposing the lace tops of my hold-ups and his fingers graze over the detail, his eyes too. 'You have no idea how much I want you right now.'

'Then take me.'

His eyes lock with mine. 'Here?'

I nod—swift, fierce. 'Please.'

His lip quirks. I can see he wants to, *feel* he wants to.

'Do you have protection?' he asks.

Fuck.

'No.'

He clamps his eyes shut and I can feel him forcing his body to stand down.

'But I'm clean.'

He opens his eyes at my assurance, stares into me like he can't believe what I'm saying.

'I'm on the pill…and we have to be tested, don't we, to be members here?' I look up to the ceiling, to the club above. 'You?'

'Coco…' He shakes his head like he's battling some momentous decision.

'I *trust* you.'

His eyes burn into mine and take my breath away. There is so much there. And I'm not just talking heat, desire. I'm talking pain. For what, I don't know. I just know that sex will make it stop, for him and for me, at least in the now.

I cup his jaw in both hands, stroke my thumbs over his stubble. 'I *need* you.' I hook my leg around his waist, pull his hardness up against me and stroke my body over him. *'Now.'*

He drags in a breath, ragged and raw. His eyes fall

to where our bodies meet, where I continue to ride his clothed hardness, and his hands take hold of my hips, gripping me tight.

'What are you doing to me?'

'This.' My hands fall to his jeans, popping open the button. 'If you'll have me.'

His head is shaking. 'I'll always have you.'

My breath catches… My eyes sting. But now isn't the time for tears. 'Good.'

I slide down his zipper, my teeth scraping over my bottom lip as I reach inside his briefs and pull him out. He's hot, thick and throbbing.

Oh, yes.

He ducks his head, takes my mouth with his, and I pump my hand over him, loving how his entire body trembles, his breath shudders, his lips lose traction with mine.

He thrusts his hands up my thighs, my dress bunched within his grasp, and I tilt my pelvis higher as I lower his cock to me, slipping aside my thong as I go.

I'm so wet his head slides in with ease, slipping past my clit, parting my lips, and inside… I throw my head back as I accept him in one blissfully sharp thrust. He's so perfect, so hot and hard as he fills me, and I clench around him tight.

'Coco…' He groans, his body stilling, his length buried within me.

I open my eyes, stare up at him. He's trying to fight, to keep control.

'Let go with me, Ash.'

I move over him, one hand pulling his head down, bringing his mouth to mine, the other pressing down between us, my fingers forking either side of his cock, buried deep within me, enjoying the feel of him there, coated in my wetness, before I pull back to circle over my clit.

I whimper into his mouth, my body shuddering around him as I let ripples of ecstasy work their way from my core to the tips of my toes. He lifts me against him, draws my other leg up and around him as he presses my body back against the car and finds his rhythm, swift and fierce, driving me crazy.

I raise my free hand to his face, run my thumb over his lips, and he dips his mouth over it, tongues it, sucks it back as his eyes lock with mine. All heat and fire. No pain. Not now.

He nips at my palm with his teeth and then flicks his head back, his neck cording with tension. His climax is coming and I'm wrapped up in his pleasure, my fingers picking up their pace over my clit.

'Fuck, Coco...*Coco...*' His eyes lock back onto mine, his thrusts turn jagged, and I grip him tighter between my thighs.

'Yes, Ash.'

Pleasure explodes through me, through him. His release is hot and pulsing, so raw and intense within me. His groan echoes off the brick walls and I cling to him, my head dropping into the crook of his neck, my body unwilling to let him go, my mind unwilling to let the outside world back in.

I listen to his heart pounding, to the rasp of his

breath as it starts to steady and slow. He lowers me to my feet and I can feel him slip out. *No.*

I look up at him, regret clear in my face as I say, 'Now I wish we were in bed.'

He gives a soft laugh as I scoop tissues from my jacket pocket and help him out with the mess.

'Lucky no one walked in on us,' I say, making conversation while I scan the car park for a bin.

'Jackson said he'd keep it secure.'

He takes the tissues from me and walks off to the corner of the garage, clearly knowing his way around. I watch him go, admiring his firm behind in his jeans, the sheer masculinity in the breadth of his shoulders, the severe cut of his hair. A fresh ripple of desire runs through me, centring around my heart.

He gets rid of the tissues and turns back to me, his stride faltering as he cocks a brow at me. 'What?'

I smile. I can tell he's read it all on my face. 'Nothing.'

His smile is tentative, questioning, as he closes the distance, pulling me against him once I'm within reach.

'Nothing?' he says, looking down into my eyes.

'I was just so sad earlier…' I stroke his cheekbones, his hair, raking my eyes over his face and seeing all that I'm falling for looking back at me.

'And now?'

'It's still there, but it's easier when you're with me.' He squeezes me against him tighter. 'Does that sound weird?' I ask.

'No, it makes perfect sense.'

Does that mean he feels it too? Is that why he understands? I wish it could be that. I really do.

'Are you going to tell me what's wrong?'

'Yes…but let's get out of here first. I could do with a glass of wine in good company.' I smile at him. When I contrast him to my company not one hour ago, I'm doing him a disservice. 'Make that *great* company.'

I sweep my lips over his, a gentle kiss before moving away, but he pulls me back.

'Coco?'

'Hmm?'

His eyes are so sincere they tug at me, pulling on strings I've never felt before.

'Just…'

I stare up at him, lost in his open expression, and then he shakes his head and grins.

'Nothing. It can wait.'

CHAPTER TWELVE

MY BRAIN IS whirling on the drive back to my place. The vehicle is keeping my hands busy but my mind is so occupied by her.

She seems more settled than she was before. So settled that I think she's likely to fall asleep before we make it back. She's half curled up in the seat, her head turned to the side, her eyes flickering between me, her hands and the outside world.

But, Christ, when I first saw her, saw the trace of tears in her over-bright eyes, her smile so genuine, so relieved, I was unable to speak. I could only open my arms to her and hold her, kiss her back as she kissed me.

And then those three simple statements: *I've missed you... I trust you... I need you.*

I tighten my grip on the wheel as the words repeat through my brain, burning deep, as I remember my hunger, so possessive as I staked my claim.

I haven't... I've never... Not since Jess—not since that relationship—have I trusted anyone enough to go without protection. It's huge. Monumental. But it felt so right, so natural, and now inside me my confession is bursting to get out.

I almost told her, there in the basement car park. And what a disaster that would've been, hot off the back of what we'd shared. She might have legged it back up top, out onto the street, where Bower would have been lying in wait, ready to get whatever detail he could to report back to that bastard Philip Lauren.

No, the timing hadn't been right. But, damn it, I want this all out in the open. I want to be there for her fully—no lies, no omissions.

I look across at her, see her eyelids heavy as she struggles to stay awake, and I stroke back the hair falling over her face. She gives me a small smile, which I return, and then her eyes are closed and I drop my hand back to the gear stick.

'Nearly there,' I say softly.

She gives a nonsensical response and cosies up deeper into her coat. She truly is at ease with me. And I would be the same if not for what I've kept from her.

I look back to the windscreen and focus on the drive, on something I do have control over in that second.

Just have faith. It will all come right in the end...

Yeah, because life's kind like that...

But if I can just get her away from here, confront Philip Lauren when she's safe from any immediate backlash on his part, deliver the threat of what I can do with the information I've gleaned and get him to call off Bower.

Because she doesn't deserve it. She doesn't deserve any of it.

And you don't deserve her...

I clench my jaw tight. That's something she will have to decide for herself, once she has all the facts and I've come clean.

Because I will…just as soon as she's safe.

I wake to the invigorating smell of coffee, the sound of cooking in the kitchen, and I roll over.

Ash's lingering scent cocoons me, and his quilt is warm and soft against my bare skin. To wake up like this every morning, not to feel alone any more…

I clutch the bedding to myself and smile into the sheets. Perhaps things aren't as complicated as he initially thought; perhaps he will change his mind about me, about us.

It felt that way when he stopped me from getting in the car last night. When he pulled me back against him and then changed his mind and said we'd talk later…

Only I'd fallen asleep.

I remember him cutting the engine, stirring enough to respond to his voice, and then he carried me here. I wanted to wake up—wanted to tell him what had happened, have him tell me it would be okay, tell me what it was that he'd stopped himself saying in the underground garage. But it was too easy to curl up under his quilt, just like I'm doing now, and let him surround me, comfort me.

And when I woke in the quiet of the night, hot and

uncomfortable, still clothed in my bra and thong, I stripped them away, and the instant my naked body curled into his, he stirred. We made love—nothing frantic, no words… Just eyes closed, mouths tasting, touching, all sensation. We savoured one another until we were sated and then let sleep claim us once more. So idyllic, so—

'Morning, sleepyhead.'

I turn at the sound of his voice—*wow!*

My mouth opens on a breathy sigh. He's walking towards me, tray outstretched, and steam is rising from two coffee mugs and a mountain of scrambled eggs. But it's not the offering that has me gaping—it's him. His sheer masculine beauty.

He's naked down to the teasing V at the base of his abs, just a pair of lounge pants hanging low, and he's barefoot, with a sexy-as-fuck grin that's as heated as I feel.

'Morning.'

It's a little gasp, and his grin widens.

'You can't be out of breath already; we haven't even started on the morning sex yet.'

'Is morning sex on offer?'

He slides the tray onto the bedside table and looks down at his crotch. I follow his eye and the sight of the tentlike bulge forming has my belly contracting.

'Guess I needn't have asked.'

'Guess I needn't bother to answer.'

'Not with words, at any rate…' I reach out and take hold of him through his clothing.

'Jesus, Coco.'

But his body bucks into my grasp, telling me just how welcome my touch is.

'The food will get cold…'

'I'm not putting this to waste,' I say, climbing up onto my knees and slackening the waistband of his pants. They fall to floor and I smile up at him as I wet my lips. 'Are you going to stop me?'

His eyes flare with anticipation. 'I can't say no to you.'

I kiss his very tip and air hisses through his teeth. His curse is fierce as his hands fork through my hair and cup the back of my head.

'Good,' I say softly, and then I press him between my lips, take one deep suck.

He's so fucking hard, and I'm already wet at the sight and feel of him, my clit throbbing fiercely with the power I hold.

He rocks and I take him further, my fingers lifting to cup his balls. His sharp intake of breath tells me it's what he wants, what he needs. And then I pull back slowly and release him with a pop, loving how his muscular frame flexes at the move and he drags in more air.

'Lie down,' I say softly.

He does just as I command, stepping out of his trousers and lying down beside me. All the while his eyes are locked in mine, lost in mine. I climb on top of him, one hand pumping his throbbing length, the other dipping between my legs, scooping up my wetness. I'm so ready for him, and I don't want to wait a second more. I slide his cock back, use his head to separate my folds and then I sink down, taking his all.

'Christ, Coco. *Yes*...' His hands drop to my thighs, his fingers biting into my skin. 'What I would give to wake up like this every morning…'

I undulate over him, hear his words chiming with my thoughts from seconds before. 'Me too.'

I ride him faster, harder, dropping both hands to his chest as my movements become more jagged. And then he rises up, holds me tight against him as I rock, rock, rock… There's that perfect hit of friction, his sheer size filling me, his body engulfing me, and then I'm gone, my head thrown back as I cry out.

I'm soaring, my body rigid and pulsating. And then he cries against me, shuddering with his own release, his forehead pressed against my clavicle, his mouth pressed into my skin. I feel so close to him in that moment, with his cock buried deep, his head so tight against me, his arms enclosing me. The need to cry is back, but it's full of happiness.

I wet my lips, find my voice. 'How's that for a good morning?'

His breath moves down my front and he breaks away just enough to say, 'The best.'

And then he's pulling me back against him again, delivering a kiss to my skin before pressing his cheek to my chest.

We stay like that for what feels like for ever, and yet I'm still disappointed when he pulls back to look up at me, his hands raking through my hair.

'Your breakfast will be cold.'

I sweep a kiss over his lips. 'It'll still be perfect.'

He laughs softly and lifts me away. Dutifully, I sit back against the headboard, give him the chance to disentangle himself from the covers, and then pull them up just enough to cover my breasts.

I give him a wicked grin. 'I'm ready to be fed.'

'You'll be waiting a little while, then; a man needs to recharge.'

I laugh. 'You *know* that's not what I meant.'

'That's a shame.' He rises off the bed and offers me the tray. 'I'll be back in a second—don't eat it all without me.'

And then he pulls his lounge pants off the floor and heads into the bathroom. To clean himself up, I'm sure. But there's a look on his face a split second before he turns away—that same pain I read in the underground garage.

He's suffering too. And I don't know why.

CHAPTER THIRTEEN

I ENTER THE BATHROOM, walk straight up to the cold tiled wall and press my head against it. I feel sick. I love her. I know I do. There's no denying it now. I don't want to wake up another morning without her here in my bed—*our* bed.

So much rides on the truth coming out and I'm scared. I haven't been fucking scared in years. I haven't felt the pain of loss in a decade, and I have no idea how I'll come out of this in one piece if she rejects me.

I take a breath and push away from the tiles. Standing here isn't going to help.

I clean up and pull on my bottoms. I take one last check in the mirror and then, happy that I don't look like the fucked-up idiot I feel, I return to her.

She's like a blushing bride, sitting up in bed after a night tangled in the sheets with her man, eagerly scoffing a piece of toast. And there goes my nausea again. Over a potential future that I want so badly and fear I can't have. The kind of future I haven't wanted since Jess upped and left.

'This is so good.'

She has her mouth full as she says it and I feel a tickle dance over the fear. My laugh is giddy and light and everything I need in that moment.

'I'm glad Her Ladyship approves enough to forget her finishing school manners.'

'I didn't attend a finishing school. How old-fashioned do you think I am?' Her cheeks flush deeper, her eyes glisten bright as she places a hand over her mouth. 'But, yes, she does approve.'

I walk to the bed and climb in beside her, taking a coffee mug off the tray still on her lap. I can't face eating. I'm scared the nausea will make a return pretty swiftly.

'You ready to talk about what happened yesterday?' I ask, lying back against the headboard and raising the mug so I can breathe in the familiar aroma, using it to gain a sense of calm.

She chews her food slowly, raking a hand through her hair as her eyes lose their spark. I wish I'd waited until after breakfast, but if I have my way I'll be taking her home to pack a bag and then getting the hell out of the city.

'My brother...my stepmother—' She swallows like it pains her to do so, her tears instant and crippling. 'They want me to convince Granny she would be better off in a hospice under twenty-four-hour care.' She shakes her head and starts to tremble.

Oh, God.

I take the tray from her lap, slide it out of the way and pull her into me. She comes easily, her head tucking beneath my chin, the tears, the sobs, racking her body as she lets go.

I rock her and hush her softly, murmuring words of encouragement—*It'll be okay... It'll be okay*—but will it, when all is said and done?

The fraud-filled boulder swells large in my chest, suffocating, heavy. I close my eyes and force myself to breathe through it.

'I don't want to do it—it's not fair, and it's not right,' she rambles through her tears. 'They just want life to continue like nothing's wrong… They don't care that being at home is a comfort to her…that it's important… They only care what effect it has on their plans, on their stupid summer soirée.'

'You don't need to do anything you don't want to,' I whisper into her hair, my lips brushing over its softness. 'You don't.'

'But I'm just tired of it—tired of trying to act like everything's okay, like I can cope, when it isn't and I can't.' She sniffs and looks up at me, wiping her nose, her eyes, with the back of her hand. 'I *never* fight with her.'

'With who?'

'My stepmother. It's not worth it. But last night I got so angry I walked out on them—created a scene, according to her.'

'I'm sure you didn't create a scene.' Wet strands of hair cling to her blazing cheeks and I brush them back as I try to reassure her. 'And even if you did, what does it matter? You have every right to be upset.'

She folds herself back into me.

'Granny wouldn't approve. Laurens don't cause a scene. Laurens need to be above reproach. Laurens don't show their feelings. Laurens sport a stiff upper lip at all times.'

It comes out in a controlled flurry as she channels her grandmother, letting rip the pressure she's permanently under. I can feel her physically cracking under the words and I'm taken over by a need to protect her, to take her away, to give her a break even for a few days.

'It's not healthy to bottle everything up.'

'But I *have* to. I have to keep up appearances. I'm not going to let her down—not while she's still here.'

'Then let me take you away—give you time to recover, regain your strength.'

She's looking up at me, wide-eyed, shaking her head.

'I can't go away—not with her so sick.'

'A few days won't hurt.'

'But what if my brother has her kicked out while I'm gone?'

'He won't.'

'You can't know that.'

I can, because I'll have people watching him. But I can hardly tell her that.

'Does she have a close friend? Someone you trust who could come and stay for a couple of days?'

'There's Grace… She's been visiting quite a bit; she'd come if I asked her.'

'There you go.'

'But you said we have to keep under the radar—your job, my…my notoriety…'

'You don't need to worry about that. The place I have in mind is quiet, peaceful. We'll hardly see a soul.'

She sighs softly and puts her arms around me, cuddling in. 'It sounds perfect.'

'It is.'

Her head-shake is softer now. 'But it doesn't feel right, leaving when she's so ill…'

'I'm talking a few days at most—a chance to recharge. You owe it to yourself and you owe it to your grandmother to look after your health too.'

She goes quiet and I wonder if I've lost her, if the idea is too much. I hold my breath as I wait.

Eventually she nods and gives me the lightest squeeze. 'Okay.'

Okay. I mentally repeat that as I relax and press a kiss to her head, staying there as I breathe her in and think.

The first part of my plan is in motion. I hope the rest can come my way as easily.

Although, I don't need easy—I just need her.

If she'll still have you when the truth is out...

'Where are we going?'

I packed as he instructed—warm clothing, enough for a couple of nights away—but I haven't actually asked until now. I think part of me is stunned that I'm actually doing it. I'm not impulsive. I don't just pack up on a whim. But one look at Granny's face when I told her I'd been invited away and I knew it was the right thing.

She actually smiled and squeezed my hand, said it was a lovely idea and told me that she and Grace were looking forward to the peace and quiet. Ever a Lauren, ever controlled, ever in charge.

I even saw Philip—albeit briefly. But it was long enough for me to make my thoughts clear once more on his attempt to move Granny elsewhere.

When I told him I'd be gone for a couple of days, he smiled. I don't want to think about what that smile meant, but I have assurances from Grace that she'll tell me if anything untoward happens in my absence, and I don't think Philip would dare—not if he wants to avoid the fuss I'd kick up on my return.

I shake off the negative direction of my thoughts and look at Ash in the driver's seat. He still hasn't answered my question.

'Come on—where are we going?'

'It's a surprise.' He smiles at me as he says it and then looks back to the road. 'You should lie back, chill… Although, don't get too comfy—we'll be getting out soon.'

'You have *met* me, right? I don't "chill".'

His smile becomes a grin. 'It's time you learned.'

I harrumph and look out of the passenger window at the rain, which won't stop falling and is making the afternoon feel much later than it is.

'I'm beginning to wish I'd said we could go away for longer—then you'd have had us in the Bahamas, or anywhere but here. It's so grey and miserable…'

'It won't feel as bad when we're up in the air.'

'When we're *what*?' I turn to him. 'What do you mean?'

His grin is still there, riding strong. 'You'll see.'

Less than an hour later, we're standing on a private airfield with a small aircraft before us and no pilot.

'Ash, what's going on?'

'You ready for some fun?'

'Fun? In that?' I point a shaky finger at the thing, which looks more like a large child's toy.

'Don't tell me you're afraid of flying.'

I spit out the rain that's gathered over my lips and pull my hood further forward, tugging my coat tighter around my neck. Our bags have already been taken on board and I know it's just me he's waiting for.

But seriously...?

'No, not afraid of flying. But that... In *this*.' I fling a hand around me at the weather.

'It's quicker this way—no traffic.' He holds out a hand to me. 'Come on. We're getting soaked.'

I slip my hand in his, but I don't move.

He gives me a little tug. 'Trust me.'

I take in the zippy-looking aircraft, bright shiny red, and I'm still convinced it's more toy than vehicle, but I trust him—I really do. I give the ground one last longing look and then climb into the cockpit, looking for a way into the back.

'Sit down,' he calls up.

'Here?' I say, pointing to the two seats that look far too pilot-worthy for me.

'Yes.'

I can tell he's enjoying this; his eyes have the playful glint to them that normally precedes a cheeky make-out session, not a flight. I sit my arse down as he closes the door. My gaze sweeps over the multitude of instruments...screens, buttons, joysticks, levers...

Oh, crap.

I'm so distracted I don't realise I've lost sight of him outside, but then he's back, and the door is opening on the other side as he climbs in right alongside me.

My eyes widen. '*You're* flying it?'

He shakes his head, eyes still dancing. 'My ego really isn't safe around you, is it?'

I can only smile as butterflies kick up in my belly. I'm nervous—I can't deny it. But as he slips into pilot mode and starts chatting to someone I can only assume is air traffic control while navigating his phone and what looks to be a flight plan, I admit to becoming awestruck.

He catches me staring and gives me a lopsided grin as he speaks into the headset. He passes me a similar contraption to wear. Then he helps to strap me in, his hands brushing over me, and all the time there's a look of concentration on his face that I find as sexy as his come-to-bed look.

If not for the fact that he's talking, I'd pounce—and, judging by the flash in his blue eyes as he settles back into his seat, he knows it too.

I force myself to behave and let him get on with

piloting, but I have so many questions. Like, how he learned to fly, *why* he learned, whose plane is this…? But they can wait—at least until we're airborne.

And even then I'm mesmerised. As we hit what he tells me is cruising altitude, I can't take my eyes away from him—the way he navigates the various controls, watches the screens, the gobbledygook he speaks into the headset. He's so confident and in control.

Who'd have thought flying could be a form of foreplay?

I've never understood the fascination with a man in a pilot's uniform before, but now I'll be right up there with heart eyes.

'Flying is in the Livingston blood.'

His voice pipes up through my headset and subconsciously I touch my fingers to the ear pad, my cheeks flushing at my inner ramblings.

'My father learned for fun, but his father was a pilot in the RAF, and *his* father before that. There's nothing quite like taking to the skies and getting out of the rat run below.'

I smile as I imagine him as a child watching his father in awe, just as I'm watching him now.

'You want to try?'

He eyes the joystick—if that's even what it's called—and I laugh, shaking my head. 'I'm happy to watch.'

'Maybe some other time?' he asks, hopeful, and my body warms.

My smile is all the answer he needs.

CHAPTER FOURTEEN

I PULL THE plane into the Livingstons' private hangar, my body abuzz.

I *knew* she'd love it. The second the Scottish Highlands had come into view, her attention had turned to the landscape, pleasure written across her face.

'That was pretty special,' she raves as I cut the engine, her eyes still bright, her cheeks warm and rosy. She already looks more relaxed, happy.

'I'm glad you enjoyed it.'

I unfasten my harness and lean across to help her do the same. Our hands collide and her eyes shine into mine as she wets her lips. I don't know whether it's an intentional move to pull me in but I'm there, kissing her. My lips are soft upon hers, nothing urgent or desperate. We have time together now. No risk of the outside world looking in, no interfering. Just us.

Her mouth parts willingly, her excited little whimper encouraging me on. I smooth a hand through her hair, my thumb across her cheek, and keep on kissing her. Soft, tender, loving… Its effect is all the more powerful below my waist, around my heart. I don't want to pull back, and I don't want to—

Rat-a-tat-tat.

She freezes. The sound comes from the glass behind me.

So much for no interfering, no outsiders…

But you chose this place—and he's no outsider.

I let out a breath and press my forehead to hers.

'Who's that?' she whispers like he'll overhear.

I shake my head and smile. 'The guy who gave me the flying bug.'

Her lips part…her eyes widen. 'You brought me to meet your *father*?'

Yeah, I guess I did.

Not that I thought about the magnitude of that at the time—only that it was the right place for her. *She's* thinking about it, though; I can see it in her face.

'Is that okay?'

'Yes—no. Yes.' She smooths out her jeans, her hair, her cheeks. 'You could've warned me.'

I grin, understanding her hesitation and adoring her all the more for it. 'You look perfect.'

She does. My father is going to love her. My mother would have too.

My head spins with the realisation, my heart pulses, too big for my chest. Fear is quick on its tail. If I have to give her up will I have to endure what my father did when he lost Mum? Is it the same kind of grief?

'I don't believe you…not when you're looking at

me like that.' She presses herself back in her seat like she's trying to hide from my father, who's rapping on the glass again. 'What's wrong?' she asks.

'Nothing at all.' I snap myself out of it, snatching a quick kiss to prevent any further protestations from her. 'But we'd best open up before he tries to clamber in and meet you himself; this is going to be fairly novel for him.'

'Novel?' she says as I lift her door handle and push it open.

'You'll see.' I turn to open my own door and spy Dad's grinning face through the glass.

Here goes...

The door lifts up. 'It's about time, you kids.'

Kids? Really?

'Hey, Pop.'

I clamber down and give him a hug, pounding his back as he does mine and whispering, 'Behave, okay?'

His eyes flash mischievously. 'Always.'

'Er...gentlemen?' Coco's voice is faint as she leans through the cockpit. 'Fancy giving a lady a hand?'

I start to move, but Dad's like lightning as he heads around the plane. 'I've got this, son.'

I laugh. 'Never seen you move so fast!'

He shoots me a look and I hear Coco's tantalising giggle.

Yes, he's going to love her, all right.

I climb back into the plane to get the luggage as I hear Dad introduce himself.

'Peter Livingston—at your service.'

She laughs a little more. 'Coco Lauren. It's a pleasure to meet you.'

She climbs down, with his aid, and I meet them a few moments later, plane locked up and bags in hand. He's telling her about the other plane in the hangar—his Cessna, the one I learned to fly in.

'She's old, but perfectly adequate, and she'll give that flash Cirrus a flight for its money.' He jerks his thumb at my Cirrus and laughs. 'It's all fur coat and no knickers, that one.'

'Dad!'

Coco is in giggles, and I swear I'm blushing. *Bloody hell.*

'You can't say that.'

'You can't say anything these days… It's a wonder we're not all mute!'

She actually snorts now, and I'm about to bollock him and demand he shut it entirely, but my eyes land on her and I'm rooted. She's glowing. Radiant. Everything I wanted her to be by taking her away, and we've only been here five minutes.

Dad catches my eye and smiles. There's so much to read in his expression. Approval is high up there and it swells within me too, to the point that I have to clear my throat to speak.

'Can we at least get to the house before you scare her off for good?'

His smile simply grows. 'Sure can—the Land Rover's just outside. Not afraid of dogs are you, Ms Lauren?'

'Coco, please—and, no, I love dogs.'

'They're going to love you.'

Dad moves off. Coco gives me a glowing smile and follows in his footsteps, and I'm still rooted, staring after them. It feels so *right*, having her here. All I need now is my brother, Jake, to turn up and the family circle will be complete.

The thought brings with it such warmth, such contentment. I know what it is because I've felt it before. There was the time before we lost Mum, and there was the time with Jess, but this is different—more profound, more real. And if it's this strong, then surely she feels it too? Surely it can survive the truth?

Surely *we* can survive it?

My God, his father looks like him…or rather Ash looks like his father.

And they're cracking me up. They're like a double act, with Ash the unwilling participant, and it's priceless.

Peter is whizzing us cross-country in his Land Rover, which looks older than me and smells fresh of wet Border collie. And he's using the trip to point out several of Ash's firsts. That's where he did his first stand-up wee; that's where he learned to ride a bike; that's where he face-planted in a cowpat… It's a brilliant tour, steeped in Livingston history. And made all the more entertaining by the colour creeping so high in Ash's cheeks that he looks sunburned.

I smile at him, sitting there in the front passenger

seat, while I grip the grab handle for dear life and take a face licking from Dotty, the youngest and most boisterous of three collies.

'You okay back there with them?' Ash asks, stroking the head of Dolly, the eldest collie, deemed sensible enough to sit upfront.

'Absolutely.'

My jeans have taken a beating, muddy paw prints galore, but my raincoat has protected my baby pink cashmere jumper from the worst. Not that I'd care if it hadn't. This is fun. *Real* fun. Even with his father's daredevil driving.

'How far is the house?' I ask, feeling in part to blame for Ash's heightened colour and thinking it might spare him any further embarrassing commentary if we discuss something else.

I look at those endearing streaks in his cheeks and my stomach flips, failing to land right when we're propelled over a mini swell in the rugged terrain.

'Just over the crest of this hill,' his father pipes up.

I lean forward to gaze through the windscreen at the sharp incline ahead and laugh. 'You call this a *hill*?'

Both men grin as they look at one another.

Clearly what constitutes a hill in Scotland is not the same as for London. But, seriously, it's essentially a mountain—and naturally beautiful with it. All green and rocky crags, with the occasional track carved out.

'Have you been to the Highlands before?' his father asks.

'No.' It's a squeak, and my grip is tightening even more as we hit a particularly bumpy patch. I fear being catapulted to the other side of the Land Rover, regardless of the seat harness.

'Ah, then you're in for a treat. You should come back in the summer, when the heather is in bloom and it's a blanket of purple out there.'

'She's not even stayed once yet, Pop.'

Ash's eyes flit to me, and the hope in his eyes chimes with my own.

'I can imagine I'd like that a lot.'

'My mother was from up here, and although she married an Englishman, her heart never left,' his father says, his voice unaffected by the rattling around us, although my insides feel like they're about to clamber up and out of my body. 'She would bring us here holidaying when I was a boy, and I bought this place not long before Ash was born. It was a bargain back then.'

We reach the crest as he says it, the car finally hitting an actual road and going quiet, smooth. I relax—only to have my lips part in surprise at the enchanting view ahead.

'It was our country retreat until I'd had enough of the city life altogether. Then it became my home.'

'But is it…? Is it meant to look like a castle?' My words are almost a whisper, as if speaking any louder will break the spell of what I can see.

'I think the wealthy trader who built it in the nineteenth century fancied himself a bit royal…' His father gives a hearty chuckle. 'And, considering the moat he fashioned around it, I'd say he was none too popular either.'

He turns to look at me briefly.

'Just don't expect much on the inside, though. It's only me and the dogs now, so I stick to the west wing. Easier to keep clean that way.'

'West wing—got it.'

Ash raises his brow at me. 'He's not kidding either, the place needs a lot of work in parts, so don't expect anything too grand.'

I nod, beaming. Truth is I'm already in love with the place.

Even as we get closer and I can make out the crumbling walls, the odd piece of scaffolding and the greenery growing where windows should be, it's still majestic. Still gorgeous in its own unique way—from the little stone bridge that crosses the water to the imposing structure itself, with its four pointed fairy-tale turrets.

'I love it.'

Ash looks at me as I say it and smiles. I'm so grateful to him for doing this. For realising I need this. I hold his gaze, spilling my all into that one look as the car slows to pass over the bridge, and the moment shatters in the bouncing excitement of my four-legged companions, who are now clambering up. Dotty chins me in the process. I laugh as I tickle her, and we look out of the window together.

The colours are beautiful. The sun is starting to set, and the water is rippling with the golden hues of the sky and the rolling hillsides.

I can almost imagine London away altogether. Is that why his father came here?

I think back to what Ash told me about his family past, the reason for his father's early retirement, and I have my answer.

His father pulls the car up and cuts the engine. 'Home sweet home.'

We all pile out and the dogs scurry off to investigate. 'Mary has made up your usual room, son. Do you want to take Coco on up and then come find me when you're done?'

'Sure, Pop.'

'Thank you,' I say.

His father beams at me and then walks off in the same direction as the dogs.

I turn to Ash. *Mary?* I mouth.

He smiles. 'Housekeeper—of sorts. She lives in the neighbouring village and comes to sort Dad out every once in a while. Her husband farms the land here.'

'It's good he has some company.'

'I think he's quite happy in his own, truth be told.'

We both watch him playing with the dogs and I wonder if we're thinking the same: Does he ever get lonely?

'Come on,' Ash pipes up. 'Let's get in before we freeze.'

I'm surprised to find tears pricking once more,

and I blink them back before he can catch them. I don't want him doubting his decision to bring me here. Not when I'm so happy to be here with him in his family home.

'Lead the way.'

CHAPTER FIFTEEN

WE ENTER THE house through the kitchen and I show Coco the lived-in areas of the ground floor: the living room, the dining room, the library—Dad's favourite room.

As we enter the entrance hall, her gasp is audible. 'This isn't grand?'

She raises her brow at me and twirls on the spot, captivated by the high-ceilinged room, with its imperial staircase, ornate features and parquet floor. But I'm one hundred percent hooked on her and her obvious pleasure.

'I feel decidedly underdressed.'

She laughs as she says it, but my head is already undressing her, wrapped up in her free and easy presence. 'That can be arranged.'

She stills and looks at me, and the very second our eyes collide, I know she's wanting the same.

'But your father…?'

'Is busy.'

I drop the bags to my feet and close the distance between us, pulling her in for a kiss that's all the deeper for the interrupted one in the cockpit. She curves into me, her soft sigh telling me she's as keen as I am.

'You ready to see my bedroom?'

She lifts her lashes, her cheeks colouring. 'It feels kind of weird. I've never stayed under the same roof as my… Well, you know… A boyfriend's parent.'

She blushes further as she puts a label to me—hell, my whole insides are blushing over it, loving it and wanting more.

'I promise you, this house is big enough that he won't hear a peep—unless, of course, I make you scream.'

She bites into her lip as she eyes me. 'Now, there's a thought.'

Heat surges south and I turn away to grab the bags before I drop her to the parquet and say to hell with any potential audience.

'This way…'

She starts after me and then stops. 'Wait—my shoes…'

'Keep them on. This place can get chilly. If it makes you feel better, you can leave them outside the bedroom; it'll save me the job of taking them off you when we get there.'

She laughs. 'Thank you, Ash.'

I frown at her. 'For what?'

'For bringing me here. It truly is perfect.'

Her voice is so soft, her eyes are the same, and there's so much emotion clouding her gaze. I curse the fact that my hands are full of baggage instead of her.

'You're welcome.'

She does take her shoes off outside the door, and I do the same, gesturing for her to go in.

She turns the knob on the door and pushes it open.

'The light pull is just to your left.'

She pulls on it and her face lights up with the glow from a central chandelier. 'Wow!'

'You like it?'

'What's not to like?'

She pads in, tracing her fingers over the antique furnishings, the window seat with its full-height drapes and then the four-poster bed.

She curls her fingers around a bottom post and smiles at me, all coy. 'This could be fun.'

The heat pulses in my groin.

Fuck.

I release the bags and kick the door closed. She straightens as I stride towards her, her smile growing, and then my arms are around her and I keep moving, walking her to the bed, onto her back, my mouth on hers, hard, urgent. My saving grace is that she's right with me, her mouth just as hungry, her hands just as fierce.

There are too many layers—our coats, our sweaters—but they're coming off. Our hands are ripping them away from each other. Our jeans are next, and our underwear, and then she shivers.

'Are you cold?' I manage to ask.

'No.' She shakes her head, her mouth finding mine and kissing away any doubt. 'I want you.'

She wraps her legs around me. I feel my cock

probing at her hot, slick warmth and I pull back, pinning my hands on either side of her head as I stare down into pools of green, dilated with desire.

She has her hands on my neck, her fingers brushing over the hairs at my nape. She wets her lips, suddenly hesitant. 'What is it?' she asks.

'You,' I say.

A delightful little crease forms between her brows.

'I'm losing myself in *you*.'

Her lashes flutter, her eyes glisten. 'I feel the same.'

I hope so.

I feel the alien prick of tears and kiss her until the sensation passes, until the burn subsides.

'Now, Ash, please.' She moves against me, pulling herself close, submerging the head of my cock in her alluring, tight heat.

'Look at me, baby.'

I need her with me—need her to see everything she has come to mean as I sink inside her.

She opens her eyes, stares up at me.

'Thank you for letting me take you away.' Slowly I enter her, savouring the feel of her surrounding me, the way her skin colours, her pleasure radiating out. 'Thank you for letting me give you this.'

She shakes her head, hooking her hands around my neck. 'I'm the one thanking you.'

She stays with me, her eyes on mine, even as I fill her completely and her head threatens to rock back. She stays locked on my gaze, clenching me tightly.

The pulsing heat is calling to me, and my eyes are trying to close as pleasure overtakes my body, my mind. I force them open. I need this. The connection. The security of it. I need it to get through what is to come. To have faith that it will all come good.

'Tell me you're mine,' I urge.

She nods her head, her eyes flashing with sincerity.

'*Tell me.* I need the words…'

'I'm yours, Ash.'

My chest swells with the bittersweet happiness of knowing what I have now and what I risk losing. I squeeze my eyes shut against the pang, scared that she will see, and when I open them again she's there…

'*Always*, Ash.'

Always. Always. *Always.*

I focus on that, rocking into her with every echo, claiming her as mine, wishing away all else. I drop to kiss her and together we rock, kiss, devour, our eyes locked together, sharing it all.

And when we come it's in harmony. Everything's perfect, exactly how it should be.

No truth can take this away. It can't…

I'm shaking. The truth of my words is tearing through me as my limbs soften around him and the waves of pleasure fade.

I love him.

I *love* Ash.

It doesn't matter that I've only known him weeks,

that we agreed there could be no future. I have fallen for him.

And if what I read in his face, in his demands, is true, he loves me too.

I grip him tighter to me. Uncertainty is creeping in. It was he who said there could be no future. He who put his job before us. Will he still?

His head lifts, and his eyes scan my face as he strokes back my hair.

'I have a few things to do. Why don't you freshen up and meet me downstairs in a bit?'

I offer him a small smile, my brain a confused rambling. *Just tell him. No, let him tell you first. Don't make a fool of yourself. You're getting high on his kindness.*

And then he's pressing himself up and off me, and heading to what I assume is the bathroom, and I'm no closer to working out where to begin this conversation because I don't want to lose what we have now.

But what if he can't give me more?

I hope a shower will clear my head, make me think straight, but I'm just as confused as I make my way downstairs an hour later. I follow the sounds of movement and the delicious scent of spices, but when I get to the kitchen it's only his father I see.

'Ah, Coco—excellent timing.' He looks up from the pan he's stirring, an apron tied around his waist, his cheeks flushed from the billowing steam.

'How so?'

I grin. I like him—a lot. I can't for the life of me

imagine him in a boardroom, though; he seems far too chilled and exuberant.

'I could do with a little helper. Ash has had to disappear to make some calls, but he shouldn't be too long. I hope you like curry.'

I breathe in the spicy aroma and nod. 'Smells delicious!'

'Good. Good…' He pops on a pan lid and stirs another two pans simultaneously. 'Ever made naan bread before?'

I laugh as I edge closer and see what he has cooking. 'No, I've never even baked—unless you count the cooking I did at school…and let's just say my home economics teacher thought I was beyond help.'

'Nonsense. Everyone can bake so long as they have the right teacher.'

It's Ash. He's back.

I turn to him. My smile is instantaneous and giddy. I'm so happy to see him again it's ridiculous. He comes straight to me and wraps his arms around my waist, pressing a kiss to my forehead. I hear the dogs patter in behind him.

'Enough of that, son. Those naans aren't going to roll themselves. Dotty—down!'

He pushes the young collie back as Ash pats my behind with a grin and slips his hand in mine to lead me to a counter dusted with flour.

'*You* know how to do this?' I say.

He positions me in front of him, his warmth radiating down my back as he takes up the dough and starts to break it into smaller balls.

'What have I said to you about my ego?'

His father chuckles and I follow suit, turning my head to look up at him.

'I'm just in awe of your skills.'

'Why do I feel like you're teasing me?'

'I'm one hundred percent serious,' I reply softly, holding his eye for a beat before taking up one of the small balls he's created. 'Right, show me the way.'

We work together, rolling out the naans and cooking them under the grill while his father tends to the bubbling pans and the dogs curl up together in the corner, having decided spice is not their thing.

It's all so easy, so relaxing, and the time just flies by. *This* is what being in a family is like. A normal family. No pretence, no walls—just existing. It's how my mother would have had it—how my father would have been had she survived.

The thought makes me sad and happy in one. Sad for losing it...happy to have found it here.

After dinner, once we've cleaned the pans and taken our wine into the library, I excuse myself to pop to the bedroom and check my phone. I want to check on Granny. There have been no calls or texts and, taking that as a good sign, I head back downstairs.

As I approach the study I can hear Ash talking, and my stride slows of its own accord.

'After Jess I just didn't want to go there—didn't want to risk going through it again.'

'Your mother never liked that girl... She saw right

through her from day one. I only wish you'd had the same insight.'

'Mum was always a good judge of character.'

'Well, I wouldn't go that far. Clive had her as fooled as the rest of us. *She* was the one who suggested he be your godfather.'

'Yeah, well...lucky for us we saw through his act.'

'*You* saw through it, you mean.'

The room falls silent and I can hear the crackling of the fire. I can't make my legs work. *Who's Jess?* I know all about Clive, but Jess... He's never told me about her.

'She reminds me of Jess.'

My heart skips a beat at his father's remark. *What?*

'She's *nothing* like her.' Ash is so vehement as he says it.

'No, no—not when you get to *know* her. But her appearance...the air she has about her.'

Ash blows out a breath so forceful I can make it out from this distance. 'Yeah, well...she's not.'

'Lucky for you, hey?' His father is all jovial now. 'Seems you picked right this time. She's lovely, Ash, truly lovely.'

'I know.'

'So why so serious, then? You look like you have the weight of the world on your shoulders when you should be walking on air.'

'It's not that simple.'

'Of course it is. Love can be that simple if you just let it in.'

'Like I did with Jess?' Ash says, and his cynicism,

the realisation that he once loved this girl, whoever she was, strikes through the very heart of me.

I press back against the wall, my hand over my chest as I try to ease the chaos beneath. I almost want to walk the other way, to forget what I've heard. It's made me realise how much I don't know about him. How much I *do* want to know and understand. Is this the pain I glimpsed? Is his heart still broken over *her*?

'*She* wasn't worthy of your love, but…'

I close my ears off and cough as I head to join them, knowing that to listen to any more isn't right. If I want answers, Ash can give them to me.

'Ah, Coco—again your timing is impeccable.' His father rises out of his chair before the fire; Ash does the same. 'I'm about to call it a night.'

'Don't leave on my account.' I feel like he's leaving because of me, and considering he rarely has company, I don't want that.

'I've had a busy day chauffeuring and catering—amazing how it can take its toll.' He grins at us both and looks like he'll say more, but then he simply shrugs and whistles to the dogs, who immediately spring to attention and trot to his feet. 'I'll see you both in the morning.'

'Night, Pop.'

'Goodnight, Peter.'

'You can call me Pop too, if you like.'

He gives me a wink and off he goes, leaving me blushing in his wake.

'He means it affectionately.'

Ash looks awkward, uncomfortable. Has he guessed I was eavesdropping, or is he still reeling from the conversation with his father?

'I know.'

I wait for the door to close before taking up my wine glass and heading over to the chair his father had been sitting in. Ash tops up his own glass and sits opposite me, but his attention is on the fire. He's distant. Thoughtful.

'Who's Jess?' I ask.

His eyes snap to me. 'You heard?'

'Sorry.' I grimace. I don't want him to think it was intentional. 'I couldn't help overhearing the tail end of your conversation, but it kind of feels like something I should know.'

'I don't talk about her at all if I can help it.'

'But you can tell me anything—you know that, right?'

He studies me, unblinking, long and hard.

'Ash?' I press softly.

He comes alive, the air shuddering from his lungs as he leans his elbows on his knees, his eyes falling to the glass he's cupping in his hands.

My gut twists. Did he love this Jess *that* much? He looks so broken…torn apart. Maybe I don't want to hear this after all. Maybe—

'We met at school. She was the popular girl every guy wanted and every girl wanted to befriend.' He gives a harsh laugh I don't recognise. 'I guess you could call me the male equivalent… I was smitten, so was she, and we were together right through school, university… I thought that was it—she was the one.'

I sip my wine, hoping it will ease the sickness inside, but instead it burns a path all the way through me. 'The one?'

His eyes flick to me. 'I was coming to the end of my gap year and she'd been doing a placement in Paris. She flew home and I surprised her in Arrivals with a diamond ring.'

'You proposed?'

He nods his head, his eyes on his drink. 'She said yes. It was sorted. We agreed we'd complete our studies and then have a grand wedding in the summer, start our lives in earnest.'

'What happened?'

'Clive happened.'

I frown at him, not putting two and two together and fearing it's because my heart is breaking with every word he says.

'The second my family's money left the equation, she walked.'

I shake my head. 'I don't believe that. No one would be that shallow.'

He scoffs. 'You'd think that, wouldn't you? Hell, I thought so too—until I ended up falling foul of it.'

'But that's *sick*.'

He shrugs. 'It wasn't just the money—it was the scandal too. She didn't want to be tarnished by it.'

'But you cleared your father's name, proved he was innocent, recouped some of the money.'

'Oh, yeah, I did all that.' He leans back in his

seat now, slumped, almost defeated. 'And she came back, all right—told me she'd made a mistake, that she loved me, begged me to understand.'

He rubs his fingers over his jaw, his eyes lost in the memories, and then I remember the night we first met—the night he told me I wasn't his type.

'That's why you were so harsh when I first met you?'

He frowns in confusion.

'When you said I wasn't your type?' I explain, softening my words with the hint of a smile. It's about all I can muster when my heart is losing control in my chest.

He cocks his head, his eyes sweeping over me. 'You reminded me of her, yes.'

'I'm sorry for that.'

'Don't be sorry.'

He places his drink down on a small side table and moves to kneel before me, his eyes soft as they gaze up at mine.

'It turns out I do have a type; *you* are my type, *she* was my type, but that's superficial...' He cups my jaw and strokes my skin. 'You see, underneath, you're nothing alike. And what I feel for you... It's more. It's real. I...' My breath hitches and he shakes his head. 'I'm not very good at this.'

I bow my head towards him, dizzy on the meaning of his words, the promise of him feeling more, the promise of his potential love...

'On the contrary,' I say, brushing his lips with my own. 'I think you're better than you know.'

And then I'm kissing him with every ounce of the love I feel inside. Because he loves me, and I love him, and we have all the time in the world to tell each other how we feel, to carve out a path together. To find a way to make our lives converge. Because I'm not turning my back on this. Not now that I have it.

CHAPTER SIXTEEN

I CAN'T SLEEP. Coco has her head on my chest, snoring softly, but I'm staring into the darkness plagued with *what ifs.*

I almost told her everything. When we were sitting before the fire and I was so lost in my thoughts, thinking of ways to explain that wouldn't impact the plan I have underway back in London.

But then she asked about Jess—a topic I could easily cover now that my past no longer has any hold over me. Thanks to her. Thanks to Coco and my love for her, I realise that what Jess and I had was never love.

But you can tell me anything—you know that, right?

Her words haunt me. The one thing I really wanted to confess I couldn't—not yet.

Soon though—very soon.

Philip Lauren will be waking up to a special delivery package today, and I expect a phone call soon after. A barrage of abuse. And then his rational side will have to win out. Or so I hope.

Then I can make real time for this—for her.

I press my lips to her head, letting my breathing ease and hoping for sleep to come and take away the *what ifs*.

I wake to the incessant buzzing of my mobile phone and an empty bed. Ash isn't far, though. I can hear the shower running in the en suite bathroom and I smile, my mind already visualising him naked and all soaped up.

I reach for my phone on the bedside table. I should hurry and join him—the sliver of light coming through the curtains tells me I've overslept as it is. But then, what's the rush? The day is ours and it feels so good.

My phone stops ringing as I pick it up and I have to activate it again to see the notifications.

Three missed calls: Grace, Philip, Grace.

Granny.

I sit bolt upright as the world around me spins. Something's happened. Something bad. My hand soars to my throat as I try to breathe through the panic.

Calm down. You don't know for sure. There could be any number of reasons why they would need to ring...

No, there's only one.

With fuzzy fingers that are far too slow to do what I want, I call Grace back.

Pick up, pick up, pick up.

It goes straight to voicemail, just as the ping of

a message arriving comes through. It's a voicemail from Grace.

'Coco, darling, it's Grace. Don't panic, but your grandmother has been taken into hospital with suspected pneumonia. She's in the ICU. I don't... I'm not... I think you should come as soon you as you are able. Philip will send you the details. Take care.'

My stomach heaves… My skin prickles from top to toe. Here I am, playing happy holidays with Ash, worrying over the state of my love life, when Granny's fighting for her life. It feels like some twisted punishment for letting go, for being selfish enough to think of myself. How could I have thought leaving was okay?

I throw back the quilt. I need to get home—now. I need to tell Ash.

I don't even dress. I head straight for the bathroom, opening the door.

Ash's dawning smile dies the second he sees me. 'Coco…?'

I can't find my voice; I'm trembling all over. I grip my upper arms and start to rub them, shaking my head.

'Coco?'

He slams off the shower and walks towards me.

'It's Granny.' I swallow as I look up at him. 'She's been rushed into hospital.'

He inhales softly and reaches for his robe from the back of the door, wrapping it around me and pulling me in close. 'Do you know what's happened?'

My teeth rattle. 'Suspected pneumonia.'

'Okay.' He's so calm, so composed, and already I take comfort. 'We'll get dressed and go. Do you think you can get your stuff together while I let Dad know?'

I nod, so grateful that I don't even have to ask to leave. He just *gets* it.

He turns away to grab a towel. 'Do you know where she is?'

I shake my head. 'Grace says Philip is going to send me the details.'

'Okay.' He wraps the towel around his waist and comes back to me, his hands firm and reassuring on my arms. 'Go and message Philip, then get ready.'

I nod up at him and move away to do as he instructs, but my mind is racing. Guilt, fear, sadness… What will I find when I get back to London? Just how bad is it? ICU means bad.

When Ash returns to find me staring unseeing into my bag, he does it all for me. His calm and controlled manner is everything I need, and as he puts his arm around me to draw me towards the door I feel his strength, his warmth, seep into my body. I know that with him by my side I can face this.

I can face anything life throws at me so long as we're together.

I'm so focused on Coco and her pain that nothing else matters as I drive to the hospital. She's sported a haunted look ever since she came to me in the bathroom, and I've never felt so powerless in all my life. Nothing can take away her pain; I can only be with her and get her to her grandmother's side as quickly as possible.

But her silence—it's killing me. She's barely said a word between saying goodbye to Dad, the plane ride and now the car journey once more.

The hospital is only minutes away now. I'm worried that she feels guilty at having gone away, and if so, that's down to me.

I mean, *Christ*, if her grandmother dies and Coco's not there, that's on my head—that's worse than everything else put together.

My hand pulses around the wheel and I realise my knuckles are white. I try to ease my grip, not wanting her to see how anxious I am, but as I look at her I see she's fixated on the passing world, her body stock-still, her eyes distant.

I suppress the ragged sigh that runs through me. I feel desperate, pained, anxious, and so full of love for her it's unreal.

'Thank you for doing this,' she suddenly says into the quiet.

Thank you? Christ.

I want to do so much more. I reach over and take her hand in mine. Her fingers are like ice and I don't want to release them. I want to give her my body heat, my comfort. I want to take away her pain.

The car grumbles, demanding a gear change, and I give her a gentle squeeze before taking my hand away.

My mind turns to Philip. I know the package was delivered this morning—what I don't know is whether he'll have opened it. From what I can make out he's been at the hospital since their grandmother was admitted in the early hours, and it's likely he'll still be there now. Which means I run the risk of being seen dropping Coco off, of having our relationship blown.

But it all seems so insignificant now. It doesn't matter that her grandmother's death is expected. When it comes to the cold, hard reality of it, life and love come first.

Will Philip see it that way?

Was my package unnecessary?

I navigate the hospital's one-way system, looking for the drop-off bay, and she turns to me.

'Park up.'

'I'll drop you at the door,' I say softly. 'You can call me, and I'll come and pick you up later.'

Her eyes widen. 'But—' She breaks off, shaking her head as she looks away.

'What is it?'

She doesn't say anything. I reach over and touch her thigh. 'Coco…?'

'I thought…'

She looks back to me, her eyes wavering over my face, trembling with a fresh well of tears.

Shit.

'Can't you come with me…please? I don't want to go in alone. I don't—' She breaks off again and hugs her arms around herself. 'Sorry, I shouldn't ask. Of course you can't—'

'I will.'

The words are tight, my heart tighter. I can't say no to her. Not when she needs me. But Philip will be there…

Fuck Philip. You love her and she needs you.

My jaw pulses and I look to the road, changing direction with carefully controlled force and heading for the car park.

Whatever waits for me on the other side of those doors, I deserve it.

She has to come first.

Always.

But can I warn her?

How do I do that without making this trip all the more devastating?

I look at her, sitting across from me, and her wet smile of gratitude pulls me apart.

'Look, I'm not sure what's going to happen when we get in there,' I try. 'Your brother… He might… Well, he might say some things about me…about us.'

She flings a hand out and squeezes my leg, her head shaking. 'I don't care what Philip has to say. I only care that you're here, by my side.'

Because you don't know.

I shake my head, my fist pulsing around the wheel.

Just tell her.

I pull the car into a parking space and cut the engine, but I'm slow to turn to her, slow to gather my thoughts. 'I'm sorry, Coco. I'm sorry for—'

'I know you are. But you're here and that's all I need; now, let's go.'

Her hand is already on the door handle, her eagerness to get in there clear, and I tell myself it'll be okay. That I'll have all the time I need to make it up to her.

If she lets you anywhere near her again...

Ash is my saviour. He talks to the reception staff, gets the necessary directions to the ICU, and his arm is a constant around me, a welcome hold that gives me heat, strength, courage.

I know the ICU is bad news. And I think in some way that impedes my step, as if seeing her there will confirm my fears. Even though I always knew it would come to this, I thought we had some time. But not now—not while I was away.

'What if she's not conscious?'

I think the words come out, but it's not until Ash speaks that I know they have for sure.

'Let's just wait and see what they say, hey?'

'But what if I don't get to say goodbye? What if she goes and I haven't told her that I love her? What…?'

I can't talk any more as the tears take over and Ash pulls me into him, stopping us altogether. He kisses my head and cups my jaw, encouraging me to look up at him.

'Remember what she always told you? "Stiff upper lip"?' He mimics me and I laugh through my tears as I nod. 'So, come on, get those Lauren genes going and put up a front she'd be proud of. You can tell her all those things whether she's sleeping or not, just as soon as you get through those doors.'

I smile. It's pathetic, but it's there, and he brushes his thumbs over my eyes, sweeping away the tears.

'Good girl. Now, come on…let's—'

'What the actual *fuck*?'

I freeze mid-sniff, sense Ash turn rigid, his face losing all colour as he looks past me to the doors we're about to go through.

I turn to see Philip gawping at us. 'Calm down,' I say. 'This is—'

'I *know* who he is, Coco.' His eyes are pinned on Ash, unmoving. 'What the fuck are *you* doing here?'

I frown, unable to understand his words. What does he mean? How can he possibly *know* who Ash is?

Before I can say anything, Ash is pushing me back behind him, forming a human shield, his hand palm-out to Philip.

'Easy, Lauren—let's talk about this later, not here.'

'Not here?'

Philip's brows rocket, spit forming with his words. I've never seen him this angry.

'I'm a bloody fool. I don't know why I didn't see it sooner. Are you two in cahoots? Is that what this is? You turning the tables on me?'

He's not making any sense. 'Ash?' I say to his back, but he doesn't even turn. *'Ash?'*

Now he looks at me, his eyes hard, impenetrable.

My brother starts to laugh, a wild, hysterical cackle.

'Oh…she doesn't *know*.' He shakes his head. 'My God, have you been playing us both? Getting Lauren money every which way?'

'Ash?'

It's a squeak now. My stomach is turning over. Bile is creeping up my throat and making it hard to breathe, to move, to think.

'Coco…'

He turns in to me, his hands reaching to cup my upper arms, but I'm stumbling back, breaking away. 'What does Philip mean?'

My brother sneers. '*I'll* tell you what it's about—'

'Shut the fuck up, Lauren,' Ash throws at him. 'This is our business.'

Philip steps towards him. 'Funny, that. Last time I checked I was *paying* you to dish the dirt on her.'

His words wash over me like ice and fire all at once. I think of Ash's job. I think of what he's paid to do. Then I think of the Ash who has made love to me, protected me. I can't make them merge and my head starts to spin, my stomach lurches, and I know I'm going to vomit as I double over with a retch.

'Coco…'

Ash bends to me, his hand gentle on my back, but I thrust him away. His touch burns me with betrayal.

'Go! Get out of here! I don't need you! I don't need anyone.'

I push past them both, fighting through the tears to make out the route to the ladies' room.

'Coco, please let me explain—'

He's hot on my heels but I can't… I can't… I can't deal with this now.

I push through the lavatory door, but Ash doesn't give up—he's in there with me.

'Get out,' I say, turning to him and backing up against the sinks.

'Please, Coco, I—'

A toilet flushes and an elderly lady steps out. She takes one look at me and the tall, foreboding man and swipes him with her handbag.

'The lady said get out! We may be living in the modern age, but the ladies' room still means it's for ladies, you brute.'

His eyes look to me pleadingly. He's barely aware of the woman shoving her little hand at him, her bag making repeated contact with his chest.

'*Please*, Coco, you have to hear me out.'

My eyes water with a fresh wave of tears and I can't even see him properly. He's just a blurry outline as he relents to the pressure of my impromptu bodyguard and backs out.

I once saw him in that role. A bodyguard. A good man, exposing bad people for the benefit of the weak and vulnerable.

I had been the bad person in his eyes.

Philip was the good.

I turn to the sink as I hear the door open and then swoosh closed. There's a muttered 'Good riddance. *That* showed him, love. Now, are you okay?'

I shake my head. How can I be? I've avoided getting seriously involved with anyone because money is always the endgame—my family's money and status. I fell for Ash because I thought he was different.

Turns out he wasn't different at all. He was after Lauren money, just as every guy had been before him. And I was fool enough to fall for it.

'If it helps, I think he looked fit to cry himself,' says my rescuer.

My head just keeps shaking, as if I can magic it all away, pretend it isn't true.

Only, it *is* true.

And there's no explanation he can give that will take away the reality that he's being paid by Philip to dish the dirt on me. And, boy, have I given him plenty.

CHAPTER SEVENTEEN

I LOOK UP at the hospital entrance across the road, my hands thrust in my pockets. It's been a week since I was last here, my world in tatters at my feet as I was forced to walk away.

Not a second has gone by without me thinking of her; even my dreams tease me with a mixture of reality and fantasy, happy and sad. But I can't take it any more.

I know her grandmother has recovered enough to be admitted to a ward and is making good progress. She may even get to go back home. I've gleaned all this by getting hold of her friend Grace's number. I haven't used my network of contacts and I certainly haven't gone to Philip. My life as a PI is over, my taste for it ruined by my thoughtless prejudice, epic misjudgement and the devastating consequences it has had on the one person I have come to love so much that every second without her physically hurts.

And that's why I'm here—to tell her. To be honest, to bare my soul if I have to—it's all I have left to give, if she lets me get that far.

I watch the doors—watch the people milling in and out, the smokers who look like they're at death's door, getting another fix, the friends and relatives taking a patient out for a stroll—and then I see her, her blonde bob dancing as she walks, head down, her eyes on her phone, focused and not breaking step.

A quick flick of the eyes up to check the road is clear and then she's crossing it, a few strides down from me. I try to call out and my voice is stuck, nerves closing my throat over. I start after her as a vehicle comes tearing around the corner, speeding for the entrance, just as she steps off the pavement.

'Coco!' I grab her arm and pull her up against me as the vehicle screeches to a halt, doors flying open, people shouting. But it's all tuned out as I lose myself in those green eyes that I've missed so goddamn much. 'You shouldn't walk and text.'

She shrugs her arm out of my hold. 'What the hell are you doing here?'

I swallow, my hand falling helplessly to my side. 'Please…can we talk?'

I know she wants to deny me; I can see it in her narrowed gaze, the hard set of her jaw. But then she turns and starts to make for the car park.

'You've got until I get to my car.'

I let go of a trapped breath and fall into step beside her. 'I meant over coffee…somewhere more private.'

She laughs, harsh and loud. 'What? So you can try to seduce your way into my trust like you did before? Tell me, Ash, how many unsuspecting souls have you seduced to get the information you need?'

I pale under the assault of her words…at how low she thinks I'll sink. 'I've *never* slept with a target before.'

'A *target*?' She repeats it thoughtfully, derisive. 'So that's what I am?'

'No, not you—not now.'

'Oh, *wow*—lucky for me.'

Her voice is so high-pitched, so angry, and she picks up her pace, her fingers trembling as she rakes them through her hair and clutches her bag tighter over her shoulder.

'How long were you following me?'

I shake my head, not wanting to tell her but knowing I have to. 'I don't know…a few weeks.'

'Every day?'

'Most days.'

'The charity galas, lunch dates, hospital visits, shopping trips? There you were, in the shadows?'

She shudders and it resonates down my spine like a chilling trickle. This is going badly—worse than even my garbled imaginings.

'Please, Coco, forget everything you think you know about us—how we met, what you think I did or lied about… Coco.' I reach for her arm but then think better of it. 'Coco, stop—just for a second—and look at me.'

She stops, but she doesn't turn.

'*Please*, Coco.'

My voice shakes, desperate, fearful. But I have to do this—I have to tell her. Even if she walks away again, at least she'll know the truth.

Slowly she turns, her tormented green eyes lifting to mine. I don't dare close the gap between us, scared of having her move off again. At least she's looking at me now. And I know I look like shit, but I don't care. I hope it will help show her what this is doing to me.

'Spit it out, Ash.'

She raises her chin and wraps her arms around herself.

'I love you.'

It trembles out of me, and it feels so good to say it, but she doesn't react. Not even a blink. Did she not hear?

'I *love* you, Coco.'

Her lashes flutter, her eyes water, and I push on.

'I love you like I've never loved anyone in this world. I love you more than you can possibly begin to imagine. I didn't set out to hurt you. I set out on a job, where everything was black and white. He was good; you were bad. You were like Jess.'

Her head shakes, her nostrils flare. 'Don't think I haven't figured that much out.'

'But you're not. *Christ*, I knew that before I even met you in the club. I'd been tailing you for weeks, falling in love with you a little bit each day.'

She looks away. 'Now you just sound like a stalker.'

'I know.' I rake my hand over my hair. 'But I mean it. I followed you and discovered the real you—the person with a heart so big you spend your days seeing that other people are happy, and to hell with your own happiness.'

'Then why didn't you just tell Philip that and *piss off*?' Her eyes spear me, fresh tears welling, and her cheeks streak red. 'Why did you have to get close to me? Why did you have to make me care about you? *Why?*'

Oh, God, this is crushing me. I want to reach for her, pull her in, make everything all right. But I know she'll run even if I dare.

'I didn't make you care about me. The person you ended up caring about is still me—how I've been with you is all real, all *me*.' I take a breath and plough on. 'That night in the club when you… propositioned me… I would've walked away had you been anyone else but you—I would have been able to. But I couldn't. I knew it was wrong, but I couldn't stop myself.'

She snorts out a laugh and wipes the back of her hand across her eyes. 'So you're blaming your dick now?'

'No, I'm blaming my goddamn *heart*!'

She sniffs, her eyes widening over my outburst. But, hell, I'm going out of my mind. Why can't I get it through to her that I love her?

'I couldn't leave you—not when I understood that Philip would stop at nothing to ruin your reputation. I knew that if it wasn't me then another PI would be hired to tail you—a fact Philip proved when he did exactly that—and there was no preventing what they'd find. Your presence at Blacks, the things that go on there… Another PI wouldn't be as bound to their own loyalties as me.'

'You mean your friendship with Jackson?'

'Yes.'

'So really I have Jackson to thank that you didn't dish the dirt?'

I shake my head, frustration mounting, my pulse racing.

'I stuck around to *protect* you—don't you get it? I kept him from getting what he needed even though I knew I was falling for you—falling for you and having to lie at the same time, hating myself for it even as I loved you.'

Her head is shaking rapidly. 'That's not love, and that's not honesty. Trust—you should have *trusted* me with it.'

'I couldn't. I was scared. So scared of what you would do. Scared that you would go straight to Philip and have it out with him. And you're too good for that. Whatever you said or did, he would always sink that bit lower, be that bit more devious. I couldn't risk it—not until I knew I could protect you, build up some information of my own.'

'*No!* You should have told me—given us the chance to deal with it together.'

She's right. I know she's right. And the real truth of it hits me like a blast of icy air.

'I was scared I would lose you.'

She says nothing. She's frozen still and I push on, my voice a mere whisper.

'I was so scared that the second I confessed you would despise me, hate me for who I am and what I did.' I reach out to cup her cheek, the impulse too strong to fight. 'I was scared that the love blazing in your eyes…' I sweep away her tears with my thumb and see exactly what I feared staring back at me '…would die.'

No, no, no.

I swallow back the rising tide of pain, blink back the tears that threaten. 'I know I was wrong—I see that now—but it doesn't mean I don't love you. You have to believe that… *Please* believe that.'

Her eyes close and she raises her hands to her ears, shaking her head. I can feel her entire body tremble beneath my touch. I'm losing her…

'Coco—'

'Don't… I can't… Don't…' She breaks away from me, her step jerky, and then she turns and runs.

I watch her go, knowing I can't follow and feeling the world shatter around me.

'Just do one thing?' I plead after her, the sound choked over the wedge in my throat. 'Speak to Philip—ask him what I told him.'

Her step falters as she looks over her shoulder, one brow raised in disbelief. 'And you trust *him* to tell me the truth?'

'No…' I take a breath. 'But he's the only hope I have left.'

I stare at my father's study door—now Philip's—my body immobile. I've found myself here more times than I can count over the past week, but this is where my courage leaves me and I end up walking away.

Ever since I saw Ash outside the hospital, saw his tortured expression, his hoarse protestations of love have hounded me every waking hour. I didn't let myself believe him—I couldn't. To do that would run the risk of opening myself up all over again, and I'm not over his first betrayal. How can I possibly hope to survive another in the future?

Problem is I can't kill the spark of hope—the idea that maybe I won't have to survive another betrayal because there won't be one, because if he loves me half as much as I love him, then our future could be as perfect as any life can be.

Because I do love him—if he's the man I got to know, the man whose relationship with his father is so heart-warming, the man whose bond to Jackson is so loyal, whose love for me kept him at my side whenever I called. I'm not blind to the fact that he came into the hospital, knowing that he ran the risk of running into Philip, because *I* asked it of him.

He did it for me. And so I owe him this. I owe it to myself too.

Just ask Philip.

We've barely spoken since the day he outed Ash. The day he outed his own devious plan too. Even now my skin prickles over his deception—anger, hurt, betrayal all coming to the fore. I need to deal with it all. I need to do this.

I take a breath and rap against the door.

It opens before my hand even drops to my side, but it's not Philip. It's my stepmother.

'Oh, it's you.' She looks me up and down, says it like I'm a piece of shit on her shoe. I so don't care.

I blame her for the way Philip is. Her, our father, Clara… They all had a hand in it.

No one forced him, though…

I give her a sickly-sweet smile and stride past her. Philip is at his desk, studying some paperwork, and I turn to look at his mother. 'Would you mind giving my brother and I some privacy?'

'I was leaving anyway.'

Her voice is unusually high-pitched as she looks towards Philip, and it makes me wonder what I've actually walked in on.

'These walls are beginning to make my skin shrivel.'

Philip's eyes shoot up, spearing her from across the room. 'In that case, maybe it's time you found yourself somewhere else to live. Perhaps you and Clara could bunk up together, Mother. You get on so very well and she'll be looking for someone else to feed off now that I've told her it's over.'

What? It's over. Him and Clara. Really?

The first ripple of hope, of excitement runs through me as his mother pales on a sharp intake of breath. I wait for her to retaliate, to hit back as soon as she's over her shock, but instead she gives a meek 'Yes…well…perhaps I should.'

'Excellent!' His eyes go back to the papers as he lifts them up. 'Don't take too long about it.'

She says nothing, her disbelieving gaze frozen on her son, and when she realises he's finished with her she flicks me a look.

'I think you can go,' I can't help saying.

I want to laugh, but that would probably take things too far. Instead, I take great delight in her heightened colour and wobbly exit.

As the door closes I look back to Philip. What the hell have I missed? I've seen her treat him in all manner of ways—trample, push, goad, belittle, the works—it's partly why he's like he is, and it's why I can't hate him for what he did. But never have I seen him stand up to her.

And as for him and Clara…?

I find my anger towards him floundering, a surprising swell of admiration building. How long have I itched for him to fight back? And not at me, but at the real purveyors of his misery.

'What?' he says.

I realise I'm staring, lips parted, eyes wide. 'Can we get her back in here and do that again?'

He takes a shaky breath and tosses the papers down, reaching for the almost empty whisky decanter on his desk and pouring a double measure. 'Look, Coco, I don't know why you're here, but I'm tired, fed up and trying to get my head screwed on straight, so if you want to lay into me please just get it over with. I deserve it—and more.'

I study him closely. He looks like he's barely slept, worry lines mar his perfect features, and the glassy state of his eyes suggests he's had several drinks already.

'What's going on?'

'What *isn't* going on?' he mutters, taking a swig and turning in his chair to look at me. 'Clara told me what a fool I'd been not to see what was going on under my nose with you and Ash, told me it just proved what a mug I was. This was after she'd informed me that Granny's deterioration was a blessing in disguise as it meant her and Mother could resume their party preparations without the worry that she would still be here.'

His voice cracks and he breaks off, his eyes falling to his glass as he clenches his jaw. His pain is so obvious and I know it has nothing to do Clara and everything to do with Granny's health.

'As for Mother…' He shakes his head as he says her name, his mouth twisting derisively. 'She's spent the last hour listing every one of my useless qualities to ensure I take full responsibility for *her* crappy existence too, as well as informing me of my failings as a husband and a future Duke, that letting Clara go is an epic misjudgement, that my darling wife makes the perfect Duchess.'

He laughs now. 'And, oh, how I know Clara agrees. She only married me for my title, you know. It's so obvious now. My title and my money.'

'I'm sorry.'

He looks at me. 'No, you're not.'

'I am.'

It's the truth. I know he won't understand it, but I am. I lived his childhood with him. I was aware of the pedestal on which I sat while he took all the shit that was thrown at him by our father as well as his mother.

He shakes his head. 'You shouldn't be.'

'Don't get me wrong, I'm still livid at what you did—what you tried to do. I still can't get my head around it.'

He pinches the bridge of his nose and squeezes his eyes shut. 'You and me both.'

'Are you saying you've had some wonderful epiphany—that you can miraculously see the horror of it all?'

His eyes stay shut and he shakes his head again. 'I wish I could go back and undo it—the whole damn lot. Go back to before Clara…before…'

He swallows hard, his skin deathly white. He looks like he's going to be sick, and even though I don't want it to I can feel my anger ebbing away.

He wets his lips, and looks at me, lost, pained. 'Is that why you've come? To have it out? To give me what I deserve?'

I straighten my spine. 'That—and I want to know what Ash told you about me.'

He gives a gentle scoff. 'As if you don't already know.'

'I want to hear it from you.'

He shakes his head again, one corner of his lip lifting. 'Fuck all, if you must know…' He leans back in his chair. 'I should've known the guy was smitten. He's supposed to be the best in the industry—it never occurred to me that he would fall under your *perfect* spell too.'

'Don't say that.' The way he drawls out the word *perfect* makes my skin crawl. 'I'm not perfect.'

'On that we must agree to disagree.'

'Is that why you hate me so much? Is that why you felt I deserved it?'

He stares at me, the silence long and strained.

'The truth is I never hated you. I *envied* you. Ash told me nothing because there was nothing to tell—because you didn't deserve it.' His voice cracks and he clears his throat, visibly trying to recover. 'But me, on the other hand…'

He leans back in his seat to open a drawer in the desk and pulls out a manila envelope. He tosses it onto the desk before me.

'What's this?' I pick it up, my eyes still trained on him.

'You might as well take a look…' He rubs his jaw, the movement awkward, shaky. 'He's probably told you it all already.'

I go to open it, but stop. It just doesn't feel right. 'What's inside?'

'You really don't know?'

'I'm assuming it's information relating to you?'

He smiles at me but his eyes are dead, wet at the corners. 'It's all my dirty laundry. Seems he was making sure I wouldn't take any steps against you. Judging by your expression, you had nothing to do with this bonus investigative work?'

My stomach twists. 'I'd never do that to you.'

He sits forward in his chair, knocking back his drink with a wince. 'No, you wouldn't, would you?'

His eyes meet mine, red-rimmed and swimming. I want to reach for him, tell him it doesn't mean he can't change, be a better person, free of the women who have tormented him for years. But I'm rooted. Unsure.

'I don't blame him, you know.' He's reflective as he says it. 'He was right to fall for you, to protect you… *Christ*, I'm glad he did.'

My eyes narrow. 'You are?'

He rakes his hand over his face. 'I don't think I could've come back from that.'

'From what?'

I want him to spell it out, to acknowledge his intent. I need to hear it from his lips, to have it out in the open and believe that he regrets it, that there's hope for us.

His eyes and his hunched-up body tremble.

'From ruining me?' I press, so softly it's a wonder he hears. But his shuddery breath, the awkward nod of his head, tell me that he has.

'I am sorry, Coco. I know it's not enough, and I don't even know if I can ever make it up to you, but…' Another breath and his eyes lock with mine. 'But I'm going to try.'

A lump forms high in my throat and I lift my chin and nod. 'I believe you, Philip. I don't need to read this.' I close the envelope without looking inside and place it back on the desk. 'We can talk when you're ready. I'm still your sister—your blood—and I don't want to lose you.'

He eyes me, disbelieving. 'How can you mean that? After all I've done?'

'Believe it.' My eyes prick as the truth hits me.

'Soon you'll be all the family I have left, and…and I don't want to lose that.'

He's across the room before the first tear falls, his arms around me, hugging me tight.

'It's not too late?' he whispers against my hair. 'For us?'

'No,' I assure him on a small sob. 'It's not.'

I only hope the same applies to Ash.

CHAPTER EIGHTEEN

I PULL OPEN the fridge for a beer. 'Bollocks.' The shelves are practically bare. No beer, no nothing.

I slam the fridge closed and snatch a glass off the drainer, a bottle of whisky next. It's not my preferred drink, especially at four in the afternoon, but needs must. And I definitely need it. I need to block out the sight of her walking away, her anger, her pain, her hate…

I'm all out of hope. She must have spoken to Philip by now. And if she has he's either lied or it wasn't enough to convince her.

I can't even blame him. This is all my fault. *Mine.*

I fucked up the best thing that's ever happened to me and now I have to face the consequences. Only I don't know how to. I don't know how to live without her.

I pour a glass as I head into the living area, where the painting on the wall teases me with the memory of her appreciation. I make a U-turn and head back to the kitchen. Not that that helps either. *Fuck.*

She's everywhere.

I slap the whisky glass down on the centre island and pour. Wishing the painful memories away. Wishing *her* away.

Maybe I should've taken Jackson up on his offer of a night out. The guy's been hounding me all week. And we could go somewhere new. Somewhere devoid of memories. Somewhere I can get hammered and forget. Even if it's only for a few hours, it has to be better than this.

Yeah, like you'd really wish yourself on him right now.

I deserve to wallow in my own sodding misery.

I take a swig of my drink and close my eyes, feel it burn down my throat and contend with the punishing ache inside.

Better.

Then the doorbell goes and my phone starts to flash up at me from the counter.

Piss off.

It's Jackson. Won't the guy just give up?

I ignore both and take another swig.

There's an incessant banging on the door now, every knock like a physical blow to my already aching head, and I wince.

Seriously, Jackson, piss off.

He doesn't, and it's driving me crazy.

I stride to the front door and yank it open. 'Jackson, will you just fu—'

The curse dies on my lips. I can't believe my eyes. This has to be some twisted trick, the booze soaring to my head…

'Ash?'

Coco frowns up at me, her beautiful green eyes flashing with what looks so much like concern. Not anger, not pain, not hatred.

She's wearing jeans and the same soft pink sweater she wore to Dad's. Memories warm me, slaughter me, but she's here. It has to mean something.

Her frown deepens. 'Ash…?'

My throat is so dry I can't speak. I wet my lips and run a hand over my face, stopping to grip my jaw as my eyes narrow and focus, still disbelieving.

'Coco?'

Her lips quirk just a little. 'Can I come in?'

'Sure.'

My voice sounds so fucking weird, so distant, but I can't function past the crazy flutter taking off inside me. I step back to let her past and her familiar scent wafts up to me, messing with my head, telling me she's real, that this is happening.

'I'll have one of those.' She nods to the drink still in my hand.

'Sure,' I repeat, swinging the door closed and making my way trance-like back to the kitchen, my ears attuned to her soft footfall behind me.

She's here. She's here. She's here.

I set my glass down and get another one for her, then reach for the bottle and start to pour. But I'm shaking so much the liquid sloshes outside the glass.

'Ash…'

She places her hand over mine. She's right alongside me, her perfume in the air, her presence radiating down my side.

Slowly I set the bottle down and look at her. It really isn't hate I see. 'I'm so sorry.'

'I know you are,' she whispers.

I go to pull her in. I need to hug her, feel her, believe that she believes me. But she steps back, shaking her head, and my stomach plummets. My hands fall helplessly away.

'But…?'

Her throat bobs, her eyes lift to mine. 'I can't… When I think about it…the idea of you following me—*all that time*—and not once telling me…' She shakes her head again, her palm pressing into her chest. 'It hurts… It really hurts. I feel sick with it.'

'I *know*.' Hearing her say it, seeing the flash of pain, of disgust, I feel sick too. 'I would do anything to change what I did. To go back and do it differently. I'd do anything not to have caused you this pain.'

'I know you would.' She breathes in deeply. 'Philip said the same.'

'You spoke to him?' My heart spasms in my chest. 'About what he did? About me?'

She nods, her hand shaking as she reaches out and picks up the glass of whisky I poured for her. I stay quiet as I watch her take a sip, my eyes desperately searching hers, looking for a sign—any sign of what is to come.

'He had his reasons—I know he did; I think I understand more than he knows.'

She swallows and takes another breath, her eyes locking with mine.

'I know about the research you did into him too—the case you built against him to protect me.'

'He showed you?'

'He tried to, but I don't want to know. I think he's hit a turning point and I'm hoping we can repair things.'

'*Repair* things?' I frown at her, feel a flare of anger, even jealousy, that she can think to forgive him while we…we flounder…

'Our relationship,' she confirms softly.

Her eyes narrow on me, reading it all, I'm sure. I shake my head. 'Are you crazy?'

'Are you being a hypocrite?' she snaps, and I realise she's right. 'You want me to forgive *you* for what you did, but not my brother?'

'I don't know.' I rub the back of my neck, cling to it as I try to make sense of what I'm thinking, of how I feel. 'I know this mess is my fault, but I blame him too—for what he wanted to do to you.' My body vibrates with anger at the very thought. 'To the woman I love.'

The pulse flutters in her neck, the glass shakes in her hand.

'I know what he wanted to do, and I know why. But his marriage is over, he's finally seen sense where Clara and his mother are concerned, and once Granny is gone…' She swallows as her eyes glisten over and she raises her chin with reignited strength.

'We'll only have one another, and I'm not giving up on him yet.'

My blood runs cold.

Only have one another.

'And what about me? Can't you have me too?'

'I want to,' she says, and I can see she means it, but I can also see the fight in her. 'I want that so much—to be able to act like it never happened, to bury it.'

'Then give me a chance to make it up to you,' I plead, my voice a husky mess of desperation as I reach a hand out to her. 'Let me love you like I've wanted to for so long.'

She exhales sharply as she looks to the heavens, a solitary tear escaping and crucifying me on its path.

'I *want* to—so badly. But I don't know how we do that when you still… When you're still…' She looks back at me, her free hand gesturing wildly. 'When you're still doing that to other people. The whole PI shit. I get why you did it, why you chose to before, but now…'

I step forward, unable to stand the distance any longer. 'That side of me is long gone.' I reach out to cup her arms and this time she lets me. 'I've already quit the business—there's no way I could carry on.'

Hope flares in her eyes as they widen. 'You have?'

'*Yes.* I didn't realise how messed-up I'd become, how blinded by the past I've been—not until you… Until I almost…almost…' I can't finish the sentence—it hurts too much. 'I hate myself for what I did, and I know I don't deserve you, don't deserve your forgiveness, but the idea of living without you, of walking away…'

My voice fails me, my eyes close as the sob rising in my throat gets too much, and then I feel her palms on either side of my face, her touch soft, soothing.

'I don't want you to walk away, Ash.'

I hear the words, hope pulsing in my chest, and I open my eyes, take in her blazing beauty.

'You don't?'

'No.' She shakes her head. 'I've wrestled with so much pain these last two weeks, every day, without you, feeling lost…empty. I can't go on like that.'

I almost don't want to ask the question, but I have to if we're to stand a chance at a future. 'Can you forgive me?'

She studies me quietly and I can't breathe as I search her gaze.

'Yes,' she says eventually, so softly I can barely hear it.

But it's there, and my chest soars, tears prick, making my vision swim as I look down at her.

'Can you… Can you love me?'

She looks to my mouth and runs her thumb over it, her lips coming next. She kisses me—a single featherlight sweep of her mouth—but I'm rigid, stock-still. Hope upon hope is building.

'I have no choice in that, Ash. I *do* love you.'

My breath leaves me in a rush, so ragged. I'm so happy hearing those words, seeing the truth of them once more alive in her bright green gaze. It's all too surreal, too perfect, too dreamlike.

'You do?'

'Yes, Ash, I do.'

I press my forehead to hers, pull her body tight against me. 'Do me a favour?'

'What?'

'Kiss me again so I know this isn't a dream?'

'I think we can go one better than a kiss…'

She rakes her fingers down my front, easing them beneath my sweater. Her fingertips over my bare skin make my stomach contract.

'We have so many lost nights to catch up on.'

'Coco...'

I can't speak any more, can only claim her mouth with all the hunger, all the love, all the pent-up pain I can now let go of because *she is here.* And she loves me. Just as I do her.

She yanks my sweater over my head and I grip the hem of hers, but she presses her palms into my chest, stopping me from going further. I drag in a breath, my eyes burning into hers.

'Tell me again,' she says, her eyes bright with desire, her cheeks flushing pink.

'I love you, Coco Lauren!' I grip her by the waist and lift her onto the counter, her resultant laughter music to my deprived ears.

'And if you let me…' I step between her thighs, drawing her against me '…I will show you just how much every day and every night for the rest of our lives.'

I seal my vow with my lips upon hers and start to show her…one stroke, one lick, one kiss at a time…

CHAPTER NINETEEN

I LOOK DOWN at the leather-bound book clutched in my hands and smile. I know this is the right thing to do now. I know I need Granny to understand my mother—her good heart and her love for my father. I also need her to know that I've found my happiness too. That I am in love and loved in return.

I turn to look up at Ash beside me.

'You okay?' he asks, his arm around my waist giving me a gentle squeeze.

'Yes. It's the right thing to do.' I've already marked out some pages in the diary—the ones that shine with my mother's love. 'Will you wait for me downstairs?'

'Sure.'

He presses a kiss to my brow and I breathe in his scent, his love, his support.

'Thank you.'

And then I turn to face Granny's bedroom door and give it a gentle knock.

'Come in,' she calls from the other side, her voice still perfectly controlled, even though I know each day becomes more and more of a struggle for her.

I blink away the tears that form and step out of Ash's embrace to open the door and walk inside.

She's propped up in bed, her eyes bright with her love for me, and the sense of doing right swells. 'Granny, I'd like to read you something…'

EPILOGUE

Eighteen months later

'If you'd told me I'd be wearing a skirt I would have said no—you know that, right?'

Philip fluffs out the sides of his kilt as he says it and I can't help erupting into a giggle.

'Who would've given me away, then?'

'I could've done it just as well in trousers.'

'And you wouldn't have been half as dashing.' I waggle my eyebrows at him. 'Haven't you seen the ladies eyeing you up?'

'You are joking.'

'Not at all, and you're quite the eligible bachelor now. You should make the most of it.'

Now he grins, his eyes seeking out one redhead in particular, currently slow-dancing with Jackson in the recently refurbed ballroom of the Livingston Castle.

'Oh, no, you don't. Cait's off-limits.'

He flashes me a cheeky look. 'Surely as your maid of honour she should be top of my list.'

'You're not the best man.'

'Best man, brother…' he shrugged '…same difference.'

'Philip!'

'Oh, dear, that's her warning tone…'

I turn at the sound of Ash's voice and feel the warmth of his hand through the white lace at the base of my spine.

'What have you done now?' he asks Philip.

'He's setting his sights on Cait.'

Ash gives a hearty laugh, his eyes dancing. 'I think that's a great idea.'

I frown up at him.

'See?' Philip blurts. 'Even your husband agrees.'

'Really, Ash?' I'd stamp on his foot if I could find my feet beneath my dress. Instead I fire him a glare. 'Not helpful.'

He shrugs. 'What's the worst that could happen? Although, he might have Jackson to get through first…'

'The question is,' Philip says, as he considers the couple on the dance floor, 'does she want a bit of rough—no offence to your mate—or does she want Prince Charming?'

'Prince Charming?' Ash mimics, choking on his giggles now, and I elbow him in the ribs.

'Right, Livingston.' Philip straightens and offers out his hand. 'Fifty I get the girl.'

I stare between them in disbelief. 'Don't you—'

'You're on,' Ash interjects, shaking his hand, his grin rivalling Philip's own.

'No time like the present to get started.'

My brother extracts his hand, rearranges his cravat and makes for the dance floor.

'Philip Lauren...' I wait for him to look back at me. 'You dare mess her around and it'll be me you answer to.'

He chuckles. 'Keep your knickers on—I wouldn't dare.'

I watch him walk off and I can't be angry. I'm too happy.

Happy that I've married the man I love.

Happy that I have the brother I always wanted.

Happy.

Just happy.

Ash leans into my ear. 'Now, about those knickers...'

A shiver runs through me. 'You're just trying to distract me from your bad behaviour...'

'No, Mrs Livingston. If I wanted to do that, I'd do this...'

He scoops me up in the air with ease, the abundant layers of my dress creating a cloud between me and his face.

'Ash!' I bat them down and laugh and glare at him all at once. 'Put me down!'

'Only when we're alone.'

He's already heading for the double doors that lead out into the hallway and the guests are parting before us, laughing, cheering and offering up smiles and salutes with their glasses.

My cheeks flush red as I plaster on a smile. 'Ash, what will they *think*?' I say between my teeth.

'That I'm desperate to have my wife all to myself.'

'Ash!'

'What?' He looks down at me as we enter the hallway. 'Aren't you keen to find out whether I'm a true Scot in a kilt?'

I frown. 'A true…?'

He wouldn't be…not all day!

'*Are* you?'

He grins. 'You'll see.'

* * * * *